Maree Giles was born in Australia and has lived in London since 1980. She has worked as a journalist in New Zealand, Australia and London. In 1997 she won the *She* magazine short story competition, and her short stories were highly commended in the Ian St James Awards. She is a member of the London Authors' Society, and runs creative writing workshops. She lives with her Canadian partner and her two children.

THE PAST IS A SECRET COUNTRY

Freya Kirby's battle to regain custody of her children takes her to her past in Australia, to a time of hidden truths — towards a spiritual heritage . . . Freya is changing. She is developing her innate gift for healing. She's going to need this gift, for one day the wounds of the past arrive in the shape of Connie. High-flying Connie is an Indigenous Australian. As unlike the fair-skinned Freya as it is possible to be . . . Passionate about her children, unsure of her future and confused about her earlier life, Freya must embark on a spiritual and emotional quest. A journey without expectations, to an unnamed destination.

MAREE GILES

THE PAST IS A SECRET COUNTRY

Complete and Unabridged

CHARNWOOD
Leicester

First published in Great Britain in 2005 by
Virago Press
London

First Charnwood Edition
published 2006
by arrangement with
Virago Press, an imprint of
Time Warner Book Group UK
London

British Library CIP Data

Giles, Maree
    The past is a secret country.—Large print ed.—
Charnwood library series
1. Adoption—Australia—Psychological aspects—
Fiction 2. Aboriginal Australians—Mixed descent
—Fiction 3. Australians—England—London—
Fiction 4. Large type books
I. Title
823.9'14 [F]

ISBN 1–84617–272–1

Published by
F. A. Thorpe (Publishing)
Anstey, Leicestershire

Set by Words & Graphics Ltd.
Anstey, Leicestershire
Printed and bound in Great Britain by
T. J. International Ltd., Padstow, Cornwall

For my daughter, Lucille,
with love

Acknowledgements

I would like to offer my heartfelt thanks to the following people for their support during the writing of this book, in particular my editor, Barbara Daniel, for her encouragement and inspired thoughts on the manuscript, my agent, Sarah Molloy, for her good advice, and my desk editors, Sarah Rustin and Jane Selley, for their hard work and courage. Also thanks to the art department, Rebecca Gray, publicity manager, and Nicola Hill, export marketing director, at Time Warner Book Group UK, and the team at Penguin in Melbourne.

To Jaime, to my mother Gloria, to my children, David and Lucille, and to my sister Lyndall — a special thanks to all of you for your love and for having faith in me. Also to Richard Gilbert, for his suggestions on humour, and to the rest of my family and friends for their love, encouragement and loyalty.

Thanks also to the following: the Australian and Torres Strait Islander Commission; Rita Catoni and Simon Fisher at Yuendumu settlement, Northern Territory; the National Wool Museum, Geelong, Victoria; the Sheep's Back Museum, New South Wales; Adoption UK; Origins, Australia; the Registrar of Births, Deaths and Marriages, Melbourne; the Adoption Information Service, Department of Human

Resources, Melbourne; the Natural History Museum, London; British Inland Waterways Association; Hart Brown Solicitors, Surrey; and Jo Dunbar, Botanica Medica, Surrey.

Several books were invaluable to me in my research for *The Past is a Secret Country: The Politics of Ritual in an Aboriginal Settlement* by Francoise Dussart; *Blood on the Wattle*, by Bruce Elder; *Daughters of the Dreaming*, by Diane Bell; *Australian Lives*, by Michal Bosworth; *The Shearers*, by Patsy Adam-Smith; *Australian Woolsheds*, by Harry Sowden; *The Great Days of Wool*, by Joan Palmer and David Symes; *The Complete Illustrated Holistic Herbal* by David Hoffman; *Interpersonal Skills for Nurses*, by Carolyn Kagan and Josie Evans; *Songman*, by Bob Randall; and *Aboriginal Art*, by Wally Caruana. Last, but not least, GOOGLE.

Nature, not man, is the selecting agent.

Ted Circuitt,
master sheep-breeder, Australia

1

Middlesex, England: March 2003

There was something wrong with the sky today. The minute Freya woke she felt it in her veins. Instead of being in control she was clumsy and preoccupied. Every time she heard a noise outside, she froze. While halving a lemon in the galley she cut her thumb. Blood dripped on to the chopping board. Even the birds seemed to sense it, swooping low over the canal and screeching.

Ever since Neill had filed for custody of the children four weeks ago, she'd had an ominous feeling of more trouble ahead. He was sure to make a surprise visit any day now, hoping to gather evidence.

A worse fate than bumping into Neill would be coming face to face with Monica Murray. Freya pictured her sneaking on to the moorings to interrogate the neighbours behind her back. An act of spite. Paranoia had become so entrenched in her daily routine that she had developed tactics for disappearing up alleys, or blending with shoppers on the busy high street.

There would not be much to unearth — at least, nothing immoral. But she wasn't sure what assumptions her neighbours had made. And the worst she ever got up to in town was a visit to her chiropractor, a matronly homosexual from

1

Manchester. People had probably drawn their own conclusions. Bearing in mind that some of the single male houseboat residents were constantly flirting.

Apart from a hunch, she might not know if Neill or Monica had been snooping around until it was mentioned at the next meeting with welfare officers — or in court. By then it would be too late to deny any errors or gossip, as her lawyer would have no planned line of defence.

Everyone knew she had a court case pending, and that the children were with Neill, and that all sorts of wild theories would no doubt be doing the rounds. Was she a child-beater? Or a husband-basher? An alcoholic? Or a shop-lifter? A mother did not just walk out on her children with no good reason. Perhaps she had been thrown out by her ex? Maybe he had insisted on keeping the children until the court case? She might be one of those mothers who wanted a child-free life with a swarthy lover in Crete.

No one ever asked about the circumstances surrounding the separation, and she didn't volunteer any details. Except to Sam Jenner, who she felt she could trust — but only with the bare facts. This was a private matter between her and Neill.

And the Family Division, worse luck.

She drew back the curtain at the main hatch and looked outside at the misty morning. The hedge directly outside her boat glistened with dew. Thank God it was dew and not frost. Last summer's bindweed was already choking her seedlings. Slugs would soon appear, voracious giants of the underworld that seemed to be born big. Next she'd be grappling with whitefly, mealy bugs and aphids. Warding off predators and pests was a full-time job. She'd thought about getting rid of the elder trees too, because of the mess they made, but she knew they had earning potential.

After breakfast she sat on a beanbag in the saloon and did a series of gentle breathing exercises to calm her nerves. It was no use. She jumped to her feet and peered through the fog at the humpback bridge for any strange cars.

There was definitely something amiss. Her heart kept skipping beats.

She opened the main hatch and popped her head outside and glanced up and down the towpath. The damp air was full of insects. Sunshine and new growth had taken the moorings from winter shabby to spring chic. Litter along the banks was at last disappearing beneath frothing wild flowers.

No one was up yet. Six thirty was too early; even the London commuters did not set off until seven, shirt-tails flying, hangovers pulsing off their scalps.

She closed the window, assumed the lotus position, and continued her breathing exercises. In, out, in, out. Her mind was buzzing. She thought of Neill and the way he had always ridiculed her knack for predicting the future. He mocked everything she did. Said her talent for sensing danger and change was all coincidence. But he reckoned it suited her profile: nutcase.

In the early days of their marriage she had

laughed at his insults, thinking he was only teasing. Since leaving him she realised he meant every word. The last time he mocked her she finally snapped.

He had just dropped the kids off for the weekend, and found her stirring a pot of borage in the galley, when she should have been waiting on the humpback bridge. He peered in at the open window, eyes smarting from the pungent fumes, and called her a weirdo, which was certainly an improvement on psychopath and schizophrenic.

'That's your opinion,' she said. 'At least I'm not a hypocrite.'

She had glared at his new lay preaching badge, pinned to his lapel. He smelled of eau de Clarissa, and Freya said so. Without another word he had turned and stormed off to his car.

God, how she wished she smoked.

Ignoring her fear of being interrupted, she got stuck into a session of yoga. An hour later she felt bright, flexible, and ready to face the world — or turn it away, if necessary.

She had just begun to braid her hair when she heard footsteps. Someone coughed. A woman. She heard shoes crunching on the gravel, as if the person was walking away. She let out a small sigh of relief. It was probably a resident after all, on their way out. The towpath was always busy after seven: mothers on the school run, unemployed men hurrying to beat the queues at the Job Centre, commuters frantic for the train at Uxbridge.

She was thankful it wasn't a needy neighbour

looking for free samples or advice. People had begun to take advantage of her generosity lately, so she had decided to start charging for her services. She just wasn't sure how to implement this change without causing offence or losing potential long-term customers. Besides which, the constant interruptions were eating into her time, when really she should be making the most of every minute to build up her supplies.

She was just telling herself to stop worrying when she heard the *clunk clunk* of heels climbing the metal landing stage. She groaned and, promptly inventing an excuse, spun around to deliver it. If she was ever going to get her kids back, 'arm's-length' had to be her new watchword.

A strange woman was outside trying to keep her balance on the top step. Gripping the lip of the roof, she bowed down and looked straight in at Freya, no qualms about the intrusion.

Freya expected to see one particularly pale and pushy neighbour, so the woman's black face made her jump.

Because of the design of the boat, and the high platform you had to climb up to get through the main hatch, Freya's eyes were level with the woman's belly, which was pancake flat beneath a perfectly pressed pleated skirt. Her limbs resembled those of an athlete or fitness fanatic.

It was an undignified way to arrive on a person's doorstep at the best of times, and impossible to make a discreet or flamboyant entrance. The elderly found the tall platform especially difficult to negotiate, even Mrs Peach, who lived on a tiny narrowboat and was used to life as a contortionist.

The woman smiled, and mouthed the word 'hello' through the glass.

Freya slid open the hatch and said, 'Can I help?'

The visitor beamed down at her. Freya looked straight up into her broad nostrils and quickly moved her gaze to her eyes, which were dark and mischievous, deep-set in a cherubic, slightly beefy face, with dimpled apple cheeks.

'Do you mind if I come in?'

Freya flinched at the sound of her strong American accent. She smelled of expensive perfume, and a rich, earthy, surprisingly pleasant body odour that triggered a strange sense of familiarity.

'Are you selling something?'

'No. I'm here for another reason altogether. I'm not selling anything, honey.' She nodded enthusiastically.

Freya glanced at her handbag, an expensive beaded clutch. There was no sign of a nylon tartan carrier, the usual choice of door-to-door sales reps, stuffed with tacky household products that broke or perished after a week. Perhaps she had hidden the bag behind the hedge and the clutch was a decoy? She couldn't tell if the woman's eyes were those of a tea towel merchant or a religious crusader, but she decided Jesus must have brought her to the moorings.

'Look, I'm terribly sorry, but I'm not interested.' She closed the door and spoke through a crack. 'My ex-husband's a religious

6

freak, but it hasn't made him a nicer bloke. Sorry.' She bolted the door.

It had begun to rain. Fine spring rain like mist from a waterfall. The visitor pulled an umbrella from her handbag and opened it, then looked through the window at Freya, like a nervous cat locked out in bad weather.

'I'm sorry, but I said I'm not interested.' Freya drew the curtain across sharply.

The woman inched her way towards the forward deck, where she peeked between the pot plants assembled in front of the windscreen for privacy.

'Freya?' She stabbed an index finger against the glass, and her eyebrows shot up as she nodded her head, willing Freya to give in.

'Are you from the Family Division?' asked Freya, wondering how the woman knew her name.

The stranger shook her head vigorously. 'No, no, no. I've got some good news for you.'

Freya was convinced she was about to be conned into signing up for a glamour makeover or a Spanish property-share scheme. She might have to take extreme measures and tell the woman to clear off.

'Can I come in?'

The woman nodded hungrily, smiled her big endearing smile, the dimples in her cheeks deepened, and the sparkle in her soulful brown eyes finally melted Freya's heart.

'All right, just until the rain stops. But I don't want to sign up for anything. And I've got no money on me. So you're wasting your time as well as mine.'

She knew it was rude. But she didn't want to be delayed; she had promised to call in and see Del this afternoon to pick up the antique jars that Del had found in her attic.

The moorings were an easy target for door-to-door sellers — residents out and about on the towpath, doors rarely locked, windows and hatches flung open. She was cornered at least once a week, and was sick of it. On top of all the other interruptions, it was sometimes too much to bear. Of course, she usually gave in — it wasn't in her nature to slam doors in people's faces, even if they were selling junk she didn't need.

She opened the door and stood away from the stepladder.

'I'm sorry if I've caught you at a bad time,' said the woman, as she climbed down the ladder backwards. 'I've only got today, I start work in the City tomorrow, you see. I flew in from New York last week and I'm on a tight schedule.'

Her feet now firmly on the floor, she turned and smiled. Her teeth were big and dazzlingly white.

Just then last night's dying fire spat at the glass door panel on the Rayburn, the back boiler burped, and an avalanche of cooling cinders fell into the ash pan.

'Pleased to meet you, at long last.'

The stranger held out a hand. Freya reluctantly received it in hers. It felt warm and firm, the palm a little gummy. The woman held on tight and tried to draw Freya into her arms.

8

Freya withdrew, alarmed, wiping her hand on her skirt. The woman looked wounded.

'I'm Connie Stanley.' Her smile returned. 'I know this will be a shock.' She was serious for a moment, then her face lit up once more. 'I thought a phone call would be cruel. You see . . . well, actually, I don't know quite how to put it.' She took a deep breath.

'Please, just say it.'

'I guess there's no point in procrastinating. I reckon you'll be real happy when you hear.'

'I hope you're not going to tell me I've won a holiday to Tenerife or a year's supply of soft drinks?'

Even as she spoke, a ripple of apprehension shimmied its way across her neck; there was something familiar about this woman, something about her eyes, the way she looked at her so — dare she think it — *intimately.*

'I'm sure this will be hard to believe, but I can assure you it's the God's honest truth,' said Connie. 'You see, the thing is, well, I'm not quite sure how to put this, it's just that . . . '

'What? What is it? Please get on with it. I've got an appointment to keep.'

Connie gulped. 'Please don't get worked up. This isn't easy.'

'What in blazes is going on?'

'It's taken me a long time to get to the bottom of everything, letters back and forth to Melbourne for years, and eventually the law changed, and it became much easier — '

'Melbourne? What's all this got to do with Melbourne? Are you a friend of my family?'

9

'Not exactly . . . '

'What, then?'

'Maybe you'd better sit — '

'I don't want to sit down. Please. Just tell me why you're here.'

'Alrighty. I will.'

Connie took a deep breath. 'There's no easy way to say it, of course. But here goes.'

She studied the back of her hands for a moment, and clasped them firmly over her skirt, then pressed her lips together, took another deep breath and said, 'I'm here to tell you I'm your long-lost sister. From Melbourne.'

She lifted her chest triumphantly.

'There. I've said it. It wasn't nearly as painful as I thought it'd be.'

Freya's mouth fell open. Her heart flipped over, and heat simmered up the length of her spine, filling her head with roaring heat.

'What? What did you say?'

'I'm your sister.' Connie nodded rapidly, then suddenly her face fell and she looked at the floor. 'That's the good news.'

She looked at Freya, her eyes full of glassy tears.

'I'm afraid the bad news is that Henry, your father, that is, your *real father* — let's get this straight right from the start — is in hospital. It's not looking good. I'm sorry.'

2

Melbourne, Australia: Winter 2003

The nurse with the fat arse and the wart on her neck brings you breakfast. You push the trolley away from your bed with the tip of your walking stick and close your eyes. You know they're doing their best but you want them to leave you in peace. The only comfort now is drifting in and out of the memories like a collapsed drunk.

You close your eyes and you are back at Tinderry.

Every morning at dawn you pulled on your boots, buttoned your shirt, and strolled outside to study the horizon. Clouds, that's what you hoped for, with enough rain in them to last two, maybe three years. You stood on the back veranda enjoying the scent of dew-soaked eucalypts. A noisy flock of galahs swooped low over the valley. In the distance the tops of the mountains glistened with snow.

Your usual routine before breakfast was to check the thermometer hanging from a length of string outside the barn. Then you checked the rain gauge, which rarely pleased you, rain being scarce in the Snowy. Squinting at the sun, already scorching at seven a.m., you half expected to see a posse of men on horseback sweeping over the Great Dividing Range,

11

bloodied swords raised to the sky, hell-bent on settling the blacks.

But when you focused your eyes against the glare you saw it was that fallen red gum near the Tambo, its scorched branches sticking up like rifles.

The isolation of the country could drive a sensible man crazy. Bigwig city psychiatrists would say it was your guilty conscience haunting you. Travel to Italy or Iceland and the same mirages would trouble you. Inverell was hundreds of miles away. But unlike Italy or anywhere else, the Snowy Mountains had similarities, reminders: fluorescent blue sky, gum trees, sheep, dust, electrical storms, locusts. History.

The only comfort was the possibility of what had happened being unrecorded history, the haunting memory of a few old-timers like you — too wizened and diseased and dependent on mealy-mouthed nurses to speak of it — the last of a dying breed who think all blacks should be wiped out.

Your father always told you to rise with the birds in order to get more things done, but the desire to comply withered when the message was delivered with a belt on your bare backside. Growing up, you couldn't stay in bed a second past sun-up or you were riddled with guilt.

These days you have to be woken for meals, and often you don't know if it's day or night.

You turn over and the catheter dislodges. You let it go — they can change your sheets later, it will give them something to do and you can

12

watch them hating you. You lie there with your eyes closed, feeling the warmth of the wet patch beneath your thigh, eyes clamped shut against this place.

After breakfast at Tinderry you went into the bathroom to clean your teeth. You looked in the mirror and cursed the sun for browning your face. You pulled your hat over your forehead and went outside to examine your flock, determined to flush out any rogue animals sprouting coarse brown wool. The sun was like a furnace.

Later, when you came in to check up on Ester and make a cuppa, she called to you for a fresh flannel and a clean nightie.

Christ. You hadn't counted on this happening.

Before her illness you had no idea the hard work she put in to keeping your clothes washed. At midday you took her thin soup made from celery and sheepshank, and helped her on to the wooden commode, then you went outside to smoke a cigarette.

She called to you again and again; she was terribly lonely, but sometimes you ignored her because you thought you had identified the odd ones out in your flock.

One evening you strode across the paddocks with your rifle, and Ester's voice, split by the crack of gunfire, lifted with the wind into the hot sky: 'Henry. Henry. Come quickly.'

You shot the rogues and left them for the birds. You stood on the brow of the hill staring hard at the homestead.

The next morning you took her porridge and sugared tea.

13

'Where were you, Henry? I called and called. You didn't come.'

'I'm sorry.'

You tried to avoid her eyes. They reminded you of white jelly.

'Come here.' She wiggled a finger.

You moved closer and adjusted the bed covers. She gripped your shirtsleeve and pulled you close to her face. Her breath smelled of carrion. Your eyes met hers and blood gushed through the valves in your heart.

'It won't be long now, Henry.'

Her voice was shaky, like that of a ninety-year-old, yet she was only thirty-four. 'I'll soon be gone, and you'll be the better for it.'

'Don't talk nonsense.'

You looked away, salty tears stabbing your eyes. She leaned up on her thin elbows.

'I remind you,' she said, her blue lips quivering. 'I remind you of those babies, and *you hate me for it.*'

3

'I say Melbourne, but I've never actually lived there, unless you count the first few weeks. Fact is, I've lived my whole life in the States, although my parents are from Yorkshire originally, but they left there a long time ago on account of my father's family, who were from America, so they went to live there expecting to find their fortune, which they did, now ain't that a dream-come-true typa story?'

Freya longed for Connie to shut up.

Her words whirled around the room and Freya's were sucked up into them like furniture in a tornado.

'Sister? I haven't got a sister. You've got the wrong person — '

'They found me when they were on a world cruise.' Connie's shoulders lifted and she smiled rapturously, like a child on Christmas morning. 'It all happened pretty fast, so they tell me, whisked me away to West Virginia, of all places. But it was a good upbringing, I was a happy child, but I like New York too, although Hopeville will always be my real home. After all, I went to school there, and my friends are there and my family.'

Freya stared at Connie's mobile lips, too afraid to do what her spirit urged: jump to your feet and declare yourself.

Without so much as drawing breath, Connie

15

described in one long sentence all the schools she had been to, her university, the athletics team she had founded at Hopeville High, the pollution-control action committee she joined through her Guide group, her cheerleading team, the mining accident that had claimed the father of her best friend.

Freya found it draining.

As Connie spoke she moved quickly around the saloon, picking up trinkets and studying them, turning her head sideways to read the spines of books, staring hard at photographs of Freya and her children, her dark eyes taking everything in. She was like a large dark flapping butterfly.

'What on earth are you talking about?'

Freya's voice came out small and choked, although she had intended it to sound firm and indignant. Her scalp tingled with perspiration. She could smell Connie's sweet, musky, familiar skin, and feel her warm breath heating the space between them.

Outside the clouds vanished and the sun appeared, streaming through the roof hatches and filling the saloon with golden light. The atmosphere was charged with fiery molecules. Freya felt the need to sing aloud a song that often came to her in a dream, rising up like secret treasure and gushing from the depths of her throat.

Instead she swallowed hard and stepped back.

'Sister, you say? Sister?'

She had to get used to the shape of the word on her tongue. Before now she had only used it in relation to her own children: Help your sister set the table. Don't do that to your sister. Look after your sister.

She moved slowly towards the door, not sure of her next move. The back of her neck was prickly and wet. She wasn't sure how to handle this, coming as it had so out of the blue. She gripped the back of a chair, feeling quite faint. A churning sensation rose inside her, and she almost threw up. She felt the blood draining from her face.

'How do you know my name?' she said, her voice weak with emotion. 'How did you find me?' Her mind was racing.

'Your father, Henry, told me.'

'Father? Bob Lacey's my father.'

'The Adoption Information Service traced Henry for me. He's on my birth certificate as being my father. But he's not — he's white. I got it from the Registrar of Births, Deaths and Marriages in Melbourne.'

'But my birth certificate says nothing about adoption. Bob Lacey is my father.'

'Bob Lacey's your adoptive father.'

'How can you be so sure? You might have made a mistake.'

'What's your mother's maiden name? It's on your birth certificate.'

'Nolan. Shirley Nolan.'

'Same as Henry's. You see, Henry is Shirley's brother.'

'But . . . it must be a mistake. Are you saying my aunt and uncle brought me up?'

Connie nodded. At least it was better than

being brought up by complete strangers. At least Shirley and Bob were family. In that way, Freya was luckier.

'When did you meet Henry?' said Freya.

'Two years ago. As soon as I got my original birth certificate, I flew to Melbourne, hired a car, and drove out to see them at Tinderry, their sheep property.'

'Is that your usual style? Turning up on a person's doorstep and giving them a heart attack?'

'I was afraid that if I wrote they might put a restraining order on me. I wanted to meet them. Desperately.'

'This is unbelievable.' Freya shook her head and ran her hand through her hair. 'I thought I had an aunt and uncle in the country, but you're saying they're my real parents? And that Shirley and Bob are my aunt and uncle?'

Connie nodded. 'That's about it.'

Freya kept shaking her head. 'What happened when you met our parents? Did you just turn up with no warning? Were they angry?'

Connie took a deep breath. She wasn't sure how to deliver the next news. She took a few deep breaths and moved to the window. She stared at the shabby tenements on the other side of the canal. A colourful paddle-steamer chugged past. The cheerful owner waved. Connie smiled and waved back.

'Henry was there on his own,' she said finally, turning to face Freya. 'I'm sorry, Freya, honey. I'm afraid our mother, Ester, is dead. She died of cancer ten years earlier.'

18

'Oh.' Freya felt she should be stricken with grief. But all she felt was a vague falling away inside.

'Since then, of course, Henry's gone downhill,' said Connie. 'He's very ill. Shame about his farm. It's in the Snowy Mountains, you know. Beautiful area.'

'I know where the Snowy Mountains are,' said Freya. 'I went skiing there once, in my teens.'

She remembered that trip clearly because it was the first time she'd been away from home. She'd thought about her mysterious aunt and uncle on their sheep farm in the mountains, and wondered how she might track them down. Then the week had gone by in a blur of activity, and on the last day she'd twisted her ankle.

'I was only thirteen,' she said. 'I thought about trying to find them. But I didn't have a clue where they lived.'

She knew at the time that Shirley and Bob would be furious with her for even thinking about it. When she had arrived home on crutches and they fussed around her, she'd felt guilty for even thinking about her aunt and uncle.

'Now I know the real reason why Mum and Dad never talked about them. It had nothing to do with them fighting.'

Someone walked past and shouted 'Morning, Freya' through the broken door. Freya dragged herself up off the chair and drew the curtains across. She sat down again, exhausted.

'I'm curious,' said Connie.

'I'll say.' Freya rolled her eyes.

'Didn't you wonder why Tinderry was on your

19

birth certificate as your place of birth?' said Connie.

Freya slowly shook her head. 'My parents . . . ' She hesitated; it suddenly seemed phoney, calling them her parents. 'They said they were living at Tinderry when I was born.'

'Yeah. That's how the story goes.'

Henry had told Connie this with great reluctance over a cup of tea on the veranda at Tinderry. She had closed her eyes at one point and tried to imagine life on the property when Ester was alive, and the shock she and Henry had felt when Connie was born black.

'Shirley came down from Inverell to visit Henry,' Freya continued. 'And stayed when she met Bob.'

'That's right.'

'I didn't even know my uncle's — '

'Your *father*,' Connie reminded her.

'I didn't know his name was Henry,' Freya finished. 'Until now. When I was growing up my parents rarely mentioned him, and never by name.'

'So Shirley told you she'd had a fight with Henry, and after you were born she and Bob moved to Melbourne?'

'Yes.'

'There was no fight.'

'I can see that now.'

Connie was impressed with Freya's grasp of things. She wanted to make Freya feel better. The intention had been to deliver the news as something positive to embrace.

'If it's any consolation, Henry actually kept in

touch with them all these years, to find out how you were. He told me he wished they'd kept you.'

Freya flashed her an angry look. 'So why didn't they?'

'I don't know. I'm sorry.'

'I still don't quite understand why my birth certificate doesn't say anything about being adopted.'

'Why would it? Only someone in the know would realise; an official at the Registrar, say.'

'Did you go and see Shirley and Bob? I mean, they're your aunt and uncle too, aren't they?'

'Yes, they are, on our mother's side, that is. They were out when I got there — '

'Just as well. My mother might have fainted.'

Connie smiled. 'Once you get that close nothing can stand in your way.'

'What happened?'

It had taken a huge effort on Connie's part to resist waiting on their doorstep. But the longer she loitered the more conspicuous she'd felt. People walking by stopped and stared. She had seen a set of curtains twitching in the house across the street.

'I didn't want a huge confrontation.' She shrugged. 'So I asked a neighbour, instead — a Mr Miller — '

'Old Eric?'

Connie nodded. She was pleased with their meeting so far, and especially with the restraint she'd managed regarding Peggy. She'd expected Freya to be shocked and upset, but considering

21

the gravity of the news, Freya was taking it reasonably well.

'I told Mr Miller I was a friend of yours from school,' Connie went on. 'And that Shirley and Bob were out, and I was in a hurry. He sent me up the road to your in-laws' house. Luckily they were in. I told them I was an old friend, too.'

'All these lies.' Freya pressed her hands over her mouth as though she was praying.

'They gave me your address in Ruislip — this was two years ago, remember. By the time I flew to England last week you'd moved, of course. The new people at your old house told me you were in Richmond. It was a shock when I phoned up and Neill said you were separated.'

'You phoned him? Christ almighty!'

'Calm down. He gave me your address and that was that.'

'Did you tell him who you were?' Freya was alarmed. 'I don't want Neill to know about this.'

'Don't worry. He thought I was a friend.'

'I still don't understand. I mean, you're . . . '

'Black?'

'Yes.'

'I prefer to think of myself as an Indigenous Australian, thanks all the same.' She said this with pride.

'I don't mean to be rude,' said Freya.

'That's all right.'

'It's all so confusing.' Freya's head felt as if it might burst. She needed a painkiller, but there were none on the boat.

Connie tried to explain. She told Freya about her first meeting with Henry at Tinderry, and the look on his face when he saw her emerge from the hire car in front of the homestead. It was a hot day, and Henry was frowning. He was thin and gaunt. His hands shook badly, and he shuffled his feet. He knew who she was immediately, and for a moment Connie thought he might chase her away with the shotgun he was holding. When she moved closer she noticed he smelled. Later he told her the dam was low, because of a long drought, and he hadn't been able to wash properly for two months.

'I was pretty shocked when I realised it was him. I was expecting a black man.'

'What did he say?'

'Not much at first. Then when he saw how upset I was about our mother's death, he told me about you.'

'Did you ask him about your real father?'

'God no. He probably would've shot me.'

Connie went on to describe the meeting, the awkwardness between them, and his eagerness to be rid of her.

Outside, birds began to arrive in Freya's garden to feed on the nuts and seeds she'd left in various feeders hanging from the elder trees.

'When I met Henry and he told me about you, I thought you'd be white,' said Connie.

'What about our mother?'

'She was white, too. I knew he wasn't my father, but because his name was on my birth certificate, I guessed what had happened out there.'

There was a long pause, filled with the shrieking of a whistle from a nearby factory

23

marking morning break, and the ear-splitting boom of a 747 approaching Heathrow.

'Are you saying our real mother had an affair with an Aboriginal?' Freya had to shout over the noise.

Connie nodded. 'I'd say that's what happened, wouldn't you?'

Freya fumbled with a button on her shirt, and kept sighing and shaking her head.

'You look very successful,' she said suddenly, keen to change the subject.

'I'm probably the first Indigenous Australian trader in London.'

'I can imagine,' said Freya.

'We've produced plenty of athletes, and a few politicians, but for some reason the financial world is a hard one to crack.'

'I bet.'

Freya's heart was suddenly filled with anticipation. But the timing was wrong. She couldn't cope with this, on top of the divorce — which would be finalised any day now — and the prospect of losing custody of the children permanently.

She turned away from Connie and jerked the hatch open hard.

The damn thing jumped off the metal runner, and she had to catch it before it crashed on to the floor. She tried to reposition it, but it was too heavy, she couldn't manage; the news had made her feel weak. How she hated the stupid hatch. It seemed a symbol of her chaotic life. She needed a man. She felt her face turning red as she clenched her teeth and lowered the door on to the floor. She leaned it against the bulkhead, vowing to have a new one fitted — the type that flew open at the flip of a finger.

The factory whistle stopped, the plane landed, and everything was silent.

'Are you sure this isn't a mistake?'

She tried to be nonchalant, but her voice was shaky.

'Oh no, it's definitely not a mistake.'

'You seem so sure.'

'I am sure. Lacey is your adoptive name. As I said, Henry gave me a copy of your original birth certificate. It says Henry Nolan and Ester Doyle of Tinderry Downs, are your natural parents. It says so, right on there. I'll show you next time we meet. You can get the original from the Registrar in Melbourne, if you don't believe me.'

Freya knew Connie was right, but it seemed wrong, somehow, to accept such devastating news without a fight of some sort.

Connie waited while it all sank in.

Freya swallowed hard and glanced away from Connie's beautiful, open face. The tips of her fingers quivered. She twisted an earring, and squeezed her earlobe until it throbbed.

'You said you met Henry two years ago. Why did it take you so long to get in touch with me?'

'I had other things that were more pressing at the time, to do with work.' Was now the right time to tell her about Peggy? She couldn't be sure. This had been a big shock; another one might be too overwhelming.

Freya remained seated. Her hands were trembling, and now and then a heavy shiver ran

25

up her spine and sent her body into a spasm. The sister debate aside, she had never come face-to-face with an Aboriginal. Connie was right to be self-conscious. There were no blacks in her old neighbourhood. Bob had once referred to them as 'a blight on Australian society'. At school she'd learned they were nomadic hunters who ate grubs and snakes. Before she left Australia, news items and documentaries focused on their rampant alcoholism and drug abuse, and degrading living conditions. There certainly weren't many Aborigines in Melbourne — none that she'd seen, at least. She had once seen one playing a didgeridoo in Covent Garden, an old man with scars on his chest and a carved, wrinkled face. She'd thought he looked wise.

'My boss reckons if the media find out I'm Aboriginal, they'll have an absolute field day.' Connie's laugh sounded like a line from a blues melody. She threw her head back and slapped her thigh. 'It was bad enough in Cambridge. The local papers were always writing stories about me.'

'Cambridge?'

Connie smiled. 'No one believed I'd get through, of course, except my parents. You'd think I'd grown up in the desert, the way people reacted.' She laughed again, and dipped her head like a shy child. 'I must admit, it wasn't an easy ride. The other students treated me like an unapproachable celebrity. And when I went on my work experience, *that* was hard. I could tell I'd never fit in over here after that. There was

26

this general feeling I couldn't do the job properly, being a woman *and* black.'

'I'm sorry.' Freya was lost for better words.

There was a long, mordant silence.

Connie pressed her lips together and rolled her tongue over her teeth. 'Of course, I wasn't the only one. The African students found it tough, but there were lots of them, so it wasn't so bad, they had one another to lean on. I was the odd one out. Except for a pygmy from Cameroon, studying law.'

Freya looked at her, still unable to find the right response.

'Anyway, I'm glad I've found you.'

'I'm afraid I haven't got room for visitors.' Freya feared a full-blown invasion. 'There's only one double bed and two bunks, but they're not big enough for an adult — '

'Don't worry.' Connie gave her a reassuring smile. 'I've got my own place in London.'

Freya chewed her lip. 'I didn't invite you here today.' It was not like her to be rude, but she couldn't think straight.

'I'm sorry, but I figured it's not the sort of thing you want to hear over the phone.'

'It's not the sort of thing you want to hear full stop.'

'I thought you'd be glad.' Connie's voice was thick with disappointment.

'I am glad. But the truth is I need some time to think. It's a lot to take in. And I really have to get going. I've got an appointment.' Freya needed to get away, desperately, to catch her breath and clear her head. She tried to steady herself, but her head was spinning with memories of a past that suddenly wasn't real, a childhood that was a lie.

She had been duped.

Heat rose up inside her with volcanic intensity, then subsided, leaving her pale and trembling, wavering between fainting with shock, and vague embarrassment at the musty boat and the untidy shelves.

'I'll wait if you like.' Connie said this as though she had a right to be there, as though she took it for granted she somehow belonged. 'I don't mind. I mean, I've come all this way, been transferred here so I could track you down and spend time with you. What's an hour or so compared with waiting a whole life-time?'

'A whole lifetime?'

'To meet you.'

'Good grief.'

'Well, I guess that's stretching it a bit. But I did sense I had a sibling. I was just never sure if it was a brother or a sister. I wasn't that surprised when Henry told me.'

'Fancy.' Freya was irritated by the frailty of her own response.

'Are you all right?' Connie frowned.

'Yes. I'm fine.'

'I shouldn't have come.'

'It's okay. I'm okay.'

Connie's persuasive eyes, the rich lilt of her husky voice — she oozed goodness and hot bread — made Freya feel giddy with happiness and anxiety.

She was remembering things she had never

thought of before: the small pearly scar on her mother's left thumb, the acute sense of emptiness she felt on Sundays when the whole of Melbourne seemed to shut down, the smell of floral tributes leaning against the garage wall before being loaded into the hearse. She had thought her past was all sewn up and pigeonholed but here it was coming back at her with a new dimension attached. She felt that her street should have smelled of gum trees, not car fumes, that the hills should have been dense with ancient trees, not sheep and housing estates and a few straggly bushes.

'Like I said, I've always known about my own adoption.' Connie's voice was matter-of-fact. 'My adoptive parents were completely upfront about it right from when I was little. I just knew I had siblings. Gut instinct. I've inherited a few skills from my Aboriginal side. Not many, mind you. Friends in Australia reckon I'm basically a coconut blackfella. Black on the outside, white on the inside. Suits me. I mean, they have a terrible life, most of them. I reckon we're the lucky ones, escaping, and anyway, I like my little luxuries, dining out, designer clothes. I couldn't imagine what it would be like to live in a humpy.' She pulled a face.

Freya sensed Connie was not going to leave until they had begun some sort of bonding process.

Connie disappeared into the galley, like a long-term tenant, and came back with a glass of water. She was an overpowering, blustery type, with a commanding, seductive presence. Freya

29

felt herself being drawn in.

'If it's all right with you, I'll wait.' Connie was determined. 'I won't touch anything. You can trust me.' She winked, and her wondrous gaze lingered on Freya. 'You're white as a sheet. I'm sorry. I thought — *hoped* — your adoptive parents would have owned up years ago.'

Freya fumbled with a button on her shirt. 'Well they didn't.' She longed to get away, to walk hard and fast till her legs ached and her heart raced, to the top of a hill where she could take huge gulps of oxygen and feel the sky — the *space* — all around her.

There was another tricky silence.

'You have to believe me.' Connie's eyes were large and unblinking.

'Do I?'

'I know it's a lot to take in.' Connie frowned, then her face lit up. 'Hey. I bet if we compared a few body parts we'd find some similarities.'

She flipped a shoe off and thrust out a stockinged foot, placing it next to Freya's. 'Take your shoes off.'

Freya leaned down and pulled off her own shoe. Connie placed her right foot next to Freya's and made a comparison.

'Well, our big toes are a bit similar,' said Connie.

Freya slipped her shoe on again, embarrassed. 'This is all so bloody unbelievable.' She pushed down hard on the urge to scream, on the flurry of emotions stirring in her heart, and forced into motion her training as a nurse. She simply had to stay in control.

'Oh, you have to believe me,' said Connie. 'There's no doubt about it. I mean, why would I make it up?'

'Oh, I believe you all right,' said Freya, gaining strength. 'What I *meant* to say was, it's incredible.'

So many things were beginning to make sense. The birth mark on her back that had always intrigued her — and Neill — was the real clincher. Neill always said it looked as if it had been left there accidentally, by the hand of an angel. More like an ironic joke.

She looked at Connie. 'I do believe you. But I don't want anyone else to know. At least, not yet.'

'What's the matter? Are you ashamed of me?'

'No. Not at all. It's just . . . it's hard to explain. My kids, I've lost them. I mean, Neill's got them, for now, but obviously, I want to get them back.'

'I'm sorry.'

'I didn't know anything about the ins and outs of custody, and now this. Being adopted. I mean, it won't go down well.'

'I guess not. How awful.'

'And you being, *you know*. I don't mean to insult you, it doesn't bother me in the slightest, some of my best friends are black. But people don't *understand*. My husband, he'll use it against me, being adopted. He'll say that's why I'm weird.'

'Sounds to me like you're better off without the guy.'

'Not that I am weird, he just *says* I am, and,

31

oh shit. It's all so complicated, and this will just make it worse. Don't you see?'

'Yes. I do.'

'I can't tell anyone. Not until I get them back. I have to get them back because he's the nutter, he's a religious freak, he's dishonest, he's a hypocrite. But no one will listen.'

'I'm listening.'

'He's a church member, can you believe it? People think he's respectable, but he's not.'

'Really?' Connie was intrigued, but she thought it was too early to pry.

'I had to get away from Melbourne, it was so boring and dull, living in the suburbs, there was nothing there. Nothing.' Freya stopped to catch her breath, amazed at her sudden verbosity. To her surprise, tears began to pour down her cheeks. 'So. They're not my parents at all.'

'That's right, honey. I'm sorry. But hey! Look on the bright side. You've got a sister.'

'I thought there was something fishy,' said Freya, 'but I put it down to the funerals. It made them very distant sometimes. But I do love them. Very much. They were upset when I left Melbourne with Neill. They didn't like him, you see. Now the tables have turned.'

She stopped, her breath coming in ragged gasps. She was shocked at how easy it was to blurt everything out.

Suddenly Connie kneeled down in front of her. She leaned right over her lap, grabbed her shoulders, and pulled her close, smothering her with perfume and musky body odour. Alarmed, Freya pushed her away.

'Don't,' she cried, 'it's too soon. I don't know you. I don't, know, you.'

Connie unfolded herself slowly and waited. This wasn't the reaction she had expected at all. She could see that Freya was very afraid.

'So you did know, underneath?' she said softly.

Freya stared at a moist patch shining on Connie's lower lip.

'Yes,' she said bluntly. 'I did guess. But it was more a feeling than a concrete fact.'

A palpable expression of guilt crossed Connie's face.

'I'm sorry,' said Freya quickly. 'I know it's not your fault. But *why*? Why drag it all up now, after all these years? What's the point?'

'I don't understand why you didn't ask them about being adopted. I mean, it would have been much better out in the open.'

Freya shrugged. 'I don't know, really. I suppose I didn't want to hurt them. And there was always the possibility I was wrong.'

'Course, I'm not surprised you knew, deep down. Most adoptees sense it. There was no confusion in my case, me being black an' all.'

Freya's temples pulsed, and the inside of her skull felt drained of blood. She thought she might faint if she stood up too quickly. She lifted the glass to her dry lips and took several sips.

'Shall I come with you to your appointment?' said Connie. 'We could go in my rental car, if you like.'

'No.' Freya's voice was regaining strength. 'No. You . . . you can't come.'

Connie looked hurt.

33

'You wait here and make yourself at home,' said Freya kindly, trying to recover her manners.

'Are you sure? I'd like to come with you. It'd be fun.'

'No. When I get back we can talk.'

Freya scooped up her jacket and handbag and made for the door. Her legs felt weak. She steadied herself on the back of a chair.

'Are you sure you're all right?'

'No. No, I'm not all right.'

'You're taking it harder than I thought you would.'

'What did you expect? A fanfare?'

'Aren't you excited?'

'I don't know what to think.' She searched her handbag for her car keys.

'I thought you'd be real pleased.'

'It's unbelievable. But I don't know if I'm pleased or not. I'm gobsmacked.' Freya's voice was hoarse with emotion. 'I mean, it's truly incredible. At the same time, I'm not surprised.'

'I realise it's a shock,' said Connie, 'but it's good news, too, don't you think? You have a sister!'

Freya nodded. 'But the timing's bad. The timing's terrible.' The back of her throat was raw. She sat down again, exhausted, dropping her handbag on to the floor.

As Freya stared at her lap and shook her head, Connie slipped on to her knees again and scooped Freya's hands in her own. Freya flattened herself against the chair back. She could hardly breathe; she hated being touched by anyone unless she had instigated the gesture.

Connie stroked her thumbs earnestly against Freya's, an act so personal it made Freya squirm. Connie didn't notice Freya's discomfort, and continued rubbing.

Freya tried to hide her distress. She thought of other long-lost sisters, and how they might react on first meeting. She remembered reality television shows about sibling reunions, and how uncomfortable she had felt at the uninhibited show of emotion between people who were essentially total strangers to one another.

She should be jumping for joy, and shouting the news from the top deck. Instead, she was paralysed with embarrassment.

Odd, how at work she could bathe the wounds of strange men with erections, stuff pessaries up the arses of constipated spinsters, shave the pubic hair of men with prostate cancer, clean the wounds of bomb victims, allow her shoulders to absorb the agony of a complete stranger's grief.

This was her sister.

She inhaled slowly, deeply, and leaned her head on the back of the chair, eyes closed. She wished again that she smoked. Valerian was probably not a patch on a Marlboro, she thought, wretched at her own stubborn devotion to good health.

'Why have you come here?' she said after a long pause, her eyes popping open.

Connie let go of Freya's hands and abruptly stood up.

'I told you,' she said. 'We're sisters.'

The warmth and tension inside the boat had altered Connie's body odour. Now she smelled

35

of coconut and sesame oil, two scents Freya associated with the tropics, specifically a roadside stall near Hua Hin in Thailand, where she had once sat with Neill under a tamarind tree eating pumpkin rice, Melbourne a dim memory.

Connie fixed her intense and patient gaze on Freya's face, sorry, now, for not phoning or writing ahead. She waited for Freya to make the next move. She picked up a copy of Philip Larkin's *Collected Poems* and opened it, her eyes scanning quickly the inscription on the inside cover:

To my darling wife, Freya, on our fifth wedding anniversary. Love for ever, Neill.

Freya's eyes flitted all over the saloon, alighting now and then on Connie's for a fleeting moment. In spite of her fear, and a gnawing feeling that her life was going to change for ever from this day on, everything was falling into place, in the same way that nature realigns itself after a storm or a fire. The dreams, the songs; it was all making sense.

Connie wouldn't believe her, she was sure of that. It would complicate matters further if she spoke about her theory.

'I can see how they got away with not telling you,' said Connie, 'being white. But they should have. It's far better to be honest about a person's adoption.'

'What makes you an expert?'

Connie dropped her eyes to the floor. 'I'm not,' she said. 'I'm simply repeating what my parents told me.'

Freya cleared her throat and summoned her authoritative voice.

'This is so sudden. I need to think it all through and work out a plan.'

'Take your time,' said Connie. 'I understand.'

Freya felt an urgent need to dash into the galley and wipe the bench tops or chop something green and juicy. Next minute she wanted to throw her arms around Connie; the impulse welled up unexpectedly and gave her a terrific jolt. She resisted.

'I just love our mother's name, don't you?' said Connie. 'Ester, without an h. Isn't that a honey of a name?'

'Lovely.'

'Of course, Peggy and I don't know who our real father is.'

Connie thought it was best to slip Peggy's name in, rather than make an announcement.

'Pardon?'

'But it doesn't matter, not really.' Connie thought if she kept talking it might not be so cataclysmic. 'It's like looking for a needle in a haystack. We've got one another, and now we've got you! That's how I look at it. And Peggy, well, she's got Forbes, her husband, who adores her, and anyway, she decided years ago to stop wondering. It was driving her to drink. Literally. But that's all history now. She's been straight ever since Forbes came along.'

'I'm sorry,' said Freya. 'I haven't got the faintest idea what you're talking about. Who on earth's Peggy?'

Connie let go of Freya's hands and got to her

37

feet slowly. She stared down at her sister, her eyes brimming with uncertainty.

'Why, Peggy's my twin, of course. She lives near Alice Springs. With Forbes. Like I said.'

'Good grief.' Freya stifled a laugh.

'It's not the sort of thing I'd joke about.' Connie looked at her sternly.

'Look, I have to go,' said Freya, 'I really do. I've got this appointment to keep. Surely you understand? I mean, this is great news, wonderful news. Don't get me wrong. But I really must go, and I think it'd be best if you left with me now. We can meet up next week if you like, in London.'

She wanted to see more of Connie, but Del was expecting her, and besides, she couldn't think straight with Connie under her feet. She stood by the door, feeling put out by Connie's determination, racking her brains for a way to get her off the boat.

'I'm sorry, but it'd just be a lot easier if you weren't here. Just in case. My neighbours are very inquisitive.'

She lifted the door and put it back on its runner, amazed she had the strength after all this. She climbed up the stepladder.

Connie settled into the sofa and tucked a cushion into the small of her back.

'I promise I won't tell anyone,' she said, eyes shining victoriously. 'I'll be here when you get back. I've got so much to tell you.'

Freya stood on the landing stage and peered through the open door. For all anyone knew, Connie could be a friend. No one would realise, unless she told them.

But she wasn't a friend. She was her long-lost sister. Someone might guess. But how?

Connie smiled up at her like a beautiful apparition.

'Are you sure you can't cancel your appointment?'

Freya was tempted. She was dying to know more about both sisters, about their childhood, their adoptive parents, their extended adoptive families, their friends, boyfriends, lovers. But she had to get away. That was the real reason now, not Del, or her paycheque.

'No,' she said, 'I really do have to go. I'm sorry.' She pulled the door across, and spoke through the remaining narrow gap. 'I'll shut this,' she said. 'In case you get unwanted visitors. And if anyone knocks, remember, you are just a friend.'

Connie looked up and winked.

'Don't you worry. Your secret's safe with me.'

★ ★ ★

Connie put the photograph album on the coffee table, and got up to make herself a cup of tea. She understood Freya's need to get away. Of course, she would have handled it differently, if things were the other way round. She'd have jumped up and down shouting, most likely, till the whole world knew.

The kitchen cupboards were jammed with ingredients she'd never heard of: puy lentils, tamarind, and dozens of large jars full of dried herbs. Was Freya one of those annoying vegetarians? There was no coffee; the cupboards were full of healthy alternatives. She took out a box of nettle tea.

She ran her fingers over the bunches of herbs hanging from the rafters, enjoying the scent that rained down on her face. Every gas ring on the hob was taken with a saucepan full of evil-looking herb mixtures. She moved one on to the bench, and put the kettle on.

When she'd made herself the tea, she took it into the saloon and set it down to cool. She lifted the lid of a large wooden trunk. It was full of brand-new fabric, all colours and patterns, and bags of lace and rick-rack. Along one wall of the saloon the shelves were stacked haphazardly with volumes on herbs and nursing and European history. There was a book about Australia called *Land of Wonder*, which she flipped through. The usual generic pictures of kangaroos, gum trees, possums and parrots. Nothing about the Aborigines. There were dozens of children's books. And a stack of worn-out board games.

Presently there was a knock at the main hatch. She went to see who it was, and as she peered through the glass panel she tried not to look at the man's crotch.

She opened the hatch a few inches and said, 'Yes? Can I help?'

'Is Freya home?'

'No, she's out, I'm afraid. Can I help?'

'Are you from the hospital?'

'No, I'm . . . a friend.'

'Do you know when she'll be back?' said the man.

She opened the hatch further and peered up at him. A rough-hewn type — unshaven, with slicked-back hair. Good-looking, though, in a dark brown leather jacket and jeans.

'She won't be long, I shouldn't think. Is it urgent?'

The man stifled a laugh. 'No, just calling in for a natter. Tell her Luke dropped by, will you?'

'Of course. Luke. No problem. I'll tell her as soon as she gets back.'

He lingered a moment, as if waiting for her to invite him in, then he stepped off the landing stage and strode towards the car park.

She settled down again, and opened the photograph album.

It made her oddly gloomy, looking at Freya's smiling face beaming out from the pictures. She was the centre of attention, surrounded by doting relatives. But she saw in her sister's eyes a look of uncertainty and sadness. Shirley and Bob were a stiff-looking couple, conservatively dressed, Shirley in twinsets, Bob in khaki shorts and long socks. Shirley had her arm around Freya in all the pictures, and an expression of love for her adopted daughter.

The photos were not dissimilar to her own albums back in Hopeville — birthdays, Christmas, picnics in the mountains. Difference was, she loved Hopeville. Didn't she? Freya had said she couldn't wait to get away from her home town. It sure showed in her face, thought Connie, staring closely at a picture of Freya,

41

aged about seven, standing astride her bike in front of the funeral home sign. Two black hearses were parked behind her on the driveway. No wonder she wanted to get away.

She closed the album and dozed for a while. When she woke she glanced at her watch. She had been waiting almost two hours. Tomorrow was her first day at work; she didn't want to be late arriving, or turn up exhausted. She decided to wait another hour, and sat back and enjoyed the view of Freya's garden. She thought about Peggy, and how excited she'd be when she heard their sister had been found. It had taken courage to front up here today, but Freya didn't seem the type to take account of that.

She opened the album again and began flipping through, fascinated by the photos of Freya's childhood. How could they not have told her? They seemed very self-assured, Shirley and Bob, unsentimental types. Although they were obviously fond of Freya, there was something missing between them; it was plain to Connie, but perhaps that was simply because she knew. No one else would notice.

Presently, there was another knock at the door. She looked across at the hatch. Another set of male legs, this time in shorts.

'Yes?' she said, sliding open the hatch. 'Can I help you?'

The man leaned down and smiled. He was better groomed than the other guy, clean-shaven and smelling of eau de Cologne.

'Is Freya there, please?' His voice was deep and sensual.

42

'I'm afraid she's out.'

'Are you Del?'

'No. I'm a friend. I'm waiting till she comes back from the shops. She popped out for some milk.'

She hoped like hell that the man wouldn't bump into Freya, who might arrive home any minute minus the imaginary milk.

'Tell her Sam Jenner called in, will you? I'll come by tomorrow, if she's about.'

'Sam Jenner. Okay.' Connie nodded.

'Are you from her work, by any chance?'

'No.'

'A herb colleague?'

'No. Just a friend. An old friend. We met years ago . . . on holiday.'

'Oh. Right. I see. In America?'

'Jamaica, actually. On a cruise.'

'Really? I didn't know Freya had been to the Caribbean.'

'It was a long time ago. Before she had her children.'

'I thought she came straight to England with her husband?'

'I can't remember the year. Must've been not long after she arrived here. Anyway, I'll tell her you called in. What was the name again?'

'Sam. From *Lady Luck*.'

'I'll tell her as soon as she gets back.'

She watched as Sam headed down the towpath and disappeared inside a large boat — the biggest along this stretch of the moorings, she noted. She saw now why Freya was being circumspect.

43

She remained at the window watching the residents for a while, curious as to how they earned a living, amused that the drinking of tea could take up so much time. Eventually she sat down and flipped through the album once more. She could already see in Freya what she wasn't: stoical, firm, quick, independent.

She's avoiding me, she thought. She's in denial. It's unhealthy, bottling things up, denying your past. She'll have to snap out of it. I did.

4

You can take the boy out of the country, but you can't take the country out of the boy.

Your father always said that, when you stumbled over your words at the wool brokerage in town. Even the cool relief of cold tiles on your bare feet in the back room at the hotel couldn't make up for the fear you felt when he introduced the hotelier's son. You didn't like meeting people.

During summer it was too hot to work after midday, so you spent the afternoons sitting on the shaded veranda at Tinderry, swatting flies and sipping Ester's home-made lemonade. Sometimes you had a beer. In those days beer was for quenching a bloke's thirst, not for turning him into an animal.

You loved the old bull-nosed tin awning and the way it hugged the house. You could have gone inside and sat in the dark drawing room, where it was cooler, but Ester became irritable when you were indoors. You heard her singing under her breath as she chopped onions or bottled plums from the orchard. She was in remission, although you didn't know it at the time. You thought she was having a final burst of life, that the tablets had a mysterious ingredient that pumped vitamins into her blood, enough to give her a temporary boost. In those days when you had cancer you had cancer, there was no treatment, no cure, and no such thing as remission. You only knew it was called that now, because these days everyone seemed to have the disease and there was plenty of information about chemotherapy and radiotherapy and new drugs.

Every square inch of land as far as your eye could see, and fifty miles beyond, was yours. You knew every chip in the bark on the stand of eucalyptus behind the dam. When a wind came in the night and broke a branch, or lifted a sheet of tin from the dog kennels, you sensed something was amiss. Like a painting, changed by the artist when you weren't looking. You knew.

Beyond the lush acre surrounding the house, with its buddleias and poplars, snow- and sun-scorched hills carved up the valleys. Mountains fell away on to heat-buckled plains. You once counted the mountains you could see from Tinderry, and carved the number on the smooth white trunk of a snow gum. It felt like Ester's bare rump on a winter night, and gave you a sense of power when it warmed under your hands.

What concerned you at Tinderry Downs was sheep, weather, feed, water.

There was nothing you could do about Ester's illness.

Not a damn thing.

Dr Roberts had come and gone many times. No hope, he said. Cancer had taken a grip. Death was inevitable.

Her little bursts of energy were a surprising

46

dividend. Mind you, she didn't think you saw it that way.

That was what hurt the most. Not her shocking deterioration. The sagging skin and protruding bones. Her cloudy eyes. Not even the smell of her skin, which reminded you of sour cheese. It was her grief that had been painful to witness. She cried every day. Her weight dropped from ten stone to six and a half in the first three months. Hell had come to Tinderry. Thank God for the sheep.

The twins were easier to give up, but the next one . . . After her, Ester's eyes became lacklustre, as though every last trace of vigour had finally drained away. You thought about keeping her, but you had a hunch. Ester kept her hidden in the nursery, under sheets. One afternoon, when Ester was in the laundry, you went into the darkened room, pulled back the cot covers, and lifted the tiny singlet.

★ ★ ★

The removal of ticks and seven-inch-thick fleece, fly-infested withers and facial wool, the nursing of injured and sick animals, the observation of weather — all this took up your time and attention.

Your private life? The sex was good. As a husband should, you had your way with her every night. She licked the salt from your skin, and breathed in the smell of your chest, thick with a layer of curling grey and black hairs. You knew she wanted more; women were never

47

satisfied. She set the table with a white cloth and silver cutlery her parents gave you for your wedding, and lit candles. But your mind was on drought, or storms, or the cast sheep you'd overlooked in the west paddock.

During the day she moved about in the laundry, cutting wedges of soap, squashing spiders with the heels of her button-up shoes, pouring boiling water into ants' nests, and scrubbing yolk and lanolin from your clothes. For a city girl she had taken to living in the country quite well. She was not afraid to wield an axe and split firewood or shove her fist up a sheep's backside to pull out a lamb.

You did not watch her or consciously listen for her. You rarely saw her from dawn to dusk. You simply knew she was there and what she was doing. There was no mystery to life on the land, no secret places she could go, nothing to tempt, corrupt or distract from the simple tasks you expected of her. And when the shearers came in you watched them the way you watched your animals, counting their heads over and over, in case one disappeared when you weren't looking, to try it on with Ester.

They seemed to know you were wary. Especially after the time you caught Rodney Browne talking to Ester, out by the gate. She had gone to collect the post wearing a bonnet to keep the sun off her face, because she burned so easily. Rodney was leaning on the post, one foot on the lower rung, so that his crotch puckered. When you pulled up in your truck your anger was so alarming you left your rifle in the back.

'Git away back to the sheds now, thanks Rodney,' you said, staring at the lump in his trousers. From that day you knew exactly where every man was and what they were doing. Your eyes swivelled around the farm like a lighthouse beam. The poor buggers couldn't even take a shit without you knowing.

In the evening you sat on the veranda and she brought you a slab of freshly baked bread surrounded by orange quarters, arranged like the numbers of a clock, on a tin plate. Neither of you spoke but the atmosphere was tense. It was destroying your marriage, this invisible tumour. One day she looked at you and said, Why, Henry? Why did you take them to that house in the city and just dump them there?

5

'I'm sorry I left you sitting there last week,' said Freya. 'But can you wait until all this court brouhaha is over and done with?'

'Of course I can,' said Connie, cradling the phone between her chin and shoulder while she checked a list of stocks. 'Give me a call when you're ready.'

She had gone back to London that day feeling deflated. But she realised Freya was in a vulnerable situation. Now she felt bad for being so pushy. She had left a note, with her phone number, on the galley table. Every evening after work she hurried home, certain that today was the day Freya would call. She was furious with herself for not taking down Freya's number. The following weekend she had toyed with the idea of taking a train out to see her again. But in the end she decided the next move had to be Freya's.

'Don't turn up unannounced,' said Freya. 'I'll let you know when it's safe. It's got to come out sooner or later, but not just yet.'

They spoke for a few minutes; Freya asked about her work at the Stock Exchange, and her flat in Knightsbridge. Connie was chatty, friendly.

Freya's voice was flat and distant. She tried to sound warmer, but she was guarded and formal. She simply needed to get over one hurdle at a time.

The day of the divorce finally arrived.

It was over in less than fifteen minutes. The build-up was contradicted by the low-key atmosphere in court. She had expected hostility, a long-drawn-out interrogation by the judge. And angry words. But Neill was civilised, almost pleasant. Afterwards, she left the court feeling strangely neutral.

She drove up to London to deliver a crate of St John's Wort flower oil to the Harrod's apothecary, and walked out feeling buoyant when the buyer put in another large order. She would have to start looking for a warehouse to rent soon. On the way home she called in to see Del. She parked the car and was suddenly aware that she was a free woman. She had expected to feel devastated and tearful. Instead, she was quite calm.

'Cool as a cucumber, that's me,' she said lightly, when Del commented on how well she was handling it.

They sat in the conservatory, enjoying the warmth, admiring Del's orchids.

Del smiled apologetically. 'I forgot you were going to court today.'

'Until today I didn't believe it. I thought Neill would back down and beg me to go back to him.'

'And of course, you wouldn't have.'

'No way.'

Del poured two cups of dandelion coffee and lit a cigarette. 'Of course, depending on the type of incident, and the individual's resilience, shock can either make or break a person,' she said.

51

'I'm glad to be rid of him, to be honest. Especially since his conversion.'

'Pay careful attention to your health,' Del warned, 'or you'll come down with depression — divorce can have a strange effect.'

'Yes — liberation. It's a rare condition for the married woman.'

'Quite right. Take what you can from this mess,' Del urged, 'because good things often come out of bad.'

Freya agreed. There was no point feeling sorry for herself. She decided to celebrate with a bottle of wine and plan her future. A future that would include having sisters.

She had thought of Connie during the drive to court, and again while driving to Del's. In fact she thought about Connie a lot, and wondered what to do about the whole situation. It was like having a secret lover getting under her skin, sending shockwaves of lust through her veins.

'At least you're away from Neill's holier-than-thou bullshit,' Del added.

'Fancy a drink?'

'Isn't that a bit risky?'

'I doubt they're following me that closely.'

'I meant your allergy.'

'Oh, that.' Freya shrugged. 'What the hell. Call it a one-off splurge. Besides, it's better than making myself ill with bitterness.'

'That's the spirit,' said Del. 'What's an itchy rash compared to cancer or a stomach ulcer?'

Freya set off for the off-licence. When she thought about the future, about being alone, biting tears sprang from her eyes like blobs of paint. In spite of that, she had to admit she had wanted a divorce for a while. She had put up with Neill's religious antics for the children's sake, but in the end realised they were unhappy because she was. It never happens as you expect it to, she thought. It creeps up on you, like the tide on a wide beach. When you try to talk about it the words are guttural and stick like mud in your throat, so you delay the moment. You freeze-frame the frustration, and push down on the petty dissatisfactions. And you long to slip into the arms of a stranger and cry, or rush for a taxi and take the first plane to anywhere.

At night in bed, when the house was quiet, Neill had curled up with his Revised Standard Version instead of *Playboy*. She lay next to him, numb with bewilderment, pretending to read *Alternative Medicine*. When he dozed off, finally, she often went for a midnight stroll. She wasn't the type to seek a lover — why should she? She was married, for God's sake. She sought solace in staring up at the stars, and the moon, which hung in the air like a stone. She touched the warm bark of a tree, smelled the damp earth in the woods, bitter with the stench of ancient battles.

She was on the verge of telling him, once, when they were on a picnic near Henley. But she chickened out. The children came running across the field shouting about a cow they'd seen, their faces sunny and creased with smiles.

When she got back to Del's, she opened the bottle of Bordeaux. She couldn't afford such an expensive drop, but hoped it would have a less drastic effect on her than cheap plonk.

'Cheers,' she said, clinking her glass against Del's.

'Cheers,' said Del. 'Here's to your future. Down with religion.'

When she woke the next morning, still dressed, on Del's sofa, her face was swollen and blotchy, and her arms itched like mad. If the child welfare person saw her now, she'd never get the kids back. She had a quick shower and went home feeling as though she was in the eye of a reckless storm.

The next two weeks went by in a blur of activity: gardening, boat maintenance, sales meetings. She bottled and labelled over fifty different herbal tinctures for her list of clients. And she managed to keep Connie at bay, saying she was too busy just yet to meet up.

'The children are coming to visit next weekend,' she said, when she phoned Connie again. 'I have to get ready for them, plan some sort of outing. But I'll get back to you when things settle down.'

'Oh,' said Connie. 'All right.'

6

You hated Melbourne. The noise, the traffic. The journey there from Tinderry was long and boring, and you resented the wool brokers in their waistcoats and brogues, dictating prices and guzzling whiskey. You couldn't wait to get home and kick off your city shoes.

After all that, here you are again, rotting in Melbourne's heart.

Ester's parents had lived here, but you lost track of them after she died. You'll rue the day you leave us for that man, Georgia said, when you proposed to Ester. Georgia didn't like your coarse humour. She was trying to teach her daughter manners.

You met Ester at a dance the shearers told you about. It took you three days to drive there over the mountains. The Ford overheated seven times the first day, but you persevered. It had been six years since your last woman; you were driving yourself insane with your little perversions.

When you arrived, the hotel was full. Men in pale trousers hung around the porch, loose-tongued and randy. You tugged the brim of your hat as you walked by, avoiding eye contact.

The whole town was buzzing. The dance was an annual shearing celebration. Everyone planned for it all year. It kept people going. Some lucky folk made a living from it: dressmakers, tailors, caterers. And there were spin-offs: weddings, funerals, christenings — cold saveloys and line dancing were chicken feed compared to six-tiered cakes and £10 wreaths.

You parked the car in the middle of a gum forest, and swam in the creek behind a timber yard. The bar of soap you bought at the Co-op would not lather. Reeds and fat eels ribboned between your legs. The leaves on the overhanging gum trees taunted you like loose-fisted boxers.

Stirring up dust, you walked towards her across the dance floor, and thought of the motes in the shearing shed, floating in the shafts of light beaming down through the roof.

You looked at her feet, feminine and petite in cream satin shoes.

You introduced yourself, and she blushed like a peach. She was staying with relatives, she said, her father's brother and his wife, on a sheep station. The Doyles. You nearly fell over. They were your nearest neighbour. She had visited every year since she was five, chaperoned by an aunt who came to collect her from Melbourne on the train. This had to be fate, you thought. She reckoned she loved the outback way of life. Said it with complete sincerity, not like a city girl with tickets on herself. You told her how you'd bumped into Cecil and Constance Doyle during your journey out of Inverell, years earlier; they were camped on the roadside near Goulburn, and when you heard they were heading for the Snowy you thought, *sounds like a good enough place to me*, and joined their party for Cooma.

You never dreamed that one day they'd be the link that would give you your wife.

Although Ester was a city girl, you were willing to give her a go. During her visits to Cecil's place she'd experienced pestilence, drought, floods and fire. You thought she could tough it out.

Your uncle probably used some of the same farmhands, you said, conversationally, but she said no, Uncle Cecil only let family work for him; cousins from Inverell, mainly, and his brothers (he had eight). He gave up employing Abos, too, when he left Inverell, on account of their deplorable habits, and the risk of rape and inter-racial breeding with the girls in the family. This last comment shook you badly, but you managed to hide your disgust.

I'd love to, she said coyly, when you asked her to dance.

You trod on her toes five times, and your arse stuck out like an ape's — touching abdomens too early in the liaison was not the done thing in those days. Now when there's a dance they call it crass names like the Whores and Sailors Ball, and what starts as an elegant evening with everyone dressed in tuxedos and gowns soon descends into a drunken orgy, with half-naked women being screwed behind the barn.

You were conscious of the smell of carbolic acid on your hands as you swung her across the dance floor. The boards and chutes in the shed were filthy when the men finished shearing last week, and you insisted on cleaning them yourself before setting off on this trip. You weren't the type of boss to stand on the sidelines giving orders. Not like these young bucks coming up, who think rounding up sheep from the seat of a motorbike is hard work.

'You smell very nice,' she said.

You thanked the Lord you had swum in that blasted creek. Your dick swelled with blood, and later you took her back to your car. She let you suck droplets of thin, sweet milk from her breasts, and you thought: *this woman is hot to trot, this filly will pump them out like rabbits.*

7

The day of the residence hearing, Freya drove into town in a fug of emotion. It was like going to her own hanging.

At the petrol station she bought a packet of chewing gum, and chewed it ferociously. In her haste, she bit a chunk off the side of her tongue. It wouldn't stop bleeding, and the pain made her eyes water.

She arrived at the court two hours early. She parked the car and sat in the driver's seat, stripping the skin around her nails like a crazed piranha.

Inside the court room it was sombre. It smelled of sweat-soaked leather and polished wood. Neill stood up and told Judge Kitty Wong, a stern, perfectly groomed woman with cerise lipstick, about Freya's odd behaviour before the separation. He made her sound like a complete lunatic.

'She wandered around the garden in the middle of the night, talking to herself. She's either possessed or mad — or both.'

'It is not uncommon for people to behave erratically during a marital breakdown, Mr Kirby,' said Wong.

Neill sat down, red-faced.

Freya waited for the verdict. She was stiff with anxiety. Judge Wong looked her up and down as if she might suddenly sprout wings.

'I have decided to award residence to Mr Kirby,' she said.

Freya stared in horror at her black eyes.

'Mainly because of the all-important family atmosphere, already established by Mrs Sheldon's four children. And the larger, more appropriate accommodation. Also, the fact of Mrs Kirby's decision to abandon the marital home before matters were settled.'

A gasp escaped from Freya's mouth, and she clamped a hand over it to stifle any other strange reactions.

'There is also the matter of her relationship with the children to consider,' said Wong, peering over her pink-rimmed Guccis at the court welfare officer. 'And of course, her drinking.'

They exchanged details as though Freya was not in the room.

While she compared her fruit print kimono top and faded denim skirt with Mrs Wong's neat black Armani suit, her life was changed for ever. The sweep of a pen on a sheet of paper. She gripped the back of a chair. Her head filled with blood and she tried to control her breathing. She sat down heavily. When she tried to speak she kept biting her injured tongue, making it bleed again. Tears sprang out and rolled down her cheeks. A minute passed. She heard noises: chairs grating on the wooden floor, hushed voices, files slamming shut, phlegmy throats being cleared.

'Your life needs a more positive shape,' said Wong. 'You need to get your act together, Mrs Kirby.'

'What do you mean?' She stared at Wong's small red mouth.

It was hard to believe her marriage was over. Now she had to contend with losing her children. Her eyes met Neill's across the room and he looked away. Clarissa was wearing a hat. She stared straight ahead, head tilted, chin up.

Freya hadn't realised Neill's interest in *Songs of Praise* would mean a major life change, an affair, a divorce, a new wife. She thought he was perving at Angela Rippon, not falling in love with Jesus. Clarissa's power of persuasion had cast its sensual, perfumed spell, and gathered him into the fold.

She thought of the children, and what they might have said to the welfare officer. Had Mrs Wong interviewed them too? These people were treating them like toys, or possessions. It was like a hideous sideshow in an Indian market, where fat Americans bartered for orphans.

And it was cruel of Neill, terribly cruel, telling the court she was an alcoholic. More to the point, it was *un-Christian*.

'Will your client be appealing?' said Wong.

Nadine nudged Freya. 'Do you want to appeal?' she hissed in Freya's ear.

'Yes, I do,' said Freya.

'Very well. In the mean time, the court will seek a further psychiatric report,' said Wong. 'Before the next hearing, Mrs Kirby, I suggest you shape up.'

Shape up. It sounded like some sort of cholesterol challenge.

'And one other thing, Mrs Kirby. You might

like to bear in mind that your children deserve to live in a proper home, not a health spa or an off-licence. There's a difference between being creative and being neglectful.'

Freya was not fazed by women in suits. 'I'm creative,' she said. 'I like to keep busy. You are misconstruing my busy-ness as neglect. And I'm not an alcoholic. I don't even drink alcohol. I'm allergic to it.'

She glared at Beverly Harris, the dour psychiatrist appointed to assess her mental state. Obviously her conclusions so far were negative. Freya wanted to wring her neck. Then she turned her venomous gaze on Monica Murray, who had visited her several times to assess her living conditions. She couldn't blame Monica. The moorings didn't give a good impression. But she still wanted to murder her. Monica fiddled with the papers on her desk, eyes cast down.

'I am not saying you neglect your children, exactly, Mrs Kirby,' continued Wong. 'The psychiatrist's report concurs with your husband's observations over a number of years: simply, you have failed to properly *bond* with your children.'

'Neill's lying. I'm telling you, he's lying.'

'It is the court's opinion that you are in need of counselling, Mrs Kirby.'

Freya grimaced. She hated the way Wong repeated her name, as if she were on her side. It was too familiar, coming from someone dishing dirt on people, changing lives on threadbare evidence and lies. She opened her mouth to object.

'Sit down,' hissed her lawyer. 'Sit down and shut up. You're making things worse.'

'I think it would be appropriate for Mr and Mrs Kirby's children to spend two weekends a month at Mrs Kirby's new address. In addition, two evenings a week. Say Tuesday and Thursday. Holidays may be split equally.'

The stenographer straightened her shoulders, looked down her nose, and tapped the keyboard with her fake fingernails. They clicked across the keys like red beetles.

Wong lifted Freya's case file papers and banged them gently on her desk, straightening the edges and setting them aside. Freya saw the writing on the spine: Kirby vs. Kirby.

Later, in the foyer, she turned on Nadine, who had been weak from the outset, in spite of pontificating about the certainty of winning.

'We can appeal,' said Nadine. 'Stop panicking.'

'It was the bottles of home-made wine that did it,' said Freya. 'If bloody Monica Murray hadn't spotted them in the larder, Neill's allegations wouldn't have stuck.'

She sat on a hard bench and buried her face in her hands. Her bones felt as if they might crumble inside her and dribble out of her toes. Her chest was cramped and sore.

'It's the court welfare officer's job to report it,' said Nadine, 'but it's not the booze that swung the decision, not really. It's your relationship with your children.'

She stuffed a file into her briefcase and placed her hand on Freya's shoulder. Freya sensed she was perhaps a little sorry.

'I don't even drink the stuff,' said Freya. 'I give it away to people, for God's sake. It's a hobby. I like picking the fruit, preparing it, stewing it, sieving it, bottling it. It's therapeutic. I'm sick of telling people this.'

'Well, if it's any compensation, I believe you. But that's beside the point. Right now you need to focus on the children.'

Nadine's hand remained on Freya's shoulder, as if to emphasise the gravity of the court's decision. It was a condescending gesture, and Freya pulled away.

'I've loved my children from the minute I knew I was pregnant,' she said, fighting back the tears. 'I lay awake at night, talking to them in my womb. I went back for two extra scans, just so I could see them floating about inside me. Neill's a jerk. He'd say anything to get his own way. He always has.'

'Think of something they're interested in,' said Nadine. 'See if you can get close through some sort of joint activity or hobby. Just because Neill's got custody, it doesn't mean you won't see them. He's not taking them to darkest Africa.'

'He may as well be. Two weeks is a long time.'

'You can see them twice a week as well.'

'That's no use. By the time I've picked them up from school and battled the traffic it'll be time to take them back to Richmond again.'

'Take them out instead. Near Richmond.'

'What are we supposed to do, sit in a bloody café till nine o'clock?'

'It'll give you a chance to talk. At least there's

not the distraction of television.'

'I don't own a TV. I left it at Neill's.'

'You must put some real effort into this. Focus on nothing else.'

'I do . . . I did.'

'No distractions.'

'It's so easy for people like you to give advice. You don't understand the emotions, the pain. Not to mention the daily hassles of just keeping going.'

'Fucking hell, Freya, losing custody isn't the end of the world.'

'No,' said Freya, 'it's not the end of the world. It's the end of family life. Mine and the children's. So don't talk to me about it not being that bad. It *is* that bad. It's worse than that bad. It's like having your soul ripped out.'

8

Del's house was set back from the river, but Freya could still smell it: tannin, soap, the wet-fur smell of dead cats, ancient mud, soggy leaves, a hint of rotting carcass, dead rat, and in there somewhere the unmistakable aroma of water. Long-lived, with balance and depth.

She allowed herself this small joke; it was her salute to Oz Clarke, the wine expert, whom she and Kirsty liked to send up. Her stomach tightened, thinking of all the little domestic rituals she would miss with the children: joking about things their teachers said or did, persuading them to help with the washing-up, games of Scrabble by candlelight in the dining room, shopping in Tesco's. By definition, custody engendered formality, organised outings, special metals. The days of Bolognese and instant puddings were history. Treating them to anything remotely extravagant would now seem like bribery, and yet she already knew she would go to a lot of extra trouble.

Out in the conservatory, Del opened a bottle of Bulgarian red.

'I'm so terribly sorry, old girl,' she said. 'How ghastly for you.'

Beads of sweat formed across Freya's brow. Her fingers trembled and she kept glancing over her shoulder, expecting someone with a clipboard to walk in.

'Relax,' said Del. 'The front door's locked.'

'To hell with the rash.' Freya clinked her glass against Del's. 'This is my requiem to marriage *and* motherhood.'

The wine was raw on her throat. She hadn't eaten all day, and it hit the spot instantly.

She cried.

She laughed.

The pain dissolved.

'Better to get things out of my system now than let them fester,' she said, and kicked off her shoes.

Del nodded. 'Nothing worse than a woman spurned.'

Freya threw down the last mouthful and banged the glass on the table.

'I know I said that was it after the Bordeaux, but I swear on my life, this is the *last time*.'

They pulled Neill apart and watched Graham Norton, and with her front teeth stained red, Freya fell asleep on the sofa, fully clothed and hugging a cushion.

★ ★ ★

Next morning her arms and legs were covered in red welts. She applied marigold cream and flushed out her system with hot lemon and water. It was worth it, though, for metaphorically sticking it up Neill.

Instead of getting maudlin, she decided to face the future (a dauntingly alone future) head-on. No point being sentimental. And Del was right: bitterness was unattractive. She would get the children back somehow; Kitty Wong had made a stupid, unfair, cruel mistake. They'd see she was a good mother. And she'd do everything by the book: make sure the children were ready on time when Neill collected them, cook healthy meals, take them on educational as well as fun outings. She'd talk to them till they could no longer bear the sound of her voice, probing their deepest thoughts, delving into the tiniest details of their friendships, their fears, their dreams. When Monica paid her next visit, Freya would bombard her with information about them.

'Neill will have to swallow his words,' she said, over breakfast, nursing a fearful headache. 'I'll prove he lied. I can handle the snooty court psychiatrist, too.'

Del smiled. 'They're a breed apart. Here, take this.' She handed Freya a glass of water and two aspirins.

'Perhaps you can give me a few tips,' said Freya.

Del ran her own psychiatric practice in Barnes, but she wasn't stuck-up or vain, she was urbane and relaxed.

'I'd be happy to,' said Del. 'I know all the tricks of the trade.'

'I never thought I'd have to prove myself as a mother. As a nurse, fair enough, or a wife. But being a mother is . . . well, surely it's instinctive?'

'For you, maybe. But not for everyone. All sorts of terrible parents pass through the courts. You're really at their mercy, especially once someone has pointed the finger.'

'As for living alone,' said Freya, 'I'm not afraid

68

of my own company. I'm not one of these women who can't bear to be without a man. I like being on my own. I can be myself. I can cut my toenails on the sofa; I can cook eggs in my underwear.'

Del smiled. 'That's the spirit.'

'I'll show them.'

'Don't get too carried away. You don't want to come across as facetious. Best to just be yourself.'

Del was right. There was no need to exaggerate her interest in the children. Monica was a cool customer; she'd soon sniff out anything phoney or forced.

'Are you missing having Neill's familiar rump in the marital bed?' said Del.

'Yes,' said Freya. 'I am. Mind you, his rump was the only thing I did have for the last few years. And I'm used to sleeping on my own, from his band days.'

He had slept with his back to Freya since finding Christ two years ago. She might as well have been on another planet. Before that he was away touring eight months out of twelve, in Europe and Japan.

In those days (she called them the BC days) she never had to worry about embarrassing herself when he brought home his mates. Musicians were so world-weary. They teased her about her Bohemian customs, and asked stupid questions like which herbal remedy was good for erections, or swollen knackers. Or which herbal tea might have the same effect as hash. Being the wife of the lead guitarist, she went along with their ribbings.

'You should remind the court, via your lawyer, about his past habits,' said Del.

'I already have. But Nadine reckons they're only interested in his behaviour now, and since that involves the church . . . well, say no more. Case closed. What hope have I got of competing with God? You know what people are like about herbalism. They think I'm a Druid, or a witch.'

'Such a vulgar, vain man.'

'Neill doesn't think so,' said Freya. 'He thinks it's natural, spreading himself around.'

'Has all that stopped?'

'As far as I know, Clarissa's the only one since the Confessions.'

When they lived in Melbourne and were saving to go to England, Neill said Australia was knocking the 'prudish pommy edges' off him. By this he meant he had discovered the joys of nude beaches and wife-swapping parties.

'How did you put up with him all those years?' said Del, topping up Freya's water glass.

'You just do,' she said quietly. 'I thought he'd get over it eventually, and go back to being normal. When I realised he was never going to change, it was too late. By then the children were involved. Perhaps if I'd been English it might have been easier. Being thousands of miles from home makes the decision so huge. Then he introduced bible study evenings into the household. The strain was unbearable.'

She had tried to be a good wife, and a perfect hostess — first to the band, and then to members of the church congregation. It was a lot

70

to take in, tight-lipped men in suits clutching bibles, buttoned-down women in floral frocks and no make-up. They scrutinised every corner of her kitchen, looking her over as if she might bite. She had to be careful not to swear. Or talk about religion in a derogatory way.

'Maybe it was partly my fault,' said Freya. 'I guess I just can't help being an oddball.'

'I doubt that,' said Del. 'He's a horrid little man. I never did like him, even when I first met you and he was telling jokes all night. I didn't find any of it funny, to be honest; I laughed because I thought you'd want me to.'

'Thanks,' said Freya miserably. 'But I wish you'd told me how you really felt.'

She had let him down badly on one occasion, and from that moment realised she'd never fit in with his new friends. She'd mentioned a patient with Crohn's disease — well, when you're a nurse, and Australian to boot, anything goes — and the assembled Christians were overcome with awkwardness.

Neill had narrowed his eyes. 'Can't we talk about something more appropriate?' Later he told her she was nothing but a hick from the colonies.

She had put the incident aside, telling herself he was feeling particularly tense, being on the short list for the new lay preaching job, which, she now realised, would put him in closer proximity to Clarissa, who played the organ.

'You don't want to believe these things,' she said, looking at Del, 'because it's a reflection of who you are, as much as who they are. It throws up your bad choices, and stupidity, for putting up with someone you're not happy with, when you know you shouldn't.'

'It's very odd for a rock musician to go so far the other way,' said Del. 'Do you think he's lost his marbles?'

'It wouldn't surprise me if he's got brain damage. He took a lot of drugs over the years.'

Thinking back, he had made their lives hell.

'At the height of his musical career the house was crammed with equipment and guitars and leads running all over the floors like worms. Drippy musicians hung around day and night, helping themselves to food and leaving a mess in the lounge room.'

'How awful,' said Del.

'I'm no domestic angel, but I was constantly emptying ash trays and clearing away debris. They thought nothing of smoking dope in front of the children or snorting a line of coke, either. Empty cans of beer were left on the sofas. Walls were damaged when equipment was shifted about. Strange women rang up in the middle of the night. I quite often found lipstick stains on his shirt collars or condoms in his pockets.'

'You poor girl.'

'Then when religion reared its smug head he banned *Top of the Pops* and MTV, and imposed Classic FM on the household. The jazz station was forbidden too.'

'You should've got out years ago, darling.'

'He began to insist on saying grace before meals. Not your bog-standard Thank You for the World So Sweet version. Oh no. That wasn't good enough for Neill. He made up his own grace, sometimes lasting five minutes — on and on about how grateful we should be for our good fortune.'

'I think I'd rather be on my own than put up with that,' said Del, her face grim.

'Oh, it gets worse,' said Freya. 'Then he'd ask God to bless everyone. He actually named people, one by one, until I picked up my knife and fork and started sighing. Finally he'd say Amen, slowly, forcing us to join in. Then he'd give me a filthy look and begin a lecture that might last the entire meal. It scared the wits out of Tom sometimes, all that stuff about being damned to fire and brimstone if he didn't eat his peas.'

'Your lawyer should bring all this up,' said Del.

'I don't want her to. It's too tit-for-tat. If I get the kids back it has to be because the court believes in me, rather than not believing in Neill, if you see what I mean.'

She knew it was going to be a battle. Apparently Monica had been at the house he was now sharing with Clarissa in Richmond when some religious crusaders knocked. Neill had actually invited them in and sat them down, and they'd talked about the Good Word over mugs of tea and plates of digestives. Monica had lapped it up, and had reported back to Mrs Wong that Neill spent all day on Sunday at church, and on Saturdays handed out leaflets in the high street about the Church Youth Group, shouting through a megaphone for hours about the evil ways of the world and the Lord's sacrifice.

'Do you know, Del, I used to bump into him occasionally when he was out crusading. It was embarrassing, but as his wife I had to say hello. He always managed to brush me aside in favour of complete strangers, who in his opinion needed saving. To me, discussing Christ's sacrifice is tantamount to pondering the mechanics of a woman's vagina.'

Del laughed.

'He was a wanker, basically,' said Freya. 'I just didn't want to believe it.'

She couldn't accept that religion alone could dampen a bloke's spirit so thoroughly.

'If nothing else, at least the courts aren't routinely giving the mother custody,' said Del thoughtfully. 'Hard-done-by dads would love Kitty Wong.'

'If I had full custody I'd never deny Neill access. Never. That wouldn't be fair on the children. I hope he doesn't pull that one on me.'

'You'll have to be clever. Play it by the book.'

'Oh, I will.'

'Mrs Wong will want evidence. Lots of it. It's hard to get the court to change their minds in these situations. Mind you, there was a recent case of a man gaining custody after his ex-wife lied through her teeth about him. So there is hope. If you can prove that Neill lied, and prove you've bonded, you'll win. The trick is, you must put the interests of the children before your own.'

'Don't worry. I will.'

All afternoon Freya was on the verge of telling

Del about Connie. Finally she decided not to. Del would be furious with her for not being more trusting. For now, it was her wonderful, scary secret.

* * *

Back at the boat she quickly changed into jeans and boots, and set off for a long walk before the sun set. She was determined to avoid her neighbours, and the inevitable questions about the outcome in court. They'd find out soon enough. One whiff and the whole community would be gossiping.

Someone was burning a piano in their garden. Smoke rose over the moorings. She hurried along the towpath before anyone could button-hole her; the fire had attracted an audience, people were standing around sipping wine and slugging beer from bottles, fascinated by the patterns and colours of the melting keys. Several wires pinged loudly, and everyone laughed. Drinking sessions weren't confined to after dark. People were only too happy to abandon their daily chores in favour of an impromptu party. She'd even seen them drinking wine with their breakfast, out on deck. There was no denying she was making life difficult for herself by living here. Sometimes she thought she might as well go along with the court's judgement. She could declare herself an unfit mother, throw all her inhibitions to the wind, and join in the nonstop party.

On the slope of a hill she sat facing the canal, enjoying the fading sunshine on her back.

Why had she put up with Neill all these years? Was she stupid? Weak? Or simply an optimist? She should have seen it coming. Thinking about it now, she had, really. Clarissa was always phoning Neill, using excuses about choir practice, bible study and church meetings. Once or twice she had noticed certain looks he gave Clarissa, his eyes resting on her rear when she stood up to take the tray of empty cups to the kitchen. A guilty exchange across the coffee table. And the way their arms touched when they pored over the parish newsletter.

Things had come to a head the day she caught him having sex with Clarissa in the larder. She'd stood for a moment like a startled deer, taking in the fact of Neill's hands down the back of Clarissa's lacy-edged stay-ups. His mouth was clamped over her left ear. His thighs slapped against her bare rump. Without a word Freya had shut the door, and withdrawn to the kitchen for a cup of camomile tea. She'd felt strangely relieved that his baser instincts were still intact.

Later, as he said goodbye to his guests in the front porch, she glimpsed Clarissa making an awkward exit through the side door. While Neill took a shower Freya went into the living room. She sat on the edge of the sofa, feeling numb. A Pisa of prayer books towered over the coffee table. She stretched out a leg and pushed them on to the floor with her foot.

Before the meeting, he had stashed her 'junk' under the stairs: unfinished herbal sleep pillows, bowls of sweet-smelling pot-pourri (she admitted these were dust-catchers), oatmeal- and clove-studded kumquats (he particularly detested the way she hung those amongst his suits), a glass jug full of unstrained herbal footbath he said looked like yak's urine and smelled like a yeti's armpit. At least religion had not diminished his lusty wit.

'It reminds me of Italy,' Freya had said. 'Pine needles, peppermint, rosemary — all those delicious Mediterranean smells. Remember?'

Neill raised one eyebrow.

'It's an excellent treatment for tired feet,' she said, eyeing the jug.

'It's nothing but a load of mumbo-jumbo,' he replied, and poured the footbath down the sink.

On their honeymoon they had driven all the way to Terracina, an undiscovered Italian town halfway between Rome and Naples. They had rented sun-loungers and a patch of sand on a raked beach. Neill swigged gallons of San Pellegrino straight from the bottle, a habit Freya knew her mother would loathe, along with topless sunbathing. In the scouring August heat her skin turned terracotta red. Neill remarked she could easily be mistaken for an Italian.

At night it was too hot in their rented villa, so they wandered through the cork pines in the park, browsing at antique lace and bric-a-brac stalls. Neill bought her a cup of lemon granita — she was easily impressed in her twenties

77

— and she devoured it greedily, sexily. It gave her chest freeze. She thought she was having a heart attack; the heat was dehydrating, the sex was draining.

She'd sat on the cut stone wall, one foot dangling in the fountain. Neill kneaded her breasts. She pretended not to mind, but really she didn't enjoy intimacy; it made her nervous, being touched.

And now she knew why. She was an adoptee. It sounded like someone sent home from a war in pieces, zipped up inside a foil bag.

Back at the villa they had made love to the tune of a dozen mosquitoes circling the room. She was aware of being more interested in the insects' blind journey than her new husband's satisfaction, and it dawned on her with a sickening jolt that her decision to leave Australia with him had been far too hasty. Apart from Roy Milton, a boy she'd gone to school with, Neill was the only other boy she'd ever kissed. Afterwards, she leaned on the windowsill and gazed at the lights of Terracina, while he kissed her neck and fed her Parma ham and pachino tomatoes. She told him he looked like a ginger version of Buddy Holly, to deflect her sexual apathy.

At midnight they made love again. This time out on the balcony — on a recliner. Now the moon captured her attention. She was thankful the noise of scooters and exuberant youths masked his embarrassing groans.

In the morning he pulled on his shorts and bought black grapes and custard croissants from the *supermercato* across the street. The dark-haired shop assistant who served him undressed him with her eyes. Freya waited outside, watching them through the window. She was terrified Neill might go off and abandon her and that she would have no way of getting back to England. He had all the money and credit cards.

When she'd noticed him eyeing a local girl who stood outside the adjacent flat, she'd said, 'Go on, I dare you, I can see you're gagging for it, get it out of your system.'

She had honestly believed that he would get it out of his system, and that she was being broad-minded for encouraging him. Not only that, she didn't want him to up and leave her in the middle of Italy. Besides, the world was changing. You could live out your fantasies and still love a person. There was the faint hope that eventually he would go off sex, and they could be like best friends. Then, when he did start ignoring her, she had wanted him. There was no justice, no logic, to love, and especially not marriage, which seemed to squeeze the vitality from a relationship.

For a while she had thought it was religion that had stunted his lust, not her. She grew accustomed to him clutching his bible in bed instead of her breasts, so his brazen, rear mounting of Clarissa was a surprise and a flashback to the old Neill, the Neill who ordered pornographic magazines from Holland and smoked hash, the Neill who was spontaneous and laissez-faire and thought sex in an open dinghy in Port Phillip Bay was all good, clean fun.

Christians did it missionary-style, didn't they? After a dinner of meat and potatoes and a cup of weak tea. But there he was, standing up amongst the shelves of home-made jam, going at it with the abandon of a gibbon.

With the smell of Clarissa's perfume still lingering in the sitting room, Freya had telephoned Del.

'If you leave the marital home the court will undeniably view it negatively,' said Del. 'Ask any lawyer.'

'Lawyers are too cautious.'

'With good reason,' said Del. 'The court will accuse you of deserting the children. Stay put, Freya, darling. Swallow your pride.'

But Freya could not live under the same roof a minute longer. She decided to take the risk. Taking the children with her was impractical, and unfair on them; they were settled at school, upheaving them to stay with her at Del's would be too upsetting. She never believed her loyalty to the children would be doubted — it was him she had to get away from, not them.

Nursing had taught her far more than how to revive a corpse — she could cope with all sorts of emergencies coolly; marriage had taught her how to unblock a drain and change a fuse, and her childhood had taught her how to be solitary. She could deal with this.

At the appeal, Kitty Wong would have plenty of positive evidence; Freya would see to that, by behaving impeccably during the run-up.

'Mrs Kirby isn't gadding off to Marrakech,' her lawyer might argue, 'or joining a monastery, or taking up hang-gliding. Her aspirations are sensible. She has left her job in nursing, and plans to use her diploma in herbalism, working from home, or perhaps modest premises in town, because she wants to run more family-friendly hours, in the field of alternative medicine. To fit in with the children. Who I am sure the court will agree should be with their mother.'

She could then mention that as an economic strategy Freya had bought a houseboat, rather than a house, and pause for effect and peer around the courtroom at the assembled officials before saying something along the lines of: 'While this might have been considered a little unconventional a few years ago, Your Honour, these days I think you'll agree it's an acceptable lifestyle. And one that seems to suit artistic types like Mrs Kirby.'

Mrs Wong was an intelligent woman. She would see the sense in such an argument.

'I think the court should reconsider their original decision,' her lawyer might continue, 'and allow Mrs Kirby a chance to prove she is a fine, devoted mother, and to demonstrate the constructive features of an unorthodox lifestyle.'

Freya could then add her bit. Talk about her efforts so far as a mother, and the difficulties of living with a man who metamorphosed practically overnight from a randy reprobate into a neurotic Jesus freak.

She could also stress the dilemma of being twelve thousand miles from her parents. She could remind the court that she was Australian, and that she had read about other custody cases in which the parents were from different countries, and the appointed judge had decided that the children should split their time equally between countries in order to experience first-hand their dual heritage.

She lay back on the grassy slope and closed her eyes against the sky.

Her children were now the only real family she had left in Britain, she could explain; Neill's side didn't count. They thought of her as foreign. Neill's father Dennis, a chain-smoking tee-totaller, had written to Freya when she and Neill were in London, and suggested she was only marrying Neill in order to get a British passport. As though having one would elevate her, somehow, to the ranks of acceptability. He had spread his suspicions by letter throughout the entire family, so that when she and Neill visited his aunts and uncles in Wales they had treated her like an asylum-seeker.

She was glad that was all behind her.

Between now and the review, all she had to do was be sensible, loving and conformist.

Keeping Connie a secret would be difficult. It was hard not to blurt it out when she was on her mind all the time. Although she was glad she now knew the truth, since their meeting a yawning abyss had begun to gnaw at her, causing an immeasurable longing for the life she had missed.

People assumed it was losing custody that was making her jittery and depressed. If only they knew. But it was too big to share, too personal, and far too soon.

She opened her eyes. It was getting dark. A bat flew low over her head and she ducked. Something shuffled through the undergrowth in the woods. She stood on the brow of the hill watching a thin new moon rising over Middlesex. When the night air made her shiver, she walked slowly down the hill towards home.

9

Along the canal, hatches banged open and bilge pumps burst into life. Through the trees in her garden Freya caught glimpses of crumpled bodies emerging from boats like butterflies, sleepy and stiff-limbed after being folded inside their chrysalis too long.

The children were grumpy this morning. The shower had been temperamental, and Kirsty had to rinse out the remainder of her shampoo at the standpipe after the main tank finally ran out of water.

'I want to go home,' she had wailed. 'The water's freezing.'

'It's good for you,' said Freya, wrapping a cardigan around her shoulders. 'Toughens you up. Prince Charles has a cold shower every morning. If he can do it, you can. Come inside and I'll make you a nice cup of hot cocoa.'

She had felt a resistance when she put her arms around Kirsty. Perhaps it was just her age. Most teenagers hated being touched by a parent. She remembered that feeling herself. Seeing her mother as a sexual being when she was becoming one herself, the repellent, embarrassing yuckiness of being mauled. It was probably even harder to take these days, she imagined, with so much on the telly about lesbians.

Monica was paying them a visit this morning, to see how she was getting on with the children.

Freya thought Monitor would be a better name for the woman charged with the task of spying.

As it was a Saturday, people were out on the towpath early, exchanging gossip and dipping in and out of one another's boats. Inevitably some were drawn to 'the lovely lady on *Harlequin*', with her potions and lotions and healing hands.

Sometimes she wished she had never bought the houseboat.

By ten o'clock, five people had already invaded her privacy. Down her garden steps they toddled, like hopefuls visiting Lourdes.

The Duchess, a middle-aged spinster with plummy vowels and fifteen cats, had no reservations about telling Freya the most intimate details of her gynaecological problems.

'It's the worst discharge I've ever had, dahling.'

A few minutes after the Duchess left (armed with a detox blend), Barge Arse from *Limerick* arrived, complaining of sore breasts.

'I don't mean cancer,' she said, rolling up her fisherman's jersey. 'They're just itchy and tender. Under here.' She lifted both breasts and showed Freya the weeping splits.

'I'll make up a lotion,' said Freya, slotting a plastic funnel into a clean bottle. 'You need to dry yourself thoroughly after a bath. A light application of talc will help, too. And it wouldn't hurt to go without a bra for a few days.'

Freya was washing the funnel and bowl in the galley when Otto knocked at the window.

'Wait in the summerhouse,' said Freya. After getting rid of Barge Arse, she went out to the garden to see what was up.

He needed something for his testicular herpes.

'You know I don't believe in conventional medicine,' he said.

He was on the verge of dropping his jeans when Freya said quickly, 'I've seen a lot of that in my job. You don't need to show me.'

If Monica turned up now she'd be sunk.

She made up a blend, and pushed the small brown bottle into Otto's palm.

He read the label. 'Will this cure it?'

'I wouldn't like to say.'

'You're a nurse, aren't you?'

'Yes, but I'm not God. You should see a specialist.'

'What's in it?'

'Echinacea, cleavers, oats, and Poke Root.'

'Poke Root? You're pissin' me?'

'No. I'm serious. Poke Root. It's a legitimate herb.'

'There'll be no poking or rooting for me, I shouldn't wonder. At least not until this lot's cleared up.' He guffawed loudly.

'And you can apply this lotion externally. Echinacea and myrrh.'

'Getting all biblical now, are we? While I'm about it . . . ' He removed his flip-flops. 'Would you mind taking a look at my feet? The skin's falling off between my toes. Have you got a miracle cure for that?'

'Look,' said Freya, biting down hard on her irritation, 'I've got a visitor arriving soon. I need to get ready. Couldn't you come back tomorrow?'

He slipped his feet back into the dirty rubber sandals and shuffled home. A few minutes later his wife Tess arrived. Freya was mortified. Why today, of all days? She had been awake half the night, thinking up excuses if anyone did call in, but when she was faced with them, eyeball to eyeball, she caved in.

'What's the matter?' she said, trying to hide her impatience.

'It's my skin,' said Tess. She hauled up her paisley skirt and twisted her leg. She had a bad case of acne on the back of her thighs, and had tried everything: salt baths, body scrubs, astringents.

'I'll make you a blend,' said Freya.

'What of?'

'Fumitory, burdock and figwort.'

'How much will it be?'

'I won't charge you this time. But next time it will be twenty pounds for a month's supply.'

'Oh, I couldn't afford that,' said Tess. 'I mean, it's not like I don't eat properly. And we've got mains water. I have a bath every day.'

It was an awkward moment. Freya knew that Tess sat around her boat all day smoking dope, and that no amount of salad or herbs or skin treatments would counteract the sinister effects of marijuana.

'Have you tried sunbathing? A little bit of sun might help. Just don't overdo it.'

A few minutes after Tess had gone, Luke Pirkel from the *Floating Gin Palace* arrived, asking for a tonic to perk him up after a bad dose of flu. Freya had had enough and sent him packing.

The sun was shining now, so she went out to the back plot and rolled up the sides of the polytunnels, to let the air circulate, then ambled through one of the tunnels, trimming dead leaves with her favourite snips. The combination of scents was overwhelming, even this early in the season.

Freya wanted the children's visits to be special; she wanted Monica to witness them *bonding*. Monica was expecting a family atmosphere. Normality, performed within the walls of a house, not some floating slum. But so far today Kirsty and Tom had shown no interest in any of Freya's ideas. On rising she had suggested they hire a boat from the nearby marina.

'What for?' said Kirsty. 'We're already on one.'

'Okay. What about going swimming?'

'We haven't got our swimsuits,' said Tom.

'I'll buy new ones,' said Freya.

'I don't want to go swimming,' said Kirsty firmly, shooting Freya a dark look.

Freya understood: it was that time of the month.

'Sorry,' she said.

In the end Kirsty sat in the garden on the sun-lounger, with a blanket draped over her legs, engrossed with her Walkman. Tom climbed a tree, where he sat in a fork, punching the buttons on his Game Boy. Freya was furious with Neill for buying them these gadgets in the first place. How could she possibly bond with them now?

She felt empty and dejected, and lost for ideas.

'Let's start again,' she had said over breakfast. 'A new way of life. Just us. It'll be fun.'

But they hated the moorings. The sludgy towpath, the vomity smells inside the boat: diesel, aquacem, coal and mould. Their new toys only amplified the distance between them.

Then she had an idea.

She loved the arty look of the moorings. She had always wanted to live on a houseboat, but it was illegal in Australia. Now she took Kirsty and Tom for a walk to the far end of the towpath, pointing out the interesting variety of boats: the dove-grey ice-breaker with brass portholes and tall smoke stack, the imposing sea-going barges, the gaudily painted narrowboats.

'Why don't you try painting them?' she said. 'I've got a set of paints on the boat, and some brushes and paper.'

'They're so old-fashioned,' said Kirsty glumly.

Tom cast his eye over the gardens. He spotted a hand-built coracle leaning against the side of a shed. Freya noticed the glimmer of interest.

'Have you got a dinghy?' he said hopefully.

'No,' said Freya, 'I haven't.'

'It's worse than camping,' Kirsty moaned after using the portaloo. 'At least campsites have proper toilets and hot showers.'

'The water *is* hot.' Freya was losing her patience.

'Call that a shower? More like a dribble.'

She decided to try and reignite their interest in gardening, with a special set of grown-up tools, and colourful packets of seeds.

'Sorry, Mum,' said Kirsty, when Freya suggested it. 'I'm listening to CDs.' She looked at the bucket of shiny new tools as if they were radioactive.

'What about you, Tom? Come on, let's make a garden like Mr McGregor's. It'll be fun.'

'Jeez, Mum, I'm not a kid any more. Peter Rabbit's for five-year-olds.'

'Yes, Mum, we're not little any more,' said Kirsty. 'You have to come to terms with that.'

'Oh, come on, you guys. Who's being boring now? You used to help when we lived at Ruislip.'

'Gardening's for old fogeys,' said Kirsty. 'Besides, I don't like getting muddy.' She pulled the hood of her black jacket over her head.

'I do wish you wouldn't sit there like that,' said Freya. 'You look like a homeless person on a park bench.'

'So?'

'We don't like gardening any more,' said Tom.

'What about Charlie Dimmock? And Kim Wilde? They're not old fogeys.'

'They're famous.' Kirsty turned up the volume on her Walkman.

'And you're not,' said Tom, from the oak tree.

'Oh well, it's your loss.'

She plunged her spade into the earth. There was nothing like a good, hard dig in the garden to burn up frustrations. It sickened her, the speed at which Clarissa and Neill had cast an antisocial spell over the children, brainwashing them with electronic toys. She might as well throw herself on the compost heap.

She let go of the spade and it fell with a thud

on the shingle path.

'What's wrong, Mum?' said Kirsty, alarmed.

'Miss Murray will be here soon; what do you think is wrong? We're supposed to be doing things *together*.'

'You can't force us to do stuff.'

'What's wrong with pretending? Don't you want to come and live with me?'

'Not down here. It's too grotty.'

'So you're not even going to give it a chance?'

'I don't like it, Mum. People are taking the mick at school. Calling me a gyppo.'

'Why are people so damned prejudiced about these things? I thought England was over its class hang-ups.'

'Not at my school.'

Suddenly Freya felt drained of energy. An icy fear raced through her veins.

'I don't like to think of you being exposed to that sort of bigotry.'

'It's everywhere, Mum. Even in fee-paying schools.'

'I'm sorry, Kirsty. I didn't think of it when I bought the boat.'

Kirsty shrugged, and turned up the volume again.

Kitty Wong had obviously thought about it. What was her parting shot? *The children deserve to live in a proper home.*

Freya dug for a while, but it was an effort. The earth was heavy and damp. Her shoulders ached, her head throbbed.

Suddenly a surge of anger pushed through her veins. She would never give up. Never.

'Please, Kirsty, Tom. Monica will be here soon. Can't you just try?'

But they did not even hear her plea. The temptation to insist welled up again, but she knew it would only make them stroppy. She wanted to rip the gadgets off them and chuck them in the canal. But that would make them resentful and angry. She gripped the handle of the spade hard, and held the words — the nag — in her throat. She wanted to improve their relationship, not push them away.

'Are you listening to hip-hop?' she said, instead.

Kirsty pulled out her ear-plugs. 'What?'

'You mean *pardon*, surely? I said, are you listening to hip-hop?'

'No, Mum. House.' She replaced the ear-plugs, and tapped the toes of her trainers together.

'Why don't you read a book for a change?' she said, turning to Tom.

'Nah. Books are boring.' He punched the buttons on the Game Boy, mesmerised.

Freya sighed. All weekend she had been analysing her role as a mother. Starting at breakfast every gesture, from pouring their milk to reminding them to clean their teeth properly, had been scrutinised. But motherhood was more complicated than frying a perfect Delia Smith omelette. If only the likes of Kitty Wong realised — she had created an even wider barrier by agreeing with Neill about the bonding thing. Now everything Freya said sounded either harping or forced, every act seemed self-conscious.

Was Neill right, after all?

She had always considered herself a capable, devoted, hands-on mum. Before Neill started criticising, she had simply got on with the job. Intuitively. She wanted them with her — didn't that make her a good mother? She made sure they were fed. Clothed sensibly, and kept safe. What about all the museums, and galleries, the kitsch theatre productions and awful panto-mimes that she had taken them to over the years? The school fairs, the firework displays, the Easter egg hunts? The list of motherly obligations was endless.

Where was Neill all that time?

Japan, Germany, Spain. Seducing a twenty-year-old fan, more than likely, who had thrown a teddy-bear or a G-string through the limo window.

She had helped with homework, entertained their friends, suffered their moods. She made sure they had sponge cake with royal icing, not wholemeal log, on their birthdays. When Tom came home from school with a black eye, when Kirsty started her periods, Neill was whooping it up in a Belgian brothel or a Berlin lap-dancing club.

Was she just being dutiful and going through the motions, when really her mind was on other things, things she didn't even understand, things that were intangible? How could she possibly explain the dreams that haunted her sleep? The complex patterns, as if seen through a kaleidoscope from a great height? The feeling she had of being disconnected from the modern world and most people. The sense of closeness she felt to nature.

How could the children grow up normal without her there beside them? There would be problems, no doubt. Self-harming, pregnancy, depression. Kirsty knew several girls who for various reasons had begun to cut their arms.

'It's like a craze,' she had once told Freya.

Neill had taken the religious thing too far. It wouldn't make up for the effects of divorce. He had become a bore. He had turned Kirsty's room into a meditation and prayer retreat, apparently, and Blutacked a poster of Jesus to the wall and built an MDF altar in front of the bay window. Clarissa had taken over Tom's room for choir practice. The box room was now Neill's office. Having to bunk in with their new step-siblings hadn't been part of the plan.

He'd really overstepped the line the day he gave a talk on Christianity at Kirsty's school.

'All my friends were talking about it,' she'd told Freya. 'They said they'd rather have an alcoholic for a father than a hell-and-damnation preacher.'

Freya would bring all this up at the appeal. It should be Neill and Clarissa's sanity under the microscope, she thought, not hers.

No wonder the children were miserable.

She kept digging, resisting the urge to down tools and do something frivolous — a trip to McDonald's perhaps, or the cinema. But she simply had to get on with preparing the garden. There was no magic wand she could wave, no muscle-bound man to take over.

Whenever she heard voices she cocked an ear for Monica.

Luke from the *Floating Gin Palace* walked past, pushing his portaloo on the communal trolley. He waved, and called out, 'Morning.'

Mrs Peach hurried by carrying a bag of cuttings for the Duchess.

Tom and Kirsty were mesmerised by their new toys. She stood for a moment watching them, wondering whether or not to tell Monica this was Neill's doing. She had to be careful not to seem bitchy or vengeful. Cursing Neill, she bashed the spade hard on the metal frame. She wished it was his head.

The children were oblivious to her gloomy mood.

Did Neill know the CDs Kirsty listened to were full of the F word? Did he know some of the games Tom was so hooked on were violent?

She decided not to push them into gardening. They needed to relax when they came to stay, not pretend or feel forced into anything.

She ran her hands through a patch of rosemary, breathing in the perfume. She let her mind wander, singing softly under her breath. Songs that weaved in and out of her dreams.

'Talking to yourself again?' Tom's voice carried across the garden, making her jump.

'No, I'm singing.'

'Please don't sing, Mum. It's embarrassing. Someone might hear.'

It troubled her now, when they teased her about her singing. Before losing custody she used to joke with them about it. Now she saw it as another reason for not bonding with them. The songs cast their spell and she was lost, until someone or something broke in.

Did Tom think she was mad, too?

A mother's responsibilities were unrelenting, she thought. Had the endless small chores that made up her days clouded her ability to see their deeper needs? When they had lived together everything seemed natural. Now their relationship was self-conscious and awkward.

To make matters more complicated, they had blood in their veins that belonged to grandparents they didn't even know. She wanted to tell them. But on top of everything else, it seemed too daunting.

'Hello, Freya.'

Freya looked up, startled. Connie was walking towards her along the rear lane. Freya dropped her spade and almost sprinted through the garden.

'What are you doing here?' she whispered, glancing back at the children, who hadn't noticed Connie's arrival. 'I thought you were going to call first.'

'I thought I'd surprise you.'

'You'll have to go. It's not convenient.'

Freya glanced over her shoulder at Kirsty. She was staring at them. Freya turned her back, and when she looked again, Kirsty had pulled her hood over her eyes and was absorbed in her music. Perhaps she thought Connie was just another weirdo resident.

'You'll have to go,' Freya repeated. 'It's too risky. The welfare officer's due any minute. I

96

can't have her knowing who you are.'

'I could be a friend.'

'You might say something. By accident.'

'No I won't. I promise. I'll make sure.'

'Please, Connie, this is important. I can't risk — '

'Mrs Kirby?'

Freya spun around. Monica was standing at the top of the steps leading into the garden by the towpath, glaring at the children, who to her probably looked bored and neglected.

'Hello, children,' she said, her tone condescending.

Kirsty rolled her eyes and said hello, her voice bitter with resentment. She wasn't a child. She was a young woman.

'Aren't you going to introduce me?' said Monica, walking through the garden towards the two women.

'Yes,' said Freya, her heart pounding. 'Yes, of course. This is Connie. A friend from America. But she's just going.'

'Oh? But she's just arrived. I saw her pull up in front of me. Don't send her away on my account. I'm supposed to be looking at all aspects of your life. Friends included.'

10

'Come inside, please,' said Freya. 'Monica's here. And this is my friend Connie, from America.'

Kirsty and Tom's shoulders slumped.

'Do we have to?' Kirsty sighed.

Freya was only too happy for them to stay outside. She did not want them asking Connie any awkward questions in front of Monica.

'Do you need to speak to the children?'

'Not really,' said Monica. 'But bear in mind that I've come today because I was aware they'd be here, and I wanted to observe them interacting with you.'

'Yes, of course. Kirsty, Tom, Miss Murray would like to see you, please.'

'Can't we stay outside?' Kirsty's eyes were wide and pleading.

'No, you can't. Hurry up, Miss Murray hasn't got all day.'

They followed the three women aboard and sat cross-legged on the floor, still absorbed in their gadgets.

Monica began to write furiously in her notebook, while Freya tried frantically to work out what she would say. And more importantly, what she would not say.

'I'll put the kettle on,' she said breezily.

In the galley she drank a glass of water, but her mouth still felt dry. She tried to think of Connie

98

as nothing more than a friend, and wondered what lies she would have to spin.

'Freya and I met in Spain,' she heard Connie telling Monica.

'Really?' said Monica. 'It's unusual for people to keep in touch after a holiday abroad.'

She's on to us, thought Freya. The woman probably doubts her own grandmother.

'Is that so?' said Connie. 'Well, I guess Freya and I are the exception to that rule. Of course, it's difficult to keep the friendship going, me being based in New York an' all, but I always try to look her up when I'm in London.'

'What do you do for a living, if you don't mind me asking?'

'I'm a trader on Wall Street.'

'That must be very interesting.'

'Oh it is. Very.'

Freya came back into the room and put the tray on the coffee table. She could hear the music screeching from the tiny black plugs in Kirsty's ears. She felt the urge to rip them out. Tom was lying on his tummy, the Game Boy screen inches from his eyes. Rather than create a scene, she poured the tea, relieved the conversation had moved off Spain. She slid Monica's cup across the table, to avoid having to offer it with a conspicuously nervous hand.

Kirsty and Tom lifted their eyes now and then, drawn to Connie's exotic aura. Connie tried not to stare at them too much. She couldn't believe she had a niece and a nephew. She was longing to tell them. She wanted to hug them close and kiss them on the cheek. When Freya went back into the galley to top up the teapot, Connie asked Kirsty if she enjoyed staying on the boat.

'It's okay,' said Kirsty, wary of Monica. 'The shower's useless, that's the worst thing. And it's a bit smelly. But Mum's looking for another boat. A bigger one. Like *Lady Luck*, I hope. Now that's what I call a houseboat.'

Monica intervened with a question about the portaloo, and whether or not it was hygienic.

Connie cut her off with a remark about New York being almost back to normal, and how disasters and problems tested your strengths. She was clever at steering the conversation off anything contentious, like politics, though she did touch on 9/11. The lie about how she and Freya had met hung in the air like a poison cloud.

Freya came back with a plate of biscuits and more tea.

'Where exactly in Spain did you two meet?' said Monica, looking at Freya.

Freya glanced at Connie and smiled. 'I'll let Connie tell you, she's better at telling stories than me.'

Without hesitating Connie said airily, 'Funnily enough, at the Café Comercial, on Glorietta de Bilboa, in Madrid.'

Freya's heart began to race. She tried to remember the layout of the city.

'Freya was at the next table,' Connie went on. 'The restaurant was all marble and mirrors, beautiful old-style decor. I noticed her in one of the mirrors. It's rather intimidating, eating on your own in a foreign city, surrounded by short

Spanish businessmen in suits. Very uncomfortable, to be honest. I think we were glad to find someone to talk to, and both being tourists, we clicked straight away.'

'After that we went to the Prado museum, I seem to remember,' said Freya. 'I'd been there already, but I didn't mind going again.'

She had stayed in the gallery all day that weekend, craning her neck at *Saturn Devouring a Child*, and *The Birth of the Milky Way*, oblivious to the drama of her own birth.

'I'd been looking forward to a quiet weekend away from the children, to be honest,' she said. 'It was the first and only time Neill ever gave me a break. I have to admit there was so much housework to do when I got back it hardly seemed worth it. I was flat out for days trying to catch up.' She winked at Kirsty and Tom, and laughed.

'Thanks, Mum,' said Kirsty.

'I don't want you to take that the wrong way, Monica.' Freya wagged a finger at the welfare officer. 'Neill made sure they didn't come to any harm. He's just not very good at domestic stuff.'

'How old were the children?' said Monica.

'Oh, I'm not sure. When was it, Connie? Ninety-nine? Do you remember, Kirsty?'

Kirsty took out her head-phones and nodded. 'Yes. I do. Dad was panicking about what to do all weekend, because it was raining. He took us to the Science Museum, and it was packed. Tom got lost. We found him in the end. One of the museum staff had him in a back room.'

Monica frowned.

Christ, thought Freya, please don't say any more. Don't tell Monica I was a day late getting back.

'You know, Miss Murray,' said Connie, 'in America most families send their children to summer camp every July and August, sometimes for six weeks. Surely one weekend without their mother can't have harmed them? I'm certain Freya wouldn't even consider going on such a trip if she thought they'd be traumatised.'

'This isn't America,' said Monica. 'So, that would have been when Tom was about eight?'

'That sounds about right,' said Freya.

'And Kirsty was thirteen?' Monica scribbled in her little black notebook.

'Before Connie and I met up, I walked the back streets of Madrid on my own, exploring all the little cafés and galleries,' said Freya, smiling at Connie as though they were old buddies. She caught Connie's wink. 'I even took a bus out to Chincon, to watch a bullfight.'

'Don't you just love the Plaza Mayor at Chincon?' said Connie. 'I went there on another trip, with an old schoolfriend. All those lovely wooden balconies overlooking the Plaza.'

'Delightful. As you already know, Miss Murray, Neill was often away,' said Freya. 'That trip to Madrid was the first time I'd ever been apart from the children for more than a few hours. Surely you're not going to put this in your report?'

'I'm afraid I have to record anything that seems relevant.'

'Well in that case, perhaps you should mention

102

Neill's globetrotting — '

'I'm well aware of Mr Kirby's whereabouts over the course of your marriage.'

Whereabouts my arse, thought Freya. I bet you don't know about his actual movements — the ones he performed on beds in Amsterdam or Hamburg.

'Have you ever been to Spain?' said Connie brightly, looking at Monica. 'I know it's a popular destination for you Brits.'

'Yes, I've been to Spain many — '

'How lucky you are to live so close to Europe. I do get jealous, living in the States. And of course, now that everyone's so damned paranoid, what with the whole terrorism threat, well, Europe's got even more appeal.'

'Europe's not exempt from terrorism.'

'Yes, I know, I know, but Europeans are so much more grounded about these things. Americans are hysterical, this being the first very real threat to their security. Tell me, Miss Murray, what do you do when you're not poking your nose in other people's business?'

'I beg your — ?' Monica's mouth fell open.

Good on you, Connie, thought Freya, smiling to herself. The expression on Monica's face was priceless. She looked as though someone had just propositioned her.

'Do you read?' Connie continued. 'Why, reading is one of my favourite pastimes. In fact, I was just telling someone at work about the library in New York, and how much I love using it. The atmosphere is wonderful, have you ever been there yourself? I'm reading *Amy and*

103

Isabelle by Elizabeth Strout right now, she was shortlisted for the Booker Prize. I bought a copy, of course, and I'm starting *The Life of Pi* next . . . '

As Connie prattled on, Monica sipped her tea, clearly amazed at the American woman's unstoppable mouth.

'Has your boat got an engine?' Monica managed to slip in at one point.

'No,' said Freya. 'Even if she did, I couldn't take her anywhere. The roof won't fit under any of the bridges. She was built in situ, apparently, and whoever built her either forgot about that little detail, or had no intention of taking her anywhere in the first place.'

Quarter of an hour passed, and Monica began to grow agitated. She dropped her notebook and pen into her briefcase and got to her feet.

' . . . *Don Quixote*'s a tome, but such a wonderful story; mind you, it's too heavy to hold up in bed. Oh, you're not going, are you?' Connie looked at her and smiled. 'Why, we were just getting acquainted. I guess you've got a very busy schedule, having such an important position. I'll see you to the door, shall I? Oops. Be careful on the steps.'

Monica's foot had slipped on the bottom rung.

'Freya, honey, be a sweetie and put the kettle on again, will you?'

'Right-o. Thanks for dropping by, Miss Murray.' Freya tried not to sound facetious. 'We'll meet again, no doubt, before the appeal?'

'I need to see you three or four more times,'

said Monica, from the landing stage. 'Next time there won't be any warning.'

'I'll look forward to it. And I'll try to make sure all my lovers have left before you arrive.' She laughed. Monica gave her a dark look.

Connie waited until Monica was standing on the towpath, then pulled the hatch across, wedging her head in the gap.

'So nice to meet you, Miss Murray. I hope I haven't delayed you with my chit-chat, oh, and do drive carefully, the traffic's something else in this country.'

She stood at the stern window with Freya, watching Monica waddle towards the car park. On the way she stopped once or twice to stare long and hard at some of the less attractive boats, in particular the *Whiskey Belle*. She was a bodge-up that belonged to Chippy, a half-blind carpenter. His self-installed windows harboured a garden of fungi sandwiched between the double-glazing. The entire boat was leaning to one side, and part of the roof was charred after a chimney fire. She had a look at the *Mary Jane*, too, which even Freya had to admit was a bad advertisement for the community, with its rusty hull and torn curtains.

When they saw Monica's lime-green VW (Freya had felt sure it would be a Datsun) rising over the humpback bridge, Freya sent the children outside. Once they were out of earshot, she turned to Connie and said, 'Have you ever been to Spain?'

'Never,' said Connie. 'But I've read a lot about it.'

Freya laughed. 'You're a good actress.'

'So are you.'

'Luckily I've been there. Otherwise I wouldn't have been able to keep it up.'

'We make a good team.' Connie smiled.

'I don't know about that.'

'Well, I think we do. I just hope she doesn't find out. Do you think she will?'

'Probably. These people will go to any lengths. Sitting in cars for hours, watching someone's house. Snooping through letterboxes. Following people home from pubs.'

'You're getting paranoid.'

'Or she could just ask Neill.'

'What will you do if she does?'

'I'll say I didn't mention you to him because he was never interested in my friends.'

'That's the truth anyway, I suspect.'

'Exactly. Thanks, Connie. You were brilliant.'

'Don't mention it.'

'All the same, please don't do this to me again. My nerves can't take it. Let me know if you want to see me. I'll come up to London.'

'She's one mean mother,' said Connie. 'I can see why you were so worried.'

Freya was beginning to like Connie. But only as a friend. She just couldn't seem to think of her as a sister. They had no collective memories or shared milestones, like birthdays or Christmases, first loves or christenings, funerals or family outings. It wasn't as if they could joke about their cousin's big nose, or their auntie's bad breath, or their pet dogs and cats over the years. Their lovers or enemies. They couldn't reminisce about anything except world events, which everyone shared.

'You're forty-eight, is that right?' said Freya.

Connie nodded.

'Have you ever been married?'

Connie had been waiting for this question to pop up.

'Too busy with my career,' she said.

Freya sensed Connie didn't want to open up. Just as well. The last few minutes had been entertaining, but she didn't want Connie to get the wrong idea. To think that the barriers had dropped enough for a familiarity to settle between them. It would take time, and a lot of careful handling. She wanted information, facts, but not intimacy. She still felt raw and exposed. And very afraid for her future as a mother. If Connie wanted things to develop further, she would simply have to back off and do it Freya's way.

Next minute, Connie went into the galley to make sandwiches. Freya wanted her to leave. She imagined if they were real sisters she'd have no trouble telling her to go. Neither the warm spring sunshine nor the fragrance of early jasmine and jonquils could soothe her irritation.

When Connie came back into the saloon with a platter of sandwiches, she had a piece of torn basil leaf stuck to her lower lip.

'Stand still,' said Freya, and tweezered it off between two nails.

The room flickered with polygons of coloured light, reflected from a shell mobile that Kirsty had given her one Christmas. Conscious of

Connie looking at her, taking in every cell, as though trying to match them to her own, Freya adopted her nurse's stance: cool indifference.

'Take a look at these,' said Connie. She pulled a large brown envelope from her leather shoulder bag. 'The copy Henry gave me of your original birth certificate, and your adoption papers.'

Freya sat down and spread the documents out on her lap. There was a sharp lump at the back of her throat. She tried to remember ordinary details that might make her adoption less painful. The sheet music next to Shirley's bed, hymns she had played on the Hammond organ in the small chapel at the back of the house for grieving families. Her father's workshop where coffins took shape in a cloud of sawdust. Her own school uniform hanging on the washing line.

Part of her torment was suddenly clear. It was probably just as agonising for them to know she was adopted as it was for her.

The papers smelled musty. Today was the last time she would ever think of herself as Freya Lacey from Windsor Meadows, Melbourne, or Freya Kirby from Ruislip Manor, England.

She unfolded her birth certificate and saw the beautiful, uncomplicated name her birth mother had given her thirty-eight years ago: *Katherine Jane Nolan*.

★ ★ ★

'You can keep them,' said Connie, 'they're yours.'

Freya put the documents back in the envelope and slipped them inside a book.

She made more tea, and they sat for a while talking about their work.

Connie sensed Freya didn't want to discuss her adoption, so she chatted instead about her own childhood. She told Freya about Peggy, how she had been working in Darwin as a prostitute after escaping from the brutal regime of an orphanage. And how Forbes, a rough diamond with a big heart, had come along one day, a bag of nerves, looking more for the human comfort of a woman's arms than cold sex.

'He took Peggy inland, away from too many white people, to his property, which actually belongs to the Warlpiri. He and Peggy set up a special riding school for Aboriginal boys who have been in trouble.'

The sun filtered through the thin curtains. Freya wondered if Shirley and Bob regretted not telling her. The passing of time would make it harder. The hoarding of a secret that wasn't terrible, that didn't involve death or mutilation. A secret that was simply sad. Though not for them. They had their child, they had what they wanted. It was Ester she felt sorry for. The shock of giving birth to black girls must have traumatised her beyond salvation.

Freya got up and fetched the documents and opened them once more on her lap. As if seeing the stained paper would make it all easier to accept. She stared at the words, pure and hard on the official stamped paper.

'When did you find out about Peggy?' she

said, looking at Connie.

'Henry told me at the same time he told me about you. He wrote a letter for me giving his permission for her to be traced. It took the Adoption Information Service five months to track her down near Alice Springs. Then they had to write to her, out of courtesy, before telling me where she was. When she wrote back and said she wanted to meet me, it was all finalised. I went to see her and stayed six months.'

'But how did you get so much time off work?'

'I work for myself, more or less.'

'Has she got any children of her own?'

Connie shook her head sadly. 'I'm afraid not. She had a lot of things wrong with her when Forbes came along. Ladies' trouble, if you know what I mean.'

She looked at Connie. 'Is Connie your real name?'

'No. My real name is Deborah. Deborah Anne Nolan.'

'And Peggy?'

'That's the name the nuns gave her. Her real name is Alison May Nolan.'

'They gave us names, but they didn't keep us.' Freya tried to imagine her parents' feelings the day they took Connie and Peggy to the adoption agency. The sense of relief and regret. A horrible mixture that could eat at a person.

She put the papers away, in a drawer this time, under a pile of bills.

The light began to fade. The children came inside. Connie looked at them and smiled, but they didn't notice.

'Next time Monica comes to visit and you're here, I'll have to insist you put those things away,' said Freya, scowling.

They went into their cabins and switched on their reading lamps. The saloon was blushed with soft evening light. She could hear them moaning about the lack of storage and struggling with drawers that had warped from damp.

Connie stood up to go. She had to meet a colleague for dinner. Freya felt like making her stay, as punishment for putting her on the spot.

'Please call me,' said Connie.

'I will,' said Freya, fighting her irritation. The woman was coming and going just as she pleased. 'I promise.'

'When?'

'Soon.'

Connie tried to put her arms around Freya. Freya pulled away. 'Sorry. I guess I'm not the touchy-feely type.'

'Do you hug the children?'

'Of course I do.' She felt defensive. She told herself again and again it was because of the funerals. Being adopted was the other reason, of course. She knew that now. As for her real heritage, perhaps it had made her cold, having the knowledge of it missing from her life, and in its place an eerie sense of not knowing herself. An elusive history discovered in dreams of bug-eyed men cartwheeling across the starry sky. Giant snakes and furry creatures scuttling through underground tunnels. Bare-breasted women dancing like banshees around glassy pools and green flames. Kaleidoscopic patterns

111

of unimaginable complexity and beauty. How could she tell anyone without staining her credibility?

What people saw they understood.

A woman watching the rain slither down a window, and a fleet of men vying for her attention.

11

Sam Jenner was hanging out washing in his varnished wheelhouse. He waved as Freya tried to slip past. Of course it was impossible to do anything on the moorings without someone noticing. She pretended not to have seen him, and hurried on to the car park. It was hard enough giving Monica the right impression, without making things more difficult by getting involved with another man. Of all the men who flirted with her on the moorings, Sam was her favourite. He knew she was interested. But his son Ryan had a crush on Kirsty, and this was causing friction.

The Citroën refused to start. She turned the key several times. The engine was completely, utterly dead.

'Damn.' She got out of the car and kicked the front wheel.

'Always in a hurry, aren't you?' Sam was suddenly beside her. He stared at the bonnet. 'Trouble?'

She nodded. The hairs on her arms bristled. He must have been right on her heels. She didn't want his help. It would establish a debt and a familiarity.

'I'll phone the AA,' she said quickly.

'Are you a member?'

'Yes,' she said. She was amazed at how easily the lies slid off her tongue lately. She'd have to stop, before it became a habit.

'Where's your sticker?'

'It must have come off.'

He gave her a strange look. He wants to talk about Kirsty and Ryan, she thought. The last time, he had tried to tell her how to handle Kirsty. She did not need anyone's advice or opinions right now, and was sick of people judging and criticising.

'It's probably something simple,' he said. 'Let's take a look.'

Reluctantly, she unlatched the bonnet and propped it open. She handed him the oily rag she kept tucked in a corner under the bonnet and they pored over the engine.

It was quiet in the car park. Not a breath of wind. She was aware of his breathing, and the sharp, jerking motion of his Adam's apple. He was wearing expensive aftershave. He wiped the corner of his mouth with the back of his shirt sleeve. The side of her head touched his and electricity sparked their hair. She withdrew and moved to the other side of the car. She tried not to look at him. She could feel him watching her. She focused on what he was doing, so that she never had to rely on him — or any other man — for help.

After a few moments she risked glancing at him. A slight frown creased his tanned forehead. His tongue flicked out and traced a moist film over the brown bristles studding his upper lip.

'What's that called?' she said.

'Carburettor.'

'And that?'

'That's where the oil goes.'

'Oh.' Her cheeks flamed crimson. 'When are you off to Cornwall again?' she said lightly.

'July. After Ryan's exams.'

She hated the way he referred to Ryan's exams, in a tone that implied Kirsty was holding him back. For heaven's sake, they had only met twice.

'He has to get through them, no matter what.' He wiped his hands with the rag.

'Of course,' said Freya. 'I already told you, Kirsty's doing her GCSEs this year. I understand.'

'They need to keep their heads down.' He held up the oil stick, studied it closely, and wiped it with the rag. 'Oil's low. I've got a full can on my boat. Wait here.'

Freya watched his back, which was broad and strong, as he disappeared behind a blue van on to the towpath. She felt foolish for letting the oil get so low, and wondered why the light hadn't come on to warn her. Just then Hamish from *Poppy* came into the car park, shouldering a bag full of heavy camera equipment.

'Problems with the fart-box, eh?' he said, nodding at Freya's car. He slid a key into the lock of his shiny Peugeot.

'How's Bridget?' said Freya, hoping he would leave before Sam came back. Hamish would gossip about them if he suspected anything more than a friendship.

'Bridget's fine, thank you,' he said. 'By the way, someone was looking for you recently. An American woman. Did she find you?'

'Yes. Thanks. She did.' She pretended to fixate on a wire under the bonnet.

'Another customer, eh? News travels fast.'

'Pardon?'

'About your talents.' He swung the camera bag into the boot, closed it and turned to her, grinning like a monkey.

'I don't know what you're talking about, Hamish.'

'Your talents. You know — '

'No, Hamish, I don't know.'

'As a witch.'

'Very funny.'

'Well don't brainwash Bridget, if you don't mind. She spends enough money in the bloody health food shop already.'

'Aren't you late for work?'

'Look at you, fixing your own car. Bridget wouldn't know a camshaft from a crankcase.'

He lowered himself into the driver's seat, turned the key, and pulled away.

A few minutes later Ginny and Eric, from *Obelisk*, entered the car park. Eric was pushing the communal trolley with their portaloo on board.

She felt her cheeks heating up as she glanced along the towpath for signs of Sam. She was beginning to feel like a character in a Miss Marple movie, hiding a sinister secret.

Eric parked the trolley between two trees, lifted the portaloo off and placed it in the boot of their Mini Cooper.

'Hi, hi, hi,' said Ginny, climbing into the passenger seat.

How could anyone be that happy, living in a floating corridor? Freya smiled politely.

'Sorry, Freya, can't stop. Sorry, sorry, sorry. In a terrible rush this morning.'

Eric got in and they drove off.

A few minutes later Sam came back into the car park carrying a tin of oil. He anchored a plastic funnel in the car's tank, and began to pour in the oil. It smelled strong and made a glugging noise.

'Don't take this the wrong way,' he said, 'but I think it might be a good idea if Kirsty stays away from Ryan for a while.'

Freya let out a long, low sigh. 'I knew this was coming.'

'God, am I that predictable?'

'I try to avoid knee-jerk reactions, myself.' She gave him a hard glare.

'You have to admit, you're on thin ice right now. You don't want to give the court any more reasons to refuse custody — '

'I didn't give them a reason in the first place. Neill did.'

'You're a good mother. I wouldn't worry about what he says. I just think you need to be extra vigilant.'

'Is that so?'

'I don't mean to be condescending — '

'But you are.'

'It seems fair enough to me, when they've got exams. And it's good for your reputation to make sure everything's above board with the children, too.'

'Anyone would think she was some sort of

femme fatale. She's only sixteen — '

'Exactly my point. Over the age of consent, I grant you, but nevertheless, she is very young. So is Ryan. We don't want an unwanted pregnancy on our hands.'

'I don't want to interfere too much,' said Freya. 'It will only make them all the more determined. All we can do is provide the facts, and give them some guidance.'

He looked at her through the triangle of light between the bonnet and the engine.

'I'd rather keep them away from one another, if you don't mind.'

'They'll hate us.'

'Not if we're clever.'

He put the oil can down and wiped his hands. 'Why take any risks at this point? Imagine if things did get out of control and the child welfare officer found out. You'd never get the kids back then.'

'You just want to spoil an innocent friendship because you think my daughter is leading your son astray.'

'Now who's overreacting? You're being too sensitive — '

'That's what insensitive people say to cover their own mean streak.'

'Be reasonable. They've both got exams. And if you must know, Ryan's smitten. He's got a Polaroid of her next to his bed. He lies there for hours gazing at her, listening to Bjork. It's quite sweet, but it's not going to get him through his exams.'

'Have you finished?'

118

She climbed into the driver's seat and turned the key. The engine spluttered. She crunched the gears into reverse and they made a terrible grating noise.

'Thanks for the help.' She gripped the wheel and put on her snootiest face.

'I think you should think about what I've said.' Sam leaned in at the open window. His face was uncomfortably close. She could smell toothpaste and soap. The hairs inside his nostrils were neatly trimmed. 'I can't help being worried. He's fallen in love with your girl.'

'Oh, give me a break. They're only kids. They're *friends*, that's all. We can't chain them to their books.'

'Look, we have to be together on this. You can't stand aside and let things fall apart with teenagers. You have to set down perimeters.'

He moved off from the door and lowered the hood. She watched him through the window, annoyed at herself for being so mulish.

He came back to the door and leaned down. 'We have to present a united front — '

'Sounds like a military exercise.' She revved the engine and a blast of soot shot out of the exhaust.

'Don't let the oil get so low next time.'

'Don't worry, I won't.'

'I know Kirsty's not here that often, but sometimes absence can inflame passion.'

'For heaven's sake, Sam, they just want to hang out together. It's normal. That's what teenagers do.'

She slammed the car into first gear. It stalled.

She turned the key, and let it idle.

'I've put a few sanctions in place,' he said. 'It won't hurt them.' He hesitated. 'And it might go down well with the court.'

'They're not going to delve that deep.'

'You'd be surprised.' Sam looked at her sheepishly.

'What do you mean? What's happened?'

'Someone from the court was here the other day, asking about you.'

Freya banged her fists on the steering wheel. 'Damn.'

'Miss Murray.'

'Christ. What did you say to her?'

'I said Kirsty and Tom are good kids, but they seem a bit unsettled. And I said Ryan liked Kirsty, but I'm keeping an eye on the situation.'

'I've heard enough.' She put her foot down and the car lurched forward. Sam jumped back and landed in a puddle. Mud splashed up and covered his chinos. Thick fumes filled the car park. The car bounced through the potholes towards the humpback bridge.

Sam ran alongside her, dodging puddles. 'I'm sorry, Freya. I didn't think I'd said anything harmful.'

She put her foot on the brake and came to an abrupt halt.

'You know what, Sam?' she said, through the open window. 'In my experience boundaries create the perfect conditions for rebellion. And by the way, next time Miss Murray or anyone else who's got it in for me comes snooping around, do me a favour and keep your big mouth shut. I don't need you or anyone else telling people my business, thank you very much.'

She zoomed out of the car park and nosed over the bridge. Before driving off down Pond Lane, she glanced out of the window across the water. Sam was still in the car park, clutching the empty can of oil, staring after her.

She mentally stuck two fingers up at him, and drove off in a cloud of exhaust.

12

It was cooler in the wool shed than outside. Even so, the men's hands were slick with sweat.

You liked to stand and watch as they stripped bare more than twelve hundred animals in one day. You loved the way they pushed their fist into the back of a sheep's knee and bent its leg, to avoid cutting its hamstring with the razor-sharp blades. After a few quick, curving sweeps with the clippers, fleece fit for weaving angel's panties lay on the floor like cloud bombs. You told the shearers your merinos were a man-made thing. You said it was hard to breed good sheep, and damn near impossible to keep them good. They seemed to want to revert back to something inferior. Because of their patchy ancestry.

The perversity of this made you all the more determined to breed out any rogue animals.

You told the men you were after pure white, continuously growing, soft white fibre.

And you'd get it.

Even if it took you a lifetime of breeding.

★   ★   ★

It is humid in this room. Through the window you can see all the other wards lined up across the hill. The same huts used for Japanese POWs, and later for those poor pommy bastards who sailed on Russian ships expecting Eden. Instead they were billeted in tin hot-boxes miles from the sea, in a dusty New South Wales paddock. Serves 'em right, coming out here and taking all the jobs.

You stare hard at a dragonfly that is trying to escape through the fly-screened door. The sill behind your bed is a graveyard for moths. The cleaners rarely visit this ward, and the nurses only dust the parts that are visible.

Twice a week a nurse wheels you outside and down, down the concrete ramp to the murky pond in a sunken garden built by the Friends of the Hospital Committee. You like to sit and watch the pond life flitting over the water.

They have changed your tablets again and the hallucinations have stopped. You can see the food for what it is: the gluey gravy, the tough stewing steak shot through with fatty veins.

Many of the other patients have carked it by now, and new ones have been brought in to replace them. You wonder when it'll be your bloody turn. The nurses tease you. Especially the one called Diane. You've still got time to flog the old pork sword, she said the other day, winking.

You lie there feeling superior because no one has died in your bed; according to the nurses, you were the first to sleep in one of six new Posturepedics.

The nurses ask about your family. You keep telling them: got none left, and who needs 'em anyway. Look at the ones who visit these other old bastards. All they want is your money.

You told your men if sheep die in drought or floods before they've given their best, it means fifteen years of careful attention to bloodlines is lost. We have to fight the seasons, out here, you said. And be on the lookout for foundering sheep. And impostors.

When you saw the sulphurous eye at the heart of a dust storm, you forgot all about Ester and the babies.

The nurses don't want to believe that you are on your own. Even though you never have any visitors. When Deborah Anne turned up you thought you were going to die from frustration, not being able to tell her to git away out of it. The nurses were watching your every move, hovering nearby with their ears pricked. When she finally left, the nurse called Diane wanted to know who she was. None of your fucking business, you said, then you promptly shat yourself to keep her busy.

13

Outside the hospital the first spring shower of the day had begun. Freya hurried to her car. Rain dribbled down her neck. She flew into the car and sat for a few minutes, catching her breath. She stared flatly at the water patterns on the window screen, then turned on the engine to clear the condensation, and listened to the afternoon play, a distressing story about a battered child. The girl screamed as her abuser tied her up.

She switched to a music station and tapped the steering wheel with her fingertips. She couldn't sit still. Her skin prickled with heat. She took out her final paycheque and did a few quick sums in her head. If she was careful, she could put some of it towards a new boat. She folded it carefully and tucked it in her wallet. She took out her hairbrush and tidied her hair in the mirror. Then she flipped through her address book, then her pocket diary. Del was expecting her at three. She wondered what Connie was doing. She kept shifting her bottom, and reaching over her shoulder to scratch her back.

The *Complete Illustrated Holistic Herbal*, which she carried in her bag, listed red clover, oats and vervain for edginess. She had tried dandelion and centaury tonic, but nothing worked. Since losing the children and meeting Connie, she was in a constant state of agitation.

She thought about Connie poring over the photograph albums that day when she first turned up. Freya the bald infant, dressed in David Jones babywear, Freya on her tinsel-covered Christmas bike, Freya at the beach holding an enormous Neapolitan ice cream. Cousins pulling her along in a wooden go-kart.

Every family has at least one annoying aunt. In Freya's family it was Auntie Maura, Bob's older sister, named after their Irish grandmother. Maura always accused Shirley and Bob of indulging Freya.

'You're spoiling that child. She'll go rotten.' As though Freya might suddenly wake up bruised and decayed.

Auntie Maura didn't visit often; she lived in 'the sticks'. When she did, Freya felt undressed by her pea-green eyes, and retreated into her daydreams. This made Auntie Maura even more critical. Bob and Shirley were always apologising for Freya's bad manners.

One day Freya was crouching behind the garages, reciting her secret language, when Auntie Maura stepped out from the shadows and glared hard at her, then stormed into the kitchen to tell Shirley that Freya was 'probably retarded'. Freya had heard them talking through the window.

The rain stopped and the windscreen began to steam. She sat for a moment, wondering what she was going to say when she finally confronted Shirley and Bob about her adoption. Then she switched on the engine, wrenched the car into reverse and sped off towards the exit.

126

During the drive home she decided that from now on she was not going to tolerate uninvited intrusions on her time. She had work to do, a business to get up and running; she had to put her life in order, and win back her children. She had herbs to plant, tinctures to bottle and label, phone calls to make, and orders to fulfil.

14

Oh yes, you told your men, one merino has two hundred million fibres in its fleece, each growing around quarter of an inch a day. That's around fifteen miles of fibre a year. If you lined up all the sheep in Australia nose to tail, they'd circle the globe nearly four times.

Your favourite roustabout, David Oatley, tossed the first of the day's folded harvest on to the wooden-rollered table with a practised flick of his wrists. The fleece went flying high through the air and landed unfolded. Greg Glasson, the wool classer, and his assistant wool roller Sandy Shugg skirted the fleece by removing inferior or dirty wool. After skirting, Sandy rolled the fleece into a compact ball, for you and Greg to grade for quality, based on the fleece's texture, colour and fibre length. After classing, the fleeces were unceremoniously dumped into corrugated iron bins, according to grade.

Around eleven, the men stopped for smoko, and stood outside in the shade of a gum tree, discussing the morning's work. Their shirts were stained with yolk and raddle. They looked like artists, and were, in their own way.

Jackie Howe, your best gun, who could strip more than two hundred sheep in a day, looked up from the pipe he was filling with tobacco, and asked how the babies were doing.

They kick a lot when Ester changes their

nappies, you said, just like that bastard of a cobbler that wouldn't keep still for you this morning, and you chipped her pizzle. You chuckled.

But are they *all right?* said Jackie, insistent, his brow furrowed with deep lines. He pulled a handful of noils from his pocket and hooked them on to the barbed-wire fence, for birds nesting in the surrounding trees.

You said, not good. Might have to take them to hospital. There's something wrong with them. Some defect or other. A birth defect.

The men stared at the ground and shifted their weight; dust puffed up around their boots. A new skirter with red hair cleared his throat, and hoiked into a handkerchief. The rest of the men looked up and glared at him. He glanced across at you, apologetically.

That's all right, mate, you said. The dust gets in your throat on the board.

You left them and went into the house to throw up, almost forgetting that your wife was there. Her stricken face turned to you from the nursery doorway.

I changed their nappies five times each today, she said. But I can't do it any more.

You put your finger on the light switch, and she said, don't.

The truck arrived to take the wool to the processing factory. You loaded the bales and silently blessed each one. You understood how far it was from the pastures to a snug woolly jumper. Then you stood with your men on the brow of the hill and watched the dust trail billowing from the rear of the truck, until it became a hazy blot on the horizon.

A good week's work, eh, boss? said Jackie. The men waited for your praise, eyebrows lifting expectantly.

That's nothing, you said.

Disappointment flitted across their faces.

One day they'll replace you blokes with robots, you said. Mark my words. They'll be able to strip off a fleece in one piece. And there'll come a day when they'll be able to feed or inject chemicals that will turn shearers into pluckers.

The men looked at you, incredulous.

That's right, you said. You'll be able to pull the wool out, just like picking spinach, or carrots. No worries about cutting the poor buggers, or damaging the fleece. Riding on the sheep's back'll be child's play. It'll put a whole new meaning on the phrase.

15

This wasn't how Connie had imagined it would be. She had expected Freya to be overjoyed. She thought they'd be on the phone to each other every spare minute of every day, catching up. Instead, Freya kept avoiding her, and never returned her calls.

She sat for a while by the window overlooking the square. People arriving home from work took their dogs into the gated park at this time. She liked to read the *Wall Street Journal* and eat her TV dinner with a fork, leaving the other hand free to turn the pages. A woman in a white tracksuit was trying to steer two white shih-tzus away from an amorous pug and its owner, a gay Dutchman with a toupee, who Connie knew lived in the next block. It was unlike them to be in the park at the same time, because the shih-tzus caused a terrible scene if another dog was there first.

The problem was, she thought, watching the dogs straining to kill one another, she hadn't included Freya's not knowing in the equation.

She kept telling herself it had been for the best, coming out with the truth right at the start of their meeting. Her parents had told her honesty was always the best policy. It had never done her any harm. As soon as she was old enough to understand, they had told her she was adopted. Freya would soon get over the shock, and come to terms with it.

After all, they'd been lucky. Especially compared to poor Peggy, whose life had been wretched until Forbes came along.

Mind you, Hopeville wasn't a perfect town, by any stretch of the imagination. Freya said Windsor Meadows wasn't exactly without its problems either.

Changes had always been planned in Hopeville, which made the inadequacies more bearable. There was always the thought that things might get better. Perhaps when the cinema was built. Or the new medical centre. A slow brown river flowed through the middle of town. Factories flanking the shores spat waste matter from stinking pipes. In summer people queued on the street to see doctors at the town surgery, which was falling apart. They complained of mysterious lumps and rashes and headaches. Fat flies stuck to people's faces, as if drunk on the air. In spite of all this, the unbearable heat in summer, the pollution and fear of disease, Connie had loved it. She especially loved the swimming baths, a patchwork of five concrete pools of varying sizes linked by timber walkways, where she used to dangle her legs and drink Welch's grape juice. She liked to flirt with the boys, skinny, spotty local kids who were surprised at her unwillingness to join in their sex games with the other black girls behind the changing sheds. The town's older inhabitants were accepting and non-judgemental of her Aboriginal origins. No one ever said a word about her black skin and the way it differed in texture and tone from other black people's in town.

'You're our unofficial town mascot,' Florence often told her. A symbol of human survival. Florence and Donald were proud of her. Their love for her was unconditional. They never called her their 'adopted daughter'. She was simply their daughter. How could she possibly be ungrateful?

There were times as a young child when she felt she was the main reason the townsfolk were so happy. Why, she couldn't do a simple errand at the post office without being stopped by half a dozen people along the way, enquiring after her well-being. Florence and Donald once showed her a scrapbook with newspaper articles about her homecoming.

Town's Finest Baking Couple Bring Home Adopted Baby, said one headline.

Their Pride and Joy, said another.

The accompanying photographs showed Florence and Donald holding her up for the cameras in front of their store, surrounded by staff and other townsfolk, all smiling.

There had never been any desire to find her real parents. If the thought ever did occur to her, she had pushed it from her mind, ashamed of her selfishness. Until the day Florence said she should track them down.

'For your own peace of mind. Because there'll come a day when you'll start wondering. Probably when you have wee ones of your own. You might as well get it out in the open ahead of time.'

She closed the *Wall Street Journal* and went across to the telephone table. She dialled Freya's number.

'I'm so glad you called,' said Freya.

Connie's heart quickened. 'I was wondering if you'd like to meet me at Australia House next week,' she said. 'On the ninth. There's a do on for expats. They're launching a new website. It should be fun.'

'I'd love to,' said Freya, and meant it. 'Thank you.'

She had never been to Australia House. She wanted to see Connie, and this seemed the perfect place to meet — away from prying eyes.

'What's your cellphone number?'

'I don't have a mobile.'

'You're kidding. Everyone has a cellphone.'

'Well, I don't.'

'Take down my number, in case you have to call me from a phone booth.'

Freya scribbled down the number.

'It starts at six thirty,' said Connie. 'Why don't we meet for a drink at six? There's a pub near Covent Garden called the Whistle and Flute.'

Connie put down the receiver and picked up a copy of *Inland Waterways* magazine, which she had bought on the way home. The For Sale pages were at the back. She had already ringed several ads in pencil. One in particular had caught her eye: a large Dutch barge with three bedrooms and two receptions. What appealed to Connie was the design of the wheelhouse, which could be folded down when travelling. 'The boat fits quite easily under the many bridges on the waterways,' the ad said. 'Recently built to high standards, with all mod cons and mains water connections.'

Freya was having a battle convincing Monica that houseboats were a respectable alternative. As long as she lived on *Harlequin*, with its dented hull and leaking windows, she may as well forget getting full custody. Connie thought the boat was charming, but Monica was unimpressed, sniffing at the bathroom when she went to wash her hands, and making comments about the cramped cabins. Connie had hated the woman the minute she set eyes on her.

She dialled the number.

'Sorry,' said the male voice on the other end. 'We sold that boat last week.'

★ ★ ★

They were sitting in a leather booth inside the Whistle and Flute, a gastro-pub full of powdered lawyers. 'When they say gastro they mean gastronomical, not gastroenteritis,' said Freya drily.

Connie laughed.

When they'd ordered drinks, Freya levelled her gaze at Connie.

'You might be my sister on paper,' she said, leaning forward so Connie could hear her over the din, 'and by birth. But you're basically a stranger. I just don't see how we're ever going to be able to make up for lost time. I mean, we've got nothing in common.'

Connie gave her a long, complicated look and

said, 'Maybe not. But we should at least try.'

They knocked their glasses of orange juice together.

'Here's one thing we've got in common,' said Connie, 'we don't drink alcohol. To us.'

'To us.'

Freya had already decided to take control of the conversation this time. 'Tell me about Henry,' she said. 'What's wrong with him?'

'Parkinson's Disease.'

'Really? I've seen quite a bit of that in my job. Very unpleasant. And difficult to treat. It has to be tailored to each individual. Quite tricky, balancing the drugs. Do you know how far advanced it is?'

'Not really. He's been in hospital for six months. And they're not planning on transferring him to a care home.'

'How sad.'

'If you're planning on visiting, I'd be quick if I were you.'

Freya chose to ignore this remark. She wasn't planning on going anywhere just yet.

'What about our mother?' she said. 'Do you know much about her?'

'Henry wouldn't tell me much that first time, out at Tinderry. And when I went to see him the second time, when I met Peggy, he was beyond conversation. He had to be spoon-fed by then. He'd lost the use of all his limbs. He could only mumble a few words at a time, and even that was an effort.'

'Was he glad to see you at least, the last time?'

'If he was, he didn't show it.'

'Of course not,' said Freya. 'How stupid of me. Parkinson's turns people into zombies, basically. I probably shouldn't say that, but it's true. Staring eyes, reduced blinking, a mask-like appearance to the face. It's rather unnerving, don't you think?'

Connie nodded gravely.

The heat in the pub was unbearable. Freya could feel sweat forming on her top lip. More people poured in, and a group of po-faced women in black suits, throwing back beer as fast as the men, parked their backsides inches from Freya's face. She felt claustrophobic, hemmed in by bodies and cigarette smoke and screeching music.

'I bought you a present,' said Connie.

'What for?' Freya did not want any sort of commitment between them at this stage.

'It's nothing fancy,' said Connie. She pulled out a box from her black leather tote bag. It was one of the latest camera phones. 'There's no privacy where you live. You can use this anywhere.'

'I can't take that,' said Freya.

'Don't be so silly. Of course you can.'

'But Connie — '

'No buts about it. Think of it as an early Christmas present.'

'Thank you, I don't know what to say — '

'Let's go, shall we?' Connie got up and squeezed through the crowd. Freya hurried after her.

Outside Connie led the way along the narrow streets behind Covent Garden, dodging frantic commuters dashing for the Tube. It was a warm evening with a full moon glowing over the rooftops. The smell of pizzas and curry wafted from restaurants. Freya's feet were swollen and tender, in shoes she hadn't worn since Neill's drummer's wedding, five years earlier.

They walked down past the BBC, stopping to look at the tourist posters in the windows of Australia House. Further along there was one of some Aborigines. Freya had a strange feeling as she stared at the photo collage. A group of Aboriginal park rangers, dressed in khaki shorts and hats, and long socks. Two policemen, similarly dressed. And another, smaller picture of some children posing in a mercurial river, with gummy grins, and brown reeds piled on their heads like snakes.

'Let's go,' said Connie, clearly irritated. She walked ahead and Freya had to run to catch her up.

Inside Australia House it was even hotter than the pub. About three hundred people were gathered in the main reception, a high-ceilinged, echoey room with marble pillars and huge chandeliers. Tables were set up along the walls, and people crowded around them ordering drinks.

'Come on,' said Connie, 'let's have a look at the books.'

At one table they were selling a book of stories written by Australian expats. They moved on to the next table. The women serving were busy chatting. A man was reading the blurb on a large hardback. He replaced it carefully on the table and moved off, the discomfort on his face barely disguised.

Freya picked up a copy. *Professional Savages*, by Roslyn Poignant. She opened it and read the jacket. Miss Poignant was an anthropologist living in London. Her book was about the circus impresario P.T. Barnum, and his collection of 'uncivilised races' from around the world, whom he took on an international tour of the metropolitan exhibition circuit in the late 1800s.

Freya turned the pages. There were photographs of Australian Aborigines, African pygmies, and native Americans, posing and performing for curious onlookers, some with scars on their chests, others with a large bone through the septum of their nose. The men were dressed in loincloths, the women in grass skirts. Their sad expressions tugged at Freya's heart. She stared at the eyes of an Aboriginal woman with a shock of black hair, posing half-naked in a circus sideshow.

Connie glanced at the books, but did not pick one up.

Behind them a woman appeared on a stage and tapped a microphone. Ear-splitting feedback filled the auditorium. The woman waited for the sound engineer to adjust the levels, then she introduced the Nobel Prize-winning professor who had come to launch the website.

Freya did not hear the rest of the introduction, nor the professor's speech. She was enthralled with the book, in particular a section about an Aborigine called Tambo whose remains were found in an Ohio funeral home in 1993 and repatriated to Australia a year later — amid much media attention and controversy. It went on to describe the cultural renewal stimulated by this event, and how it made people in Tambo's community examine more closely the causes of today's social and economic injustices.

Connie peered over Freya's shoulder. 'It's all too much for me, seeing pictures like that,' she said.

Freya replaced the book, the temptation to buy a copy suddenly gone.

'Come on,' she said. 'Let's look at that table over there, with all the leaflets.'

As they moved through the crowd Freya noticed people's eyes sliding away from Connie, and the way they looked at Freya straight after, in that way that meant 'what are you doing with *her*?'

'Let's get out of here,' said Connie suddenly, grabbing Freya by the arm and leading her towards the exit. 'It's too hot.'

They walked down the Strand towards Trafalgar Square, and found a small café in a side street, with tables and chairs on the pavement.

'This'll do,' said Connie, plonking herself down on a chair.

Freya was beginning to feel bullied. She had wanted to stay a while at the launch, and talk to some of the Australians gathered there about current attitudes to the Aborigines. Her desire for knowledge was growing with every minute of her new identity.

Connie was in a quiet, reflective mood. She

disliked being in London. She was glad Freya had come, but she wanted to go home now and be on her own at the apartment.

A sullen Italian waitress took their order.

'Thanks for inviting me,' said Freya. 'It's great to see so many Australians doing well over here.'

'I don't want to go home,' said Connie irritably.

'Home being?'

'Australia, of course. I know I'll have to go again, to find some peace of mind. And I want to see Peggy.'

'So what's the problem?'

'People treat me better in West Virginia and New York than they do in Australia. As soon as I land there some people either stare at me with hatred or they look away embarrassed. I know I'm a curiosity in America, but I'd rather be a curiosity there than a stranger in my own land.'

Freya looked at her. Should she tell her what she now knew in her heart to be true?

The waitress banged their cappuccinos on the table and gave Freya a quick, fake smile. When she had gone, they sat in silence for a few moments, Freya weighing up the pros and cons of confessing, Connie thinking about the difficulties of her life.

'What would you say if I told you I think I've got Aboriginal ancestry, even though I look white?' said Freya. 'That I think our father is the same man?'

Connie looked at her, incredulous. 'I'd say it's impossible. I know our birth certificates say Henry is mine and Peggy's father, but that can't

141

be true. I mean, the man's as white as a lily. He's definitely your father. And he's definitely not mine or Peggy's.'

'Then why is his name on the birth certificates?'

'I told you. Because Ester had an affair with an Aboriginal. Obviously. Back then they employed blacks to work on the farms. She may have been lonely. And Henry was probably mad at her, and ashamed. So he put his name down.'

'Well, it wouldn't surprise me if it turned out we had the same Aboriginal father. It's possible I could have more of our mother's genes, and that's why I'm white.'

'Possible. But highly unlikely.' Connie's eyes grew dark. She frowned. 'You want to be careful who you go saying this to. Especially in Australia. People would say you're an impostor, making out you've got Abo blood. It's like those white Australians claiming convict ancestry, like it's trendy or something. Can you imagine people boasting about being related to a common thief who was transported out there by ship? Now people are coming forward and claiming Aboriginal heritage, and some are trying to get in on the land claim. I'd be very, very careful if I were you. It's not something you say lightly. It's an insult.'

Freya wished she had never brought it up. She had sounded presumptuous, and vain.

'I'm sorry,' she said softly.

Clearly there was a lot she had to learn about Aboriginal culture and recent attitudes. She decided not to mention her theory again. Not to Connie, not to anyone. Not even Del.

16

Around the time you drove yourself into the city to the hospital, there were exciting developments in the wool-growing industry. It pissed you off, having to chuck it all in. But you'd had a good innings. What really irked you was not having a son, or sons, to take over.

In October that year you read about a merino ram from Collinsville stud in South Australia that sold for $330,000. Wool growing was on the brink of a radical breakthrough in artificial breeding and genetic engineering. You sat by the fire reading the *Snowy Mountains Gazette*, dumbfounded. The newspaper was six months old. You bought it last time you were in town for supplies. Even so, the news was immediate and exciting.

Semen could now be stored for more than fifteen years and transported around the world. One ram could inseminate up to ten thousand ewes, instead of a hundred, each year. Stud breeders were queuing to buy frozen semen and embryos. Scientists in Sydney were on the verge of producing genetically engineered 'super' sheep by splicing additional growth hormone genes into the chromosomes of single-celled embryos, things called zygotes. They were trying to find ways of genetically enhancing wool growth, and had isolated bacterial genes which, when transferred into sheep, could put fifty per

143

cent more wool on each animal.

Fifty per cent.

You let out a long, low whistle.

Long before these breakthroughs, you leaned on one of the posts in the shearing shed, chewing sweet resin from a gum leaf and running a lock of wool between your index finger and thumb, and you told your men that one of your best merinos at its peak could cut over forty pounds of soft, bright wool.

The men agreed your animals were non-stop fibre factories.

You smiled, and said, that's what's so marvellous.

17

Parent was ordinarily a simple six-letter word that implied unconditional love and stability. In Freya's case it was a word crammed with chicanery. She wondered if she would ever feel the same towards Shirley and Bob. What would she say, next time they met? What would she call them?

Three days had passed since she and Connie had met up in London. Every day after finishing work in the summerhouse and the garden, she set off on a long walk to try and clear her head. She felt crushed in the confined space of the boat. The summerhouse was not much better, measuring ten feet by eight and facing north. It got little light and was overshadowed by a large elder tree.

Some days she lingered on these walks too long, and found herself coming home in the dark. Today she set off soon after breakfast. At least she was still eating. Some people might lose interest in the four basic food groups after such a major trauma.

A few miles along the canal the houses thinned out and gave way to open fields and low hills. The sun was warm and the banks of the canal were buzzing with insects. Wild flowers spilled over the towpath. She loved the sound of the narrowboats putt-putting along the canal, forcing their way through a skin of green duckweed. Several powerboats chugged past, causing a wash that slapped hard against the banks.

She passed the canal-side pub, closed at this hour, and felt relieved that she did not have to sneak past any tipsy neighbours.

A warm breeze came up from the south, and the mist melted away over the water. A moorhen darted into the reeds, and a swan landed up ahead with the grace of a drunk ballerina.

The beauty of this stretch of the canal made her quicken her pace. The smell of watercress beds and onion weed was strong and pungent. The sky was colourwashed with flimsy clouds. She felt as though she could be a thousand miles from London.

In the distance a group of youth volunteers were mending the edge of the canal. Sam Jenner was with them, supervising.

When she saw him, Freya almost turned off the towpath, but there was no way over the barbed-wire fence. Her usual route via a stile and across a field up into the woods was just beyond where Sam was working.

He smiled as she approached. She waited until the last second and offered a stiff hello, wincing at the steeliness of her own voice. He stood in the middle of the towpath, making it difficult for her to pass without pushing him aside.

'You look as though you've got the weight of the world on your shoulders,' he said. 'What's wrong?' He worked his jaw.

'Nothing,' she said airily. 'You know what it's

like, being on the boats. Not enough fresh air, sometimes.'

She felt guilty for being short with him, and decided it could not hurt to stop and chat for a few minutes. Surely the court didn't expect her to live like a nun?

'I see you've bought some paint for your hull,' he said. The tins were stacked outside *Harlequin*. 'You know, there's a lot to be said for using a high-performance two-pack paint in your bilges, and a corrosion inhibitor for your engine. Frosty winters can take their toll.' His face was solemn. Before she could make an excuse and get away, he went on to warn her about electrical faults caused by outmoded switch panels, and how corrosion could produce seizure. 'Especially on older boats that weren't built properly in the first place. Like *Harlequin*. And then of course you need to overhaul your gas connection.'

Her eyes grew heavy. She wanted to learn about boats, in particular her boat, but Sam could be such an anorak. Why couldn't he simply say you need to paint your boat with special paint and service your electrics?

'What got you into this?' she said, nodding at a pile of sticks and hazel rods piled next to the path.

'It's just a part-time job, for a local consultancy,' said Sam. He and the other 'river doctors' were installing the sticks to strengthen a section of crumbling bank. 'Part of a lottery-funded upgrade programme.'

Just then a Dutch barge slipped by doing two knots. Sam became agitated, pointing out the potential damage caused by its wash.

'Even at one knot, the daily battering leaves its mark. Shoring up the banks with concrete or steel is effective, but not exactly environmentally sound or attractive.'

They leaned over the bank to inspect the damage.

'Look at the difference here, where we put in faggots. It's only twelve months, and already the marginal plants are well established, and wildlife has returned.'

'They look lovely,' said Freya. 'Like baskets. They must be very strong.'

'Oh they are. It's a green solution to the erosion problem, and one that's taken a lot of research to get right. It's not just a matter of knocking in a few sticks and throwing in some hazel, soil and plants. The trial runs took months in fast-flowing, high-energy chalk streams.'

'I like the way they blend in.'

She was surprised at her willingness to get drawn into the conversation. The warmth of the sun and the clear sky made her feel expansive. There was something solid and enduring about Sam. He made her feel protected and relaxed.

'They're practical as well as ornamental,' she said.

'Exactly.' Sam beamed. He seemed determined not to mention the children. He was friendly enough, and was definitely pleased to see her, but a formality had developed between them.

They chatted at length about the history of the canals. He was knowledgeable and enthusiastic.

148

She lost track of what he was saying, and focused on the deep and pleasant timbre of his voice. At one point his arm brushed against hers and she pulled away. Because her body did not feel like her own, she felt reluctant to share it. She almost cried when she thought of the deception. Heat travelled from her stomach, weaving its way through her chest and along her arms, stopping short of her fingers, which remained strangely cool. The back of her eyes burned with suppressed emotion. She had begun to think about her transformation from the old Freya to the new, and found that it often made her nauseous. It seemed profoundly unnatural, moving from the familiar to the unknown. Yet in other ways it felt perfectly right.

'I must say, you're acting very odd lately,' he said. 'Is it something I said?'

'You practically accused Kirsty of being a tramp.'

'I did no such thing. You're being ridiculous.'

'Am I?'

'I think we should sort this out once and for all. Wait here.' He sounded cross.

He left her standing under a willow tree and helped the others finish off a section of faggoting. She stared at the fields beyond the canal, yellow with corn and early rapeseed flowers. Her eyes were drawn back to the murky water, eddying and swirling as the nearby lock filled and emptied, boats emerging as if from the gates of heaven.

She had been thinking about Shirley and Bob all morning, and wanted to continue her attempt to reshuffle her memories and get used to her new persona as Katherine Nolan. Bumping into Sam was not part of the plan.

She had been picturing her whole family — aunts, uncles, cousins, second cousins — assembled at Christmas, pretending they were related to her. They must have known it was a lie, that her life was a lie, and her 'parents' were liars.

She decided there was no point in thinking about the possibility of sharing all this with anyone. She had to be icily rational, get on with her life and keep it to herself. Connie had made it clear that Peggy would not tolerate Freya's fantasies. Connie herself had seemed irritated with her theory about having Aboriginal blood.

Besides, if Neill found out she was adopted, he would latch on to it as the likely and logical reason she had never bonded with the children. He would associate Bob and Shirley's aloofness with the reality of their function: as adoptive parents, not genetic. Freya being adopted would be a neat little dysfunctional jiffy bag for his defence.

She wandered off a short distance, debating whether to tell Sam she had changed her mind. She was distracted by the abundant plant species along the canal. She put on a pair of cotton gloves from her pocket and picked a large bunch of nettles, stuffing it into the calico shoulder bag brought along for the purpose. She stood for a moment admiring the English landscape. Water-lilies and tall reeds fringed the banks of a distant pond. A rippling stream emptied itself into the canal from a dark tunnel near her feet. Larks drifted like kites high up in the pale sky.

'Fancy a drink?' Sam came up behind her.

She turned and gave him a hesitant look. 'I don't drink.'

'Come on,' he said, 'let's cut all this crap and behave like adults.' He smiled, his irritation gone.

Freya felt a surge of something verging on affection. He was trying hard, but he would probably mention Kirsty and Ryan again, and there would be more fireworks. She didn't want another argument.

'Did I say you look lovely today?' His eyes wandered over her body.

'Thank you,' she said, smiling shyly. When she had left the boat she'd looked in the mirror and noticed that her brown eyes were shining with good health, and her dark wavy hair was glossy. It was all those seeds and raw vegetables she had been nibbling in place of cooked meals. But it was difficult to stay in a good mood, with so much on her mind.

'There's a nice pub over the hill,' he said. 'It's a good walk. Are you up for it?'

'All right,' she said.

'Good. It's a steep hike, but worth it. They do a very nice steak and kidney pie.'

Freya hated steak and kidney pie, but said nothing.

They left the canal and followed a track of flattened mud that became drier and harder as they climbed. Eyebright and comfrey brushed their legs. Hoverflies hung in the air. Behind a broken fence a carpet of primroses stippled the mossy roots of alders and young oaks.

They clambered over a stile, and entered the tomb-like stillness of the woods. A thick blanket of rotting leaves squelched underfoot, releasing a rancid smell. All around them dark branches were sprouting tender leaves. The undergrowth here was still shrugging off winter's mean temper.

The path became steep. Their feet searched for footholds between the twisting roots of fat trees. Freya's heart quickened. The roots reminded her of the Dandenong mountains near Melbourne. She slipped past Sam and strode ahead.

'*Pura-mi*,' she whispered.

'Beg pardon?' said Sam. He watched her march ahead, and frowned.

Freya dared not answer. She did not understand the word herself, let alone know where it came from.

A cool wind whipped through the tops of the trees. The branches rocked to and fro, grinding wounds into the bark. Not a blackbird or robin stirred in the shrubs. High up in the canopy, too, it was quiet. As though some strange creature had passed through and cast a spell.

★ ★ ★

On those Sundays when Shirley and Bob took her out for the day, Freya could hardly wait to leave the inner sanctum of the Lacey family and disappear into the rainforest.

They always parked in the same spot. At the

foot of a broad, fern-lush gully. Lizards sunned themselves on fallen logs. Tadpoles swam around rain-filled holes in black rocks, like sperm on a futile mission.

Shirley would busy herself setting the picnic table with a red and white checked cloth, while Bob wandered off to find baby ferns to dig up for the fernery behind the mortuary. He took a cloth bag to put them in, and was on the lookout for the ranger.

On one occasion Freya had dashed off, ignoring her mother's calls, and scrambled over the rocks to the head of the stream. A fine mist pricked her face. The sweet smell of the bush sharpened her appetite for a deeper adventure. Under the lee of a waterfall she stuck out her tongue. The force of the drop was too great. The water slapped her face, making her retreat into the dark recess of the ledge.

She was gone for hours, ducking inside caves, folding herself under mossy outcrops, climbing trees and swinging like Jungle Jane from vines. Bob finally found her sitting by the edge of a stale tarn, daubing her legs with ochre. It trickled over her knees. She was transfixed by the intensity of the colour.

'Where the heck do you think you've been?' He stepped out from behind a tree, eyes blazing, arms stiff by his sides.

'*Kawarirri-mi*,' said Freya. '*Warnirri japiya*.' She looked up at her father and smiled. '*Mully-mully wandurk*.'

'What the . . . ?' Bob stood over her, his broad shoulders casting a shadow over her face. 'You've

153

well and truly done it now, young lady,' he said.

He hauled her out of the water, folded her over his thighs and spanked her hard on the bottom.

'Now wash that bloody muck off, before your mother sees you and thinks she's got a ruddy nutcase on her hands,' he said, standing up and catching his breath.

* * *

At the summit the ground was wind-dried and brittle. Sam led her to a treed slope dotted with spongy, mossy mounds and sharp vertical slivers of rock. Shafts of light fell through the branches, spotlighting each headstone. A cold shiver rippled over Freya's neck.

Sam was in a pensive mood. Perhaps he too sensed the strangeness of the woods, the desolation. He walked ahead now, pointing out dangerous protrusions and rocks. Freya studied his closely cropped hair and the solid outline of his shoulders. She thought about reaching out and cupping her hand over his smooth neck. Or linking her arms around his waist and spreading her hands over his firm stomach.

A cool wind rustled her hair, and a dark foreboding engulfed her. She felt the urge to forge ahead and leave Sam behind, to run over the hills without stopping. What if someone saw them — someone she knew?

Sam chatted away about the history of the Anderton Boat Lift, and the cessation of commercial traffic on the waterways, and how sad he felt about this. His voice was like a Radio Four announcer's, thorough and rehearsed.

They left the woods, and followed a flint path that Sam reckoned dated back to Roman times. The hill was exposed and raw. Freya scanned the valley, in case someone had followed, but there was no one about. The canal was a thin silver ribbon in the distance.

Sam spread his jacket out on the grass, and they sat quietly enjoying the view. After a while he began to prattle on about a dredging operation he had volunteered to help with in late autumn, and a nature reserve planned further north. Suddenly he stopped talking and frowned hard. He broke off a length of grass, twirling it between thumb and index finger, as if it helped him to concentrate. It was an intensely irritating habit.

Freya knew he was building up to something. She had to sit on her hands to stop herself from snatching the piece of grass.

'The problem won't resolve itself, you know,' he said grimly.

She looked away, and tried to block out his voice.

Last night he and Ryan had argued, he said. 'I found him gazing idiotically at Kirsty's photograph, when he was meant to be revising for an exam. It's a crucial age, seventeen. Especially for a boy.'

'What's the difference?' Freya gave him a sharp look.

'You know what boys are like. They love to show off. Things can easily get out of hand. One little mistake can jeopardise a person's whole future.'

'Hard to imagine I'm under an English heaven,' said Freya. She turned away and gazed at the hills rolling off towards Watford.

'I say we make a rule,' said Sam.

'Kids hate rules.'

'They don't have to know. It can be an unspoken rule.'

'They're not stupid.' She lay back and closed her eyes.

'Let's make sure they're never alone together.' He put his hand over hers and squeezed it. She pulled away.

'Kirsty's a sensible girl,' she said. 'She doesn't need me telling her what's what.'

'Sensible doesn't come into it. It's a matter of getting carried away.'

'That implies lack of self-control.'

He leaned on his elbow and studied her face. Her smooth skin glowed like brandy on ice.

She could see him watching her through the slits in her eyelids. She pretended she had not noticed, and bent an arm over her face.

'The sun's hot for April,' she said.

'I want Ryan to get four A levels,' he said. 'That means a lot of work. He doesn't need any distractions.'

'He has to have a life,' she said. 'A balance. They need to know they are trusted.'

'It's not that I don't trust Ryan. I just know how easy it is to get caught off guard.'

Freya scrutinised the strong, angular line of his unshaven jaw.

'Did you train as a child psychologist before turning to youth work?' she said.

'Very funny.'

'I'm serious.'

'You're very anti-authority, for a nurse.'

'I'm not a rebel, if that's what you mean.'

Sam slid his eyes over the curves of her body. 'You certainly don't look like a revolutionary, with that figure.'

A surge of desire pulsed through her veins, startling her. She longed for Sam to put his lips firmly on hers. To feel him exploring her mouth with slow tenderness. She wanted to reach out and lift his hand on to her breast. Then push it slowly down to a place that she had almost forgotten existed.

'People are right about you,' he said. 'You're sassy, and independent. It can put a man off, you know.'

'I'll take my chances.'

'What was that strange language back there? Are you bilingual?'

Freya shrugged. 'I often talk to myself.' She laughed, trying to make a joke of it.

'I know you think I'm being neurotic about the kids,' he said. 'But I have to do my best to keep Ryan on track. That's part of being a parent.'

'You don't have to tell me how to be a parent,' she said. 'These things will take their course. You'd be worried if Ryan showed no interest at all in girls. They're normal, healthy teenagers.'

'It'll serve us right if something goes wrong.'

'Will it?' She sprang to her feet, suddenly fed up with the whole conversation.

He sat up abruptly and shaded his eyes with a hand. 'What's wrong?'

'This is ridiculous,' she said. 'I think I'd best head off.'

'Don't go. I'm sorry, Freya. I don't mean to insult you or Kirsty. It's just that I want Ryan to pass. That's all.'

'With you watching his every move, I'm sure he will.' She brushed the grass off her clothes and turned away. 'Meanwhile, I don't want to hear any more of your views on the subject, if you don't mind.'

She left him sitting on the hillside, twiddling a blade of grass, and marched across the fields towards the moorings, which right now seemed to her like a sanctuary. At the bottom of the hill she hid behind a tree and looked back to where they had been sitting. Sam was gone. She had hoped he would follow her. Take her into his arms and kiss her, as if marking her out as his.

She climbed the stile, remembering the heat of his hand on hers when he'd helped her over earlier.

When she got to the towpath she stood for a while looking at the hazel faggots, thinking about his voice, the strength of it, the respect he showed her, the tact. She was furious with herself for being so touchy. As a nurse who was known for her diplomacy and clever manipulation of difficult patients, she was failing miserably with her handling of Sam Jenner.

She would have to make an effort next time to be charming. Before it was too late and he gave up.

18

It was only three weeks since Connie had come into her life. So much had changed in such a short time. Good and bad.

Although she was a little annoyed with Connie for foisting a mobile phone on her, she was beginning to enjoy the privacy it offered. She used it to call Connie several times a week. The noise of the Stock Exchange in the background gave Connie an air of great importance, but she had to shout over the din. Freya held the phone away from her ear.

She wanted to talk to Connie more often, every day in fact, but she resisted; Connie was busy, and she didn't want to be a pest. It was almost like having a secret lover, except the thrill was sisterly, not sexual.

Connie invited her to Knightsbridge. 'We could go to Harrods first, if you like. It's only around the corner.'

'I'll show you where they sell my products, in the apothecary,' said Freya.

'I'll definitely have to buy something of yours,' said Connie. 'What do you recommend?'

'You don't have to do that. I'll bring something with me.'

Connie was very excited. She began to giggle. 'Why don't we have lunch at the oyster bar?'

Sometimes her eagerness repelled Freya; Connie was assuming a depth between them that didn't even exist. On top of the uncertainty and reticence she was already feeling, it was a bit hard to take. One minute she was all for them getting to know each other, the next she wished Connie would simply go away.

'Please say you'll come,' said Connie. 'I've thought about you every minute this past week.'

'All right,' said Freya, trying to hide her reluctance, 'I'd love to.'

She turned the phone off and sat for a moment watching the canal glinting in the sun. In normal circumstances Connie wouldn't be her type. Freya didn't like businesswomen, especially those to whom making a lot of money was paramount. But she could see that under Connie's glitz there was an ordinary woman with terrific spirit. A lonely woman who, like her, felt on the outside of life looking in.

It was amazing how much work Freya had done lately. She'd bottled and labelled enough products to fill four dozen crates, and stacked them in her shed. At night she hardly slept, labouring over the stove instead. Breathing in the herbal oils made her head swim and her eyes steam, but the scents of the herbs were energising, pushing her on to achieve her goals.

Time seemed to stand still in the hours between one and six, before the first sounds of people stirring on the other boats reverberated down the canal, and up into *Harlequin*'s steel hull. Freya felt suspended in time, the only person in the world awake. Sometimes she felt deeply at odds with herself, as well as the world. She knew she had to watch herself closely, in case her inner turmoil turned to malice.

She thought about telephoning Sam, or knocking on his door. When she lay awake on her bed, she thought about him being here with her, holding her close all night, the sound of his voice deep in her skull.

Sometimes she nodded off while sitting at the dining-room table writing labels. Her dreams made her sweat profusely and cry out. Giant men with unnaturally long legs and short arms taunted her with bloodshot, pulsating eyes. One dream in particular was so disturbing it made her scream: a huge serpent with rows of serrated teeth, swallowing a steady flow of tiny human figures, eyes wide with fear. They tumbled down the animal's throat, regurgitated as wild-eyed animals and birds.

On waking she busied herself in the garden or the shed, telling herself she was normal, that the dreams were simply a manifestation of her fears. She pushed them from her mind. Like the timid Cryptanthemis, an underground Australian orchid she had read about recently, which tried and often failed to penetrate the earth's surface to scatter its seeds, she kept sealing up the cracks and shrinking from the light.

19

The children were like rag dolls when Neill dropped them off for their weekend visit, listless and sulky. She thought perhaps it was because she had asked them to leave their gadgets at Neill's.

'It's not because of that,' said Kirsty.

They're under a lot of strain, thought Freya, sharing bedrooms with their step-siblings (strangers), being restructured by Clarissa and indoctrinated in the ways of the Lord by Neill. These were the moments Monica should witness.

But she feared that her own efforts weren't up to much, either. They seemed so distant and neutral when she tried to rally their interest, even for the big things — the museum outings, the shopping trips.

'You'll fall over your bottom lip if it hangs any lower,' she said to Kirsty, as they waited for the train to London on Saturday morning.

'Ha, ha,' said Kirsty. She walked further along the platform and sat on a bench, staring at the tracks.

She had been wearing her hair in plaits when Neill dropped them off this morning. Freya quite liked them, and said so. Kirsty had rolled her eyes and groaned. As soon as Neill's car heaved over the bridge, she pulled off the rubber bands and shook them out.

'Dad made me wear them,' she said.

Tom was wearing a new pair of brown cord trousers that he obviously hated. He kept looking down, and kicking out his feet so that the hems, which were too short, covered his shoes. His hair had been cut in yet another new style. He showed Freya a church brochure with his picture on the cover. He was smiling shyly at the camera, hair combed in a way that Freya could only describe as churchy.

'Who took the photo?' she had said lightly, trying not to show her dismay.

'Dad,' came the despondent reply.

On the train she tried to draw them out, talking about her new business venture as a medicinal herbalist, and how it was already starting to take off. But Kirsty said, 'The Body Shop's got the natural cosmetics industry all sewn up.' (Business Studies had made her an expert — kids were so cluey these days.)

Tom said simply (pulling a face) that he hated 'all that girlie stuff'.

'I'll be concentrating on the medicinal side of it,' said Freya defensively.

'How do you expect to make a living doing that?' said Kirsty. 'People will think you're a witch.'

How Freya hated Neill for brainwashing them.

'It's coming back in, herbs for healing,' she said. 'People are under a lot of stress these days, and anything alternative always attracts attention.'

They sat in silence.

'How's school?' said Freya when the impasse

became intolerable.

'Okay.'

'All right.'

At the Science Museum they perked up a bit, experimenting with light boxes and activating the wheels on model trains. Freya hung back from the exhibits, observing some of the other mothers, and the way they related to their children. She tried hard not to stare, but couldn't drag her eyes off a doting woman in designer jeans who kept hugging her little girl, bending down to describe each display in rapt tones. The child responded with smiles and giggles, and whoops of delight, as the various machines burst into action. The woman was oblivious to the other visitors, focusing entirely on her daughter's pleasure.

When the children were hungry, Freya took them to the museum cafeteria. Normally she would pack sandwiches, but this morning she couldn't be bothered, because Kirsty had reminded her of the last excursion, when they had gone soggy. Kirsty and Tom ate their baked beans and jacket potatoes in silence. Screaming children drowned out Freya's attempts to talk about the displays. She felt sure they were the only family in the entire building — in London — not connecting. As she looked across the table at them, she saw two strangers sitting in front of her. They were as English as mist and rain.

Should she tell them about Connie? They had a right to know. But they might let it slip out in front of Neill. Would it really matter if she didn't tell them, at least until everything

164

had been sorted out?

They were oblivious to her inner turmoil, and saw only the mother they were used to, every inch of her as familiar as their own breath. Freya, though, felt that she was seeing them clearly for the first time. Thanks to Neill and the court, she now doubted intensely her own ability as a mother.

When they had finished eating, they laid their knives and forks neatly across their plates and sat with their hands clasped on the edge of the table. This was a new habit Neill and Clarissa had obviously instilled. Table manners.

Freya sipped her cappuccino, wondering what to say to break the ice. Was it always going to be this way when they got together? Tense for the first day, then by Sunday a little more relaxed?

She stared at their hands, suddenly fascinated by the shape of their nails, the size of their knuckles, the texture of their skin. She had never noticed the small wart on Tom's thumb, nor the large freckle on Kirsty's wrist. A guilty spasm shot through her chest. What if something happened to them, and she was asked to identify their bodies by particular moles or scars?

'Can we go and see the old fire engines?' said Tom. His eyes were wide and languid.

'Can't we skip that bit, and go to the section about space?' Kirsty sighed heavily.

'Tell you what,' said Freya, 'how about we do both?' She smiled and reached across the table, squeezing their cupped hands.

They pulled away and buried their fists in their laps, sitting back so abruptly that their chairs almost toppled. Kirsty's cheeks glowed pink. She glanced around, in case anyone had seen Freya's embarrassing little act.

'What's wrong with you today, Mum? Stop touching me all the time.'

'All the time?' A small laugh slipped from Freya's lips. 'Twice. I touched you twice. And anyway, what's wrong with that? All the other mothers hug their children. Look, there's one over there with her arm around her boy's shoulder.'

'Mum. He's a toddler.'

'What's age got to do with it?'

'Everything.'

'I just thought we should try and be closer, that's all. So that we can live together again.'

'Dad'll never let that happen,' said Tom gloomily. 'I heard him telling Clarissa.'

'Do you like her?' said Freya blithely.

'We don't let her touch us, if that's what you mean,' said Kirsty. She pulled a face.

Freya's heart lurched. Was it too late to reverse the status quo? How could she bond with them if they weren't willing to let her? Even without the Game Boy and the Walkman driving a tangible wedge between them, they were untouchable.

★　★　★

They walked to the Natural History Museum and wandered through the galleries. Freya was conscious of people looking at them — possibly thinking she and the children were fighting or foreign (or both) — because they were not

166

speaking to one another. Several times she felt the urge to slip an arm around Kirsty's waist or squeeze Tom's hand, and resisted.

Because of their different interests, they decided to separate, agreeing to meet in the museum shop in an hour's time. While the children ran off to find the Earthquake Experience, Freya, unsure of her bearings, roamed through the galleries, feeling out of sorts. She found herself in the new Darwin Centre, staring up at a seven-storey atrium full of specimens. The place made her think hard about her own origins, and gave her an instant headache. Her own history was too much to take in. The weight of it made her move slowly; she felt unnaturally tired.

Walking past the exhibits, she stopped to look at various preserved animals: a Komodo dragon, loggerhead turtles, huge spotted rays, an Amazonian giant fish. A collection of invertebrates collected by Captain Cook on his *Endeavour* voyage. This she found especially interesting. She stopped one of the guides.

'Excuse me, can you tell me where I might find anything about Australian Aboriginal people?'

The man had an air of superiority, and a name tag pinned to his chest. A look of alarm flitted across his face. He stepped back as though she had struck him. Then, in an instant, he changed his stance. He had noticed Freya's slim figure and warm dark eyes. He leaned in close. Hesitating once more, he glanced over his shoulder at his colleague, who was chatting

167

animatedly to a litter of Japanese students. Then he put his mouth close to Freya's ear.

'Actually, madam, that's a bit of a sore point here at the museum.'

'Really? Why's that?' She smiled, eager to keep him on side.

'In terms of exhibits, there's nothing on the Orstralian Aborigines any more. They took down the displays in the late nineteen seventies.'

'But why?' Freya was surprised at her defensive reaction.

'Matter of fact, some of the items that we have in storage are in dispute.'

'Artefacts?'

'Not exactly.'

'Go on.'

'I'm not supposed to be telling you any of this, because negotiations are ongoing.' He glanced at his colleague again.

'How interesting,' said Freya.

He moved in closer. She could smell coffee and chocolate on his breath.

'Bones, actually,' he said. 'Kept in special conditions. Dating back to the eighteen hundreds. There's been a big controversy about how they were obtained in the first place.'

'What do you mean?' Freya tilted her head closer to his. She could feel the heat pulsing off his scalp. It smelled of sweat and hair gel.

'Some of the bones may have been dug up soon after they were buried.'

'You mean grave-robbing?'

'Look, it happened a long time ago. And Orstralia's a big place. It was easy to get away

168

with that sort of thing in those days, I imagine. Anthropologists and scientists thought they were doing the world a favour.'

'You know a lot about it.'

'I've worked here for seventeen years.'

'When you say the remains are 'in dispute', what do you mean, exactly?'

'They want them back, don't they. There was a big furore last year, some of them came over. Elders and that.'

'Has the museum agreed?'

'It's not that easy. Although there's new management here and they are more amenable, it's not an overnight decision. There are arguments on both sides.'

'But surely after all these years they've done enough research?'

'We haven't got the power yet to just hand them over. But it's coming. And we've argued for it.'

'Do you think the museum is cursed because of the bones being here?' Freya stared deep into his eyes.

He laughed nervously. 'Look, love, if it was down to me I'd send them all back, no question.'

She gave him a seductive smile.

He returned the smile, and moved his shoulders in around her conspiratorially.

'How many bones are we talking about?' She had him now.

'A lot.' He moved even closer, his arm against hers. 'Until recently there was a race on to find a link between the Aborigines and Neanderthal

169

man, but they've discovered there's no such link, that Neanderthal man was a completely different species to *Homo sapiens*, different bone structure, the lot.'

'Fancy that.'

She tried to sound chatty, but her heart was in turmoil. The pupils of her eyes shone large, glassy and nocturnal, as if she could see the skeletons beneath the stone floors of the museum, labelled and kept in special wooden boxes on high shelves in controlled tempera-tures, for eternal preservation.

'Some items are in private collections, so it's hard to coordinate repatriation,' he said. 'Like I said, we all think the remains should go back. I mean, if the scientists wanted to do any more tests they only need a small piece of bone. Not an entire skeleton.'

Freya shivered.

Sensing her discomfort, he said, 'What's your interest, if you don't mind me asking. Are you a mature student?'

'Oh no. Nothing like that.'

'You're not one of those Abo-wannabes, are you? I came across a lot of them when I was over there touring a few years ago. Byron Bay's full of them. They haven't been any further inland than twenty miles. They haven't got a clue what it's like in the outback.'

'I've never met a real Aboriginal,' said Freya carefully. 'At least, not the sort who lives in the bush. The only one I know grew up in America. She was adopted. So I suppose she doesn't count.'

The man raised one eyebrow and stepped back involuntarily.

'Did she send you here?'

'No. Stop worrying. I'm just curious.'

'How long have you been in England?' He gave her a long, suspicious look.

'Twenty years.'

'That long, eh? You still sound very Orstralian.'

'Do I?' said Freya flatly.

He looked at her strangely now.

'Some people are not really interested in the museum, you know,' he said. 'They come here just to get out of the house. You seem more intelligent to me. Not jaded.'

'Thank you,' she said. 'I'll take that as a compliment.'

'You won't say anything about this to the papers or anything, will you?'

'What difference would that make? Surely they already know?'

'I don't want to lose my job.'

'Don't worry,' she said, moving off. 'I won't say a word.'

20

Being an academic, Del found the whole sister-turning-up-out-of-the-blue-with-Aboriginal-ancestry thing fascinating.

'Psychiatry taught me to be ready for all sorts of freak shows. Especially these days.'

'Thanks,' said Freya, and laughed.

'Only last week the tabloids reported a story about a white woman who gave birth to a black baby,' said Del. 'A bit different to your sisters' story, I know; this was a case of IVF going horribly wrong. Imagine that.'

Freya was on the verge of telling Del her secret. Del was worldly and unshockable, but Freya was afraid if she said it out loud she might not be able to stop. It might slip out at the corner store and spread like smoke. Mr and Mrs Patel were terrible gossips. Or she might mention it casually to one of her customers. Once it was out in the wider world Neill would eventually hear. He had inbuilt antennae.

They were sitting in Del's kitchen. The sun came out and they moved into the conservatory. Del poured Freya a mug of dandelion coffee.

'Comparing yourself to someone worse off to soften your own pain doesn't help,' said Freya. 'I should know. People with stomach ulcers don't feel better when they meet someone with cancer. If you know what I mean.'

Del smiled. 'Life sure is throwing a few

172

punches your way lately.'

'I'm not looking for sympathy.'

'Did you believe she was your sister straight away?'

'Not at first. Then it began to make sense. Because of the feeling of not belonging anywhere.'

'They did a good job of hiding it from you.'

'You mean lying.' Freya's eyes flashed.

'Did she show you any evidence — a birth certificate, adoption papers?'

Freya nodded.

'Where's she living?' said Del.

'Knightsbridge.'

'Must be doing all right for herself.'

Despite the warmth in the conservatory, Freya began to shiver.

'You're shaking,' said Del.

'It's my nerves. I don't even know what to call them any more. 'Mum and Dad' doesn't seem right.'

She rummaged in her handbag and pulled out a letter from Shirley and Bob. She handed it to Del.

'Are you sure . . . ?'

Freya nodded, and Del unfolded the single sheet of stiff paper.

Dear Freya,
Your father and I are both well and trust you and the children are, too. It seems like such a long time since you all came to visit in 1997.

We are always here if you need us; remember that. We miss you very much and hope

173

*you'll be over again soon so we can see
Kirsty and Tom, as well as you, of course.
They look so lovely in their school photos.
Thank you for sending them.*

*We're both well, you don't need to worry
about us.*

*We're very proud of you making a life for
yourself as a nurse, and now as a herbalist.
It's all the rage out here, too. There's a
new herb farm opened up in the Dande-
nongs, we'll take you there when you come
over.*

Take care of yourself, Freya dear.
Love always,
Mum and Dad

'They're angry,' said Freya. 'Because I wanted
to get away. I can read between the lines.'

'And now you're angry with them.'

'I feel betrayed, really. As for leaving so
suddenly, I *had* to get away. It was no life, living
in that house.'

'It wasn't their fault, being undertakers.'

'They could have done it somewhere else.
Kept it separate.'

'Perhaps they couldn't afford to.'

There was a long silence. Freya felt suddenly
ashamed.

'You can't begin to work through the shock of
all this until you accept that they did what they
thought was best.' Del reached across the table
and held Freya's hand.

'I'm not sure I want to see them again.' Freya
sighed, and withdrew her hand from Del's.

'What do you know about Aboriginal people?' said Del.

'I've seen documentaries. Artefacts in the British Museum. Churingas, boomerangs, digging tools.'

'They seem very downtrodden, from what I've seen on the television.'

'Connie's not. She's strong and confident.'

'Her adoptive parents must be good people.'

'I think she was born that way. It's so weird, to think I've got Aboriginal sisters.' Freya could not meet Del's gaze. She looked at her lap and turned her hands over.

'Is there something you're not telling me?' said Del.

'My whole life is false.'

'I have to agree it's an unusual situation,' said Del. 'But it's not false, darling. You lived your life as the person you thought you were. People who deliberately live a double life, now that's false.'

She poured more coffee. The noise of it drilling into the cups was amplified in the transparent room.

'It's different for Connie,' said Freya. 'Her adoptive parents didn't need to tell her. It's obvious she's adopted.'

'I doubt it's been any easier for her.'

'I'm sure you're right. But at least she's grown up with the truth. As well as it being out in the open, it was right there in front of her in the mirror, every day.'

She leaned back in her chair and looked up through the roof of the conservatory. High up, the sky was marbled with wispy cloud and jet vapours. A flock of starlings screeched past and settled on a Victorian chimneypot. In the distance she could see a church spire piercing the sky, and sooty buildings.

She didn't belong here, in London, in England. But where? Where did she belong?

'This isn't as unusual or dramatic as you think,' said Del. 'Mixed-race families are nothing these days. One of my clients has got three children by three different fathers. One's West Indian, one's Japanese and one's Irish.'

'Pick 'n' mix.'

Del laughed. 'I think it'd be rather exciting, having twin sisters. Having Aboriginal twin sisters is terribly interesting.'

'She's really nice,' said Freya. 'But she's very involved with making money. You know how I am about corporate stuff. It's so boring and shallow. I'm going up to meet her next week, for lunch. I'm looking forward to it but I'm not sure we have anything in common. Besides, I'm more concerned about Kirsty at the moment.'

'Oh?' Del frowned.

Freya sipped her coffee. She wanted to get off the subject of her adoption, in case the whole truth slipped out.

'What's going on?' said Del.

Freya felt like a traitor, talking about Kirsty's private life. It was bad enough discussing it with Sam. But Del was so wise and Freya felt she could trust her completely.

'Sam reckons Ryan and Kirsty are getting a bit carried away.' She blurted it out, and immediately wished she could suck the words

176

back into her mouth.

'Oh dear. What are you doing about it?'

'It's hard to strike a balance. I don't want to ban them from seeing each other. Although Sam would like to. But I don't want Kirsty falling pregnant, either.'

Now she felt really awful.

'Don't get me wrong,' she added quickly, 'I do trust Kirsty. But you never know. Things can go wrong very quickly when you first fall in love. And sometimes I wonder if she might have inherited her father's randy habits.'

Del leaned back in her chair and laughed.

'It's possible,' said Freya grimly. 'Just because she's a girl, it doesn't mean she's going to be like me in those areas.'

'Are you frigid, Freya dear?'

'No. Of course not.'

It had been a long time since a man had made love to her, but she was sure the desire was still there, somewhere.

'Well, in my experience the more you try to control teenagers, the more they rebel,' said Del.

'Exactly.'

'How does Sam know? Is he spying on them?'

Freya swallowed hard. Kirsty would think her a terrible turncoat for telling anyone, even Del.

'He called in last week and confessed he'd caught them in Ryan's cabin a few weekends ago. He didn't want to tell me at the time because I was being defensive. When I asked Kirsty about it on the phone, she said they were just listening to CDs, but Sam said they were kissing. Kirsty said it's none of my business. I like to think she's got her head screwed on about these things. But you can never be sure.'

Del lit a cigarette. She got up and propped the door open with a flowerpot.

'Have you talked to her?'

Freya shook her head. 'Not about this. We've talked about the facts of life, but lately she won't even look at me. I tried to hug her the other day, and she recoiled in horror.'

'But Freya, you've never routinely hugged the kids. What's brought this on?'

Freya shrugged. 'I thought that's what Neill and the court wanted.'

'It's got nothing to do with hugging them. It's much more than that.'

'Neill's idea of bonding is using his credit card.'

'That should be part of your argument. Show the bastard up.'

'I'm afraid it would sound like sour grapes.'

She was convinced every line of defence would be twisted by Neill. He would accuse her of jealousy, because he lived in a big house, and because he had the children, and a new wife. She had to be so careful what she confronted him with. And Kitty Wong had probably heard every trick in the book.

'The child welfare officer will have to investigate if she finds out about Kirsty.'

'She won't find out. I'll make sure of that. Besides, I doubt there's anything to it. So they were kissing? So what.'

'You could tell the CWO that Neill is spoiling the kids. Buying their affection.'

'It's all getting so tit-for-tat. I hate it.' Freya banged her cup on the table.

'Look, *I* know you love them,' said Del. 'And *you* know you love them. It won't be that hard to convince the court.'

'How?'

Del took a deep breath.

'Don't take this the wrong way, but you must talk to the children. Really listen to them. That's the sort of thing the CWO will look for.'

Freya shook her head emphatically. 'They don't want to talk to me. They're only interested in computer games and music.'

'Don't you have fun when you're with them?'

'We used to have fun. But since Neill won custody, since Connie turned up, things are weird between us. I can't be myself.'

'The court relies heavily on evidence, but they'll also give you a chance to express your opinion. And if the evidence is thin on the ground the magistrate will ask lots of questions. Unexpected questions. They're very clever.'

'I seem to be pushing them further away.'

Del studied Freya's face. 'It's natural, you know, growing apart from your parents. It happens to everyone.'

'I know that.' Freya stared at the contents of her cup and swirled it as if searching for something amongst the dregs.

'The judge confused your free-spiritedness with irresponsibility,' said Del. 'Now you have to show her she was wrong.'

'I don't know who I am any more.'

'Why don't you go to Australia and visit your

179

parents? And meet your other sister?' said Del. 'It might help put things in perspective.'

Freya looked at Del and smiled. 'I know you're trying to help, and I'm grateful. But it might complicate things with the court. Imagine if Neill found out I'm adopted. He'll use it against me. He'll say it's the reason I never bonded with the kids.'

'No one has to know about your adoption. He won't find out. You could just say you're going home to visit your parents. That's perfectly reasonable.'

'But what if being adopted *has* affected me, without me being aware of it? It does make people act strangely. I've read about it. It can make you afraid of physical contact.'

Del stubbed out her cigarette in the ashtray.

'Now you're being defeatist,' she said crossly. 'I've met a lot of adopted women who manage to bond with their kids. I think it's your job that's made you uptight. And living in that ghastly funeral parlour.'

'Uptight? You think I'm uptight?'

'Sometimes.' Del's voice was subdued. 'But you're being too hard on yourself, darling. You're also very giving. Very compassionate.'

'Now I'm confused. How can I be uptight and caring at the same time?'

'I don't know, sweetie. But you are.'

Freya leaned over the table and buried her face in her cupped hands. She tried to cry, she needed to cry. The pressure behind her eyes was so strong she thought her eyeballs might pop out.

Del reached across and laid a tentative hand on her arm.

'It's not easy for you,' she said. 'But you must look at the good that might come out of all this.' For a few uneasy moments she left her hand on Freya's arm. 'You can't move forward till you accept the truth of your past. It might help you bond with the children more than anything else. Facing your roots.'

'What are you talking about?' Freya pulled her arm away and the atmosphere stiffened. 'I can't go to Australia. The CWO would use it against me. And I can't risk Neill finding out about Connie. She was at the boat when Monica Murray called in. We had to lie to her. We said we met in Spain. It was a very tricky meeting. I think we managed to pull it off, but I don't want it to happen again, just in case.'

'Oh dear. That does put a different spin on things. I hope Monica doesn't find out you lied. She'd view it badly, I think.'

'I told Connie to keep away, but she couldn't help herself.'

'Look, when it all comes out I'm sure the court will understand why you haven't been yourself. Some people would go right off the deep end. You've managed to keep going. You're getting on with your life, and trying hard with the kids.'

'Del, there's something I haven't told you,' said Freya urgently. 'Something I've never told anyone.'

'What is it, Freya? Tell me quick, before you change your mind. I know you.'

'All my life I've had this spiritual feeling. I know it sounds crazy.'

'You're not going down the same path as Neill, are you?' Del frowned.

'No,' said Freya. 'It's not that. Not religion per se.'

'Thank heavens for that.' Del waited, eyes wide and expectant. 'You're just over-emotional right now.'

'Yes, I admit that. But it's something else. It's as if there's another person inside me. Like a thin person inside a fat body. That sort of feeling.'

'That's probably a normal reaction. I wouldn't read too much into any of it. You'll go through a lot of strange phases, I imagine. Just run with it. You'll soon see that fundamentally you are the same person. Even if you'd been brought up by your real parents. Environment is a factor, of course. And attitudes passed on by your carers. But if you want my opinion, basically you'd be the same person inside. Don't you agree?'

'No. You don't understand, Del. And it's so hard to explain without you thinking I'm barmy. It's something I've felt for years. Long before Connie turned up.'

'You mean you had a hunch all along?'

'More than that.'

Del frowned. 'Perhaps you need to see a counsellor.'

'Thanks.'

'Don't be so prickly. It might help put things in perspective. I'm sure there are lots of adoption support groups you could get in touch with.'

'No. I don't want to talk to strangers about this.'

'Lots of people are adopted, Freya darling. It's not that unusual. It's just that the majority of them know from an early age.'

'I think I probably did know. But I couldn't put my finger on it.' Perhaps Del would think she needed more than a dose of counselling if she came clean.

'Are you having second thoughts about seeing more of Connie?'

'No. I want to see her. And I'd like to meet Peggy. I suppose I'm just being silly. I should just get on with it and stop analysing.'

'You're very hard on yourself, you know. Try and look at the positive side. When you eventually bring it out in the open, the children will have two aunts. And if Connie and Peggy have children of their own, you'll have a little band of nieces and nephews. Isn't that something you've always wanted? An extended family?'

'Yes. But it's all so sudden, I can't get used to it. That's all.'

'Be patient,' said Del. 'Pretty soon you'll be wondering why you made such a fuss.'

Freya did not want to come across as a spoilsport. Del was one of the few people who still believed in her. She decided not to let her secret out after all.

'Sorry,' she said. 'I don't mean to whinge. I haven't been myself for a while.'

The irony of those words hit her hard.

'I always thought you were a schizophrenic,' Del joked.

'Is it obvious I'm adopted? It feels obvious. As if I'm wearing a sign. 'This person is not who you think she is.' '

'I'm only teasing,' said Del. 'Mind you, I'm not that surprised. You don't look at all like Shirley and Bob, from the photos you showed me. Even though Shirley's your aunt, you're nothing like her.'

'In what way?'

'Everything, really. Your eyes mainly.'

'Mum . . . Shirley said they're the Italian in me,' said Freya. 'But she never told me where in Italy, or rather, who. There's no one else in the family with brown eyes. 'A long-lost ancestor' she always said, and left it at that.'

21

The shower slowed to a dribble, and finally stopped.

Damn.

She was halfway through washing her hair.

The electric pump strained and whined. She pulled the little switch to turn it off. She could hear the pump that drew water from the main tank into the header tank, buzzing deep in the bilges. She had filled the main tank two days ago — hadn't she? A full tank usually lasted five days, if she was careful.

How she longed to live in a house again.

The weather had turned unseasonably cold during the night. When she looked out this morning a thick blanket of snow covered the gardens.

She wrapped her soapy hair in a towel, put on her dressing gown, and went into the saloon to switch off the pump. She stared at the floor, wondering what to do, then she sat down on the sofa, defeated.

A copy of *Waterways World* was open on the coffee table. She had ringed an ad for a Dutch Tjalk, a sailing Skutje with no mast, fully converted to residential, with mahogany wood panelling, generator, inverter, diesel central heating, in exceptional condition with beautiful lines — priced at £35,000. She would phone the number later and set up a viewing. She could just about manage it, at that price, if she could sell *Harlequin* for around the same amount.

If only she'd looked into the plumbing side of owning a boat. The previous owner had said the shower was in good working order. He didn't tell her the tank would keep running dry, or that she would have to go outside and attach the hose to the tap in all weathers. She'd known nothing about mains water, or header tanks, or pumps. She was a landlubber. He had seen her coming a mile off.

She opened the hatch and looked out. The towpath was deserted. Smoke billowed from chimneys. The air smelled of burning coal, and the sound of traffic from the M25 was muted, while over at Heathrow air traffic had ground to a halt.

She stepped outside and padded through the snow to the standpipe. Little dags of ice stuck to her sheepskin slippers. As she screwed the hose running from *Harlequin*'s hull on to the tap, a biting wind blew icy tentacles between her thighs. She turned on the tap, and waited. The standpipe juddered violently. It was frozen solid. Now she would have to borrow water from a neighbour, and boil up her kettle.

She had an appointment with the estate agent at nine. After that, she was taking the train up to London, to meet Connie at Harrods. This was the last thing she needed.

She turned the tap again. It shuddered and groaned, but not a drop of water came out.

'Having a spot of trouble?'

Freya swung round. Sam was standing there,

dressed in a woollen jacket and striped beanie. She had not heard him approaching; the snow absorbed his tread.

He stared at her breasts.

She looked down. Her dressing gown was gaping open, revealing her cleavage and ivory lace bra. She tugged it together, and looped the belt tight around her waist.

'I could have sworn I filled the tanks two days ago.'

She leaned forward and reassembled the towel on her head. A spiral of hair near her temple was stiff with ice.

'I've got an appointment at nine, and my hair's got shampoo in it. I'll look like a scarecrow.'

Sam laughed. 'Come on, you can use my shower. I'll boil up some water and get this lot working.' He nodded at the standpipe.

She hesitated. 'Is that a good idea? Taking a woman on to your boat at this hour? Someone might see. I don't want anyone to get the wrong idea. It might get back to Neill, or Monica Murray.'

'It'll take hours to fill the main tank, and another few to fill the header. You know that. You'll still be sitting about in your dressing gown this afternoon. I doubt if anyone else is even up yet. And if they are, they'll be too busy sorting out their own problems. But it's up to you.'

'What about Ryan?'

'He's staying at a friend's for a few days.'

He strode off towards his boat, snow bursting up around his boots in powdery explosions.

187

He was right. If she didn't take up his offer, she'd have hours of waiting for the tanks to fill.

On board *Lady Luck* Sam handed her a towel. 'I'll meet you back on your boat,' he said. 'I'll check your pump while I'm about it.'

The perfect gentleman.

'Thanks,' she said, smiling.

She made her way along the companionway. Ryan's door was ajar. She stopped and peeked in. The walls were adorned with music posters. There were remnants of his childhood: teddy bears on the bed, a wooden train set displayed on a shelf, a box of Lego, a bowl of marbles, a basket of Action Men. There was a photograph of a woman next to his bed, and Freya realised it was probably his mother, who Sam said had gone off with another man when Ryan was only six. He said Ryan didn't remember much about her, which was just as well because she'd been a heavy drinker.

Ryan's door had a porthole in the middle of it, inset with clear glass. There was no lock. Sam could easily keep an eye on Ryan and any guests.

The bathroom was lined with cedar wood, like a sauna. It smelled of a sultry pine forest on a summer's day, with a hint of sweet vanilla. There were potted palms, and black-and-white framed photographs of Italian lakes and French waterways. Various bottles of aftershave and upmarket men's deodorants were arranged neatly on a glass shelf, along with large tubs of body scrubs, exfoliating creams and bath salts.

Lady Luck's plumbing was connected to mains water; frozen pipes were never an issue.

Freya stepped under the shower, savouring the tingle of hot water on her numb skin.

Outside, the snow was falling steadily. She opened the porthole a fraction and an icy blast whooshed in, dissolving the steam. She shivered and closed it again in case someone passed by and saw her standing there, naked.

She glanced around for any signs of female visitors — discarded thongs, perhaps, or make-up — but there was nothing. A framed newspaper photo from the *Cornish Echo* hung above the loo. Six lusty youths were posing in a speedboat. Sam was in the driver's seat, grinning. Two of the teens had a hand each on his shoulders. The headline said: *Local Adventurer Big Hit with Troubled Youths*.

She pulled on her dressing gown, and hurried back to *Harlequin*. Sam was banging about in the bilges.

'Everything all right down there?'

'Almost done.' His voice was muffled. 'Pump needed cleaning too. Bit of a blockage.'

Freya took her chequebook out of her handbag, and in an act of reckless bravado and wilful pride began to write. She needed every penny right now, but she was not a sponger.

'You can put that away,' he said.

He climbed into the saloon through the open hatch, his fingers stained with oil. He helped himself to a handful of tissues from a side table. He smelled of diesel and peppermint. She saw that he was sucking a mint.

'There's no need for that,' he said. 'We all chip in down here.'

189

Her pen moved quickly over the cheque. 'Is thirty pounds all right? That covers the car, too.'

'I'm not taking it.'

'I insist.'

He shook his head in quiet frustration. 'Do you charge every Tom, Dick and Harry for a neck massage, or a jar of cream? Of course you don't. Everyone on the moorings knows that.' He thrust out his chin.

'That's different.'

'No it's not.'

'People have been kind to me.'

'Okay,' he said, thoughtfully. 'How about we swap favours?' He winked, then clearly regretted it.

'What?' Freya gave him a sharp look.

'Sorry. That wasn't funny. A tub of that lime body scrub you're famous for will do nicely.'

Freya relaxed. 'I noticed all your jars and bottles.'

'I don't see why men can't indulge in a little pampering. Do you?'

'Not at all.'

'It's admirable, getting these bargees interested in their appearance and health. They're such a scruffy lot. You're an angel, handing out your bottled miracles.'

She tried to give him the cheque, but he put his hands behind his back.

'I refuse to take it,' he said, shaking his head emphatically. He waited, calm and relaxed now against her rising impatience.

'Okay,' she said, softening under his grace. 'I'll put something special in your letterbox.'

As he moved towards her, she pulled her dressing gown tighter, but she couldn't tear her gaze away from his. His hand came up and cradled her jaw.

'Don't,' she said, her voice hoarse. 'It's too risky. I . . . I can't.'

'But you do want to.' His breath was warm against her cheek, and he moved his face deep into the curls of hair around her ear. She felt him breathing her in.

He lifted his head and looked at her, then tilted her face and slowly moved his mouth over hers. His lips felt firm and hot. She resisted a little, and he pulled her closer. His solid, strong arms made her soften and mould into his body.

He gently prised her lips apart. It felt good. She was afraid she might have forgotten how to kiss. Sam was the only man she had ever kissed properly besides Neill. It felt sinful, but the attraction flowing between them was strong, and real, and overpowering.

She forced herself to relax a little, to give in to the surge of emotion and desire beating through her veins. She told herself she didn't care if anyone caught them. She was entitled to a personal life with a man of her choice. The court would understand that a woman needed to be loved. Having a relationship did not have to compromise her role as a mother.

He put his arms around her waist, then ran both hands down the length of her back and over her buttocks, resting them there and pulling her tightly into him. She closed her eyes and surrendered.

Still kissing her, he manoeuvred her back-wards to the sofa and gently laid her down, then kneeled over her and lowered himself.

She opened her eyes and stared long and hard into his. She felt consumed by those deep green eyes, hypnotised.

He pushed harder on her mouth, probing, tasting, exploring, and she was lost in rolling waves of pure, carefree pleasure.

When they finally stopped, Sam whispered, 'I love you, Freya. The minute I set eyes on you, I knew.'

Her heart lurched. She hadn't been expecting this. Not love.

'I know you don't feel the same way. At least not yet. But in time, I hope you might.'

She didn't know what to say. She felt deeply attracted to Sam, but it was all too sudden. So much had happened these past weeks, and now this.

'Take your time,' he said. 'I'm not going anywhere.'

They heard footsteps. Someone hurried by.

'Wait here.' Freya stood up and opened the hatch, and looked up and down the towpath. As she clambered outside in her dressing gown she had a feeling of being watched. She often felt someone was spying on her, but she had so many strange feelings and hunches, she could not afford to be intimidated by them all. Hearing more footsteps, she peered through the swirling white mist. Bridget from *Poppy* emerged from the fog, a vampy vision in black and red.

'I was just coming to see you,' she said, eyeing Freya.

Freya sniffed hard; her nose was running. Bridget's perfume smelled harsh in the icy air.

'You look as though you've had a rough night,' said Bridget, nodding at Freya's dishevelled hair.

'Do I?' Freya made an attempt to tidy her curls. 'I haven't had time to do it yet. Too busy trying to defrost the standpipe.'

'Is this a bad time? I was hoping you could look at this rash I've had, on my back.'

'Yes,' said Freya quickly, climbing on to the landing stage, and reversing into the saloon. 'It is a bad time, I'm afraid. I'm going out, as a matter of fact. I've got an appointment, and I'm late already. I'm terribly sorry, Bridget. Can you come back later?' Her heart was thumping hard. Bridget was one of the pushier residents, talkative and demanding.

'It won't take a minute.' Bridget mounted the landing stage and followed Freya into the saloon.

Sam had disappeared.

Freya glanced towards the steps leading into the cabins. The cushions on the sofa had been straightened. There was nothing in the room except the whiff of his aftershave.

'I like that perfume you've got on,' said Bridget, inhaling.

'Would you like some?' said Freya. 'It's a vanilla and frangipani cream perfume.'

She reached for a jar on the sideboard. She unscrewed the lid and scooped out a small dollop with her fingers.

'Try this.' She rubbed the cream into Bridget's wrist, hoping to cancel out Sam's lingering smell.

'Lovely,' said Bridget.

'Now, what can I do for you?' said Freya politely, using a tone that implied haste.

Bridget lifted her jumper and turned around. 'It's very itchy.'

'Probably a heat rash.' Freya gave her a tub of herbal ointment. 'These boats can get terribly hot.'

'How much do I owe you?'

'Nothing,' said Freya.

Bridget hesitated.

Why did people assume the self-employed were always available? thought Freya.

'Is that all for now?' she said.

'Have you got time for a cuppa?' Bridget looked at her hopefully.

'I'm afraid I haven't. Not today.' Freya moved towards the hatch.

'Sorry for holding you up,' said Bridget. She did not sound at all apologetic. 'Oh, and say hello to Sam for me, when he comes out of hiding.' She looked at Freya and grinned.

Freya was going to say, *I don't know what you mean*, but Bridget was already on the towpath, and she didn't want to continue the conversation through the open hatch.

'I'll be seeing you,' said Bridget lightly, and was gone.

Freya watched her disappear into the mist, and thought how sharp she was, and how easy it was for the residents to spy on one another.

At that moment she dreamed of owning a movable boat that could take her and Sam away from this place, somewhere private and quiet, miles from these meddlesome amateur detectives.

22

Michael Laine, a spotty twenty-year-old estate agent in a dirty suit, drove Freya to view an empty shop. It was at the end of a stylish parade of designer boutiques.

It was perfect: whitewashed walls, inset ceiling lights, two back rooms that could be used for storage and treatments. But the rent was exorbitant, and on the corner next to the shop stood a self-flushing public toilet. A yellow-and-brown rivulet ran from the toilet door across the footpath and into the gutter. Freya imagined punters from the nearby racetrack battling with the inner workings of the aluminium Tardis, putting any potential customers off their stroke. Worse, it was an ideal spot for perverts to hang out, being partly screened by a man-made rock waterfall that looked like a huge wart. It wasn't the sort of outlook she'd envisaged.

They drove on to a former tobacconist's, next door to Tesco.

'No, it's not right,' she said. 'Plenty of passing trade, but too noisy, too busy.' By eleven she had had enough. Everything he had shown her was either too expensive, too small, too big, in the wrong position or falling apart. They said goodbye, and she took the train up to London to meet Connie at her apartment.

At the door Freya handed her sister a smart gift bag full of herbal products.

Connie threw her arms around Freya. 'Why, thanks,' she cried, planting a loud wet kiss on Freya's cheek.

Before Freya had a chance to peek over her shoulder at the inside of the apartment, Connie had shut the door and ushered her into the caged elevator.

Over lunch at the oyster bar in Harrods, Connie was animated as ever, chatting away about her job. Everyone stared at her, because of her colour and her accent. She didn't look at all like a black American. People were trying to work it out. She didn't look African, either. If anything, Freya thought, she looked Polynesian. The thought crossed her mind that Australian Aborigines did not even have a distinctive name for themselves as a collective ethnic group. After all, the word 'aboriginal' simply meant 'native', according to the dictionary. It wasn't a reflection of their individuality or nationhood.

She found Connie irritating today for some reason. Probably because of the attention she seemed to attract. She was glad when they had finished their meal and took the lift to the first floor, to look at the designer fashions.

Connie bought several expensive outfits. Suits, mainly, and a chiffon ensemble that took her ages to put on. It had tiny buckles and straps and flowing tails that she couldn't work out. They both giggled when she put her head through an armhole and almost choked.

Freya began to relax. So far, her heart had not been in the outing. She wanted to be with Sam today, but he was taking a group of handicapped children on a cruise to Little Venice.

Downstairs again, she took Connie into the apothecary.

'These are beautiful. Very stylish. You're so clever, Freya.' Connie bought a tub each of Freya's hand-made lime and rosemary salt scrub, and elder flower body mousse.

'You don't have to do that on my account,' said Freya. 'I've already put the same ones in your goodie bag. They're sixty-five pounds a tub, Connie. Please don't worry.'

'Oh, but I want to,' said Connie. 'They smell good enough to eat. And I love the packaging and the brand name.' She turned a jar over and read the label. 'The Natural Nurse. Did you think of that?'

Freya nodded.

'All natural ingredients. I'm very impressed,' said Connie. 'I'll have to get in touch with the buyers at Macey's for you.'

'That'd be great. Thanks, Connie.'

After they'd spent half an hour in the food hall, Freya said her feet were killing her.

'Come on,' said Connie. 'Let's go back to my apartment.'

They walked through the back streets and arrived at a pretty square with a lush rhododendron garden and tall plane trees.

'It's beautiful,' Freya breathed when Connie opened the door of the flat.

All the furniture was white, even the sofas, which were enormous and scattered with blue and white cushions. There were several antique pieces, and chandeliers, and huge windows overlooking the park.

'This is my favourite spot,' said Connie. 'Right by the window. I can watch the world go by.'

She made a pot of tea, camomile, especially bought for Freya, and they sat at the window table watching two lean couples playing tennis, and people who looked like their dogs strolling around the inside perimeter of the gardens with poop scoops.

'I've got something for you,' said Connie. She took an envelope from her bag. 'I knew if I left it up to you that you might put it off. And I know you probably can't afford it right now. So I took the liberty of buying you a ticket myself.' She handed the envelope to Freya. 'Go on, open it.'

Inside was an open-dated return air ticket to Australia. And two domestic tickets. One from Melbourne to Alice Springs. The other from Alice Springs to Sydney.

'I thought you'd like to see your parents in Melbourne first. And maybe meet your real father. And Peggy is near Alice Springs.'

Freya was speechless. She read the details, and placed the tickets on the table. She sighed. She'd been right about Connie. She was overbearing.

Connie looked at her and smiled. 'I know you think I'm being pushy, but I figured you need to sort this out. Talk to your parents about your adoption. And seeing Henry will clear a few things up for you too. I knew you'd want to meet Peggy. She's a character. Forbes is too, although he struggles a bit with white people. There's a history in his family of Aboriginal abuse. His great-great-grandfather helped slaughter a group of Aborigines up near Darwin. He's racked with shame over it. But he's a good man, and he looks after Peggy. That's the main thing.'

'I can't take these,' said Freya.

'Why not?'

'It's not fair, you paying for them. They're first-class tickets, Connie. They cost a fortune.'

'Don't be silly. It's nothing to me. Look at this apartment. My parents are very well off. And I make a lot of money now myself. You don't need to worry.'

'I'd feel awkward, meeting Peggy without you.'

'I'll be there, Freya; you just book the date. I can take a holiday any time I like. I'm basically my own boss. I can come and go as I please. You can too, now that you've ditched your husband. I won't be pushed around by any man. You shouldn't be, either.'

23

The day arrived. Ester put two nappies on the twins, to save you the bother — for a few hours, at least. You placed them in a wooden crate lined with sheepskin, toe to toe, and put it on the rear seat of the Ford.

Ester tried explaining about the bottles, but you only half listened. You did not intend stopping, except for fuel. They won't bloody well starve, you told her.

You placed a folded tablecloth on the passenger seat, to drape over the box at the petrol station, in case the attendant or another driver peeked in and saw. You did not want to face any awkward questions, or rude stares. Ester had put aspirin in their milk, to make them sleep.

After today we'll make 'second time lucky' our motto, Ester had said. Her voice sounded strained and high-pitched, as though a hand was squeezing her throat.

She stood on the veranda as you drove off. You were so intent on watching her in the rear mirror that you veered off the road into a paddock. At the gate you put your arm out of the window and waved. When you poked your head out to catch her return wave, you saw that she had already gone inside.

You slowed the car, and wondered if you should go back and make sure she was all right.

The minute the car stopped, flies shot through the windows and settled on the babies' eyes. You reached behind and fanned them clear with a hand, but they kept coming back, as flies do.

You are a country boy. You know all about fly strike, droughts, dust storms, snow storms, bush fires and floods. You know how to kill animals and how to give them life.

Your hands had been busy that week; ten days of wool classing had left them unusually soft and supple.

Soft as a baby's bottom. Ester had whispered this when you ran your oily hands over her naked body in the back seat of the Ford, after the dance — the night you first met.

Aren't you just, you had breathed, sliding a hand into the dark recess between her thighs.

You put your foot down on the accelerator. It was as if you were trying to break away from the back half of the car, which at that moment seemed to hold all the reasons for your anguish. Your breathing was sharp. Your stomach felt bruised.

When you did finally pull over for petrol, you prayed they wouldn't squawk. A man in a blue boiler suit leaned down at the window and said, 'Off on a picnic?' He glanced at the checked tablecloth covering the crate.

You threw your head back and laughed. 'No,' you said, thinking quickly. 'I'm delivering wool to a weaver in town.'

As you drove off, he watched you through slitted eyes.

Once the garage was out of sight, you pulled

over and got out. You stood where the pump attendant had stood, emulating his position, and stared at the back seat. Tufts of sheepskin poked through the bottom slats of the crate, and there, just above the second slat, was a tiny black and pink toe.

You spread your map out on top of the roof, and wrote an X next to Melbourne in bold black pen. Then you got in the car and revved the shit out of it. The engine purred with pleasure, practically driving itself all the way to the city.

24

When Freya thought of Shirley now, she pictured some fiendish Boris Karloff character in the back room of the funeral parlour.

She sat in the saloon on *Harlequin* with the lights off, remembering Shirley's strange domestic habits. They had irritated her in the end. Her collection of miniature tea sets and thimbles locked in a polished cabinet. The kitchen cupboards stuffed full of empty plastic bags and Tupperware, tins of Heinz soup, sachets of Heinz soup. The fridge with its labelled leftovers. The laundry bag on a hook behind their bedroom door, heaving with used stockings.

Shirley was a collector of things, but most of it never got made into anything useful or decorative. It was as if by hoarding objects she was holding on to life itself. Her wardrobe was bursting with musty coats and misshapen shoes dating back to the twenties. The bathroom cabinet harboured fossilised deodorant sticks, manufactured long before the modern world had invented 'use by' labels. Bottles of solidified Calamine lotion used years before on Freya's grazed knees festered in a wooden first-aid box, alongside rusty tubes of vile yellow ointments. In the kitchen there was a collection of empty cobalt-blue formaldehyde bottles, lined up on the windowsill to catch the light. Sometimes when Freya went into the kitchen it was like walking into a shimmering blue aquarium. Bob strung more blue bottles from a tree in the garden, to deter crows, who seemed to know there were bodies inside the house.

There was always the hope that Shirley might suddenly want to make something, or play something, with Freya. But her haunted hands had been inside death all day. How could those same hands mould plasticine or turn the pages of *Alice in Wonderland* for an eager child?

Freya sat in her armchair and examined her own hands. She stroked the palm of her left hand with her right thumb, tracing the life lines. She was beginning to feel more aware of her body — its rhythm, its history.

There was nothing she needed right now, except to hear the even breath of her children around her. If Sam came to her, she would turn him away. She did not want him here when the children were staying.

She steeled herself against the lonely night ahead, when she would toss and turn, fighting her dreams, fighting her desire to know who she really was, fighting her need to feel Sam's arms around her, fighting the feeling of disappointment and betrayal she felt towards Shirley and Bob.

They had been at Sam's all evening. It was Ryan's seventeenth birthday. She had chatted to everyone but Sam, aware of him watching her across his garden. He had gone to so much trouble to make the night go off with a bang. His garden and boat were strung with fairy lights, he had set up some speakers in the branches of a tree, and bought Ryan a snooker table for the summerhouse.

Freya had not wanted to go, because she was afraid everyone would know about her and Sam. No one said anything, but she felt people watching her, waiting for some exchange between her and Sam to give them away.

In spite of that, she was glad they had accepted Sam's invitation. For Kirsty and Tom's sake. They were beginning to settle into the community, she thought, and seemed to like it. Kirsty had spent the evening playing snooker with Ryan and his friends, while Tom had gone for a night walk into the woods with the other children, Sam leading the way with a lantern. Freya felt as though she was getting somewhere with them at last.

The boat was stuffy and hot. She pulled the curtains across, and locked the door. She would let the fire fizzle out of its own accord; sunshine was forecast for tomorrow. She pulled open the hatch on the opposite side of the boat, and sat on the sill, watching the surface of the water ripple under the light of the moon. A cool breeze fanned her face. The steel hull was cold on her thighs.

In the distance an orange glow hung maliciously over London. Voices — shouting — rose up from the middle of the nearby tenements, and something — someone — moved in the shadows on the opposite bank. The bushy tip of a fox's tail disappeared into the undergrowth.

There was a tap at her window.

She froze. She didn't want to speak to anyone right now.

Tap, tap, tap.

'Freya. Past. It's me, Sam.'

She pulled back the curtains and slid open the window, with the intention of giving him the brush-off. She didn't want to wake the children, or be seen by anyone on their way home.

Sam crouched down and smiled.

'Did they have a good time tonight?'

Freya nodded. 'Yes thank you. They did.'

Sam hesitated. 'What about you? Did you enjoy it?'

'Yes thank you, it was fun.'

'I'm really glad you came.' He smiled.

Something deep inside her stirred. It would be good to talk to a man about things for a change, to get a different perspective. But she couldn't risk it. Bridget had watched her every move at the party. She might even be watching now, from the front window of *Poppy*.

'So am I,' she said. 'But I'm not so sure you should be hovering outside my boat in the dark.'

'Luke told me you're still looking for a bigger boat.'

'Yes, I am. I meant to phone up about one I saw in a magazine, but I haven't got around to it. It's probably been sold by now.'

'I'll ask around. Some mates of mine work at a boatyard a few miles away.'

There was an awkward silence. She wished he would go but did not want to nag him into it.

'Kirsty and Ryan behaved themselves tonight.' Sam shifted his weight.

She caught a glimpse of the bulge between his legs, and looked away, suddenly overcome with shyness.

'Kirsty always behaves herself,' she said crisply.

'It can't be easy for Ryan. Kirsty's a good-looking girl.'

Freya had seen for herself this evening the extent of Kirsty's flirting — it was innocent, and entirely appropriate for a girl her age.

'I'd better get to bed,' she said, wanting him to leave.

'Big day planned?'

'I'm taking them up to London tomorrow. There's a Picasso exhibition at the Tate Modern.'

'I can take a hint.'

'I don't mean to be rude. It's been a long day. I'm not used to having the kids around all day any more.'

Stating it baldly like that made her temples throb. She needed to talk, to open up fully and tell someone how confused she felt.

'You must miss them in between their visits.'

'Yes, I do,' she said quietly. 'On the other hand, I didn't see much of them anyway. You know how kids are, doing their own thing. And I was always busy working.'

She decided she didn't want to confide in Sam after all. They had jumped in too soon the other day, before they had really had a chance to get to know each other. Basically they had only ever talked about the children and boats.

'How much were you thinking of spending on another boat?'

He had some good connections on the waterways. Perhaps he would find her a bargain. But she did not want to get that involved. Human beings are so fickle, she thought, having sex one minute and the next behaving like strangers.

'The mooring fees are going up,' she said. 'Luke was complaining about them. So I'll have to be careful.' She wasn't going to tell Sam — or anyone else — how much she had to spend on a boat.

'Luke complains about everything,' he said. 'But he's quite well balanced — he's got a chip on each — '

'And coal isn't cheap these days,' she interrupted. 'Still, boats aren't as expensive as houses to heat. What about your boat, it's quite big, do you go through a lot of fuel?' As long as Sam hovered, she would keep him talking about anything except her personal or financial situation.

'It's not too bad. I get a delivery every fortnight in winter. All the pipes are lagged and . . . '

As he talked, his minty breath came at her through the window and his chest hairs lifted in the breeze. Freya wanted to reach out and put her hand there and feel the warmth of his skin. She backed into the galley, putting some distance between them.

He stared hard at her, mouth open to form the next words, but something made him falter.

'Well, I'd better be going,' he said finally.

'Thanks again for a lovely evening,' she said.

She gave him a warm smile, and he perked up.

'Are you sure you don't want me to come in?'

'No. I'm glad Ryan had a good time,' she added, trying to sound light.

'He wasn't expecting so many people, actually — '

'Lovely. I'm so glad it turned out well.' She moved about the galley, straightening jars and wiping the benches. 'Thank you again for inviting us. Mind you don't trip over anything on your way home.'

He reached into his pocket, pulled out a small torch and flashed it, nearly blinding her.

'Wouldn't be without my trusty torch. Brilliant invention, works on solar power — '

'Good night, Sam.'

She turned her back, and began filling the kettle, before he could launch into another of his product descriptions.

'Right. Well, see you around,' he said uncomfortably.

He moved off and she quickly shut the window and drew the curtains across. Then she switched off the lights.

She heard his footsteps crunching down the towpath, and longed to run after him. She ached to feel his mouth moving over hers, pressing down, devouring her, but she could hear her father telling her, 'You be strong, girl. Stick to your guns about things you believe are right.' She was surprised at how easily she still thought of Bob as her father, and realised that his and Shirley's advice quite often came at her head-on from the deep recesses of her mind.

In her heart she knew it would be wrong to go after Sam, to risk being seen. She didn't want to do anything else that might harm her chances of getting the children back. Besides, they wouldn't like it if they knew about her and Sam. It was all too soon. Even though it had felt natural to her, they might see it as disloyal to Neill and she did not want to make a worse mess of things.

She had thought about asking Bridget not to tell anyone, but decided to let fate take its own course. The whole population on the moorings probably knew by now. She hoped it would soon be forgotten. People had their own lives, their own daily hassles, their own secret loves. Even so, when the sun appeared above the tree line at six thirty she would wake Kirsty and Tom, and take them to London on the train, long before anyone had stirred enough to remember the gossip that Bridget had probably spread at the party.

She thought of Sam alone in his bed. Her skin was on fire. She hugged the hand-embroidered cushion Shirley had sent for her birthday.

To love a person, she thought, is to let them work through difficult times in their own way, without interfering, without demanding some-thing that cannot be given until everything else is resolved.

Her last thought before she fell asleep, her breath rising and falling in time with the children's, was: Please don't give up on me.

25

It was dark when you pulled up outside the adoption agency. You parked the car and leaned back in your seat, too tense to eat, too tired to think. The journey had taken four days.

The smell of the nappies was overpowering. Ester had given you eight extras, but by the time you were halfway there they were all dirty. Along the way you threw them one by one into the lantana next to the road. You kept two and stopped to wash them in a creek. You hung them over a branch in the midday sun and they were dry in less than ten minutes.

Before you entered Melbourne's sprawling suburbs and picked up the main road into the city, you pulled over again and washed the twins in the cool brown water of a pond. They kicked at the coldness on their skin.

You didn't want the agency to think you were a bad father.

You avoided looking at their eyes, and pinned the clean nappies around their dimpled bottoms.

Thank God they didn't cry. You put it down to the rocking motion of the car, and transporting them in one crate. You imagined they were well aware of each other, with their toes touching.

When you found the right street you parked a few doors away, behind a tree growing out of the pavement. You watched the building from under the brim of your hat. It was a brown Victorian terrace with dark green iron lacework verandas.

When the sun came up and the kookaburras began to laugh, you waited for signs of life.

The sun burnished the windows of the house like mirrors. You could see the whole street reflected in them at odd angles, the plane trees shimmering with bronze light.

You wondered if you had come to the wrong address. You reversed up the street and read the sign — Balmoral Crescent.

You pulled up outside the mansion once more, and waited.

Presently a tall woman wearing a pale blue suit opened the front door. She leaned down and placed a crate of empty milk bottles on the doorstep.

Good morning, you said, a few minutes later, when the same woman opened the door and smiled. I have two packages for you.

26

The following day Kirsty and Tom seemed brighter. She assumed it was because of the party. They seemed to be warming to the idea of their mother living on a houseboat, and even helped her change the gas bottle stored on the stern deck. It irritated her to think she had to take them away from the moorings just when they were beginning to relax and make friends. But she needed to get away. She felt hemmed in. Only when she was on the other side of the humpback bridge did she feel any sort of immunity.

She and the children took the Tube to Waterloo and walked along the river. Before going inside they sat on a bench in front of the Tate Modern, resting their burning feet. Perplexed tourists overwhelmed by the enormity of the building stood about studying floor plans and exhibit brochures. Art-lovers and eager students scurried in and out of the cavernous space like ants on a mission.

It seemed the right moment, now that they were out in the open, away from the boats, to ask a few pertinent questions.

'Are you okay, living with Dad?' she said. Even this sounded like some sort of veiled grilling. She chewed her thumbnail.

'Dad promised we'd get our own rooms,' said Tom miserably. 'He *promised.*'

Freya felt a surge of simple pity. She could feel the unfairness, and knew it must be even more real and painful to the children. They had to fall asleep listening to the breathing of strangers.

And they were off, describing all the different situations, big and petty, that got on their nerves. One day Tom had had to ask Clarissa to pass him toilet paper because the roll was empty. Another time Kirsty had to borrow sanitary pads from her — the ultimate humiliation. And Tom had been forced to get undressed under his bed covers, because the other children had teased him about the hairs growing around his penis.

'The deal was you would have your own rooms,' said Freya.

She was trying to avoid the pitfall of criticising Neill. So many divorces ended in recriminations and bitterness, making things worse for the children, innocent piggies-in-the-middle.

'Jack keeps taking my things,' said Tom. 'I don't mind, but he breaks everything. I loaned him my Game Boy and he trod on it.'

Freya was secretly glad. She hated the damn thing. 'Never mind,' she said, trying to sound genuine.

'Dad's getting worse, since everything happened,' said Kirsty. She was bursting with grievances. 'He and Clarissa have bible study twice a week. And we spend nearly all day Sunday at church, because Clarissa plays the organ at both services. Instead of going home, we have to stay and help with chairs, and set up the cups for tea.'

'Doesn't Dad realise you've got homework to

do on Sundays? And friends you'd like to see? And outings that would help with your school work?'

She suddenly saw how difficult it was for them, that her wanting them back was justified, that Neill wasn't providing the perfect environment.

'I think your father's gone a bit mad.' She bit her lip; she hadn't meant for this to slip out, but she couldn't be diplomatic all the time.

Neill and Clarissa were being dishonest, promising one thing, doing another. Imposing their religious beliefs and rituals. She had argued with him about this time after time, before leaving. 'Religion should be a personal thing,' she had said. 'It should be a completely private matter, a quiet affair with the God of your choice, precious, intimate. Not something to foist on people, or manipulate them with.'

'I just remembered something, Mum,' said Kirsty. 'I've got a cooking assessment in food technology tomorrow. I need to buy the ingredients.'

'Surely your father's got stuff in his cupboard you — '

She had to stop doing this. It was wrong. Running Neill down in front of them would only reinforce their dissent. Monica would accuse her of trying to influence them. She had to remain impartial.

'Clarissa said I have to get my own ingredients,' said Kirsty.

'Oh she did, did she?'

It was coming out wrong. She should have

216

said, fair enough, and kept her real thoughts to herself. The depth of her anger worried her. She was helpless in the teeth of it. All the nursing training she'd had was useless now. How to be polite, how to be tactful, how to recognise and deal with cognitive dissonance using persuasive appeals and social cues. It all seemed so false and premeditated.

The court would say she had no influence on what went on under Neill's roof. And that if she did have a gripe she should channel it through the CWO.

It was getting complicated and distressing, being under scrutiny, being controlled, having a go-between to communicate the important stuff with her own children, to tell her when she could and could not see them, talk to them, laugh with them, shop with them . . .

'Can't you cook next week instead and catch up with your written work this week?'

'No, Mum. I have to cook six times between now and the end of the year. I've got three to go, and my teacher said I'm running out of time. Clarissa said she'd give me a container, if I got the ingredients.'

'That's big of her.'

Damn. Shit. Bugger. She had to control herself, or it would come back to bite her.

'Please, Mum.'

'Stop panicking.'

She walked ahead and tried to calm down. When Kitty Wong had made her decision it had been a shock, but she had pulled herself together quickly. She hadn't expected it to get harder. She was slowly being ground down. Her head was roaring. She thought of Clarissa leaning over their beds to say good night, and running their baths and washing their underwear, when they should be with their own mother. Wasn't it their birthright, to be with her? To be told off by her, to be bossed and nurtured and encouraged by her? Where was the justice, the sense, in splitting them up? They were becoming more and more like possessions. But she had to try — for their sake — to be tactful.

She turned around and waited until they caught her up. They looked so fed up and defeated it made her heart ache. Kirsty was pouting. Tom hung his head and kicked stones, and deliberately stepped on brittle leaves.

'We'd better head back early,' she said, trying to sound cheerful. 'Most supermarkets close at five on Sundays. If we leave at three, we'll make it in plenty of time.'

'We don't want to upset Dad,' said Kirsty suddenly. 'Or you. We're torn.'

'Don't worry about me and Dad. It's you I'm worried about.'

'We're not used to it, sharing with other people, and Dad doesn't — '

'Understand,' Freya finished. 'It must be a pain, mucking in with kids who are younger than you.'

Perhaps by airing things they might feel better.

Was there something else? she wondered. Tom seemed depressed. Were they afraid? Had they seen Neill and Clarissa *at it*, in the larder — or the bathroom? He had a fondness for sex in odd

218

places. How unbearable for the children, knowing their father was sticking it up some strange woman with a small red mouth and hair the colour of a field mouse. Then dispensing ten baked beans each on a slice of stiff toast, and a strong dose of the Lord's Prayer.

Tom looked at her sheepishly.

'It's okay,' she said. 'You've got to stop worrying about me and Dad.'

'But we want to live with you. Can't we come home with you today?'

'No. You can't. I have to go back to court first.'

It was all so unjust, the clipboards, the power of pens on dotted lines. Time could be a great healer, but it could also aggravate wounds.

'I'm sorry things haven't turned out as you'd hoped. Perhaps when I get a bigger boat you might like to come and live with me? If I can convince Dad, and the CWO . . . '

'Really?' they said together. Their eyes lit up.

'Is it that bad at Dad's? I mean, you don't even like where I live.'

'Yes we do. We didn't at first. But we do now.'

'Do you get on at all with Clarissa?'

'Not really,' said Kirsty. 'She's so uptight.'

'She's not hurting you or anything, is she?' Freya's voice was tinged with alarm.

'No. She's horrible, that's all,' said Tom. 'We didn't want to say anything, in case we got told off.'

'In what way is she horrible?'

'She gives all the treats to her kids. And we never get as much to eat. Little things, they get nice cereal, we just get corn flakes. And she won't let us have a bath when we want one. We have to wait till the weekend. She says they can't afford the hot water. And she never gives us any lunch money, we have to make sandwiches. And we have to sit at the table until we've eaten every morsel. And we're not allowed to talk at the table — if we do, Dad grounds us. Oh, and Clarissa rapped Kirsty over the knuckles once for licking her knife.'

'Not allowed to talk at the table?' Freya shook her head in disbelief.

Why was she more concerned about this than Kirsty's knuckles? It seemed deliberate, whereas the knuckle-rapping was no doubt spontaneous.

'They're always going on about the bible but they're so mean,' said Kirsty. 'Rebecca and Melanie are horrors. Always having tantrums when they don't get their own way. Clarissa spanks them.'

'But I thought you wanted to live with Dad,' said Freya.

They shook their heads solemnly.

'What about the moorings?'

'It's a bit yucky,' said Tom. 'But we're getting used to it.'

'I was under the impression you didn't want to live with me. That's more or less the conclusion the court came to, after speaking to you.'

'All we said was you're a bit weird,' said Kirsty. 'We always say that about you. It's a joke. We've said it to your face. The judge took it the wrong way.'

'But why didn't you say something to Dad about not wanting to live with him?'

'We didn't want to hurt his feelings.'

A pang in the pit of her stomach made Freya flinch. Didn't want to hurt *his* feelings? She realised then that she had been terribly upset by their choice, and it *was* a choice, as much as an outsider's decision. But they weren't to know that things could have been different. She was furious with Kitty Wong, with her painted lips and sleek hair. The quiet, controlled questions, and the way she scribbled in a notebook as she spoke.

She would have said, in the quiet atmosphere of her chambers: 'And how do you feel about your mother?' In a way that seemed harmless, chatty and obsequious, leaving out two vital words: 'living with'. Two little words that could have made all the difference to the children's interpretation of the question. They were so clever, these legal eagles.

'Is that why you've been a bit quiet?'

'We'd rather live with you, Mum,' said Kirsty. 'Wouldn't we, Tom?'

Tom nodded. 'Dad's turned into an old fuddy-duddy. He's so strict. He used to be fun. What's happened to him?'

Freya shrugged. 'That's religion for you.'

'At church he's, like, a complete nutcase,' said Kirsty. 'He and Clarissa sing in some mad secret language and waggle their tongues like complete loonies.'

'Really?' said Freya.

She lowered her eyes and fumbled with her handbag. She felt hot around the neck. Had they ever wondered about her secret language? They

221

probably thought she was batty, too.

'Come on, let's go inside and look at the art.'

They wandered through the galleries. 'Don't you worry,' she said, handing them each a map. 'Things will work out for the best. You have to be strong. Don't give in to your feelings and get involved in anything dangerous or unhealthy.'

The small side rooms were stuffy and crowded. Reverential whispers filled the space. She felt as if she was sealed in a flask of hot air.

Kirsty and Tom were quiet and noncommittal about the art-work. Some of the pieces were unbelievably complex: tortuous mindscapes, too fertile with ambiguity for anyone other than the artist to grasp. Instead of interpretation being a reasonable challenge, it became a burden for the average punter, who turned the pieces into jokes.

'Look at that bloody monstrosity,' said an American tourist. 'Looks like a giant vomit.'

'What about that one?' said her husband. 'Litter inside a clock? Absolute rubbish.'

Freya smiled to herself.

After an hour or so they went outside and walked along the river. A brisk wind whipped across the water, making them shiver. Halfway across Tower Bridge the sun came out briefly. Freya put on her sunglasses.

Tom and Kirsty smiled at her camera.

'Say Hickleberry Funn.' They laughed and she pressed the button.

It was a huge relief to know they wanted to live with her after all. She was not the sort of person to wallow in self-pity, but losing custody had crushed her confidence. She couldn't help wondering if, in their eyes, she was merely the best of a bad choice: should they live with the religious freak, or the herb and houseboat nutter? How could she ever know the truth without observing them in their new home?

The titanic sprawl of London always made her feel tiny and insignificant. But today its overwhelming scale seemed merciless. She walked behind the children in a state of bewilderment, watching the back of their heads, measuring them against each other. They seemed to be growing an inch a fortnight. She was unsure if her relationship with them was simply going through a natural progression that all parents experienced — of pulling away and growing up — or if there was more than a grain of truth in Neill's accusation about them never having bonded properly.

In spite of wearing sensible shoes, her legs ached. She loved the sense of empowerment walking gave her, but she longed to be up on a hill, looking down, rather than in the shadow of the city. Today the architecture and history of London depressed her; it seemed suffocating and arrogant, and she wanted to get out.

They pressed on through the unfamiliar bodies, past the strange, uninviting buildings, watched over by the ever-present veil of grey sky. Her mouth was full of foul air. They sat down on the freezing steps in front of St Paul's, huddled together, barely touching, like the three wise monkeys.

'I'd hate to live in the city,' said Tom. 'It's too noisy.' He tossed a few crumbs from his sandwich bag at some pigeons.

It was uncomfortable on the step in front of the cathedral. Freya thought of piles and kidney infections and cystitis. She felt weighed down by the force of the buildings, and the humid spring air, and the knowledge that she wasn't Freya Lacey at all, but someone taken in by strangers, like a dog rescued from a pound.

A man with no arms stood nearby, begging.

'How's he going to pick up his plate full of money?' whispered Tom. 'You know, when he wants to go home?'

The man was wearing a placard that said: *A land-mine in Afghanistan did this.*

'I don't know,' said Freya. 'With his mouth or his feet I suppose. Don't stare. Here, give him this.' She handed Tom all her change.

He approached the man nervously. As he bent down to place the coins in the dish he looked up at the man, and they exchanged smiles.

Tom scrambled back up the steps and sat next to Freya. She could feel his skinny arm trembling against hers.

'Can we go now?' he said. 'This place gives me the creeps.'

27

Your father Joseph was a garrulous bastard. He liked to boast to the shearers. He told the story about the massacre in the same way he talked about rabbit or kangaroo shooting, with the vocabulary of a hunter.

You hid behind the straw bales, bony knees tucked up to your chest. He'd have skinned you alive if he'd caught you, but you thought it was worth the risk.

The bit about women wrapped in possum skins with nothing underneath was the best. When Joseph told how these half-naked whores visited the stockmen's huts in the evening, his men went whoo-ar, and laughed heartily.

Back in the 1830s your great-grandfather, Fred Mace, and his wife Jessica had taken up a squatting run called Chestnut Vale, near Green Swamp, which these days is known as Inverell. A real pioneer. Rough life. Dangerous. Bloody Abos made it harder.

Fred and Jessica lived in a slab hut. There were no regular supplies, no support in emergencies, no 'how to' manuals. There was the constant threat of attack by bushrangers and natives. The local tribe kept stirring up Fred's cattle.

Then something happened that enraged him. Something one of the native policemen did. Fred went after this fella. Name of James Ganabidi. James had worked for Fred occasionally as a bark cutter, before joining the force. In those days the blacks were easy to lure with the prospect of a small wage, a uniform and a horse.

Fred wanted James strung up and sliced down the middle like a sheep to slaughter.

This James had been fooling around with a young white woman. It wasn't the done thing, especially in those days. The men could have their way with gins, but they were only vermin with pussies, after all.

New men who joined Fred's team were always keen to hear his version of the Myall Creek massacre, which he'd also been involved in. But they preferred the more personal angle of his secret rampage.

You explained the reasoning behind Fred's outlook to your own men: the unreliability of Aborigines, their uncivilised habits, the guilt by association when a white was attacked by a black.

Mainly he blamed their weakness for rushing cattle and spearing sheep. It always came back to that, as if they were doing it to deliberately stir up trouble.

One of Fred's men once said he didn't mind some Aborigines. Fred went into a blind rage. He went out to the wood shed and tore it apart, plank by plank, with his bare hands.

You thought your father Joseph was clever, the way he told his story over and over, to different sets of shearers, without saying the truth.

He said that when a group of hardened convicts from England went on the loose killing Aborigines a few years before Myall Creek made headlines, Fred had been disgusted. He hated the filthy animals, but there was no need to slaughter them wholesale.

But then, Joseph explained, you know how things are in the bush. Things happen. Bushmen can't afford to be sentimental. In the end, when Fred was pushed too far, he changed his mind about slaughtering Abos. He decided it was a necessary evil, said Joseph.

Anyway, Fred's posse searched the banks of the river, then the forests, where other Aboriginal men were bark-cutting, looking for James. They hunted down and shot twenty-three Aboriginals before rooting him out.

He was cowering in a bark humpy, crying.

Joseph always laughed about that. That was the only part you didn't enjoy, hearing him cackle like a warlock.

We might be riding on the sheep's back, you told your men, but my great-grandfather rode on the back of the Myall Creek massacre. It took the sting out of his guilt, I reckon.

Joseph always went into details about the weather and the difficult terrain, and the Aborigine's stealth in the bush. He went on like this for half an hour or so, just to soften the blow. Then he described the scene in the stockyard, after the slaughter.

This was your favourite part of the story.

You'd never laugh about it like Joseph did. But you were fascinated by the sheer bloody adventure of it, the folklore mystery Joseph lent it with his theatrical turns.

Once he placed a handful of black wool on his

227

head and crouched in one of the stalls, cringing like James. The men thought this was hysterical.

You'd seen Westerns, when you went to town, and since being in hospital you've sat in the TV room watching war movies, a favourite choice from the box of dog-eared videos in the cup-board. But nothing, not even *Apocalypse Now*, or *Saving Private Ryan*, could compare with the sound of your own father's gruff voice telling his men about the killing.

A pile of black bodies lying in a river of blood. Flies everywhere. The sickly-sweet smell of blood. Severed heads resting on fence posts with bullets through their eyes. A woman's breast nailed to a tree and used as a target.

When he got to this bit, Joseph sucked hard on his hand-rolled cigarette.

Fred and his blokes used knives and swords, Joseph said.

He looked around at his men's reactions. There was nothing that amused him more than watching hardened men flinch.

When they got in the way, babies and children were decapitated and their heads thrown around the yard, he said. Some — women included — were tied to posts and set alight. You could hear their screams all the way to fuckin' New Zealand, so he reckoned.

At this the men would push their hats back, scratch their beards, suck their teeth, or fold their arms. Crouching behind the hay bales, you held your breath. A sheep bleated. Jeez, boss, someone would say, that's a bit rough. Yeah, Joe, fair suck of the sausage, another might say. Ah well, Joseph always said, their glory was short-lived. After Myall Creek, it all changed.

Oh yeah?

Yeah. Seven of those poor blokes were hanged in Sydney. People couldn't believe it. The bloody government thought the hangings would be a deterrent. Thought they were being clever buggers. But the killings still went on. People were more careful, that's all. Kept things quiet. It became a matter of death by stealth. People had no choice: a dead Aborigine was worth the risk for the sake of a safer flock or herd.

You thought you could leave these stories behind when you left Inverell and went south. But they came back to haunt you when your wife had the twins.

It took another ten years till you found the courage to have another go at getting Ester pregnant.

Courage and faith.

It was a bit like working out what stocking rate the country could stand, without stripping its vegetation. Acting on gut instinct and selling off sheep before a dry spell. You had to look twelve months ahead, although you knew that was never enough. Five years was more like it.

You couldn't measure the impact over the short term.

28

On Monday, Freya met Michael and he showed her another selection of unsuitable properties. One was situated between a busy pub and the railway station in Twickenham. The other was a former off-licence on a dangerous intersection in Isleworth.

'Can't you show me something more . . . peaceful?' she said.

'Hmm,' he replied. 'I've got something that might suit you in Richmond.'

It was a tiny gift shop opposite a department store, set amongst a row of rickety olde-worlde boutiques. The location was ideal, near the river and the common, and within spitting distance of the high street. But the rent was exorbitant. Freya's heart sank. Then she realised that Clarissa or Neill might walk past one day, and she was glad she couldn't afford it.

As she walked back to the car park she glanced into the churchyard opposite a new Moroccan restaurant. There was a tea shop next to the church she knew was run by women on the church committee. She wondered if Clarissa was there nibbling scones and imparting her joyous aura.

In the afternoon she drove down to East Sussex to buy some plants at an organic herb farm. She opened the windows of the car. The air was warm and silky. As she left the motorway and headed along the winding country roads towards Rye, her thoughts began to unscramble. The rolling hills and clear expanse of sky filled her with optimism. The haunting sense of failure, the emptiness, began to dissolve a little.

After loading the boot and back seat with plants, she parked in a lay-by and went for a walk in a wooded valley. What a relief to walk without fear of bumping into anyone.

When she got home it was late. She went straight to bed and for the first time in months slept soundly.

In the morning she took the train up to London to see Nadine. She called her before she left home, to tell her the news.

Nadine pounced. 'This will make the appeal easier,' she said briskly.

A rush of elation swept through Freya. She sat on the train like a person with things to do, a successful woman on a mission. As she walked through the underground she felt rejuvenated: she smiled at strangers, tossed her hair, and braced herself against the hot railway wind.

In her tiny office, tucked down a narrow alley near Oxford Street, Nadine was like a bower bird in a paper forest. Scraps of wafer-thin snakeskin and cicada cases, collected on an African safari holiday, lay amongst musty books on buckling shelves. Like the bower bird, she favoured blue objects, to match her penchant for indigo power suits. Her blue-rinsed hair flicked out at the back in feathery tails and her fingers were laden with jade and peridot and turquoise rings, huge pieces that made her fingers seem small and pinched.

'Well,' she said, leaning over her desk, 'now that the children have admitted they hate living with their father, and Clarissa is not the prim-and-proper Christian we all thought she was, we might actually win this appeal. The judge will still want a report from the CWO, but basically, this is your ticket to full-time motherhood. It will change everything, and put the court and your ex-husband firmly in their place. You know, the court is always at a disadvantage, relying on reports from outside sources. Even the CWO can't make an in-depth assessment after a few short visits to a person's home.'

'You're telling me,' said Freya.

Nadine's enthusiasm depressed Freya. It seemed predatory and smug. Here at last was her chance to have what she wanted — her children. Nadine was talking as though the court had already made their decision. It seemed so easy. Too easy. Freya had been gearing up for one hell of a battle. After a long moment she sighed heavily, shook her head and looked at Nadine.

'I know this might sound strange, but I don't want to bring any of this up at the appeal after all,' she said. Her voice was shaky.

Nadine's pencilled eyebrows shot up like exclamation marks.

'I suppose I should be overjoyed,' said Freya. 'I was overjoyed — when the children told me. But I'm not now. I wouldn't care if the children were living in the Congo or Iceland or Philadelphia — I'd still want them to be happy. Using their unhappiness to get them back, just to get my own way, would be wrong.'

'Really, Freya, aren't you being a bit dogmatic?'

'Neill lied in court, and they believed him. They believed the CWO. But she doesn't know me, not really. None of them know me. You don't know me. I want to prove I'm a good mother. On my own merits.'

'Pride is a blocking emotion, Freya. You should know that.'

'I don't want them to give me custody if they still think I'm a bad mother. We shouldn't just give in to Tom and Kirsty.'

Nadine lit a cigarette. A ribbon of smoke settled above her head.

'You can't leave it to fate, my dear girl.'

But Freya was firm. 'If we tell the court what Kirsty and Tom told me, they might misconstrue it. They might think I primed the children, that I got them to say they're not happy, to please me.'

'Surely your main consideration should be the children's welfare?'

Freya sensed Nadine's irritation.

'Of course. But I'm not ready to let them live with me yet. I thought I was, and I am in some ways. But this is too easy. It might backfire. Before they come back I have to buy a bigger boat and set up my own business. And I have other things to attend to, things I can't talk about just yet. That's actually proof of my love, if only the court used their wits. Sorting my life out properly before having them back. That way, when they do come back, everything will be in place. I'll be ready for them. I mean, a good mother wouldn't want them to live on a leaky old rustbucket, would she now?'

'I'm not sure I understand. But it's your decision, and as your lawyer, I can only advise you.'

'Being given custody because they hate it at Neill's wouldn't prove anything,' said Freya. 'It wouldn't prove that we've bonded, or that I'm perfectly sane, and teetotal.'

Nadine clasped her hands over her mouth and sighed into them. After a moment she looked up.

'But which is the lesser of two evils? Living with their father who is making them unhappy, or living on a damp boat? Why make them suffer under his roof when they could be happier with you on the houseboat?'

'Look,' said Freya, leaning forward, 'I love my children. I'd give up my life for them.'

'You don't have to convince me.'

'I want them back. But not until it feels right.'

'You're making a big mistake,' said Nadine.

Freya slumped back in the chair. Nothing seemed real or right or honest any more, she thought. Her entire life was a lie. Neill had lied. The CWO had done a half-arsed job of getting to the crux of issues.

How could she know her own children, when she did not even know herself?

'You don't understand,' said Freya. 'It's complicated.'

'What does it matter, if they misjudged you?'

'I'm not being stubborn or conceited, if that's what you mean.'

She wasn't going to get into it with Nadine, it

would only confuse matters. This was her secret. Besides, Nadine would think it all very odd, in spite of her Kenyan safari trips and her cruises down the Nile.

Freya looked out of the small Gothic lead-light window at the black fish-scale roofs. Since arriving at Nadine's office a pall of grey cloud had covered the city. Not one beam of light lanced the gloom. She sighed. The city had exhausted her. She wanted to go home and rest.

'I just need some more time,' she said.

'What for?'

'To find a better boat. To set up my business. To get my thoughts together. To prove I'm not mad or hopeless or indifferent.' She banged her hand on the desk.

Nadine frowned.

Freya withdrew her hand and buried it in her lap. She stared hard at a flock of swooping birds, dipping, rising, flying off to a less hostile place.

To find out who she really was would mean dismantling and rebuilding her entire life: every thought, dream and memory.

'Well, if it's any consolation, I think you're a good mother,' said Nadine.

After a long moment, Freya lifted her eyes slowly and said, 'Just remember to tell that to the court.'

29

Freya needed to see Connie, to ask her more questions about herself and Peggy. But she had to stay focused on the custody appeal and give Monica plenty of reasons to write a glowing report.

'I won't be calling you for a while,' she told Connie one night when she phoned. 'I'm keeping a low profile for now. I'm sure you'll understand. Just until after the appeal.'

Connie was disappointed, but she agreed. 'As soon as it's all over, maybe then you'll think about using those tickets.'

Sam seemed to have taken the hint too, and was keeping to himself. She was grateful for this, and it made her feel something deeper towards him than mere sexual attraction. He was a good, kind man.

One morning she saw him mucking about in his dinghy. He did not even look her way.

Various residents dropped in to collect their orders and ask her advice. She kept herself busy preparing, packaging, gardening, and felt constantly tired. Not even her own herbal remedies helped her sleep. She tossed and turned, dissecting every remembered detail of her life up to now, spinning it all like a Rubik's cube, trying to view herself reinvented.

★ ★ ★

'What's that horrible smell?' said Kirsty.

'Bilge water, I expect,' said Freya.

'Can't you spray some natural air freshener around?'

'I'll light a scented candle.'

Kirsty flopped in the armchair.

'I'm having a new sofa bed delivered today,' said Freya. 'I bought it in the sales. You can sleep on it if you like. There's more air up here in the saloon.'

Kirsty brightened.

'I thought we'd stay home this weekend,' said Freya. She didn't want to keep frittering away her savings on outings. 'You can help me clear a space for the new sofa, then do some studying, or finish any projects that are due in.'

Kirsty rolled her eyes. 'Can I see Ryan?'

'You can see him tomorrow. Let's spend today together.'

Kirsty pouted.

'Oh come on, Kirsty, we're supposed to be bonding.'

Kirsty delved into the pocket of her combat trousers, pulled out a mobile phone, and tapped the keys.

'Where did you get that?' said Freya.

'It's an early birthday present. From Dad.'

Freya sighed. 'I thought he was broke.' She stopped herself from saying any more.

'Everyone at school's got one, Mum. I want to get a camera phone next.'

'What's wrong with that one?'

'It's crap.'

'It's *what*?'

There was a knock at the door. They all rushed at once and Freya drew back the curtain that covered the main hatch. A burly man in green overalls was standing on the landing stage with a delivery note.

'Sofa for Mrs Kirby.'

He leaned down and came face-to-face with Freya, then cast his eyes over her head, clearly amused by the houseboat.

The sofa, a large Chesterfield with bulky armrests and exaggerated wings, was parked on the towpath. Two men were sitting on it in dirty boiler suits, catching their breath.

'Quick, Kirsty, help me clear a space.'

'Does this door slide open any further?' said the boss.

'A bit.' Freya pushed it open as far as it would go.

The men turned the sofa on its side, and lifted it up to the hatch, but they could not get it through. They tried every possible angle, but it was no use. They put it on the grass verge and sat down, exhausted.

'Did you measure the bloody thing when you bought it?' said the boss.

'Open the roof hatch, that might work,' said Tom.

'Good idea,' said Freya. She gave him a quick hug, but he pulled away.

She lifted the hatch, creating a large, L-shaped open space stretching over the roof and down the side of the boat, and the men tried again. Still the sofa wouldn't fit. The wings were the problem.

'Why don't you chop them off with an axe?' said Tom.

The men roared with laughter.

Freya laughed too. There was no point getting angry.

'Looks like you've bought yourself a white elephant, darlin',' said one of the men. They exchanged mocking looks.

Freya felt foolish.

'Shift it on to the grass again, boys.'

'What on earth are we going to do?' said Freya. 'I'm not sending it back.'

'You mean what are *you* gunna do.'

'There's no way I could get it aboard on my own, and the kids aren't strong enough.'

The boss tutted. 'You should've thought of all this before you bought the bloody thing.'

He got out his tape measure, measured the sofa, then the opening.

Freya glanced along the towpath. She could hear the sound of a drill coming from somewhere inside *Lady Luck*. Sam would help, but she didn't want to use him.

'Would you guys like a cup of tea and a slice of home-made carrot cake?'

'Wouldn't say no to a cuppa,' said the boss. 'I'll skip the carrot cake though, thanks all the same.'

'Got any digestives?' said another man.

'I've got some Australian biscuits. Chocolate.' She had bought them in Covent Garden and kept them for special visitors. Turning on the charm, she decided, was the only way to keep the men captive until the sofa was inside.

'How do you take your tea?' said Freya quickly. 'Sugar? Milk?' She took their orders and sent Kirsty in to boil the kettle, then sat down on the landing stage, her mind racing. She simply had to keep them here until the sofa was safely on board.

The men settled back on the sofa and lit cigarettes, while Freya tried frantically to keep the conversation rolling. Where were they all from? Had they ever been on a houseboat? Did they enjoy their work? This question was a mistake.

'We've got other stuff in the van to deliver besides yours, darlin',' said the boss.

'I bet you've come across some funny situations, trying to fit large pieces into small houses?'

There was a collective rumble and the stories flowed: pianos that wouldn't fit up staircases, beds that had to be lowered through roofs, wardrobes that had to be dismantled, sheds that had to be taken through terraced houses piece by piece.

They asked about the ins and outs of living afloat — the usual questions about toilet arrangements and water, and whether or not she froze to death in winter.

Kirsty came out with a tray and offered the men their tea. The boss scooped seven teaspoons of sugar into his mug. The other two men emptied the plate of biscuits.

'Are you Australian or South African?' the boss said suddenly, one ear leaning hard into the timbre of Freya's accent.

'Australian,' she said.

'Jesus,' he said. 'What the fuck are you doin' livin' 'ere?'

Freya looked at him, taken aback by the question.

'I really don't know,' she said, shaking her head. 'Perhaps I'm mad.'

★ ★ ★

The ruckus outside *Harlequin* began to attract the neighbours. Everything and anything attracted the neighbours.

Pluto and Harry, two gays from *Me Old China*, settled themselves on one end of the sofa, eyeing up the youngest of the three delivery men.

'I love your boiler suit,' said Pluto.

The young man shifted uneasily.

Next door, Ginny and Eric opened their hatch and popped their heads out.

'Fancy a cuppa?' Freya called out. She couldn't ignore them; Ginny's expectant face demanded an invitation.

'Would you like a hand?' said Eric.

'Yes please,' said Freya. Good old Eric. She did not want to socialise at all right now, but if the delivery men decided to take off, at least everyone could lend a hand. 'I'll put the kettle on.'

It was warm inside the galley, and peaceful. She wished she could shut herself away, the sofa installed, and get on with her day.

When she went out with the tea, Sam and Ryan were just arriving. Ryan made a beeline for the forward deck, where Kirsty was now sunbathing in a singlet top and jeans. He sat beside her, hugging his knees. She adjusted her top.

'Would you like some tea?' said Freya, rolling her eyes at Sam.

'Not for me,' he said, sensing her desire to get rid of everyone.

She glanced towards the bridge for signs of unwanted outsiders: court officials, ex-husbands, the CIA, the FBI. Christ, how she hated living here sometimes.

The delivery men gulped their tea and demolished the biscuits. The boss reached into his pocket for another cigarette, and spilled tea on the arm of the sofa. He rubbed it with his elbow, which was stained with grease.

Presently Chippy arrived, then Sharon, then Rick. The simple delivery of a sofa was turning into a party.

'This is what I was talking about,' said Sam, winking. 'You're never alone on the moorings.'

Luke had arrived, she noticed, and was showing Tom a fancy torch. Now and then he flashed the torch at Sam, making him wince. He was enjoying the logistical superiority — sitting on Freya's boat with her son — over Sam's inconsequential position on the towpath.

Freya thought the rivalry between them over her was petty and childish. Sam became prickly in Luke's presence, which was silly — how could he possibly think she would be remotely attracted to someone like Luke? She'd made it clear to Luke weeks ago that she thought of him as a friend, no more, after he'd declared his feelings for her were more than just friendship. But he hadn't made much of an effort to curb his desire, serenading her when he walked home from the pub, knocking on her door at all hours asking for a refill of an ointment she'd prescribed for a rash.

Chippy passed around cans of beer. If she didn't act fast, the party would be in full swing and she'd never get rid of them.

'Sam, get my electric jigsaw from the garden shed, would you?' She handed him the keys.

The delivery men were having an in-depth conversation about football.

'You boys can go now, if you like. We'll sort it out.' Freya gave the boss a small tip, and they departed.

Sam came back with the saw and ran an extension lead from the saloon. Freya held the saw firmly and switched it on. It vibrated dangerously. She began to cut through the timber super-structure next to the main hatch. The noise of the saw shredding the air sounded obscene, and sawdust flew all over her face. Suddenly she lost control. The machine veered off on its own merry way. She quickly turned it off.

'Here, I'll finish,' said Sam.

She smiled gratefully.

He steadied the saw and effortlessly guided it along. Rather than hover like a school teacher, she went inside and made more tea. These people had an endless capacity for the stuff.

When Sam had finished sawing the hole,

instead of getting the sofa on board, everyone sat about chatting. Freya looked around at them, dismayed. She wished they would leave; it made her edgy, all these men. They were terrible flirts, every one of them, even Eric, who liked to pat her bottom.

'Don't do that,' she always responded, and he laughed.

Luke jumped off the boat and began to stack the jigsaw segments in a neat little pile on the grass. He looked up and winked at Freya, a spicy look in his eye.

Kirsty and Ryan went inside and put on a CD. Music filtered through the window and echoed over the canal.

'Turn it down please, Kirsty,' Freya said through the window.

'It's not even loud,' Kirsty retorted.

Freya gave her a dark look and Kirsty turned the dial.

'Thank you,' said Freya.

She looked around at the gathering — nearly all men. Luke had climbed back on to the forward deck and was holding an elaborate Swiss army knife.

Tom's eyes became round and shiny. 'Cor,' he breathed.

Sam set to work sweeping up the sawdust.

'Come on,' he said at last. 'Let's see if we can get this sofa inside, and mend the hole.'

'This is what you might call a débâcle,' said Eric drily, staring at the gash in the super-structure.

'It's not that bad,' said Sam. 'Once we get the

pieces glued back and give it a lick of paint, no one would even know.'

'Until the whole lot pops out again when a big cruiser steams past.'

'Don't be such a pessimist,' said Sam. 'It'll be fine.'

Freya looked at him, alarmed. 'Do you think I've made a big mistake, sawing the hole?'

'It'll be fine,' said Sam again. 'If it's not then I'll sort it out with a new sheet of marine ply.'

'But that's a huge job.'

'Let's hope it won't come to that. Come on, let's get the sofa inside before it rains.'

Freya looked up. Clouds were coming in from the south. 'Christ. Come on, everyone.'

'Give us a hand will you, Luke?' Sam gestured for Luke to climb aboard, and they waited to guide the sofa through the hatch. Everyone else got into position and lifted. This time it slid through the opening quite easily.

'Phew. Thank God for that,' said Freya. 'Well done, everyone, thanks for your help. I'll see if I've got some wood glue in the shed. And I'll bring a tarp, in case it rains before we can get the hole glued up.' She hurried into the garden.

When she came back on to the towpath a few minutes later, arms loaded with the folded tarpaulin, Neill was standing there, thin-lipped and scowling. He looked out of place, in his neatly pressed chinos and blue-and-white checked shirt from Pink's. Everyone was quiet.

'Hello,' said Freya. 'What are you doing here?'

She stood very still, trying to gather her thoughts. At the same time she was thinking, how dare he turn up like this, without calling her first.

It was typical of Neill — master of the unexpected.

'I thought I'd come and see for myself the children's second home.'

You mean come and gather more evidence, thought Freya.

Neill looked at Tom, who was holding the splayed army knife. It looked menacing and lethal; the blades glinted in the sun.

'Put that thing away,' said Neill sternly. 'Before you hurt someone.'

Tom handed the knife to Luke, who folded the blades inside the casing and slipped it into his pocket. 'Don't get your knickers in a knot, mate. I was watching him.'

'I'm sure you were,' said Neill.

'What's that supposed to mean?'

'It means, I'm sure you were watching him. But I don't want my son playing with knives no matter who is watching, thank you.'

'What are you doing here?' Freya repeated.

'Where's Kirsty?' he said. Freya felt the blood rising in her cheeks.

Coldplay were not a particularly weird or blasphemous band, but with Neill standing there their music seemed subversive. She moved to the window and peered in. Kirsty and Ryan had disappeared. She leaned down at the galley window. They were not there, either.

Now she moved with the briskness of a nurse in an emergency, striding through the garden to check the summerhouse, then around the path to the herb garden. She popped her head in the polytunnels, and looked towards the woods, but the teenagers were nowhere in sight.

'She must have gone for a walk,' she said, back at the towpath. She smiled ingenuously at Neill and handed the tube of glue to Sam, who set to work mending the hole.

'Nice little party you're having in the middle of the day,' said Neill.

'We had a spot of bother getting my new sofa inside.'

Neill sniffed cattily. Typical, he was probably thinking, another of Freya's impulse buys that didn't fit or match, or was uncomfortable, or badly made. The house had been full of her shopping disasters.

Luke was showing Tom how to tie Turk's Head knots with lengths of blue, red and green silk rope. An antique earring in his right ear and a diamond in his front tooth sparkled simultaneously in the sun.

'You can decorate your mother's tiller with these,' he said, pushing the finished knots on to a cardboard toilet roll. He glanced at Freya and winked.

God, how she wished he would stop it.

Neill noticed the wink. 'Excuse me, mate,' he said, pushing Sam aside.

'Watch it,' said Sam.

Neill climbed aboard. 'Mind if I use your bathroom?'

'Help yourself,' said Freya. 'Turn right in the saloon, down the stairs, third on the right. Excuse the state of the loo, I haven't had a chance to empty it today.'

Neill crinkled his nose. 'I thought it went straight into the canal?'

'What do you take us for, mate, fuckin' animals?' said Luke.

Neill was stuffy about swearing and drinking. It was okay to screw Clarissa behind the church organ, but God forbid if anyone said the F word.

Freya gave Luke a sharp look.

Neill disappeared below decks. Freya imagined the smells that he would be experiencing. And the dust he might notice. The pile of dirty laundry she had forgotten to bring up from the bathroom this morning.

She and Sam sorted through the cut-out marine ply, sizing up the hole and gluing each piece back in its original position.

'I was a boy scout, Freya; I know how to fit the contents of a suitcase into a matchbox.' He nudged her gently in the ribs.

She smiled, but inwardly she was full of tension.

Before Neill would have had time to even unzip his trousers, he was back in the saloon with his head out of the door.

'I found Kirsty,' he said, his voice even and crisp.

'Oh?' Uh-oh. Freya gulped. 'Is she asleep?'

'No,' said Neill. 'She's with a young man. On your double bed.'

30

On rising next morning, Freya noticed the stern was lower in the water than the rest of the boat. The saloon floor sloped alarmingly. She went down the steps into the galley. To her horror, the floor was an inch deep in water. The main leak was worse than she'd feared. She would have to bale it out by hand; the bilge under the galley floor was too shallow to be pumped.

She was suddenly businesslike, down on her knees, scooping the water into a bucket. When the bucket was full she emptied it out of the window. It made a loud splash as it hit the canal.

Young man.

Since when did Neill talk like that?

An expensive, tricky expedition into dry dock was looking likely. Sam had once offered to tow *Harlequin* to the marina if ever it became necessary. She had politely refused. She would find another way — hire a pony, or a tug boat.

After yesterday's fiasco, with Neill making a to-do and taking the children home early (as though they were in terrible danger of corruption or drowning), and Sam giving her an *I told you so* look, she was even more determined to be independent.

She sat on the steps linking the saloon to the galley and dining area, and stared despondently at the flooded floor. The water slapped against the kitchen units like a persistent tongue.

249

Orders had come in from two top London department stores this week; she couldn't afford to get behind. She went outside to work, leaving the flooded galley till later.

It was too chilly to work in the garden, the weather was unseasonably (as well as unreasonably) cold, so she went into the summerhouse. She loved working there; the exposed timber walls and rustic rafters hung with bunches of herbs gave it a Swiss chalet atmosphere. The scent of lavender, rosemary and witch hazel was overpowering in the small room. It made her feel light-headed.

She was in the middle of pouring a tincture into a bottle when the extension phone rang. The green light bleeped. Neill's number flashed on the incoming calls panel.

She picked up the receiver.

'Hello?'

'I thought you'd like to know what your daughter's getting up to,' he said. 'In view of your inability to keep tabs on her.'

Freya said nothing. What was the point in arguing?

'After what happened yesterday, I thought I had better take a closer look at Kirsty's life.' His voice sounded threatening.

'What do you mean? I hope you haven't done anything stupid, Neill.' She still couldn't get to grips with the change in the man. He was like a total stranger. She had no time for do-gooders. 'You're being silly. Nothing happened. They were just talking. Don't you know your own daughter? Kirsty's a sensible kid.'

'You're the one who's lost touch with where she's at.'

'There's not a lot of privacy on the boat. They probably wanted to be alone.'

'I bet they did.'

'Look, I don't want to argue.'

'I've got my own methods of finding out things, you know.'

Her heart sank. 'What have you done?'

'I read her diary.'

Freya gasped. 'You'll push her away doing that.'

'If you can't look after the children properly, then perhaps you'd better not have them to stay at all in future.'

'You can't do that.'

'Let's see what happens at the appeal.'

'They were just talking,' said Freya. She held back the urge to scream *fuck you* down the phone, took a deep breath, then said calmly, 'Teenagers don't want to hang around adults all the time. You have to cut them some slack, or they resent you.'

'I'm not in a popularity contest.'

'It's a matter of balance. And Kirsty's not stupid.'

'How do you account for this, then? *I wonder when I will lose my virginity? When will Ryan kiss me? Rebecca says she'll ring him up for me, but I don't know his number.*'

'I don't want to hear this. It's private.'

'This isn't just fantasising. Listen to this: *I wonder what our babies will look like?*'

His tactics were repugnant, but she had to

251

admit it made her uneasy. She *trusted* Kirsty; this was simply the teenage mind playing make-believe, wasn't it? 'It sounds like pure imagination to me.'

'You're not taking this seriously.'

She sighed. 'Of course I am.'

'You're a hopeless mother, you know that?' he said. 'Really hopeless.'

She almost slammed the phone down. She took another deep breath and said evenly, 'Look, Neill, you'll lose her respect, reading her diary.'

'I've got every right, as her father, to make sure she's safe.'

'You're being ridiculous. Kirsty's a normal teenager.'

'Under-age sex is not normal. It's illegal.'

'I doubt if the police would care these days. They've got far more important matters to deal with. Murders, for instance.'

'As I said, you're irresponsible.'

'No I'm not. I'm reasonable.'

There was a long pause, then Neill said, 'You'll be sorry. She'll end up pregnant. How do you think she'd cope at her age? She can barely wash a cup properly.'

'You underestimate your own daughter.'

'You don't see what I see every day. I live with her, you don't.'

A nasty, creeping prickle passed under the skin on Freya's neck. He had to rub it in, didn't he? 'That's right,' she said. 'I don't live with Kirsty. But I'm still her mother, whether you like it or not.'

'You've got no idea the stress we're under with

six children to rear.'

'Well I'd be happy to help you out, but you've got custody.'

'Just spending two days with you every fortnight undermines what Clarissa and I have tried to instil. Clarissa is constantly picking up after Kirsty and Tom, and that's because you don't teach them any respect for their surroundings.'

'What crap. Look, if you're that hard pressed, why don't you hire an au pair? They only cost thirty quid a week. Slave labour, in my opinion, but there you go. I'm sure all your neighbours have got one. You should look into it.'

She put the phone down and sat for a long time with her head in her hands, her heart falling away inside her. After a while she got up and, referring to a list of orders, began to fill a basket with creams and bottles of tinctures.

When she had finished, she walked back quickly along the towpath, fearful of bumping into someone, but glad of the fresh air and exercise. Arriving at *FGP*, Luke's boat, she put a jar of aloe vera ointment on his step. He had burned his hand on his fuel stove weeks ago, and the skin wasn't healing. As she was about to move away, she heard someone groaning, and looking down at a porthole, she was taken aback to see a foot in a filthy grey sock, the sole of which was covered in blobs of Blu Tack. Long grey and black hairs stuck out from the little rounds of blue and a big toe, the nail of which had a nasty black bruise across it, had worked its way through a tattered hole. Thank God it was only a toe at the porthole and not some other part of Luke's anatomy.

Luke was sobbing.

It was not new to her, hearing a grown man cry. Many of her male patients had bawled like babies. She had learned to adopt a sympathetic but brisk approach, egging them on to joke about their predicament, or compare their fate to others on the ward much worse off, or changing the subject on to a positive aspect of their life.

Luke sounded desperate. He'd lost his daughter in a car accident fifteen years ago, but it still upset him.

The healing, caring part of her nature made her want to knock on the door and give him a shoulder to cry on. The Australian in her said this would be a perfectly natural gesture, extending the hand of open goodwill. But what if someone saw her going in? What if Monica turned up unannounced? After yesterday's setback, she did not want to risk it. She hovered near the porthole, watching Luke's twitching foot. His big toe flexed and wiggled as the pitch of the unbearable weeping rose, then fell. She couldn't stand the thought that anyone could be that depressed. And yesterday he had been kind to Tom, keeping him occupied.

She was just about to open his door and climb in when she heard a loud splash. At first she thought someone was breaking canal etiquette and emptying their portaloo into the cut. But the sound was oddly sleek, like an otter slithering off a bank.

She dumped her basket on Luke's forward

deck and scanned the canal. It was perfectly still and smooth, not a ripple.

Suddenly a young boy's face broke the surface of the water near her feet.

Freya lurched backwards.

He sank for a few seconds and came up spewing water and spittle, eyes bulging with fear. In them she saw the eyes of her own children, and the horror of loneliness, loss and confusion.

The boy scratched frantically at the grass verge like a dog digging a hole, but the leaves were too slippery and he could not get a grip.

At last Freya broke into action and with one clean movement scooped him up on to the towpath. He hung there in her arms like a puppet, limp and dripping, then coughed hard. His Wellington boots squelched and dirty canal water slurped over the rims. He was whimpering like a small puppy. He was too weak to hold himself up and his bony body shivered uncontrollably. She drew him against her stomach and thumped him firmly between the shoulder blades. Then she laid him down gently on the path and rolled him on to his side, checking his mouth for obstructions with her little finger and his head for bumps. She took off her jacket and placed it over him, and pressed her fingers against the pulse on his wrist until she was sure he was well and truly out of danger.

'Where's your mum?' she said softly.

'Asleep.'

She pulled his boots off and flung them on to the verge, then lifted him up and carried him home. His small fingers clung to her lapel. They were blue with cold. His teeth chattered and his bloodless lips quivered.

Rather than put him down, Freya extended a leg, twisted it, and knocked on *Poppy*'s main hatch with her heel. A few minutes later the hatch flew open and Bridget poked her head out. Her hair was a frightful frizz and she was wearing a thin sleeveless nightie. She squinted at Freya and her dripping wet son. Her mouth gaped.

'What on earth . . . ?' she said weakly.

Adrenalin pumping through Freya's veins always brought out the Australian in her. 'You'd better start keeping an eye on Charlie instead of other people,' she said. 'He nearly drowned just now. If I hadn't been walking past he'd be a dead bloody duck.'

Charlie curled himself into her.

'Make yourself useful and run a hot bath,' she added, looking down at the boy's pale face.

Bridget gave her a wounded look, sighed dramatically and hurried off along the corridor.

'Grab a couple of towels to wrap him in,' called Freya after her.

When Charlie was bathed and dressed in a clean pair of pyjamas, Bridget settled him down on the sofa in front of the TV with a cup of hot chocolate.

Once she was sure he was okay, Freya ushered Bridget into the galley.

'I know what you're going to say,' said Bridget. Her thin nightie clung to her legs. She seemed vulnerable, like a torn moth.

'Look,' said Freya, 'a child's life is *everyone*'s business.'

'I never wanted to live here in the first place,' said Bridget miserably.

Freya couldn't believe what she was hearing. Charlie had almost drowned, and Bridget was complaining about her own misery.

'I suggest you keep a close eye on Charlie if you want to avoid a tragedy.'

'You won't tell anyone?'

'Ordinarily I'd report it to Social Services. But if you promise me you'll be more careful from now on, we'll keep it to ourselves.'

'Oh thank you, Freya, thank you.'

She knew how it felt, to be under the thumb of the authorities. She wouldn't wish it on anyone, unless that person was dangerous.

'You have to put Charlie first, Bridget. He's precious. He's got his whole life ahead of him. You'd never forgive yourself if you lost him.'

31

Freya drove into town and met the estate agent, who had a few more properties to show her. Once again they were all unsuitable.

Later, she walked along the high street in a strangely dreamy mood. The noise of the traffic seemed far away and muted. People she saw every week looked straight through her. She thought again about the way Londoners ignored one another. It was one of the reasons for buying the houseboat, to be part of a community. She looked at people's cold faces, noticed the heavy overcoats that old people wore, too bulky for spring, as though they were anticipating rain, and thought, what am I doing here? Who are these people? I don't belong, I don't fit in.

Inside the newsagent's she bought a copy of *Exchange & Mart*, which advertised houseboats for sale.

Outside, the sun was shining but the faces seemed peculiar and unyielding.

An overpowering desire to get on a plane to Australia came over her. The crooked half-timbered buildings around the market-place, the cobbled lanes, the harsh shout of a fruiterer flogging Spanish strawberries, the blue language of a trucker delivering crates of homogeneous cakes to Starbucks, and the inclination people had of sliding their eyes away when she looked at them, while she hoped for some small recognition, a smile perhaps, or a friendly *Nice day*: it was like walking through a silent film. Was this what it was like to be homesick?

She wandered into a small, mean café next to the Job Centre, and joined the queue. The smell of baked beans and stale clothing was over-powering in the tiny room, with its streaming windows and artificial plants. She bought a rigid Danish that resembled a glazed cow pat, and a cup of tepid decaffeinated coffee. She sat by the window, staring out at the figures hurrying past. She wondered if they opened up to one another in the comfort and privacy of their own homes, or if they remained guarded the way they were on the streets.

'Excuse me, Sister Kirby, I thought it was you,' said a distant voice.

Freya turned slowly, not sure if she had imagined it, but there, squeezing between the tables, was Ursula, a nurse who had left the hospital to work at the Job Centre.

'Mind if I join you?'

Freya smiled and said hello, but her voice was lukewarm.

'I hope you don't mind,' continued Ursula, parking herself opposite Freya.

Freya stared at the red nose stud in Ursula's right nostril. 'How's the new job going?' she said.

Ursula stirred her mug of tea. They both stared at the swirling murk as if they expected it to offer up an answer.

'Interesting,' said Ursula thoughtfully. 'There are some very sad cases, of course. In some ways it's more satisfying than nursing. But I do miss the excitement of the hospital.'

'What is it you do, exactly?' Freya glanced at the wall clock, which was dripping with greasy condensation. She did not wish to be cornered like this, but had only taken two sips of her coffee, and had not even nibbled the cow pat.

'I advise the disabled,' said Ursula importantly. 'And people with chronic — but not totally debilitating — diseases. I tell them about job possibilities or, if they're beyond getting work, I sort out their benefits and make sure they're not being short-changed.'

'I guess there's a lot of paperwork.'

Ursula nodded. She smelled of Joop perfume. 'I'm glad I bumped into you,' she said, taking a long draught of her tea.

'Oh?'

Ursula gave Freya a sympathetic look and, stretching her hands with their short nails across the table, cupped them over Freya's and squeezed. Freya whisked her hands out and dropped them on to her lap. A hot prickly sensation stabbed at her armpits.

Ursula dipped her head down conspiratorially and said, 'I just wanted to say how sorry I am, really.'

'About what?'

'Your husband.'

'That's all in the past.'

Ursula gave her a strange look. 'I mean, just when you wanted to start afresh and make a new career with your herbs. It must be a terrible blow, thinking you could rely on your other half to help out while you get things up and running.

Still, the main thing is he's getting treatment for the diabetes, and I've gone through all the benefits you're entitled to as a family with a fine-tooth comb. In the end you'll probably be better off than you were when you worked at the hospital and he was teaching music.'

Freya almost choked on her coffee. Benefits? What was this?

'I had no idea you had so many children,' Ursula continued. Freya tried to compose herself and fought back the urge to speak. 'How do you do it?' said Ursula. 'I think you're amazing, with six kids . . . '

What? Freya managed to look as if she knew exactly what Ursula was talking about.

'No wonder you gave up your full-time job at the hospital,' said Ursula. 'What's that other thing you do, with the massage?'

'Shiatsu.'

'Yes, that's it. I'm never sure how to pronounce it.' Ursula giggled. She gathered up her bag and coat, still talking. 'Anyway, I won't stop, I'm only allowed ten minutes for morning break. I just wanted to say you don't need to worry, there's lots of support these days for this sort of case. Next time Mr Kirby comes in I should have a few jobs he might like to consider, easy positions teaching adults, although I don't want him to feel under any pressure. No one's forcing him to get a job. If he doesn't feel up to it, well, that's his decision.'

She gave Freya a pitying smile, and was gone.

32

That afternoon she drove to the marina.

Gradually, as the shock subsided, she had begun to expand with anger. It was unbelievable that Neill was claiming benefits when he earned more than enough as a web designer. If he was caught he would be in terrible trouble. It would bring shame to the family, to the children, if the media found out. She could use this against him in court to get them back.

She thought about his diabetes. He would need support eventually. He would probably have to give up working, even from home. She had known for years he was heading for trouble with his health, the way he gorged on sweets and carbohydrates. His diet was appalling. She had tried to encourage fresh food, but he hated vegetables and salad, and whenever she bought grapes he thought it was because someone in the house was sick.

He had not even told Ursula he was divorced. He had sat in the Job Centre, hands clasped morally in his lap, and pretended they were still married. Freya's name would be on the claim forms as his spouse, and not Clarissa's.

The truth would have to come out eventually. Someone would catch him unawares. A Job Centre veteran with more experience than Ursula, most likely.

It was all so seedy.

She decided against telling Nadine, who would pounce on his little scam and puff herself up like a blowfish in court, as though it were *her* discovery, *her* investigative skills that had caught him out. It would be too easy. Freya wanted to be judged on her own merits at the appeal. Neill would come unstuck eventually. She just had to sit tight.

★   ★   ★

At the marina she met Sam's friend Jason, who showed her a new boat he was fitting out, a handsome broad-beam narrowboat. In spite of the pristine interior, it wasn't what she wanted.

'I want an old barge that needs doing up,' she said, sweeping her fingers along the buffed woodwork. 'I like character, history. A boat that's been lived in. A boat that can sail. A boat with a heart.'

Jason — a tall, intelligent young man with a shock of unruly black hair and designer stubble — gave her a derisory look.

'You'll be buying trouble,' he said. He wiped his greasy hands on the front of a filthy pair of grey overalls.

'Oh, I'm used to that.'

As she walked along the jetty towards the parade of shops, tears filled her eyes. Everything became a smoky blur. She wiped them on her arm, marking it with tiger stripes of mascara.

At the forecourt next to the lock she sat down on a bench. The air was thick with the smell of diesel, Calor Gas, and charcoal. Clouds of

263

sawdust spewed from the open doors of a nearby timber yard.

In the car park she stood for a moment staring at the interior of her car. A white sachet of dried herbs dangled forlornly from the rear-view mirror. The patchwork cushion on the driver's seat, which she had sewn herself, bore the imprint of her backside. The ashtray was open and held a packet of echinacea cough sweets. The rear seat was stacked with boxes of ginger and elder flower moisturiser. A copy of *Mosby's Handbook of Herbs and Supplements and Their Therapeutic Uses* and the American magazine *HerbalGram* were on the passenger seat. Paper strips stuck out of them, marking pages of interest. There was a particularly fascinating article in the magazine about the use of cultural items for science being unacceptable.

'Native people have a social and sacred relationship not only to their ancestors, but to the heritage and objects they have created,' the article said.

Reading this last night had put her in a strange mood. There were photographs of cave walls in the state of Utah, decorated with ancient petroglyphs, and intricately engraved ceremonial shell cups.

She had thought she was being clever and mature, with her just-get-on-with-it attitude. The truth was, she was lonely. How stupid of her not to have seen it.

33

The comforting sound of the children's steady breathing flowed through the cabins.

Neill had dropped them off on the humpback bridge, reversing into the road and turning the car for home without even acknowledging her.

She stood at the top of the steps that led below decks, sipping a mug of herbal tea. The sun was setting and the sky was wrapped in tissue-pink clouds. She wondered if she would ever feel normal. How could she let go of the seeds planted so maliciously in her mind by Neill and the authorities?

Earlier, the children had been terribly wound up. Tom in particular could not sit still. Freya wondered if he had attention deficit disorder. The irony of the expression made her feel quite ill — was it *her* attention he needed? Was she giving either of them enough? Had she ever?

'Sit still,' she had snapped when he knocked a glass of orange juice over. He had left the table, toast and jam uneaten, and curled himself into a foetal ball on the sofa, sucking his thumb.

Freya was shocked. She felt helpless. She stared at him lying there like a wounded lamb, her heart contracting.

'Don't suck your thumb, Tom. Only babies do that.'

'Shut up. I can do what I like,' he exploded.

265

She looked at him, stunned. He had never shouted at her.

'Well,' she said, clutching at the remains of her dignity, 'is that how you've learned to behave at Dad's? I suppose Clarissa's kids speak like that and you think it's okay? Well it's not okay in my home. Understand?' She wasn't sure how to deal with this new behaviour, coming from a deep place inside his skinny, still developing body.

'We're fed up with living at Dad's,' said Kirsty, stepping in. Sweet Kirsty, trying to defend her little brother. 'He said he's going to claim money from you to help support us. And he's hired an au pair. I don't want to be looked after by a stranger.'

Freya listened quietly. 'That's probably my fault,' she said. 'Your father was moaning about the extra workload with six children. He suggested you two might chip in a bit and clean up after yourselves.'

'You're joking. We're not allowed to make a mess, or Clarissa grounds us. She's put a list of chores for everyone on a noticeboard in the kitchen.'

'Yes, and we've got the worst jobs,' said Tom. 'I have to clean the downstairs loo. And Kirsty has to take out the garbage.'

'Where's the au pair from?'

'Poland, where else,' said Kirsty. 'They're always from Poland.'

'Is she nice?'

'She's all right, I suppose, but I can tell she doesn't like living here.'

Freya calmed them down with mugs of hot

chocolate. She lit some aromatherapy candles and put a Shostakovich CD on the stereo.

'Let's play Scrabble,' she said.

She let them beat her, and made them laugh with Australian colloquialisms: *blot* (as in 'sitting on his blot all these years'); *bingle* (a car crash); *grouse* (excellent, outstanding); *a house like a pakapoo ticket* (an untidy house). She had them in fits with the expression *ugly as a hatful of arseholes*. She felt strangely guilty about this last one; the court wouldn't approve and nor would Neill. She couldn't believe her ex-husband was so prim.

Eventually they had gone off to bed feeling happy. She tucked them in, stroked their hair off their foreheads, and leaned down to kiss them. Tom let her plant a light peck on his cheek, but Kirsty turned away. 'I'm too old to be tucked in,' she said, her eyes heavy with sleep.

'You're never too old for some TLC from your mother.' Freya smiled. She gave her a hug, and put her cheek against Kirsty's, enjoying its silky softness. 'I love you, Kirsty,' she said.

'I love you too, Mum.' Kirsty had smiled contentedly and closed her eyes.

The love between them was solid. No one could argue with that.

She stood at the top of the steps until the sky was completely black and her cup of tea was drained. Mist drifted over the canal. Ducks settled in the reeds. Swans landed on the watery runway after a long day on the lake.

She wished the boat had an engine. She would sail it to France and disappear with the children to a new life somewhere anonymous. It had all seemed so simple when they were together as a family, the complexity of everything building to a climax unnoticed by her until it was too late.

★ ★ ★

The rest of the weekend was spent at the houseboat. She tried to cheer them up, but they were miserable and sat quietly reading, and playing board games.

'Don't worry,' she said on Sunday evening, 'it won't be long before you can come and live with me.' She should not have said this, she thought, in case it never came true.

They were standing on the humpback bridge waiting for Neill.

'When?' said Tom, eagerly. 'When can we?'

'Soon.'

'Why can't we come now? I don't want to go back to Dad's. Why can't we stay now?'

'Yes,' said Kirsty, 'why can't we stay now?'

'It's not that simple, I'm afraid.'

'We're your children, why can't we stay with you if we want to? Why has it got anything to do with anyone else?'

As Tom turned his large hazel eyes up at Freya, she stifled a gasp. Until this moment it had not occurred to her — his eyes provided more evidence that Connie was wrong about Henry being her father.

Tom's expression alarmed her. He was harbouring a secret. 'What is it, Tom? Is there something you're not telling me?'

He shook his head. Kirsty sniffed and gave him a disparaging look.

'He doesn't want to get into trouble with Dad.'

'If there's something wrong you should tell me.'

'It's Clarissa. She's a bitch. She keeps clipping him around the ears when he doesn't sit up straight at the table, or if he doesn't put the lid down on the toilet, or if he forgets to turn the tap off properly in the bath, little things, stupid things, things that her kids do but she takes no notice.'

'Is that true, Tom?'

Tom nodded. He looked at his shoes.

'The other day she made him stand in the corner for being happy,' said Kirsty. 'He was laughing at something on the telly. I told her she was being, like, totally unfair, and she told me to shut up and mind my own business.'

'What?'

'Don't say anything,' said Tom. His voice was small and strangled. 'Dad'll get angry.'

'Come here.' Freya held open her arms. Tom fell into them and she hugged him close. Tears slid down his flushed cheeks.

'You have to be brave right now,' she said. 'I know it's hard for you, but we have to do as the court says, or it will make things worse. Much worse. If you want to come and live with me, we have to be very clever and very careful.'

'I want to live with you now.'

'I'm trying my best to get everything organised. We have to be patient.'

She crouched down in front of him and tilted his chin up, then put her hands on his cheeks and kissed him firmly on the forehead.

'I love you both more than anything in the world. Remember that. We'll get this sorted out soon, I promise. For now, let's keep this a secret. If we tell on Dad and Clarissa, it will turn into a nasty big fight. Understand?'

Tom nodded. She hugged him again, and his body yielded to hers in that trusting way that only a mother and child can share. At last the tension between them had dissolved. Kirsty came over and volunteered a hug. 'Thanks, Mum,' she said. 'I'm sorry we've been moody.'

The lights of a car appeared at the end of the road. It was Neill.

Rage smouldered in Freya's stomach. She felt she could quite easily punch him right now. She unclenched her fists and took some deep breaths. That good old nurse's staple, control, would save him from getting a black eye.

She said goodbye to the children. Neill's mouth gaped when she hugged them. Normally she patted them lightly on the back and blew them kisses. He sat at the wheel, incensed.

She leaned over the wall and waved. Their faces looked small and anxious at the rear window.

The truth of their love for her was going to hurt Neill far more than playing dirty or fighting.

34

Clarissa's three-storey Victorian house was situated on a narrow, winding street overlooking Richmond town centre. It had a gentrified air. The red brick walls were cloaked in Virginia creeper. It reminded Freya of an orphanage or nursing home, the sort you might see in a Bette Davis movie, with secrets in hidden rooms and locked cellars, and an attic crammed with string-bound documents and trunks full of musty clothes and sepia photographs.

The front door was painted navy blue. It had a brass knocker in the shape of a conch shell. Now there was a doorknocker she would never use. She was burning to walk through that door and rifle through the other life her children lived. She wanted to unearth further evidence against Neill and Clarissa and prove that it was they who were unworthy, not her.

She had parked her car in the shadow of the trees on the opposite side of the street, two houses down. She sat low in the driver's seat, wearing sunglasses and a woollen scarf, even though it was a warm day. She pulled the scarf up over her nose, and propped today's copy of the *Independent* on the steering wheel. If anyone saw her they would be immediately suspicious. She knew she looked silly, but she didn't care. Her heart had raced all night, thinking of the cruelty within. She couldn't bear to think Tom

271

and Kirsty felt unwanted and picked on. At the side of the house was a gate, sturdy and strong and freshly painted. Beyond it stretched a high brick wall mossy with damp and gripped by variegated ivy, marking the boundary between the next-door neighbour's property and Clarissa's. Either side of the gate and curving over it was a stone arch with a bug-eyed gargoyle. A sign on the gate said: *The Vicarage*. Trust Clarissa to live in a house with holy credentials.

Deftly, silently, she pushed the car door shut and locked it.

No doubt they were all just getting up inside. Neill would emerge around ten to ferry Clarissa's children to their various clubs and lessons. Kirsty and Tom had given up their Saturday music classes after the custody hearing, because Neill said they were costing too much. Twisting the knife, he included the excuse that it would be a hassle for Freya to bring them all the way back to Richmond every second Saturday for lessons, as it would interfere with their fortnightly visits, which he was sure she didn't want shortened by unnecessary activities.

She knew she should stop being obsessive and drive home, but the desire to see for herself what it was like inside her children's new home was overpowering. If she saw or heard something she did not like she would barge in and confront them.

Warily, she opened the gate and tiptoed around the side of the house, along a spongy path that led past a white-painted shed, on through a shadowy tunnel of leaves, to emerge on to a broad expanse of perfectly mown lawn bordered by flowerbeds, shrubs and trees. An ugly, incongruous conservatory protruded from the rear of the house like a transparent boil. It was full of plants that climbed up its sweaty walls, their suckers clinging to the glass panels. It made the house seem as though it was trying to eject some horrible matter it no longer needed.

Freya shrank into the shelter of the leafy lair and watched the downstairs windows. Beyond the Laura Ashley curtains she could see the oak kitchen where her children sat with their step-siblings, eating cereal. Even from this distance she could see that Tom and Kirsty were silent and brooding over the contents of their bowls. It was irrational, but she imagined Clarissa had served them cold, lumpy porridge full of weevils, and given her own children Coco Pops or Frosties. She breathed in the warm, damp air and the scent of jasmine. The sky was a bland pale grey this morning; it hung low over the whole of London, like gauze on a belligerent wound.

Thinking she was completely alone, she was surprised to see a figure moving about at the bottom of the garden amongst the shrubs.

It was Neill.

He was tying bamboo stakes together, forming a wigwam. He hated gardening but had taken to it out of spite some years back, to prove he could grow something more beneficial to the family than the 'useless herbs' that Freya produced. Then he discovered it was a good way to get out of other chores, like spending time with the children.

She watched his back as he bent over to push the stakes into the soil. His movements were slow, deliberate. She imagined he would be reciting some sort of Christian mantra, blessing the soil to ensure a hardy crop.

Though he was tall and broad-shouldered, from Freya's position in the shadows he seemed frail and vulnerable. He looked ill; his face was pale and drawn. But he was digging the garden; that took energy, muscle.

It amused her to see him in the garden at such an early hour. He would have come out here willingly, telling Clarissa he wanted to sow now for an early crop, giving the impression of a man who loved gardening and whose knowledge of plants was impressive. He would have said he wanted to grow organic vegetables for the family. Freya knew better.

As she stood in the silence pondering the inner workings of Neill's new household, the sound of a twig snapping made her spin round.

A woman was behind her, closing the gate. She clicked the latch and whirled around, waving a crowbar over her head. Then she looked at Freya, lowered the crowbar and leaned it against the fence.

For a moment they stood staring at each other like sparring cats. Freya tried to speak but her jaw was locked.

Clarissa was a prim-looking woman, with black bobbed hair skimming a pair of sharp bright blue eyes. The skirt of her black suit was too long, too staid, and her shoes were clumpy. Her small, unnaturally rosy mouth was the only sexy thing about her, although Freya thought it looked more like the mouth of a gerbil than a sex-pot.

'What are you doing here?' Clarissa's eyes did not waver from Freya's stricken face.

'Sorry,' said Freya, collecting her wits. 'I was just passing. I wanted to drop some money off for the children.'

'Why not knock on the front door like most people?' Clarissa's plummy vowels made Freya conscious of her Australian twang.

'I did, but no one heard me, act-u-ally.' She tried to enunciate her words without sounding like a hick and cursed herself for even caring. She had often put on an English accent at the hospital, to fend off the tiresome jokes about kangaroos and emus and corked hats.

'I find that hard to believe,' said Clarissa. She narrowed her eyes. 'The knocker is loud enough to wake the dead. Did you try the bell?'

'The bell?'

'Yes. The bell.' Clarissa moved slowly towards her.

Freya shivered. An eerie desire for the truth about her past crept through her veins. She knew perfectly well what it was like inside the big house. She did not need to spy. She needed the facts of her own life. Facts harboured by people she did not know, who had invisibly shaped her character.

She felt a shift of power over her own destiny. She was surrendering at last to strong emotions not honestly faced until this moment, which had been sneaking up on her ever since Connie dropped her bombshell.

Behaving like a stalker, one of those detestable people who focused all their energy on someone else's life because their own was empty, would only make things worse, although she wasn't a stalker, she was a concerned mother. It was a natural reaction to the children's complaints. Perhaps she should have done the sensible thing, and asked Monica Murray to investigate. Neill and Clarissa would be clever, no doubt. They would say the children were happy as Larry, loving the big house, their new siblings — no complaints.

She had told herself she wanted to see with her own eyes that the children weren't being beaten or half starved, but the truth was, she thought they were exaggerating. She had come because she felt it was her duty to make sure. She could not help envying Neill and Clarissa's cosy little world, flawed or not, because it was a world that her children were part of without her.

She looked at the smooth skin on Clarissa's face, the small silver cross around her neck, the large diamond ring on her finger with a gold band next to it, the neatly pressed clothes. She was conscious of her own unruly appearance, the long, crumpled skirt grabbed from the ironing basket (the bottom of which she had not seen for at least three months), her curly hair hanging loosely over a faded denim jacket, her scuffed, muddy shoes, her chipped fingernails.

She squared up to Clarissa, whose attitude

was gratingly superior. 'I thought I'd find Neill in the garden,' she said. 'He always did hate Saturdays. House full of squawking kids, all those silly little domestic jobs to tackle. He loved escaping to the garden when it got too much for him. But he hates gardening, really. Still, I suppose you've found that out by now.'

She rummaged in her shoulder bag and pulled out two ten-pound notes. 'Could you see that the children get this, please? I forgot to give it to them last weekend. It's their fortnightly pocket money.'

She handed the notes to Clarissa, whose cheeks had turned pale.

'As if that's enough to cover the expenses,' Clarissa snorted.

'Maybe you should talk to your husband occasionally,' said Freya. 'If you did, you'd discover that I already pay him maintenance every month. Voluntarily. And if you're that hard up, perhaps you should ditch the au pair. The poor thing's probably hating it anyway.'

'Well really,' Clarissa huffed. 'How dare you speak to me like that.'

'How dare you steal my husband.' Freya's voice came out thick and congested. She pushed past Clarissa and opened the gate. She was elated at having spoken her mind. She felt bold enough now to give warning. 'Be very careful how you treat Kirsty and Tom,' she said. 'They tell me everything, you know. And they'll tell me if you punish them for letting me know, so don't even think about it.'

Clarissa was nursing the spot that Freya had

bumped, as if bitten by a snake. Her mouth was half open trying to form words, but nothing came out except air.

Freya turned and strode across the street to her car. She pulled away, her hands trembling, and when she glanced in the rear-view mirror she saw that Neill and Clarissa were standing at the gate staring after her.

35

Connie removed her suit jacket and flung it over the back of a chair. She threw off her shoes and checked her answer-machine. There was an old message from her boss, and one from her mother. She deleted these and went into the kitchen to heat a chicken and vegetable ready-dinner in the microwave. She took it across to the table by the window and watched the street as she ate.

A medley of bubbly tourists squeezed through the arched door of the pub opposite. She pictured the grizzled locals eyeing them disdainfully in the darkened interior with its snugs and stuffed foxes. When she'd first gone there for a drink on her own one night, she had expected it to be full of cool professionals. Instead there were bigoted old men leaning on the bar eyeing her as though she had just flown in from the planet Jupiter. She wondered where they lived now that the area was so expensive and overrun with foreigners. She imagined they had clung on to flats or houses bought decades ago, when properties here were cheap. The one night she had ventured in and ordered a gin sling, a man with peanut nuggets in his beard made a comment to another man about Connie's 'rubber dinghy' lips. She had overheard a few remarks like this at work, about her looking out of place in the City, and being more at home in the desert with a spear and a piccaninny hanging off her tit.

A woman weighed down with Harrods bags glided past the pub. Connie half expected to see Joan Collins or Madonna sashaying down the street with a chihuahua on a leash. Unlike some parts of London, the streets here were clean and shiny. She imagined some poor soul down on their hands and knees in the middle of the night, polishing the cobbles. Neat window boxes stuffed with expensive bulbs on white-painted ledges. The locked garden in the middle of the square was choked with valuable flowers, and every day a man arrived in a van to empty the dog bin.

She was disappointed there was no message from Freya. Perhaps she had lost her phone number? Connie thought about ringing her, something she considered every evening when she came in from work to the empty, silent apartment. But she was afraid Freya might get annoyed and break contact completely if she made herself into a nuisance. She clung to the thought that Freya might be building up to phoning, that it was just taking her a while to accept things and get her life sorted out. Four weeks had passed since their last meeting, and with every week the phone calls had dwindled.

She did not feel like socialising tonight, but her boss had insisted. He said it would do her good to meet other Australian businesswomen. The usual argument. Connie had reluctantly agreed. Now she had changed her mind. Things were tense at work, she felt unwelcome, colleagues ignored her at meetings and in the cafeteria. Even her equals were indifferent and cold. She felt much more at ease with her American friends. They fussed over her, made her feel special. Five nights out of seven in New York she was out at parties and dinners. Tonight she would stay in and pamper herself with a long bath, and sit up in bed writing home. Her parents expected a letter every week.

At eight the phone rang. She let it click into message mode and listened to her boss, Graham, berate her affectionately.

'I know you're ignoring this call, young lady.'

Connie cringed.

'Get yourself along to that function and meet some fellow Aussies. Make some contacts. Next time you go and see Peggy, you can combine it with business. I've got my eye on some small companies in Australia. You need to network with them tonight, set up a few meetings if poss. Off you go.'

Perhaps Graham was right. She might feel more herself if she met a few Aussies. Perhaps if she made a real effort to start conversations they would see that she had half a brain. She thought about Hopeville, and how undemanding life was there, how popular and visible she was, how cherished.

'All right,' she said to the machine. 'I will go.'

She changed into a black dress, and tied her hair back in a smooth braid. When she looked in the mirror the person she expected to see wasn't there. Instead, a trendy New Yorker stared back.

'Special,' she said softly. 'In Hopeville, I am special.'

★ ★ ★

An official at the main entrance pressed a sticky-backed name tag to Connie's chest. The party was gathering pace in a large stifling room at the back of the Down Under pub near Covent Garden.

'So pleased you could make it,' said a girl as she entered the room. The girl's eyes did not leave the clipboard she was holding. 'Name?'

'Connie Stanley.'

The girl put a tick next to her name.

Connie was the only black woman present, but she was used to the sly looks and overheard comments. She drifted from one cluster of guests to another, like an enthusiastic worker bee, sucking up titbits, never quite replete. She tried several times to join in, or start a conversation, but people glanced sideways at her as though she had gatecrashed the wrong party.

Some people asked her the usual tedious questions with their silent subtext.

'Wasn't it strange, growing up in the States?' *Didn't people mistake you for a black American?*

'Wouldn't you rather be in Australia, with your own kind?' *Eating grubs and lizards?*

'If you don't mind me saying, you remind me of Cathy Freeman before she got fat.' *They all revert after their moment of glory.*

'You're not related to Evonne Goolagong, are you?' *She's the only Aborigine I've heard of who made something of herself.*

'It must've been hard, being at university.' *All Aborigines are thick.*

'Do you ever wonder where your real parents are?' *You probably don't want to, in case they're alcoholics living under a sheet of corrugated tin in the dust, sharing their mattress with an equal proportion of dogs and flies.*

A few people managed to keep the conversation neutral, but Connie knew their curiosity was bubbling beneath the small talk.

She wanted to tell them about the training farm where Peggy and Forbes taught local Aboriginal boys social skills and a sense of responsibility through learning to ride and care for horses, and about how civilised it was, for the outback, with its broad, shaded veranda. She thought of the camp a few miles down the road, the glue- and petrol-sniffing that took place there, the empty turps bottles, the dogs and rubbish and sand flies and the atmosphere of despair, and decided it was too tricky a subject.

A large woman with the build of an elephant and bare white legs stood in front of the guests and rang a small brass bell.

'Good evening, everyone, I'm Tracey Hickman and I work for Jones and Noble.' She tugged at her tight black skirt. Her voice was harsh and nasal. 'I'd like to welcome all you Aussie battlers tonight, and talk a little bit about the role of Australian business-women in London. I've been in London for two years now and the general consensus is we're known for being brash. My experience here has taught me that we need to

283

capitalise on this national quality to get things done. We have to promote ourselves as straight-talking and honest.'

A few people stretched their spines and raised their jaws, nodding in agreement.

'I'm not talking about being rude,' she continued. 'I'm talking about being frank. Cutting out the bullshit, basically, and getting to the point. Some of the meetings I go to here are so long-winded I can feel my hair growing.'

Laughter rippled through the gathering.

During question time, a podgy woman with a bleached bob and diamond jewellery (who Connie thought looked more like a croupier than a financial expert) said that when doing business in Britain they ought to bear in mind the difference in cultures. 'Just because we all speak English, it doesn't mean we do things the same way or have the same outlook. I think we need to respect their customs.'

Tracey Hickman's face turned pink. 'Oh, I'm not saying we should steam-roller their traditions. What we can do is find subtle ways of directing our energy, taking the lead, so that others naturally follow.' She lifted her glass and sipped the contents slowly, then set it down again. 'I don't mean go around behaving pompously. Let the poms do that. I mean use our brashness as a tool of manipulation.'

'You mean be devious,' someone at the front remarked.

'Not at all. I mean use it as an interpersonal communication skill. We weren't endowed with our bouncy charm for nothing.' She looked around at the uncertain faces. 'A better word would be assertiveness. Yeah, that's the word I'm looking for. Be assertive. Use positive messages. With a smile and a joke.'

Later, Connie would remember this night as a turning point. For now, she sipped her juice and fixed her cool gaze on the speaker's face. As the next presenter took his place in front of a vast map of Australia, with place names like Yuendumu and Timber Creek and Lajamanu and Streaky Bay, she slipped away unnoticed, scooping up a kangaroo-meat canapé in a serviette to nibble in the taxi.

★ ★ ★

It struck Freya as ironic, being summoned to the hospital she had worked at for years, to be assessed psychiatrically.

Beverly Harris's office was on the fourth floor. She made Freya wait over an hour, then finally appeared at the door with a clip-board. 'Freya Kirby?' She looked at Freya over the top of her glasses, and when Freya stood up she disappeared from the door, leaving Freya to pursue her like a naughty schoolchild.

Beverly's manner was dour and uncompromising. She wanted to know everything about Freya's life, in particular since losing custody.

'Just be yourself,' Del had advised Freya last time they spoke. But how could she be herself when a complete stranger was cross-examining her, the implication being that she might be mad?

Freya stared through the window at the tops of the trees and the washed-out sky. Beverly's voice hammered her brain. She answered the endless questions vaguely, her mind on other things. The time was coming when she would have to go home to Australia to find out who she was. The urge to get on a plane tugged at her daily now, the reminder constant as jets rose from Heathrow and dipped over the canal.

'Of course, you could agree to an allergy test,' said Beverly, 'to prove you're allergic to alcohol.'

'I'll be damned if I'll do that.' Freya was suddenly alert. 'If the court can't accept my word about this, then tough luck.'

'It's all about genetics, a lot of it,' said Beverly. 'Pot luck.'

Freya gave her a sharp look.

'What you inherit, who you are.' Beverly smiled.

'Neill's a liar,' said Freya. 'And now he's regretting it because he can't cope with six children. He had to hire an au pair. I will tell you again, Miss Harris, I am not an alcoholic and never have been. It disagrees with me. And neither of my parents ever touched the stuff either. They had to stay stone cold sober. They never knew when another body might come in and need sorting out.'

'You're very defensive. You need to calm down, get a grip.'

'Of course I'm defensive. These are my children we're talking about.'

Beverly asked about her parents and her relationship with them. With an enormous effort

286

Freya managed to say all the right things. 'We got on really well. It was a bit weird, growing up in a funeral home, but I was used to it. I didn't know anything else. And they made sure I was well looked after and happy. They were very good parents.'

'What do you mean were? Are they dead?'

'No. They're retired. Same difference.' Freya laughed at her own joke. Beverly smiled. 'Sorry,' said Freya. 'I'm a bit wrung out right now. That wasn't funny. Seriously, they are great parents, I had a wonderful childhood. There was no abuse or anything, if that's what you're thinking.' She slid a thumb under her collar, and pulled it away from her neck. Then she picked up a magazine from the table behind her and fanned her face. 'It's hot in here.'

'I'll open the window.'

Freya made a deliberate attempt to relax. A cool breeze wafted through the open window. A fat pigeon landed on the sill and pecked at some crumbs. Freya could smell freshly cut grass.

'Are you depressed?' Beverly gave her a long, measured look.

'A bit down. But I'm not clinically depressed, or mad.' It's my background that's up the wop, she thought. In different circumstances she would feel inclined to open up about it to Beverly, and perhaps ask her advice about how to cope. 'I feel like hell sometimes. I miss them. Does that sound like a mother who hasn't bonded?'

'You worked throughout their childhood, is that right?'

'Yes. Isn't that what the government wants?'

'Did you have an au pair?'

'No. I managed with Neill's help, and friends. And I sent them to nursery as soon as they were old enough. When Neill was away my friend Del helped out. When she couldn't take over I had a network of friends from the hospital.'

'Would you say this has affected your relationship with them?'

'Obviously it has. But it doesn't mean I don't love them, or that we haven't bonded. They want to live with me, if you must know. They've been asking me for weeks.'

Beverly wrote furiously in a notebook.

'I believe in letting them make their own mistakes,' Freya went on, 'as long as they're not in dire danger of losing life or limb. Perhaps people get the wrong impression because of that. I don't mollycoddle them. The world is a tough place these days, they need to learn how to manage themselves without me propping them up all the time.'

'What about the whole erratic behaviour thing? Mr Kirby said you were acting rather oddly in the run-up to the separation.'

'I guess I was pretty upset.'

'What exactly did he mean by erratic?'

'I couldn't sleep. I rigged up a light so I could work in the garden. The neighbours complained because the light kept them awake. After that I didn't bother.'

'Is that it?'

Freya nodded.

'Well, I must say I've heard of worse things,'

said Beverly. She considered Freya for a moment. 'You seem to have everything under control, in my opinion. Are you sleeping well?'

'Not really. But I do a lot of yoga and my diet's good, so it doesn't affect me too badly.'

Beverly asked more questions about the children, and what they did together and talked about. Freya answered as best she could, but she wanted to go home and telephone Connie.

'There is something in the CWO's report about you talking to yourself. Do you ever hear voices?'

'No.'

'Are you aware of this habit?'

'Yes. I do it to wind the children up. It's a joke, that's all. Sometimes they don't listen, you know, when they're preoccupied with music or computer games, so I start talking to myself. It catches their attention, that's all.'

'I see,' said Beverly.

When Beverly finally let her go she was faint with the strain of it all. She dragged herself back to the car and sat in the driver's seat for a long time, staring straight ahead at a brick wall.

She could not be sure Beverly would write a favourable report. Psychiatrists seemed to notice things that the patient was not even aware of, particular nervous tics or inconsistencies in their answers to questions. She went over the hour-long interview three or four times, trying to remember every word, putting herself in Beverly's position, assessing the likely judgement of her mental and emotional state.

No matter how hard she tried to reassure

herself, she could not help thinking the meeting had gone badly. She had been too defensive, too stroppy. As if she had a chip on her shoulder. She felt tempted to march back in to Beverly's office and apologise.

After a long time she turned on the ignition and drove home.

36

When Freya and the children arrived at Sam's boat the following weekend for the cruise he'd invited her on weeks ago, he was ready to leave immediately. The eastern sky was still turquoise with the last of night, and the air felt damp against her skin. Her mother would call it a sparkly day; everything seemed freshly washed, even the council tenements. A warm, light breeze was plump with the summery smells of jasmine and watercress and warmed timber. Even the constant purr of the distant motorway traffic seemed clean and efficient.

Freya had forgotten her wallet. She looked at the children and said, 'Wait here. I'll have to go back, Sam, sorry.'

'The waterways get busy after nine,' he said, checking his watch.

'I'll be back in five minutes.'

'You needn't worry about money.'

'It's okay, I won't be long. Promise.' She ran down the towpath, careful not to trip on hoses and ropes. She did not want to spend the day penniless in case they stopped at a village or café. She had forgotten her jacket, too. Her head was in a scramble. It had been another restless night, dreams coming at her thick and fast. She was excited and nervous about going on this cruise with Sam and his mother, whom she'd never met. The day had started out sunny and

291

warm and Sam said it would probably stay that way. 'But you never know,' he had added. 'English weather can change suddenly.' An innocuous comment, yet it had stabbed at Freya; the realisation that even Sam thought of her as an outsider.

He had gone to a lot of trouble: a full fridge, nibbles on the breakfast bar, bowls of fruit on tables throughout the boat. His mother, Adele, seemed like a nice person, friendly and unaffected, a tall dark-haired woman in a navy-blue windcheater and jeans. Freya was looking forward to chatting with her as Sam negotiated the canal and locks.

When she reached *Harlequin* she almost fell down the stepladder into the saloon, such was her eagerness for the day to go well with Sam by her side, arms touching, eyes meeting across the wheel. In her excitement she had felt a twinge of apprehension, as though something else might happen today, but she could not be sure; she had been racing all morning to get ready on time and did not have time to stop and listen to her intuition.

Before locking up once more she checked her hair in the mirror. She thought about Sam's dimpled chin and his firm, smiling mouth, and what it would feel like, with immense tenderness, to put her lips on his, this time with meaning. She straightened her hair and applied a light layer of pale lipstick. She had never felt this way with Neill.

Someone banged on the door. There was an urgency to the knock that made her heart thump. She turned around to see who it was. Luke was on the landing stage, peering in, his face pale and gaunt.

'What is it, Luke? You don't look well.'

'It's Mrs Peach.'

'Is she sick?'

Luke nodded. 'She's very ill, I'm afraid. But she won't let me call an ambulance. She's gone a terrible colour.'

'I'll call a doctor.' Freya lifted the receiver and began to dial, but Luke climbed aboard and begged her to hang up.

'Please, just come and see her first.'

'But Luke, if she's sick, she should see a doctor.'

'She's terrified they'll refer her to Social Services for long-term care. She doesn't want to be means-tested, in case they sell her boat to pay for a nursing home.'

'But I'm just off out. They're all waiting — '

'Please?'

'Can't you keep an eye on her till I get back?'

'I'm not a nurse.'

'Oh, all right,' said Freya, sighing. 'You go and tell Sam what's happened. Tell him I'll call him on his mobile later. Maybe I can drive up and meet them at one of the locks further north.'

★ ★ ★

Freya climbed aboard *Midnight Star* and made her way through the narrowboat to where Mrs Peach lay dozing. The boat smelled of damp underwear draped over radiators, and charcoal and peanuts.

Mrs Peach looked up as Freya entered the cabin, and a look of relief registered on her face. She was aptly named: pale ginger hair, apple cheeks dusted with golden rouge, small green eyes like two perfect peach leaves.

'Hello, dear,' said Freya. 'Luke tells me you're not feeling well.'

Mrs Peach smiled. She was too weak to talk. Freya thought she needed a good all-round vitamin supplement, and a daily serving of steamed vegetables and fresh fruit.

She took her temperature; it was raging.

'I'll be back in a few minutes,' she said. She hurried home to put together a herbal first-aid kit and fetch her medical bag.

Mrs Peach had mild bacterial pneumonia. She would need constant care until the worst was over. Freya's first thought on seeing her condition was to ignore her anxieties about being put into a home, and call the hospital.

Back at her bedside she suggested it, gently, as a sensible option. 'It doesn't necessarily mean they'd make you sell up and go into a nursing home. If you make a good recovery, which I'm sure you will, you'll be back home on your boat in no time.'

Mrs Peach was adamant. 'I'm not leaving. If I'm going to die I want to be at home.'

'You're not going to die, Mrs Peach. But you need looking after.'

'If you call the ambulance I'll die all right. I'll make sure of that.' She gave Freya a dark look.

Freya decided to give it twenty-four hours. If there was no sign of improvement after that, she would call an ambulance.

In the galley she prepared a decoction. Using her own glass saucepan she blended dried boneset, cayenne and hyssop, finally adding chopped fresh garlic, comfrey and pleurisy root with a little water. When it came to the boil she placed a lid on the pan to stop the release of volatile oils. While it simmered, she made up a hot-water bottle. After fifteen minutes the mixture was ready to be strained.

Back in the cabin, she took Mrs Peach's blood pressure.

'Any trouble with the old ticker?'

Mrs Peach shook her head. 'Strong as an ox.'

'Are you taking any other medication?'

'I hate all that artificial rubbish.'

'Good. We're on the same wavelength.'

Freya soaked a large square of gauze in the decoction and placed it between two sheets of plastic. Gently unbuttoning Mrs Peach's pyjamas, she placed the compress on her chest. It was an old-fashioned remedy; Freya had used it when the children had chest infections, and swore by its success. When Mrs Peach dozed off, she made an infusion of white horehound, which would act as an expectorant, elecampane, which had wonderful anti-bacterial properties, and echinacea and ginger to build up the immune system.

'Ooh, lovely,' said Mrs Peach, stirring. She smiled at Freya, showing a row of perfect false teeth. Freya gently placed the hot-water bottle on top of the compress, to keep it warm and help release the healing oils.

As she leaned down to steady the cup to Mrs Peach's blue lips, Freya could hear quite clearly the telltale rattle of pneumonic lungs. She had nursed many elderly patients with chest infections back to health, without the use of herbs. Administering to someone outside the hospital was a huge risk, not to Mrs Peach's health, but because if anything went wrong Freya could be blamed, and she would never forgive herself either. But when the tension vanished from the old lady's face she decided it was worth it. She had every faith in the effectiveness of herbs, in spite of bad reports in the media and the hocus-pocus reputation herbal healing attracted. And she knew that sending her to the hospital was not a guaranteed cure. She could just as easily languish on a stretcher in a cold corridor, allowing the illness full rein.

Mrs Peach fell into a peaceful sleep. She did not stir at all when Freya replaced the gauze with another warm piece. After a few hours the fever had not improved, but nor had it worsened, which pleased Freya.

She decided to try a poultice using solid plant material instead of a liquid. In the galley she made a paste of herbs and roots using her own home-made apple cider vinegar. Rather than placing the mixture between two sheets of gauze, she applied a little olive oil to Mrs Peach's chest, to protect the skin and make the poultice easier to remove later, then placed the ground herbs directly on the skin, covered them with gauze, and put the hot-water bottle on top.

Every hour or so she woke the old lady and got her to drink another infusion. Later she applied a soothing liniment to her chest, a blend of eucalyptus, thyme, lavender and tea tree.

Luke came by at six thirty, on his way home from work. 'I told Sam,' he said.

'Oh God.' She had forgotten all about the trip. 'I hope he wasn't too upset.'

'He said not to worry, call him later. I said I wasn't sure if you would, because Mrs Peach was so poorly.'

'What about the kids? Did they mind?'

'Tom was okay, he went with them. But your daughter insisted on staying behind in case you came back to your boat.'

'*What?*'

'It's okay. Ryan's there. He jumped ship when they got to Cowley lock. He said his dad was pretty angry, but he promised he'd look after Kirsty.'

'Well, I suppose they'll be okay.'

Seeing the uncertainty on Freya's face, Luke said, 'It's okay, my love, they were listening to CDs and playing Scrabble when I looked in on them a few minutes ago.'

Freya winced. She wasn't *his love*. 'It's not the kids I'm worried about, it's Sam's reaction. He seems to think the minute our backs are turned they'll be at it like rabbits. Still, I suppose he'll be back soon.'

'Stop worrying,' said Luke. 'It won't be dark for ages yet, so he's still got plenty of time to beat any canal traffic. Tom's in good hands. Sam knows the waterways like the back of his hand. And his mother will make sure Tom's fed and watered. As for Kirsty, she looks like she can handle herself.'

Freya smiled gratefully.

Mrs Peach moaned.

'Shhh,' said Freya, pressing a finger over her lips and ushering Luke out of the room. At the main hatch she slipped £10 into his palm and asked him to take Kirsty and Ryan something to eat. 'Get them some fish and chips, or a pizza. Tell Kirsty I'll be home later to get my nightclothes. Can you come back afterwards to keep an eye on Mrs Peach while I collect my things?'

'Of course.'

'See you later,' said Freya, pushing him firmly through the door.

She went into the saloon and lay on the sofa, and wondered how on earth she had got herself into all this, after her promises to keep to herself and lead a normal life.

★ ★ ★

When she woke around ten o'clock she was pleased to find Mrs Peach still sleeping soundly. Luke hadn't come back as promised, and she was furious with him. She went to collect her nightie and dressing gown from *Harlequin*. Ryan and Kirsty barely looked up when she came on board; they were engrossed in a game of Scrabble. Freya felt greatly relieved.

'Is Mrs Peach okay?' said Kirsty.

'She'll be all right after a good rest and some of my potions.' She gave Kirsty a cheeky wink. Kirsty rolled her eyes and stared at the board game.

'What time did your dad say he'd be back?' Freya looked at Ryan.

Without taking his eyes off the Scrabble board, he shrugged and said, 'Dunno. Looks like he's decided to make it an overnighter.'

'Perhaps I should phone.'

'You can't. I've got Dad's mobile. It's in my pocket. He loaned it to me this morning to text a friend, and I forgot to return it.'

'Damn. Well I suppose you had better stay here until they get back. Find a sleeping bag for Ryan, please, Kirsty. He can bunk down on the sofa.'

'When will you be back?' said Kirsty.

'Mrs Peach is still not right. I'll need to stay with her. Hopefully by tomorrow she'll be a lot better. Do you think they've broken down?' She looked at Ryan.

'Nah,' he said. 'Dad's boat's pretty sound. Even if it did break down he'd soon have it going again. They've probably gone too far north. The canal gets busy on weekends. The locks jam up with traffic and when that happens he usually decides to stay overnight and come back early the next morning, before it gets too busy.'

Well, thought Freya, if no one else is panicking, I won't. 'If he does come back can you please tell him I'm still with Mrs Peach and I'll catch up with him tomorrow. And Kirsty, please give Tom a hot snack and make sure he goes to bed straight away.'

They nodded.

Ryan pored over his Scrabble letters. Freya looked at Kirsty, as if to say, Are you okay with all this? Kirsty gave her a look that meant: Don't worry, you can trust me, Mum.

Freya hurried back to her patient, feeling she was on a journey full of annoying glitches and irrelevant obligations, pulled this way and that by people who meant little to her, as if shredded like a moth in an electric fan.

★ ★ ★

Mrs Peach was over the worst. Freya had been up all night. By three o'clock the following afternoon she was exhausted. She left Mrs Peach to doze and went into the saloon to lie down. She was soon asleep and did not wake until Luke arrived. Freya thought it was around five o'clock, judging by the light outside, although it was so hard to tell in the middle of an English summer; the days were long and light, like two days rolled into one with no night in between. She sat up and yawned. 'What time is it?'

Luke checked his watch. 'Coming up for six.'

'Six? Oh my God. Neill's due to collect the children any minute. I'd better get back. We have to meet him on the bridge. He'll be furious if we're late. I hope Sam's there. Is Tom okay?'

Luke nodded. 'They got back early this morning. I just called in. Sam said he didn't want to disturb you and he'd see you later. And he said don't worry, Tom's fine.'

'Thank God for that.' She gathered up her belongings and said goodbye to Mrs Peach, who was sitting up in bed reading a copy of *Woman's Own*.

Back at *Harlequin* there was no sign of the children. She hurried along the towpath and knocked on Sam's door. 'Sorry for missing the trip. Are the children here?'

Sam shook his head. 'They've gone.'

'Oh God.' Her heart sank.

'I fetched Ryan home this morning,' said Sam. 'I have to say, I didn't think it was very wise, leaving him alone with Kirsty all night.' She could hear a Van Morrison track droning on about loss and pain in the background.

'They were fine,' she said defiantly. 'I looked in late last night. And Luke kept an eye out too.'

'Luke? I wouldn't trust him.'

'Calm down, will you? They were fine. You have to learn to trust them.'

'Let's not get into that again.'

'Where have Tom and Kirsty been all day?'

'Back and forth between your boat and mine. I gave them breakfast, and lunch. Neill came for them just now. You missed him by three minutes. He looked a bit angry.'

'Did you speak to him?'

'I was about to explain, but he stormed off.'

'He's so unreasonable. I honestly don't know what's wrong with him.'

'The kids were on your boat at the time. They were perfectly okay, but I guess he didn't think so. I'm sorry, Freya. I didn't know he was picking them up. They forgot to mention it.'

301

'Oh God. Was Ryan with them?'

He gave her a reproachful look. 'Now who's being paranoid?' he said. 'I sent him down to check on them and he stayed for a while to keep them company. I was just about to go and get them all, actually, to give them supper, when Neill arrived.'

'Don't get me wrong,' she said. 'You know I trust Kirsty. And last night I saw that she was absolutely fine on her own with Ryan. But Neill will jump to conclusions. He'll say I neglected them, leaving them to be looked after by an unreliable stranger all day, and then finding Ryan there . . . I just hope they were doing something innocent when he showed up.'

'They were listening to music in the saloon, according to Ryan. Oh, and just for the record, I'm hardly a stranger any more.' He looked hurt. 'You can easily explain, you know. Surely Neill's not that obstreperous? Give him a ring.'

'You don't understand. He's vicious right now.' Thinking about Neill exhausted her, as if warding off his mean-spiritedness was sacrificing her health.

'He is rather unpleasant, I must say.' Sam gave her a pitying look which made her even more irritated.

With a huge shrinking of her heart she wondered if the whole enterprise of getting the children back was an impossible dream. For every step forward she seemed to be taking five back. Without thinking, she began to open up — too much, she knew, as the words tumbled out uncontrollably.

'He said if Kirsty and Ryan were left alone again together and he found out, he'd take her to the doctor for a pregnancy and HIV test.'

Sam looked alarmed.

She had laughed down the phone at this suggestion and told Neill to stop being ridiculous. Now she was seriously worried. Kirsty would be mortified if Neill kept his word and marched her off to the doctor. What if he took her to a VD clinic? She was beginning to regret helping Mrs Peach. She should have called an ambulance, like any sensible person. Neill would be gripping the steering wheel all the way home like a man coming back from winning a war, smug, gloating, triumphant. She had given him exactly what he wanted, that extra bit of evidence he needed to maintain custody. The proof that he was right: his ex-wife was crazy, and negligent to boot.

37

She woke to the soundless hush that accompanies snowfall. It was mid-June, officially summer. The weather was so unpredictable in Britain, and right now it seemed to reflect her life. She put her head out of a window under the lee of the ledge, blinking at the white world outside. After making a cup of tea she stood in the saloon, staring in shock and disbelief at the sugary garden. She dared not go outside in case all was lost. She could not bear any more disappointments or disasters. She hoped it was snowing in Richmond. The children would be standing at their bedroom windows, where they had a view right across the Thames Valley towards Heathrow. She imagined them grinning like monkeys, watching the snow fall over the trees next to the river. It was a leafy, almost rural view that the children loved, a view that belied the density of traffic and life buzzing through the suffocating streets. She longed to telephone them and share their excitement, the way she had during other snowfalls. Her heart felt heavy at the idea of communicating her pleasure down a phone line.

She thought of the magical effect snow had on people. It forced them to stop and reflect on the power of nature and reassess their frantic lives. Traffic was restrained and slow; drivers surrendered to delays and tuned in to Radio One, or phoned their wives or lovers, or read the paper over the steering wheel as they inched along the M25. Snow on the railway tracks and roads could not be argued with. Trapped in their vehicles and railway carriages, people happily accepted their fate. They could be late in and not be sacked. Animals in fields lifted their heads in forlorn surprise. It wasn't supposed to snow in June. The only people who panicked were officials, glumly forecasting huge losses of revenue. Morose schoolchildren suddenly became hyper. Somewhere in a maternity ward a young mother stared at her newborn child, then at the huge flakes falling against the murky window. It did not take much to turn the world upside down and make people think.

After dressing she went outside. The brightness made her lift her arm over her eyes, as if repelling a thug. She plodded into the garden, enjoying the silence and the soft crunch of her shoes. It was bitterly cold, a shock after the warmth of the last few days. She could feel the skin on her face tightening.

Many of the more delicate herbs were beyond rescue, and a whole row of basil had been reduced to brown slime. These plants were important to her plans. Now she would have to order bottles of tincture from her supplier in Bristol. She would need to dip into her savings.

When she had finished cloching the plants that were still alive, she went into the summerhouse to do some work. It had been a long and lonely week so far. She had thought about phoning Neill to explain, but she knew he wouldn't listen.

She sat at the table sticking labels on bottles, trying to keep her spirits up. But it was no use fighting it. She laid her head on her folded arms and wept. When the tears had subsided she fell asleep in a pool of salty mascara.

By mid-afternoon the snow had melted. She washed her face under the standpipe and stood on the towpath surveying the scene. There were traces of snow in hollows and crevices and on roofs. Water trickled off trees and branches bounced back to their original positions. Spirals of steam rose from boat decks like white flames. In the distance a siren wailed, and the roar of traffic was amplified as wheels spun through the slush.

The phone rang from inside the boat. She hurried aboard and picked up the receiver. It was Neill.

'Tom's school are having an arts and crafts sale today, but I've got an emergency church meeting to attend,' he said. 'Part of the roof has caved in after the snow. Could you go along in my place? Ania will be there; you can introduce yourself. She's very friendly and speaks quite good English.'

There was no point mentioning last weekend. He was convinced he had the upper hand, she could tell by his supercilious tone. She did not like being asked to stand in for him at the school, and felt annoyed that she had not been told about this event earlier and given the choice about attending herself. She felt superfluous and humiliated.

After putting down the phone, her irritation

soon melted and in its place came a rush of adrenalin. She dashed around the boat getting ready. Halfway through showering, the water ran dry. There was no time to replenish the tanks. She hurried outside and filled several saucepans, carried them inside and heated them on the hob. Eventually she was able to rinse her hair over the sink.

In her haste to make up for lost time she kept dropping things. While cleaning her teeth in the cramped bathroom, she knocked a jar of bath salts off a shelf and it smashed in the bath.

She stopped for a moment and tried to steady her nerves. Her breathing was shallow and her fingers trembled. 'I love my children,' she said out loud, with absolute conviction, tears welling up. Her voice had a throaty, primeval quality, gushing from the depths of her being.

★ ★ ★

The school hall was choked with pushchairs, and mothers all talking at once, and children rushing about tugging at skirts, and people hovering over tables groaning with home-made crafts.

When Tom saw her walk through the door he bolted towards her across the room. For a split second she thought he was going to fling his arms around her, but he stopped short, and after a bright 'Hi, Mum' hovered close by, suddenly awkward in front of his friends.

Freya made her way around the tables, examining the handmade goods, alert for

307

someone with a Polish accent. Later, she and Tom sat in one of the classrooms, which had been turned into a café for the event, eating home-made chocolate rice cakes and bland cucumber sandwiches.

'There's Ania,' said Tom, pointing at a leggy girl in a mini-skirt. He waved and beckoned her over.

'Hello,' said Freya, standing up and holding out her hand. Ania took it in hers and smiled. 'I'm Freya, Tom's mother.'

'Yes, yes, I have seen picture of you,' said Ania.

'Would you like something to drink?'

'No, please. But cake would be nice.' She winked at Tom.

He offered her a rice cake and she bit into it hungrily.

'Why don't you go and find something for Kirsty?' said Freya. She handed Tom two one-pound coins and he dashed off.

'Has the snow made you homesick?' said Freya.

'A little,' said Ania shyly.

'Is this your first trip to England?'

'No, I have been before many times, as au pair.'

'Are you a student?'

'Yes.'

Freya sensed Ania was unhappy. She seemed tired and rundown.

'I hope my two aren't causing you any trouble,' she said.

Ania's face brightened. 'Oh no, Mrs Kirby.'

'Please, call me Freya.'

'No, it's not the children.'

'Are they working you hard, Clarissa and Neill?'

'The English are very strange. They work, work, work all day long. There is no time to relax.'

'Do you get your weekends off?'

'Only Saturday. On Sundays I go to the church with the family. It takes long time in morning to get ready. Six children. All those clothes.'

'Do you cook for the children too?' Freya knew she should not be asking so many questions, but she couldn't help it, and Ania seemed lonely and only too willing to open up.

'There are no breaks in the day, and you rush at everything, especially eating, and especially lunch. Mr Kirby stands at the kitchen bench stuffing a sandwich down. In Poland we enjoy our food so much more and we always try to eat something hot in the middle of the day. The weather I can put up with, but the food in this country is terrible. When I go home I eat and eat until I almost burst.' She laughed.

'Isn't Clarissa a good cook?'

'She cooks frozen meals only. The funny thing is she watches all these programmes about cooking, all extravagant dishes, but I have never seen her cook. The children eat chicken nuggets, pizza and chips. Freezer to oven. She buys too much at the supermarket, sometimes we need two trolleys. But there is a lot of waste. Only your Tom and Kirsty eat vegetables, so Clarissa does not buy them because she says it is

309

uneconomical. And fruit goes bad and has to be thrown out.'

'Really?' Freya did not want to take sides in too obvious a way, but secretly she was appalled.

Ania continued, 'You know, the children are lovely, although Clarissa's can be difficult. They are very spoilt. They all have computers and televisions in their rooms and DVD players and videos. Children in Poland would not believe it. And to school they take their mobile phones, computer games and Walkmans. I know our cultures are very different and this is a much wealthier country, but it is madness to give a child so much. They appreciate nothing. In one house where I worked in Ealing the daughter had twenty-five Barbie dolls and they were all thrown in a toy box. It's very sad. They never play outside, not even when it is sunny. Everything is timetabled, violin lessons, ballet, swimming, tap dancing. They cannot do anything alone, an adult has to be with them all the time. So they do not go out. Not even Kirsty. She should be out with her friends, but she is not allowed. The children have no imagination, no conversation. Parents have no time to give the children and they feel guilty, so they buy them things. The house is wonderful, so big and comfortable and cosy. But to be honest . . . ' She glanced over her shoulder and lowered her voice, 'I do not like working for your husband and Mrs Kirby. They are alcoholics.'

'What do you mean?'

'Every night they have a bottle of wine with their dinner and then they start arguing. It's terrible. The children have to stay in their rooms straight after dinner. The atmosphere is very sad. As soon as Mrs Kirby returns from work she has a glass of wine, and for dinner they always open a new one.'

Freya was astounded. She tried to be nonchalant, but it was hard to hide her surprise.

'In Poland young people do not drink,' Ania continued. 'I have seen Mrs Kirby offering your daughter alcohol at the dinner table. She said it is a European thing to do, that in France and Italy drinking is encouraged so that when children turn eighteen they do not go crazy. And you know the other children never listen, and they nag and nag until they get their own way. Mr Kirby tries to be strict, and he punishes them, but the children are tough as nails and do not care. You know, Mrs Kirby — Freya — your children are not happy living with their father. Mrs Kirby is unfair with them.'

'So I've been told.' Freya felt a stillness in her heart. She turned and scanned the room for Tom and caught a glimpse of him at the jewellery stall. She looked at Ania, the gravity of this information made her feel ill. Here was something she could and would use to win the children back — the same excuse that Neill had given the court for justifying custody. Of course he and Clarissa were not alcoholics. A bottle of wine with dinner between two did not constitute an addiction. Although Neill did seem to have a low threshold with drink, probably because of his diabetes. She was furious to think he had accused her of something he did himself, even if it was in moderation, and she no longer felt pangs of guilt for calling him a hypocrite.

Ania continued to moan about conditions at other homes she had worked in, but Freya was not really listening now. She wanted to rush outside and telephone Nadine on the mobile Connie had given her. She wondered if it might be a bit dramatic, dashing out to make the call? She could easily ring tomorrow, from home. But she felt an overwhelming urgency. She shifted uneasily on her chair, not sure what to do, rage burning her throat.

She breathed deeply and sat back in the chair, trying to relax her shoulders.

Ania said, 'Of course, Mr and Mrs Kirby go to church every Sunday, so that is good, I like that. At home I go too, with my family. And they are very strict about the children saying their prayers. But it is very bad that they drink so much. They should go to a Catholic priest and confess.' She pushed the plate of cakes away and flicked her long hair off her shoulders. 'Of course, there is one thing I like about the English. They know how to enjoy themselves and they have good sense of humour. But they do like to . . . how do you say it? . . . take the mickey out of people, especially foreigners. That I do not like at all. The joke wears thin, you know?'

'Yes,' said Freya quietly, 'I do.'

★ ★ ★

Kirsty grinned as she came out of a side door and spotted Freya. She kissed her cheek lightly, like a baby bird pecking its mother, and Freya looked at her, surprised. It was not like Kirsty to show any affection. Freya smiled and they linked arms. Walking to the car, she stopped and, glancing around, said in a low voice, 'Did Dad take you to the doctor this week, by any chance?'

'Yes, he did,' said Kirsty. 'How did you know?'

'He mentioned he might.'

'I ran away,' said Kirsty. 'I got the bus home. He was furious.'

'Was it your GP?'

'No, Mum. It was an STI Clinic. I knew what it was as soon as we went inside and sat in the waiting room. There were posters about it. I asked him what we were doing there, and he just looked at me and said it was because of Ryan. I couldn't believe it. There was no way I was going to let any of those people touch me, so I ran out the door. He came after me, but luckily a bus came along before he could catch me up.'

'What happened then?'

'He grounded me for the week, but that's not exactly going to affect my life; he won't let me out anyway, so big deal. He's full of crap, Mum.'

'Don't use that word.'

'Why not? It's the truth. He's stupid.'

'That doesn't mean you have to swear.'

'You believe me, don't you, Mum?'

'Of course I do.'

'I'm not like that. Me and Ryan are just friends. I don't even like getting changed in front of my friends at the swimming pool. There's no way I'd want to be seen by a boy. Especially Ryan. You know how much I hate my legs.

Besides, I couldn't handle anything like that yet.'

No, thought Freya, overcome with shame, I didn't know that you hate your legs.

Inside the car Kirsty and Tom chatted away happily to Ania. After the initial excitement a familiar atmosphere settled over them, as Freya eased the car through the afternoon traffic. She asked the usual questions about school and thought of all the other mothers doing the same, wondering if they used a different tone of voice to hers — more bonded, more attuned to their children's fears, hopes, dreams. There would be so much she would never share as long as they lived apart. She could not bear to think of Clarissa being privy to their intimate secrets and milestones before she was.

Tom got out a new Game Boy and began stabbing the buttons. Kirsty put her head-phones in and nodded along to the music.

When Freya stopped the car outside Neill and Clarissa's, Neill appeared at the front door as if he had been watching for them through the window. Without thinking, Freya raised her hand to wave, then lowered it slowly into her lap. He did not want her friendship, he was finished with her. She had to accept it and move on. In spite of this, she began to get out of the car. She wanted to explain about Mrs Peach being ill and not wanting to go to hospital, and that the children had been perfectly safe, and that Kirsty had confided her personal vow of chastity.

The children kissed her goodbye and ran up the path and through the front door. They did not stop to greet Neill and he clearly did not

314

expect any gesture of affection.

'Nice to meet you,' said Ania. She looked away from Freya guiltily and hurried up the path. At the door she nodded curtly at Neill and slipped inside. Before Freya had a chance to even open the gate, Neill had turned and followed Ania inside, slamming the door hard.

Freya stood for a moment, trying to decide whether or not to knock. It would make no difference what she said; he was in a mood with her and that meant he would not listen. Telling Nadine was her only hope.

She went back to the car, climbed in and pulled away from the kerb, tears biting her eyes as she tried to remember the route home.

38

There was an air of uncertainty in the office this morning. People were fretting over the unstable market. There was talk of capitulation. Heavy indiscriminate selling in Europe yesterday had prompted some analysts to suggest that the markets had finally reached the point of defeat.

Connie sat at her desk in her twelfth-floor office studying share price graphs in the *Financial Times*. Like everyone else in the building, she was feeling uneasy about the future. Investors were nervous, bankers were nervous, everyone was nervous.

She was feeling disillusioned with the business world. It had started creeping up on her when war was declared on Iraq. This was the second time she'd doubted her career. Three years ago her faith in capitalism had been shaken after the mobile phone and dot com boom. Companies her investment trust had turned down because they had no merit had gone on to achieve soaring valuations. Some of the excesses and the way companies were sold were, in her view, outrageous. Her faith was restored a little when some of the biggest culprits went out of business. 'Capitalism works when people don't stuff other people,' she told a colleague at the time. 'You have to deal with the same people next year, and in five years' time. Focusing on this year's bonus just proves that people have lost their values.'

She remembered this conversation because she was surprised at her own reaction. She often thought of it, especially in times of uncertainty. She had not realised she would feel so strongly about opportunism and greed.

When she had discussed it with her parents, Donald said her attitude made perfect sense. 'We raised you to be honest, fair and hardworking. I'm not saying what you do isn't hard work, but it seems a bit too cut-throat for someone with such a gentle nature.' She knew they were disappointed in her decision to go into finance. They had expected her to get involved with the bakery, but she had had enough of hot bread and American suburbs. She wanted to live in the city and travel.

Feeling flustered by the crowds in the underground and the stifling air, she made her way home and changed into jeans and flat shoes, and went for a walk through Regent's Park. It was busy with nannies pushing prams, and au pairs supervising toddlers, and fat Middle Eastern women in black robes watching their offspring dart across the lawn spooking pigeons. She felt every pair of eyes following her as she hurried along the footpath that led straight across the park to the zoo. She noticed that everything smelled sharper: the warm tarmac and the distinctive scent of freshly bedded pelargoniums. She sat for a while on a bench and her nostrils were assailed with the smell of dog shit and a rubbish bin full of half-eaten hamburgers and greasy fish and chips. She got up and strode away, feeling a little sick, and presently the path opened on to a bitumen amphitheatre with a fountain in the middle and water gushing from the mouth of a lion. She sat on the edge of the fountain enjoying the sound of the water and the sun on her face.

I am sick of working with people who look straight through me, she thought. I need to go back to where I belong, even if I don't understand what any of it's about.

When she got home it was still light. She knew what she had to do, and nothing would stop her now that she had made the decision. Feeling perkier than she had in a long time, she put a ready-meal in the microwave and treated herself to a glass of white grape juice from a bottle she kept in the fridge. After dinner she had a shower and dressed in a tracksuit. She sat by the window writing postcards to her friends in New York. They would stick them on their fridges alongside the ones she had sent from Australia of Aboriginal art.

There were no messages from Freya. She stared at the phone for a long time, then suddenly it rang. She jumped, startled by the noise. She pounced on the receiver, hoping it was Freya.

It was her mother.

'Hi, Mum.' She tried to sound cheerful, but her voice was thick with emotion.

'Are you okay, Connie?'

'Yeah, Ma, I'm swell.'

'We're so proud of you, dear,' said Florence. 'It can't be easy over there. We know London isn't the friendliest of cities.'

'I'm real fine, Mum, honest.'

'Have you been to Buckingham Palace yet?'

'I've been to Australia House twice. And the National Gallery.' When she was a student at Cambridge, they'd nagged her to visit all the historic sites, but she'd been too caught up with studying and never got around to it. This trip was supposed to be the time for sightseeing, but the thought of trailing around looking at the fruits of colonialism and the Empire made her blood run hot through her veins.

'We're so proud of you,' said Florence once more.

'It's all because of you,' said Connie, for the millionth time. 'I don't know where I'd be without you and Dad.'

She meant this, she really did. But her gratitude was laced with loss and longing. She stood by the window, talking into the phone, watching beautifully coiffed women pushing their waxed legs into BMWs and Mercedes, and slim men in crisp black suits marching home from the Tube station with a copy of *The Times* under one arm, briefcase stiff in the other hand.

Florence filled her in on all the news and gossip from home. Connie was only half listening. Her head felt foggy. The apartment smelled of artificial air freshener — the cleaner had just been. Connie felt a strong desire to fill the rooms with the smell of something real, like vegetable soup or mown grass. Sometimes, when she sat by the window, she thought she saw Ester in the square below. Back in Virginia she once thought she had seen her in the supermarket checkout queue, and on another occasion in one of the aisles at the library. She saw a nervous woman, anguish eating her eyes. In the rhododendrons surrounding the square she imagined a group of white-coated professionals trying to work out how to sneak up on Ester and, with the least degree of fuss, dispatch her to a hospital.

She sighed. All her life Ester must have been grieving for daughters who were not even dead.

'Have you met your sister?' said Florence.

'Yes,' said Connie. 'I've met her.'

'Are you happy?'

'Of course I'm happy.'

'What's she like?'

'Very pretty, with a noble nose. She's nothing like me. She's white.'

'Do you get on with her?'

'Like a house on fire, Ma.' Connie wasn't at all surprised by Florence's lack of reaction to the news that Freya was white. She had often said colour was never an issue for her: 'I can see past all of that, and so can your father.' Connie believed this wholeheartedly, for they had proved it time and again with both customers and friends.

'I'm glad,' said Florence. 'I'm so happy you've got two sisters. Now you must make sure you keep in touch with them both. You'll be able to write them. They might want to come visit you here some day.'

'I'm sure they will, Ma.'

'Your father and I miss you.'

'My contract is up in July. I was thinking of

paying Peggy a visit. And I'm hoping Freya might come and meet her too. I won't spend too long there. I'll be home before you know it.' She hated herself for lying, but she did not want to break the news of her decision to stay in Australia for good just yet.

'We'll be waiting,' said Florence, in the customary tone that emphasised Connie's duty. 'Your room is always ready for you. The house isn't a home without our beautiful daughter.'

39

Peggy was out at the pens, her bare, purposeful feet gripping the ironbark railing, when her mobile phone rang.

'When you comin' home again, aye?' Her giggle rippled down the line.

Connie had been to Australia twice since her adoption. The last trip was just prior to arriving in London. She had stayed six weeks at Paradise, Peggy's home; in naming it, Forbes had taken his characteristic ironic humour to extremes, for the station was dusty, hot and plagued with flies.

Peggy had kept reminding her Australia was her true home. 'Not that place,' she always said, waving an arm in the general direction of America. Connie had laughed and said, 'You reckon?' Underneath she hated the place, and in spite of her attempts to get to grips with her spirituality, she was no closer to feeling Aboriginal than she was to flying. The kinship system, the Dreamings, the complex Laws, it all left her baffled. She wanted to understand and tried hard, but no matter how many hours she spent in the shade of the casuarinas with the Elders, listening to their tireless stories and teachings, she just didn't get it. Sometimes she insulted the Elders with her stupid questions and they punished her by ignoring her for days on end. She would sit in the homestead kitchen, watching them through the window as they painted their bodies with ochres and sang up Dreamings. They stayed there all day, merging with the darkening blue pools of shade under the gum trees, and Connie would gaze at them until her jealousy made her break something, a cup or a plate, and then someone would finally come running in from outside to see what was up, satisfying her fierce need for attention. She was confused by her own behaviour; it had changed as soon as she got off the plane at Alice, as if she had stepped into the bitter skin of a lemon, and yet the ferocious desire to be there was undeniable.

'What are you doing today?' she said down the phone.

'Watchin' the old coot break in Pepper, his new bay colt, aye.'

Peggy laughed like a drain and Connie could hear her slapping her thigh. Peggy was always laughing. She laughed if one of her boys tried to mount a horse on the wrong side. She laughed when one sat in the saddle as though he'd been born on a horse. She laughed at a boy's broad grin when a bucking horse responded to his voice. She laughed when her husband hugged her, or when a new boy cried for his dog. And sometimes she laughed at nothing.

Connie held the phone up towards the ceiling so that Peggy's lovely rich voice lived in the apartment for a moment.

'You there, sister?' said Peggy.

Connie pressed the receiver to her ear. 'Yes. I'm here. I'm coming to see you again. Might stay for good this time.'

'I've got your bed ready for you, aye,' said Peggy, not a bit surprised. 'Forbes said we can go bush if we want to. He don't mind. So long as I cook 'im up somethin' at night. He's a good bushman, but he can't boil an egg without burnin' it, aye.'

She let out a long peel of laughter, rounding it off with a loud snort.

'Can I bring someone else for you to meet?' said Connie.

There was a long pause.

'Freya? You bringin' her?'

'I have to tell you something,' whispered Connie, as if someone might be listening. She glanced around the empty apartment. 'I don't want you to get a shock, so best I tell you now.'

She held the words back for a moment, almost too afraid to say them aloud, then, with a rush said, 'She's not black.'

'Cooo . . . That's funny, aye,' said Peggy.

There was a long silence at the end of the line.

Connie could hear horses whinnying in the background, the soft clicking of hoofs in the dust, a whip cracking. She could almost smell the eucalyptus trees and sweaty saddles, the strong body odour of young men out riding all day, and coming home to sausages sizzling on the huge barbecue near the back veranda.

'Henry's her real father,' said Connie firmly. 'I'm sure of that, now we've met. This means we've got a different father to her. What do you think about that?' She tried to sound passionate, to lend the news about Freya the sort of emotional weight it deserved.

Connie waited; Peggy said nothing.

'Don't get too excited. She might say no when I suggest she comes with me. She's just getting back on her feet after her divorce. And she's trying to win her kids back. Her husband's got them.'

'We've still got the same mother, aye,' said Peggy softly. 'Got the same blood.'

'Yes, I know. But she's in shock, seeing me. Confused. She might be heading for a breakdown.'

'You taking her to see Henry?'

'Nah. I'm coming to see you. She can go and see him on her own, if she wants to.'

'Are you and Freya gettin' on?'

Connie waited a minute, not sure how to answer.

'When I ring she makes excuses about being busy,' she said at last. 'She's pretty caught up with her neighbours and their problems, and worried about getting her kids back. But we went out together a coupla times.'

'Sounds like she needs a proper friend, aye.' Peggy's voice was thoughtful.

'She's got plenty of friends.'

There was another long silence.

'What are you thinking?' said Connie.

'You bring that girl here.' Peggy sounded worried. 'She needs to spend time with her sisters.'

'I can't force her. She's got the tickets, I bought them myself, as a gift. Anyway, what about Forbes?'

'Don't you worry about the old coot. I'll sort

him out.' Peggy glanced around and saw Forbes lifting a box of oranges — the boys' morning tea — on to a table under an old peppermint gum.

'How is he?' said Connie, conscious that Peggy was watching her husband as she spoke.

'Stubborn old bugger.' Peggy laughed, her voice louder so Forbes could hear her teasing. 'If Forbes was running this country it'd be all blacks and we'd all be breeding bloody horses.'

Connie could hear a muffled response in the background. 'What'd he say?' she said.

'He said the boys give 'im a bloody headache. Just a minute.' She put the phone down on a table, and Connie could hear her telling the boys to line up for their oranges.

When she picked up the phone again, she began to tell Connie about some of the new arrivals since her visit.

'Two boys from Melbourne with an alcohol problem; another one from Broome with light fingers, and three brothers hunted out of Darwin for stealing petrol, and next month we're expecting some fellas who have been living rough for three months. Some tourists found 'em and brought 'em in, aye.'

To Peggy's boys, she was their emotional salvation. She knew that. They all got plenty of love and regular meals. She washed and mended their clothes. They each had their own bed with a small cupboard. Some of them called her Mum. She was always available with a willing shoulder for tearful boys unsure of their future and ashamed of their past, her devotion to Forbes and the boys equalled only by her contagious sense of humour.

'The government's talking about shuttin' us down, but we'll keep going somehow. We don't need their fuckin' help.'

Connie had not heard a word Peggy had said. 'I'm not sure you'll like her,' she said.

'Aye?' said Peggy.

'Freya. She's pretty weird.'

Connie bit her lip against the strange ache in her heart. She didn't want to give Peggy the wrong impression of their sister. But there was something odd about Freya that she couldn't put her finger on, something that riled her.

'Might be best if she doesn't come. She's got her own life now. I don't think she took too kindly to me turning up out of the blue. It's given her a goddamn shock.'

'Nah,' said Peggy. 'She's just playin' for time, I reckon. Same as I did. Same as you. It takes a lot of guts, facing up to your real self. She'll be here, you watch. I reckon the place'll soon get under her skin. Same way it's gettin' under yours, aye.'

40

Deep inside *Harlequin* Freya lay on her bunk and stared vaguely at the mould growing around the rim of the porthole. She had cleaned the windows four weeks ago and already the fungus was fighting back. She was just dozing off when the phone rang. She hurried up the steps into the saloon.

It was Connie. Her voice sounded small and hesitant.

'Peggy and me, we'd like you to come and spend some time with us at her farm,' she said. 'You've got the tickets. It's just a matter of booking the flights. Please think about it. Peggy's dying to meet you.'

'Oh,' said Freya. She did not know what else to say.

'Please, Freya? It'd do you good. And you said the appeal might take twelve months to come up.'

'I'm very busy at the moment, but maybe in the future.'

'Well, at least think about it.'

'I have been. But I've got a lot to organise before the appeal.'

'Why don't you forget everything for a while and come away? Find someone to look after your boat. Peggy thinks you should come home.'

'Is that right?' Freya wished she could find the courage to tell Connie she didn't want anything

328

to do with her or Peggy until after the appeal. And that she was afraid to confront her past because it would alienate them if she spoke the truth about being part-Aboriginal. It was easier to ignore it for now and get on with life as she knew it, rather than try to create something from a life that didn't exist.

'Please don't take it the wrong way. It's the timing. That's all.' She was trying to be dignified and kind about the whole thing.

'Why are you being so cruel to me?' Connie felt bitterly disappointed by Freya's reticence.

Freya thought about this remark for a moment. It took her by surprise. Connie was normally so jovial and easy-going.

'Self-preservation, I suppose,' she said finally.

'I don't want to hurt you, Freya. I thought it might help if you came home and got to know me and Peggy.'

'We haven't got anything in common. None of us have, if you think about it. Why try and force something that's not there?'

'That's not true. We may be a different colour, and we grew up apart, but we've still got the same mother. The judge would understand, I'm sure. This is a big thing in your life. Finding out about your past.'

'You don't know what they're like, these welfare people. They don't care about me, or Neill. It's the children they want to see sorted. That's all I ever hear: 'We will do whatever's best for the children, Mrs Kirby.' That's how it should be, I know. But the only interest they have in me is whether I'm a fit mother. If I go gallivanting off to Australia they won't look on it favourably.'

'Why don't you talk to the welfare officer? Try and get her on your side?'

'I'd rather set alight to myself than confide in Monica Murray. She thinks I'm a lowlife because I live on a boat. Even my GP wrote in my notes that I live on a houseboat, as though it's a reflection of my intelligence. I had no idea when I bought the boat that people would be so judgemental about it. I'm sorry, Connie. I just can't leave England at the moment.'

'Why don't you tell Monica you are going to visit your parents? That's a reasonable kinda desire, to spend time with your family. I mean, the judge can't be that callous.'

'In some ways I don't think it would matter what I did now. Neill seems to have twisted the knife enough to make it stick.'

'Isn't there anything I can do to persuade you?'

'I'm afraid not.'

Connie's mood was flattened. 'I'll write to you when I get to Peggy's.' Then she said, 'I love you,' and there was an uncomfortable pause, during which Freya cringed, because she realised Connie was waiting for her to say *I love you too*.

After hanging up Freya had to practically peel her fingers off the telephone receiver, she had been gripping it so tight.

She padded outside in her slippers and dressing gown, to collect the mail. As she usually did before stepping outside, she glanced up and down the towpath to make sure no one was lurking.

Inside the box there was a letter postmarked Knightsbridge, addressed in neat, small handwriting. A letter from Connie. She went inside and opened the creamy envelope with a knife. A handwritten letter in tiny modern script, no loops or fancy dots, on a sheet of unlined paper.

Dear Freya,

In case I couldn't reach you by phone I'm writing. We'd love to see you in Australia. I've enclosed Peggy's address near Alice Springs, and her mobile phone number.

Please think about it. You won't regret it, I promise. Peggy's a wonderful person. You will feel better about everything if you come home. It will make you stronger.

I've loved meeting you. It's been a dream come true. I only wish we could've spent more time getting to know one another. I do understand what you're going through, Freya. But please trust me. Peggy and me, we only want what's best for you. Peggy says you need to meet her. Until you do, you'll be stuck.

Take care of yourself. Let us know if you change your mind. We'll be waiting.

Love from your new sister,
Connie

She sat down. An uneasy feeling crept through her. A dream come true? How horrible I've been, she thought. I could have made Connie's trip here so much better, if only I'd been more willing, and if only the timing had been better.

An overwhelming urge to cry for the mother she had never met suddenly gnawed at the pit of her stomach. This was the first real emotion she'd felt for Ester. She waited for the tears to well up but her eyes remained dry.

Her prevailing emotion was a no-nonsense curiosity. Ester was from a world she had never shared, except in her imagination. There seemed little point in wasting energy on something she'd never experienced. She also felt an odd desire for the life she had lived to be eclipsed. At the same time she wanted to feel isolated from her unlived past, yet still be able to spy on what she had missed. Her emotions were confused and her head was bursting with images. She was slowly getting used to the mixture of emotions and making sense of where she stood, a process of elimination and acceptance that couldn't be rushed.

A welcome sense of relief settled over her now as she stared at Connie's letter on the table. Her heart rose up within her, suddenly lighter. The painful yearning she'd felt since meeting Connie began to dissolve. Connie was treating her like someone too confused or ill to make their own decision. She felt protected and loved. The choice had been made for her; Connie's persuasive personality had worked its magic.

She could go. Why not? She had enough stock to supply the stores who sold her products. She could set up the sales before leaving, so that no one ran out. Connie was right. She did have a right to visit her family. And she would, just as soon as she could get organised.

Freya put the letter away, had a shower, and set off for Richmond. Before booking flights and doing the million and one things she'd have to do before leaving, she wanted one last shot at finding out the truth. She would just come right out with it, like any straight-talking Australian.

'So,' she'd begin, squaring up to Neill, 'what's all this I hear about you claiming benefits for all six kids?'

She had a perfect right to ask such a question. Especially as she had let so many other things slip: the religious burden he put on the children, the expensive gadgets he bought them, which she now realised were his way of keeping them occupied, their complaints about Clarissa's favouritism, what the au pair had said.

She expected him to be so shocked that he wouldn't be able to answer. The truth would show in his shamed expression. He never could keep a secret.

She'd go on to say, 'You're earning more than most men who graft up to London every day. You'd better come clean, or I'll have to discuss this with my lawyer before we meet in court.'

All the way to Richmond she practised her little speech. By the time she nosed the car over Richmond Bridge she had perfected every word. Her stomach was churning. She focused on her breathing, sucking oxygen deep into her abdomen and holding it for a few seconds.

She parked the car along the street from the house. She stared at it for a few moments, picturing Neill sitting at his computer. A boiling anger rose up and she said out loud, 'I love my

333

children. They're mine,' in a hard, bright voice that sounded like someone else's.

It startled her, and she looked over her shoulder, expecting to see someone sitting in the back seat. She repeated the words, louder this time.

The front of the Victorian mansion seemed more ominous than the last visit. The glossy leaves of the creeper were a dark summery green. The rose beds were freshly turned and weeded. Neill had obviously been spending lots of time in the garden.

This house would never be his, or the children's. The children knew it. Perhaps he did too. Perhaps that was what drove him out into the garden, away from the walls pressing in on his resentment. Every inch Clarissa's, right down to the High Gothic vaulted stonework and the blue-and-white Minton tiles on the front porch. Even the flawless plastic-coated milk crate with its order indicator had her stamp of virtue on it.

When Freya gripped the knocker, a dark dread engulfed her and she began to tremble. She stepped away from the porch, into the sunlight. What if Clarissa came to the door and made her feel small? She hated Clarissa's beady, round eyes drilling into her, and her prim red mouth with its small pointy teeth and too much gum when she laughed. She always looked at Freya as though she was the epitome of evil.

Freya turned and walked towards the gate. Halfway down the cobbled path she heard shouting coming from upstairs. She glanced at the window of the room she knew belonged to

Kirsty and Rebecca, and caught a glimpse of a child throwing a pillow. An innocent enough sight; she imagined they were having a game. She wondered if Tom and Kirsty were included. Burning with curiosity, she ducked sideways on to the lawn for a better view. She stepped backwards, craning her neck for a glimpse of the children, her legs buckling as the back of her knees came into contact with the edge of a low stone wall. She almost fell, but just managed to keep her balance. She glanced around, red-faced, in case someone had seen. She decided the whole exercise was too risky.

As she dashed through the gate on to the street she bumped straight into Neill. He was on his way home from the corner store, carrying two Londis bags bulging with milk cartons and cereal boxes.

'What are you doing here?' he said.

Freya took a deep breath. 'I've come to see you, actually.'

'Did you speak to Clarissa?'

Freya wasn't sure what to say. He was so quick to judge her and gather harmful evidence. But he'd ask Clarissa, so there was no point lying.

'I was just about to knock and thought better of it.'

'You're supposed to phone first. Tonight's not your night.'

'Look, Neill, I'm not a bloody criminal. I'm your ex-wife, for God's sake. Can't we be civil? Does it matter if I call in on a day that's not on their schedule? Do we have to do everything they tell us to? They're not going to lock us up if we have minds of our own.'

'I don't want you creeping about — '

'I came here to speak to you.'

'Well here I am. Talk away.'

'All right. If you insist. It's about a conversation I had with a woman I know from the Job Centre.'

Neill's eyes grew dangerous. 'I see,' he said. His voice was low and cautious. 'What about? Are you claiming benefits?' His face brightened.

She knew this trick. He always tried it when they argued, turning things back on her.

'No,' she said. 'You are. Before you go off the deep end, don't worry. I didn't let on. But I might tell the court. You're making plenty of money; surely you don't need to stoop to this?'

'Plenty of money? Have you any idea how much it costs to feed and clothe and educate six children?' He lifted the shopping bags. 'This little lot came to twelve quid. Our food bill alone adds up to two hundred a week, and that doesn't include cleaning products and toilet paper and school supplies and clothing, not to mention all the other stuff, like power and gas and telephones — '

'That's no excuse for fraud.'

'If you say anything, I'll put in a claim for more support from you.' He narrowed his eyes.

'I'm already giving you plenty.'

'It's not enough. Don't forget, they're still your children and — '

'I know that.'

'And I'll tell the court you keep snooping around. That you're stalking us.'

Freya sighed heavily. She looked at Neill; a great surge of pity welled up for them both.

'If you need more money, just ask,' she said. 'You don't have to air our private business with strangers or resort to fraud. I just don't understand, Neill. With you and Clarissa both working, you must be raking it in.'

'Well you thought wrong. We need at least another fifty quid a week. Richmond's not cheap, you know.'

'Maybe you should buy a houseboat. They're very economical.'

'You must be joking.'

'There's nothing wrong with it. People are so snobby about it.'

'I'd rather stay here and take the extra fifty quid, if you don't mind.'

'I can't really afford it, Neill. But if that's what you need, fine. Consider it done.'

She wondered how many more shocks she could take. She couldn't afford to give Neill more money. But she had faith in her products, and orders were coming in every day. Anything to shut him up and stop him from spoiling her chances. He pushed past her; the shopping bags grazed her legs, and he made for the gate.

'Are you going to tell the CWO?' she said, turning after him.

He looked worn out, she thought, watching him struggle with the gate. Hair uncombed and in need of a cut, jaw unshaven. Like a man who worked from home in his pyjamas. Computer-weary eyes, wrinkles that seemed etched with dirt. Mouth severe, authoritarian. It was hard to believe she had ever put her lips on his and enjoyed it.

'About what?' He kicked open the gate and it almost came off its hinges.

'My being here.'

'Maybe.' He shrugged.

The gate banged shut before he had a chance to duck through. He kicked it again, harder this time. It flew off its hinges and landed with a clatter on the concrete.

'See what I mean? The place is falling apart. We can't afford to pay a handyman. I have to do everything.'

'Well, are you going to tell Monica or not?'

'It depends on how soon your cheque comes through. What about you? Are you going to tell her about my claim?'

'It depends,' said Freya.

'On what?'

'On you. It depends on you.'

'You'll never get them back, you know.'

'You seem so sure.'

'Oh, I am. I'm very sure. I mean, the court only needs to take one look at you to see you've got baggage, you've got issues. It shows all over your face. You're weird and screwed-up. I should know. I lived with you.'

* * *

Freya snipped the seal on a bottle of essential lavender oil with her nail scissors, poured a few drops into the filled water chamber of a terracotta oil burner, and lit the candle inside the pot. She had an overwhelming desire to fill the boat with the therapeutic aroma of nature. After a few moments the water and oil mixture began to heat, and fragrant vapours trailed around the saloon.

During the night she had become more and more conscious of the sour pongs inside *Harlequin*. She had opened all the hatches and portholes, and before retiring had lifted the portaloo into the garden ready for emptying the following day. She was even thinking about not using it at all, and going into the woods instead. Or walking to the pub when the urge struck. Totally impractical, but tempting.

She had scraped the fungus from the portholes yet again, ripped up the damp coir matting and thrown it on the compost, washed and ironed all the curtains. The smells were ingrained. She had also emptied two guns of filler, sealing the leaky windows. The entire boat was held together with the stuff. She was thinking about renaming it HMS *Mastick*.

She wanted to make it pleasant and presentable and *normal*; even if it meant ripping the guts out of the bilges, stripping out every damp slat of timber and replacing anything that smelled or looked remotely kooky.

★ ★ ★

Over the next few weeks she went about her daily chores in a haze. She pictured Connie and Peggy in the outback, and Kirsty and Tom creeping about in Clarissa's house like intruders,

339

afraid to speak, afraid to join in.

She posted a cheque to Neill, enough to cover three months, and hoped it might shame him into keeping his word. But Neill was a stubborn bastard. And he never could keep a promise. Freya doubted his relationship with God would make a blind bit of difference.

★ ★ ★

It didn't seem possible. Great flocks of screaming cockatoos and budgerigars. Desert dust, rock drawings, clay pans, stone churingas.

Who was Freya Lacey? She wasn't the Katherine Nolan her birthright had intended her to be. She was not Shirley and Bob's child, yet they seemed to have taken her role as their daughter for granted and expected her loyalty.

She wanted to ask Connie, *why, why, why did you have to come?* What was the point in stirring up a past that could not even be remembered?

The warm days passed. She checked the postbox every morning for postcards of emus and kangaroos, but none came. She thought about Connie and Peggy riding into the desert together on dusty hacks, burning their shoulders under the open skies and wondering if Freya might arrive in a bus.

When the children came to stay she felt disconnected from them, as though someone had unplugged her from the socket in their veins. Instead of the whole bonding thing working, they seemed to be growing further apart. She took them to the model village in Beaconsfield.

340

'Why did you sneak around the garden like that?' Kirsty stared at the model playground with its miniature swings. She squatted and, reaching a hand over the plastic field, pushed the swing gently. Its stiff occupant fell off. Kirsty quickly replaced the tiny figurine and steadied the swing. She stood up and looked at her mother. 'Well?'

Freya blinked. 'I don't know,' she said. 'I wanted to give you your pocket money.'

'Dad said you've lost your marbles, sneaking around their house.'

'Your father doesn't know what he's talking about.' Freya smiled. 'Take no notice. You know I'm not mad. A bit eccentric, maybe. But not crazy.'

She didn't want to alarm Kirsty, and saw the uncertainty in her eyes. She felt terribly sorry about everything, and angry with herself for going anywhere near Richmond.

There was something wrong with the air today. It was humid and heavy in the sheltered village. The damp was upsetting her hair. She caught a glimpse of herself in the window of a storage shed and realised she looked as bad as she felt. She tied her hair back with a ribbon and pinned the wisps off her face, and they continued the tour of the village in silence.

Later they had scones and jam in a teashop in Beaconsfield. Kirsty pulled out a pile of brochures sent to her by the welfare department. One was entitled *My Family's Splitting Up*. Another had a cartoon face of a perplexed child and a drawing of a worried child in front of a

341

brick wall. There were two large brochures full of blank spaces for drawings: Draw a picture of some of your favourite things. Draw a picture of where you live now, and where you used to live. Colour in the faces which show how you feel on different days.

Freya picked up a pamphlet called *My Family's Changing* and opened it.

Is my family normal? But what is normal? Families come in all shapes and sizes. 'I live with my mum in the week and with my nan on Friday and Saturday nights.' 'Me and my brother live with my Dad and his girlfriend and her three children.' 'I live with a family who look after me, and sometimes I see my mum.'

Towards the back of the booklet was a quiz.

Every time you come back from a weekend at your mum's, your dad tries to find out how she is getting on with her boyfriend. Do you:

1. Make up stories that things aren't going well even if they are?
2. Tell him to stop hassling you and storm off?
3. Explain to him why talking about it makes you feel uncomfortable?

You go and stay with your dad every weekend. You get on well but often miss out on what your friends are doing. You don't want to hurt his feelings. Do you:

1. Continue going to your dad's as usual?
2. Not turn up on the weekends that your friends are doing something more exciting?
3. Explain to your dad that even though you still want to see him, you'd like to see your mates sometimes too?

She closed the booklet.

'I'm so sorry,' she said. 'I don't know what to do any more.'

She couldn't bear to think her children were in the same category as the ones quoted in the brochures, confused little waifs shunted from one home to another, never knowing where they belonged, full of apprehension over which parent they should be loyal to, and not able to grasp the emotional implications of having a foot in two camps.

Tom began to fill in the blank spaces. Kirsty pulled out a copy of *Romeo and Juliet* from her bag.

'We're studying this for GCSE,' she said.

'It's a great play. Do you like it?'

Kirsty nodded and opened the book.

Freya watched silently and sipped her tea. Tom drew a lovely picture of *Harlequin*, and three stick figures on the forward deck, *Kirsty, Me, Mum*. At the top of the page he wrote: *My home*. Then he drew a picture of Clarissa's house, covered in swirling vines. Under this he wrote the caption: *My dad lives here with his new wife and her four brats.*

★ ★ ★

'You're jealous.' Del steadied her gaze over the top of her cup.

'No I'm not.' Freya stared at the contents of her own cup. She could see a watery image of her face. She put the mug down and fidgeted with her spoon.

'You're jealous of Clarissa and Neill having the children. And of their big house.'

'No I'm not. That's ridiculous. I'm upset because they keep trying to tarnish my reputation to get their own way.'

'You have to admit, Freya darling, anyone would think you're a bit odd, sneaking around their garden like that.'

'I was curious, not crazy. And certainly not jealous. I was worried about the children. They're so unhappy, Del. I had to find out for myself if they were telling the truth.'

'The court won't see it like that. The psychiatrist won't. And the welfare officer most definitely won't. You should know better.'

'They can talk. Turning up unannounced. It wouldn't surprise me if they had hidden cameras on my boat and miniature microphones in my shoes.'

'Now you're being silly.'

'At the last meeting I could tell Monica Murray was on Neill and Clarissa's side.'

'It's amazing how religion can influence people.'

Freya swept her hands over her face.

'Look at you,' said Del. 'Look at the way you're letting all these other things get at you. The solution is so simple.'

'Is it? How would you know? You've got your husband, your house, your successful career.'

'You've still got a lot of positive things in your life.'

'Have I?'

'I don't understand you, Freya. I thought you were such a practical person. A bit airy-fairy, but basically you're very sensible. Ever since Connie turned up you've become nervy and unsure of yourself.'

'You're wrong,' said Freya. 'You're so wrong. I'm not jealous. I'm lonely.'

'Well do something about it.'

'The timing's wrong. I don't want to complicate things with another man in my life.'

'I don't mean that.'

'You mean my sisters?'

Del nodded. 'And your adoptive family. Some people would be thrilled to have both. Especially people who have neither. Like me.'

'Del! I'm so sorry. I forgot. Please forgive me. How selfish of me.' Freya reached across and cupped her hands over Del's. It was an unexpected gesture, and Del looked at her, surprised. Freya had completely forgotten Del's parents had died in a car crash several years ago. Now she felt awful. 'You're right,' she said softly. 'I do need to see them. And I suppose I'm never going to feel settled until I spend

345

some time with my sisters.'

'Get it out of your system,' said Del. 'By the time you get back it will nearly be time for the appeal.'

'Do you really think I should? What if the court says I took off and left the children — again?'

'If you can come to terms with your background, and admit it with pride, I imagine they'd view it positively. Just make sure you tell Neill first, and let Monica know too.'

Freya smiled.

'Thanks,' she said. 'I've been trying not to think about it. But it's driving me crazy. I keep reading the travel pages.'

She told Del about Connie's letter, and the tickets. Sitting in an envelope in a drawer.

'Out of sight, out of mind. But you're right, Del. Thank you. Until I go to Australia I won't be able to get on with my life.'

'That's more like it.'

Del looked away and chewed her bottom lip. She was holding something back. Freya knew her well.

'What is it?'

'Nothing,' said Del quickly. Then, 'There is something else — '

'What? What is it?'

Del looked as if she wanted to confide a terrible secret. But finally she just looked at Freya and said, 'I'll take you to the airport.'

★ ★ ★

Driving through the dark towards the moorings, Freya cried. For her children, for herself, for Shirley and Bob. Everything spooled past in a blur of colour, light and noise.

She had no idea what she was heading into. She didn't know this stranger from America, her *sister*. The outings in London had not brought her and Connie any closer. Connie still felt like an acquaintance. Would it be any different in Australia? As for Peggy, what if they didn't get on? What if Peggy guessed her secret and hated her for it?

Later, after packing her suitcase, she lay awake, trying to convince herself she'd made the right decision. No matter how hard she tried to wheedle her way out of it, she kept coming back to the facts. Until she confronted her past and truly accepted the *other* Freya, she would never be able to offer her children what they deserved: a mother who was content with herself. A mother who was whole.

★ ★ ★

The day of her departure was one of those long summer days that seemed endless. Freya had been awake since five, making last-minute lists for Sam, who had promised to look after *Harlequin*. Everything was in place. Monica had tutted, but Freya could tell she was glad: as far as she was concerned, the trip to Australia confirmed Freya's slack attitude to motherhood. If Monica was called as a witness at the appeal, Freya expected the trip to be cited as firm

347

evidence. But she was past caring. The excitement of leaving everything behind for a few months took over. She would face the consequences when she got back.

'How were Kirsty and Tom when you said goodbye?' said Del on the way to the airport.

'Not as upset as I thought they'd be. Neill bought them each a second-hand computer last week.'

'He's doing all right then?'

'Yes. He's doing fine.'

'Did they cry?'

'No, thank God.'

'Children are very resilient.'

'You're not having second thoughts, are you?'

'Once I get there I'll feel better.'

41

Listen here, you say. I'm from the country. Things are different in the country. People from the city just don't get it.

Take dogs, for instance.

Had one I picked up on the road. Thought I could tame it. Not as a working dog — it was some sort of Rottweiler, crossed with something else. Kelpies make the best working dogs. Anyway, the rotten mongrel — and it was literally a bloody mongrel — kept getting into the rubbish pit, dragged stuff all over the yard. I had to tie the bastard up day and night, and that's not good for a dog or his master. In the end it was kinder to get rid of him. Shot him in the head. Didn't feel a thing.

Gave him a proper burial, you add, noticing the look of horror on the woman's face. City slickers. They just don't get it.

You could have avoided the whole subject and said, Nice day for a funeral, or Can I have this dance? But she might not get your sense of humour, which has become more cynical since you arrived at the hospital.

The way the nurses looked at you that day you first came here. It made you tear at your face with your fingernails in the privacy of the ward bathroom. They pitied you, bringing yourself here in your beat-up ute, with your blue heelers tied up in the back. They led them to a Hills

349

Hoist near a tree. Stained sheets and flannelette pyjamas hung from the lines. They tethered the dogs and gave them a bucket of water. Later you asked how they were faring, especially Minstrel, your favourite kelpie, who was old and riddled with cancer.

The day after you got settled, a dumpy nurse with food between her teeth said the animal welfare people had removed the dogs. You tried to punch her in the mouth but your arm was rigid on the bed.

Katherine perches her bum near your feet. There's a chair she could sit in. Why doesn't she use it? You can feel the heat from her body through the bedcovers. When she was a newborn baby you looked at her tiny face from the doorway and cursed her. Now she sits on your sickbed, a grown woman, and you are polite. Polite!

You feel it's probably time to explain, but you won't. Especially as she's white.

I'm a country boy, you repeat. What do you want for your money? A striptease? You try to wink, but your eyelids are stuck. She just gives you a blank look.

Look, I can't help who I am, you say. I was born on the land.

She pours a glass of water from the jug on your cabinet, and sits there sipping it, like she's got all the time in the world.

Connie and Peggy — well, what can I say? she says, after a long silence. Our mother must have been very lonely, living on a farm, she says, shaking her head. She gives you a funny look, as if you're to blame.

She was a city woman too, you say. I understand, she says.

But you know that she doesn't. That she never will.

You're not sure what to do. It's not as though you can behave like a father, with a catheter in your dick and feet that won't do what your brain tells them to. You can't leap from your bed and carry her on your shoulders, or place her on the back of a horse, or help with long-distance learning. You can't take her out on the ridge behind the homestead and explain the moods of the wind.

You know you should reach out a hand and touch her. Or take her in your arms and hold her. But the desire it not there, only the sentiment.

All the way from Old Blighty, eh? You look at her and try to smile, but the muscles around your mouth are rigid with disease. You can see that she wishes you would stop staring, with your milky eyes that fix on a person until a nurse snaps her fingers or turns your head.

You can see she is tired. You know the tiredness is not jetlag, but sadness. You examine her hair and the way the light streaming through the window isolates maroon and ginger shades amongst the curls. You dislike these colours intensely. You wish you had a pair of shears.

What's with the mahogany hair? you say, and she looks at you as though you have put a knife in her heart.

Her eyes are dark. Her hair has golden lights

351

amongst the red hues, the colour of corn, like Ester's. You concentrate on these. She has a small brown mole on the ridge of her upper lip, like Ester's. She doesn't smell like Ester, although this could be your imagination. She smells like you. You caught a whiff of her skin when she reached across to place a Get Well card on the locker. It is a smell you blamed on forty-degree heat and dusty dogs and the lanolin from sweating sheep.

Your wife noticed it and said it was none of these things. It's you, Henry, she said, it's your special man-smell.

She liked to press her face into your chest and breathe in your musk, but it made you angry, this smell. You washed yourself in the dam three or four times a day in the summer when it was particularly strong, but nothing quelled it.

You imagine Katherine has fantasised about this moment, expecting you to provide her with details of a handsome tribal Elder who could not help falling in love with your wife, so she can toddle off and tell that black bitch Connie and her filthy sister who their father is.

Better to let her leave here today none the wiser. What she doesn't know won't harm her.

You show her a photograph of Ester. It's the least you can do. You only have one picture. The rest are in a box in the loft. One day you will tell your lawyer where they are, and send him to get them.

In the photo Ester is sitting under a tree on a rock, behind the shearing shed. The dappled shade cast flickering shadows over her skirt that day, but in the photo the shadows have gone and her skirt is pure white. It matches her face. She hated the sun and always stayed inside. Sometimes her cheeks were flushed with pink after stirring laundry in the outhouse copper all day. Ordinarily they were pale and bloodless. She practically ran from the back veranda to the laundry, cowering under her straw hat.

Her eyes seem dark, but it's hard to tell in a black-and-white photo, Katherine says.

You can feel her backside pressing into the mattress. The intimacy of it riles you. You hate the astrakhan collar on her sweater. It reminds you of those floor-length ponchos that models wore in the seventies at the annual Wool Collection shows in Melbourne. You always sat in the middle row, the hairs on your neck bristling, as they sashayed towards you on the catwalk. You bought a ticket to see your wool woven into smart brown worsted suits and herringbone jackets, not overblown itchy tents.

What colour were they? Katherine looks at you, her face expectant and keen. My mother's eyes?

Blue, you say. Like cornflowers.

Your eyes are blue, she says.

My mother had blue eyes, you say, looking away.

My children have dark brown eyes, she says. Neill's mother had brown eyes too.

You can feel your bladder filling. You don't want her to see your blue-veined feet with their cracked heels and horny toenails like Brazil nuts. The overhead fan stirs the fetid air like an egg beater in cream.

A fly the size of a bumble bee commits suicide on the window pane and falls on the sill, where it fries. You can see a lizard sunning itself on the concrete ramp outside. It is so still it looks dead.

Ester was loyal. Ester was good.

You want to hit Katherine, so haughty and sure in her hippy garb, for thinking Ester was so unhappy with her marriage that she let a bloody savage touch her. Instead, you give her a square-on look and say, I hope you'll forgive me and your mother for giving you up. It's just that we were hard up in them days, and being miles from anywhere, you wouldn't have had much of a life. You were better off with my sister.

She smiles and straightaway says, That's all right, I had a good life in Melbourne. I'm just glad to have met you after all these years. I'm glad to know what you look like.

You always made sure Ester had everything she needed. You brought home bolts of cotton from the city. Boxes of thread, needles, thimbles. You put her black Singer sewing machine on the back seat of the Ford and took it hundreds of miles to be mended. You gave her perfume and an opal necklace and a velvet headband for Christmas. At night you held her hips and lifted her gently on to you, and whispered I love you into her curls.

The nurse comes and you tell her, as politely as you can, that your feet are numb with pain. She gives you a bemused look, as if to say, bloody whinger. You are never courteous in this place. You ache to be home. Mending the tumbling gate out in the sheep yard; raking straw from corners of the races where the wind blew it through the open doors of the barn; checking your equipment, especially the wool press, which needs regular lubrication. You fret for your hens and your sheep, even though your broker told you it had all been taken care of. In your mind the sheep are still there, sniffing at empty troughs, baulking at the electric clippers dangling from the ceiling, struggling to turn in the narrow races.

The nurse rubs your feet, but not for long. She rushes to the far end of the ward to draw the blinds, and disappears through an unmarked door.

Katherine looks at you and says she will do your feet.

I'll finish massaging them for you, she says.

You'll do no such bloody thing, you say.

You struggle to bury your feet amongst the covers, but they are petrified.

She says she is going to meet Peggy.

Are you expected to say, Peggy, eh? They sent her to Queensland, didn't they? How was it for her? Did she have a nice time, in the Deep North?

She asks you where Ester is buried. There is no letting up with this woman.

Burned, you say. She was burned. Cremated. Her ashes are in a small box on the mantel over the fire at Tinderry.

You lean forward and flick the wing of a dead fly from the grey blanket.

Wind has inflated your belly. You clench the

cheeks of your bum, but nothing can stop it now.

Don't you worry about that, Katherine says, not flinching a muscle. Flatulence is common in people who are bed-ridden.

You look at her and say, You're a bloody expert, are you?

She nods and says, Yes, as a matter of fact, I'm a trained nurse.

42

It was a relief to be away from Henry. Freya sat in the hospital grounds on a white bench in the shade of a wattle tree, reliving their conversation, enjoying the scent of the pale yellow flowers. She wiped beads of sweat from her nose. The air smelled of coffee, which was everywhere in Melbourne. It was wicked of her, she knew, pretending to believe Henry was her father. He was too sick to care, obviously. She'd known as soon as he looked up from his tray of liver and mash. His blue eyes were the giveaway. If they'd been brown, well, then she would have been confused. Especially as his skin was so dark. She put this down to being on the land, out in the blazing sun all day.

She stepped out on to the street and ducked between the traffic, almost running to the train station. To think she'd travelled twelve thousand miles to meet that rude man. She was glad he wasn't her father. She felt sorry for her mother and didn't blame her at all for falling in love with someone else. Even if he was nothing but an itinerant farmhand, he was probably kind to Ester.

It was so strange being home. It almost didn't feel like home, in spite of the familiar smells and sights.

She wandered up and down the platform, looking at faces she had never seen before.

The sun belted her face. She thought of Neill and Clarissa, bossing Tom and Kirsty under a dull English sky. She wished she could be home in England right now, so she could pick up the phone and know the children were only a few miles away at Richmond, or drive to their school and watch them from the safety of the car.

'Thank God he's not my father,' she told Del the following morning on the phone.

'What do you mean?' said Del.

Freya caught the insincerity. 'You knew all along, didn't you?'

'Yes, I did,' said Del softly. 'I mean, it all added up. When you scratched your back one day, and I saw your birth mark . . . well, you know. I put two and two together. You must have felt strange, meeting Henry. I imagine it's hard for you, though, still not knowing who your real father is. If it was Henry, your quest would be over in many ways.'

'Henry's typical old-school conservative. Been on the farm too long.'

'Sam called. I said I hadn't spoken to you yet. He said everything's fine on the moorings.'

'That's good.'

'Your boat hasn't sunk. And everyone's been asking after you.'

'That's nice.' She felt detached from the ins and outs of life on the moorings, and suddenly saw how intense it had all become before she'd left, how all-consuming.

'What's the matter?' said Del. 'Aren't you relieved to have solved one piece of the puzzle?'

358

'I'm tired. It was a strain, seeing the old boy. He's very ill.'

She was lying. It wasn't his illness that had made her tired, it was his attitude, his quick eyes moving from hers.

Far below, on the streets of Fitzroy, she could see people scurrying in and out of a row of colonial buildings, renovated and painted in trendy shades of khaki, aubergine, turquoise. The original foundations had been arrogantly solid, but now the damage was, in some cases, irreparable. Crumbling walls, triple-light sash windows buckling under the weight of sagging roofs, crooked chimney pots, ogee guttering fractured and rusting. Brickwork oozing damp.

'What's next on your agenda?' said Del.

Freya opened the French doors and stepped out on to the balcony. The noise of the traffic hit her. The sun was warm on her face and bare shoulders. Some of the houses on the street still had their original colours, she noticed: biscuit walls, deep green shutters, Indian-red iron roofs, peeling and anaemic after one hundred years of solar penetration and neglect.

'I want to visit my parents,' she said. 'Then I'm flying to Alice Springs, to meet Peggy.'

She stared at the houses, forgetting for a moment that Del was on the line. It was as if the buildings harboured nasty secrets and were suffering the effects of a poisonous guilt.

'Are you still there, Freya?'

'Yes. I'm here.' She imagined life inside the houses unchanged, like a living museum.

'Freya darling, why on earth didn't you tell

Henry about your suspicions? He may have been able to point you in the right direction.'

'Connie already asked him. He just got angry. It's obviously a sore point. Besides, it happened a long time ago. Whoever our real father was, he's long gone. Henry's ashamed.'

'Of you?'

'Of my mother. For being unfaithful — with a black.'

'Maybe he's ashamed of giving you away.'

'He's not the type to have a conscience.'

'What are you saying?'

'You know.'

'You mean a redneck?'

'Yes,' said Freya. 'Not the sort of man who would take kindly to his wife having it off with a black man.'

They talked for a long time about everything, about the changes all this would make to Freya's life, to her personality.

'You know me so well,' she said finally. 'Thanks for being such a good friend.'

'I hope you work everything out.'

'So do I.'

When she finally put the phone down, Freya immediately dialled Neill's number in Richmond.

'How much longer are you going to be away?' he said.

'I've only just arrived, for heaven's sake. Why? Is there something wrong? Are the children okay?'

'Yes, yes. They're fine.'

'I was planning to spend a few weeks catching

up with old friends from work,' she lied. 'But if the children want — '

'Have you found another houseboat?'

'Not yet. Why?'

'Just wondering how the search was coming along.'

'Why the sudden interest?' Freya was suspicious. He sounded unnaturally concerned about her life.

'I know someone who's selling a barge. Brand new. Big. Very big.'

'How much?'

'A hundred and fifty thousand. But to you, a hundred.'

'I can't afford that. But it's nice of you to mention it.'

'He's a boat-builder. Puts them together in no time — whole fleets. He's got cheaper models. But not the size you want.'

'I'll wait till I get back. Something will come up. Even if I have to renovate one.'

'That aside, have you decided whether or not to bring up the other thing at the appeal?'

'Look, Neill, if you're that worried perhaps you should sign off benefits, before they catch up with you.'

'I can't,' he said. 'We need the money. Like I said, bringing up six kids is expensive.'

'You should have thought of that before getting on your high horse about having Kirsty and Tom. You only wanted them to spite me. You know that's the truth. It's so unfair on them. Now it's probably too late. The court won't want to uproot them unless it's absolutely necessary.'

'I don't want them living in that awful place.'

'It's not as bad as you think. There are lots of families on the moorings. Decent people who work hard to make ends meet. People who have had hard lives. People who would do anything for their friends and family. Ordinary people. Just like us.'

'Well, we'll see what happens when you get back, shall we?'

She replaced the receiver. Something about Neill's voice had disturbed her. She wished she could get on a plane to London right now. She had a hunch he was up to something.

43

Walking up her old road, Freya was assaulted with the smells and sights of her childhood. As if no time had passed since the days when she skipped home from school, satchel strapped to her back.

Last night when she'd climbed into bed at the hotel she'd known they were thinking about her. It made her so uneasy she had to turn the light on again at four a.m. and watch television. She rehearsed what she would say to them over and over, then she lay awake with her heart pounding, not sure if she was doing the right thing after all by confronting them.

They'd done their best for her. Why ruin the image they probably had of themselves as good people, who only wanted a child they could call their own? They'd done Henry and Ester a favour, too.

As she turned the corner she was taken aback to see them out the front of their red-brick house, dressed casually, Shirley in pedal-pushers and T-shirt, Bob in khaki shorts and short-sleeved shirt. They seemed to have shrunk in height to half their original size, though they'd filled out in typical Australian style, around the middle mainly. It was odd, seeing them on the driveway dressed normally and looking relaxed, instead of in ceremonial attire and funereal mood. It brought her up sharp.

They were laying a new driveway with the help of a man in obscene shorts.

She waited, breath caught at the back of her throat, which felt parched. She didn't want them to spot her too soon, ruining her planned speech. Glancing around for somewhere to hide — a tree, a hedge, a shrub — the starkness of the neighbourhood struck her.

The sun's rays beat down on her shoulders from a fluorescent blue sky that seemed to reinforce the significance of the moment. She squinted, fell away from the footpath and crouched behind a car, as if under a police searchlight. She suddenly longed to escape into the water-dappled shadows of her houseboat, claustrophobic though it was, where she could figure out who she was in private. At her own pace.

A silent refrain rose up inside her, synchronising with her speeding heart:

I am coming back to parents
who are not my own,
They live in a house
that was never a home.

Their stoical relationship with her was a blessing, she realised. If they'd been all pally and affectionate with her as a kid, she'd have found it even harder to confront them now. It wasn't that there had been no love. They just didn't show it in the usual way. The way other parents did, gushing and physical.

She heard footsteps, and a woman walking her

poodle came round the opposite corner. Freya pretended to check the car's tyres, aware of the woman's eyes drilling her back. She had parked the hire car in Whipbird Street, walked down Galah Close and ducked through the lane into Lorikeet Avenue, so as not to draw attention to herself. But it was impossible to hide anything in Windsor Meadows.

Because of the funerals, the house had always been the estate's main curiosity, even outstripping the loud Sicilian couple in Bowerbird Crescent, who had twelve children under fifteen and grew olives and lemons and car parts in their front yard.

As a child she sneaked in and out undetected, not only out of respect for the mourners, but because she did not want anyone to know she lived in a funeral home. She'd have gladly frightened any rivals with her father's books on embalming, but her friends wanted prestige, not black tongues and spilled gizzards. To these she made the excuse that her mother was ill, so that not one of her schoolfriends ever set foot through her front door.

One sly route home had been through a stand of forlorn paperbarks on the empty block behind the back yard. She ripped strips of bark off the trunks as she went by, savouring its soft texture between her fingers. Then she tiptoed into the concrete courtyard, squeezed between the parked hearses, touching the sunburned roofs with flattened palms, as if tempting fate, and slipped through the kitchen, helping herself to biscuits, then along the hall to her room, clamping her nostrils against the smell of disinfectant, wet newspaper, blood and body fluids.

One day as she went across the courtyard, she glanced into one of the hearses and noticed the lid on the coffin inside it was bulging. She told her father gas had probably caused the eruption, hoping he'd be impressed with the knowledge gleaned from his books. Bob was insulted, to think a child was pointing this out to *him*, a professional. She had crept to her room feeling ashamed, and later heard the relatives complaining loudly, angrily. She sat on the edge of her bed shaking. But Bob never came.

She had developed the ability to occupy herself for hours, particularly on Saturdays, when her parents were flat out with funerals. She wrote slogans and drew animals on sheets of bark and gum leaves, captivated by the smooth grooves made by her favourite thick-tipped biro. On the vacant block behind the house she drew colourful 3-D tapestries of sinuous lines, concentric circles, U-shapes and dots on the bare rock, with chalk.

Most of the children in the street avoided her, because of the ceremonies, and the bodies toing and froing. There was a mongoloid she played with sometimes from number 18, who didn't understand death.

Mostly, she played alone.

She liked to eat the sour-sweet lilli-pilly berries that grew in the paddock. And pick bunches of morning glory and nasturtium, arranging them on rocks like blobs of paint. She lay on a worn rock watching lizards darting in and out of holes, or simply stared up at the sky. On weekends and holidays she lingered all day, breathing in the smell of sandstone and ants and rain-filled rock pools.

She never got bored with nature, but sometimes she longed for someone to talk to.

She had been terrified to go home sometimes, in case a widowed woman was wailing, or a motherless child was sitting silently while its new carers sorted out floral tributes and coffin prices with Shirley.

Once, she took home Christmas bells and flannel flowers, which Shirley displayed in the reception area, a dour green room with pictures of artificial sunrises, and French fields battened with unnaturally large sunflowers. The flowers provided a conversation point, Shirley said, a distraction for people seized by sorrow. Freya smiled when Shirley told her about the admiring comments.

New houses now crammed the once-vacant block, like grandiose Italian crypts.

She had been crouching down so long her legs were beginning to ache. It occurred to her that Shirley and Bob probably wouldn't recognise her immediately. She had filled out a little, and her hair was longer.

She glanced at them through the car windows. They were preoccupied with cement. She walked along the road, away from the house, until she was out of sight, and sat on the brick wall outside number 68, enjoying the warmth on her back. It was a miracle how the sun could diminish a problem.

In the distance, all she could see were houses and more houses. Melbourne's city-scape was no longer visible. She could see clearly now why she had longed to escape.

Somewhere in the middle of the new houses, a dog howled. A child's crying drilled the vacuous air.

Suddenly she was aware of her mother's voice.

'The powder's a funny colour,' said Shirley.

Freya took a deep breath and approached the gate. They still hadn't noticed her, so intense was their focus.

'The powder's turning a funny colour,' Shirley repeated.

They were staring at the glistening paving. Bob scratched his head in his familiar way. Shirley waited patiently for her husband to speak, conscious as ever of not emasculating his authority.

What a team.

Bob had done the embalming and most of the reconstruction — a difficult, gruesome job, especially if there had been an accident — and he had built the coffins. Shirley manned the phones and comforted the clients. Bob had talked her into doing the make-up on the bodies for viewing — Catholics, usually.

'There's more to it than merely applying powder and rouge,' she once said to Bob, who couldn't understand why it was getting her down. 'Cheeks need stuffing with cotton, teeth need mending, ears have to be sewn on.'

Shirley bent over, lifted a foot, and scraped the

368

sticky concrete mix from the sole of her shoe with a small garden fork, frowning as she did so.

'It's gone black,' she said, clicking her tongue at Bob. 'Look.' She held the end of the fork in front of Bob's face. He recoiled.

'She'll be right,' said Bob. He pushed away Shirley's hand and sprinkled grey powder over the wet concrete. 'I'll hose it down till we get that weathered look.'

The man in shorts poured another barrowload of wet concrete over a prepared area. When he shut down the concrete mixer, suddenly the street was silent. Freya thought she saw Bob glance at her. She held her breath, but there was no flicker of recognition. He laid the hose down and stamped a brick pattern into the wet concrete with a large rubber pad, working his way up towards the front of the house.

Now and then he bent down and, tilting his head sideways, gently lifted the stamp, peering under it cautiously to see if the impression was crisp and permanent.

'It's supposed to be a biscuit colour, love,' said Shirley. She frowned and shook her head. 'That doesn't look like biscuit to me.'

'You're right, darl,' said Bob. 'If it is biscuit, they've been overcooked.' He chuckled.

'Burnt, more like it,' said Shirley, grimacing. 'How will you get it off? The broom's not much use.'

'Murray the gyprocker had the same problem with his patio. When a good hosing didn't work he used acid. Got it off, no worries.'

'That foul-mouthed wretch,' said Shirley,

laughing. 'Pity he didn't use a bit of the same acid on his loose tongue.'

Bob grinned. 'You're the only lady for miles who doesn't go ga-ga over Murray. When he gets up on those stilts of his to fit gyprock the women practically swoon.'

'I think I'd find it most disconcerting, coming face to face with Murray's crotch.'

'The ladies love it.'

'Why would I want the likes of him when I've got you?' She gave him a wink, then moved to the head of the drive, guiding him as he positioned the stamp, urging him a little to the left, or right, until the edge of the stamp was aligned with the previous shape.

The sun was so hot Freya's skin felt as though it was melting into her bones, taking with it the disillusion she felt about their sincerity, leaving a prickly residue of regret. She wished she had not ignored them all these years. What if one of them suddenly died? Or got ill? She'd have to come back and look after them. But then, they'd always looked after each other. They might not want her interfering.

Shirley and Bob had known Neill was a bad egg, but what teenager listens to their parents on these matters? Freya was surprised when they objected to her choice and her plans. All she saw was a knight on a shining scooter.

Find out the hard way.

Those were Shirley's last words when she left. Freya still carried them with her, like a disease. She had fought the truth of those words, determined they would not trip her up.

370

In spite of the heat, her hands were trembling. Beads of sweat assembled under her breasts. Several times she almost turned around and walked back to the car.

She found it hard to define herself by this suburban house with its stark garden, the memories of black cars gliding in and out and the sombre atmosphere pervading the rooms. She wanted to run from it right now, just as she had the minute she'd set eyes on Neill and seen in him the possibility of another life. She had to confront them, find closure for her guilt, give them a chance to explain, so she could forgive them, and understand. Although they were not her biological parents, they had cared for her. She owed them her respect for putting themselves out on her behalf.

She opened the gate. The hinges screeched. They were already staring at her, their mouths drooping at odd angles. Water poured from the hose on to a pile of sand.

'Watch it,' said Bob, noticing.

Shirley reached for the tap, her eyes still on Freya, and turned it off.

'Hello, Mum, hello, Dad.'

She walked towards them, unsure about whether to hug them. In a flash she decided she would. She put her arms around Shirley. Shirley's arms did not leave her sides. It was like hugging a warm mannequin.

Freya felt foolish suddenly, expecting them to reciprocate. She began to panic. She cursed herself for not phoning ahead. She had wanted to surprise them.

When she put her arms around Bob, he lifted one hand and placed it limply on her waist. It was the restraint you might expect of someone accosted by an affectionate stranger.

Freya suggested they go inside and put the kettle on. 'I'll make it,' she said.

'We can't drop everything just because you've turned up,' said Bob.

She wasn't sure how to take this.

Then he said, 'This concrete'll go off if we don't finish.'

'We've been saving up for years for this driveway,' said Shirley. 'You'll have to wait.'

'Can I help?' said Freya.

'You must be joking,' said Bob. 'This is a job for the experts.'

Feeling like a child, Freya stepped aside and watched them finish the drive. After a while she could no longer bear being ignored. She chattered away about how nice the driveway would be when it was finished, and how hot it was in Melbourne compared to London, how well they both looked, how strange it was to see the sign gone, and the roses, and the new shopping centre at the end of the street, and the new café on the corner, with its cosmopolitan choice of drinks and food . . .

Normally with her patients, once she got into her stride the conversation flowed. She tried to make her voice sound natural and friendly, but it came out stilted and forced. She was conscious of her slight English accent.

Finally she gave up and retreated to the only bit of shade at the side of the house, under the eaves. She wished she smoked. Her hands felt conspicuously idle. She studied her nails, and watched small lizards dashing in and out of holes in the brickwork.

Eventually Bob popped his head around the corner and said, 'Stuart's going to finish up for us. The majority's all done. You'd better come inside.'

It was dark in the house, even though a hole had been knocked in the lounge room wall leading into the former office, and an archway fitted. The knick-knacks on the sideboard were in the exact positions they'd always been in. Everything Freya touched was covered in sticky black dust.

Shirley pulled on the same blue cardigan she'd bought in Woolworths years ago. Bob took off the same pair of brown leather moccasins he kept for gardening and slipped on a pair of brown tartan slippers. The rooms smelled of perm solution and Airwicks.

As they sat sipping tea from Shirley's best rose teacups, Freya couldn't help wondering if they'd have given her a different, more ardent greeting if she was their genetic child.

They asked about their grandchildren. Freya handed them some recent photographs. She noticed with a pang the framed pictures she had sent of Kirsty and Tom when they were little, alongside others of her as a child, arranged in neat rows on the mantelpiece and sideboard.

Bob reached into his top pocket for his glasses. He had not worn glasses on the last visit.

'They look more like you than ever,' he said.

'Do they?' said Freya. 'I thought they looked like you.' She forced herself to look him in the eye, and smiled.

Bob returned the gaze, but not the smile. It struck Freya how thoroughly they had convinced themselves she was their daughter. There was no question of not loving her. She bit her lip and looked at her lap.

'I'll make more tea,' said Shirley brightly. She leapt up and dashed into the kitchen. Freya heard her humming a little tune, and recognised it from her childhood. Blood and genetics, the arse-splitting pain and natural love that characterise childbirth — these were not part of their perspective. Their love for her was unconditional. They just couldn't express it. Not in a conventional way, at least. They were still holding back the truth of their feelings.

Shirley's hands were twisted with arthritis; her fingers were crabbed like deformed claws, as though the tension of burying her sadness manifested itself through this physical defect.

'I'm sorry I couldn't come before this,' whispered Freya.

She kept her voice low out of habit. Shirley had trained her to tiptoe and murmur, and to watch television lying flat on the floor, her face an inch from the screen, the volume right down and barely audible. Because of the funerals. Everything was because of the funerals. 'Shhh,' Shirley would say, 'there's a service on.'

'You were right about Neill,' said Freya.

'Has he been unfaithful?' said Bob.

Freya nodded.

'We knew he'd end up hurting you,' said Shirley, not at all surprised.

'There was something rotten in that man from the start,' said Bob. 'He had the sort of face you want to thump. Any man whose head is flat at the back needs watching.'

'You never would listen to us,' said Shirley. 'We tried to tell you. But you wanted to do it all your way.'

'We didn't expect anything in return for what we did for you,' said Bob. 'We just thought you were too young to go off. Far too young.'

'I couldn't help it,' said Freya. 'I wanted more than Windsor Meadows or Melbourne could ever offer.'

'It's not such a bad place,' said Bob. 'A bit cut off from the world, but we've got an Italian café now. As for Melbourne, it's got more cafés than London. I read it in *The Age*.'

'We wanted you to meet a nice young man,' said Shirley. 'A gentleman. Neill was such a . . . yob.'

'It was just bad luck that he wanted to go back to England. But at least I've had the chance to live in another country.'

'We were always upset because of the funerals,' said Shirley. 'We tried to keep a brave face on it all. I suppose we thought if we showed our feelings we'd break down and have to give it all up. People come to rely on you. Just when we thought we might be able to sell up we'd be inundated. Remember that little girl who was knocked off her bike by a truck right outside? That's the sort of funeral that makes you want to keep going. The ones that hit you personally.'

'And I've got two lovely children.' Freya wasn't listening. She lowered her eyes and willed herself to be careful. She didn't want them to know the children were living with Neill, that she had lost custody. 'And I've done a lot of travelling,' she added. 'I worked in a London hospital . . . '

'Well, we're just happy to see you,' said Shirley. She looked at Bob. 'Aren't we, Bob? Six years is a long time.'

Bob nodded. 'Very happy. We never could tie you down. You were always off on your own, exploring and running wild. Any bit of vacant land and you were away with the bloody birds.'

Freya managed to get them off the subject by asking about the rest of the family. Her cousins were all married with children now, her aunts and uncles had various health complaints, nothing serious.

While they prepared dinner, Freya went into her old room to investigate. She lay down on the narrow bed and considered again telling them she knew about her adoption. And about Connie, and Peggy. But it would be too hard on them. It wasn't the sort of news they'd want, let alone understand. They loved her. Nothing else mattered.

Back in the kitchen she sat on a stool at the breakfast bar, watching as they went through the same little rituals in the kitchen, and the lack of self-conscious fuss that dominated events in other households.

When Freya said there was something she

wanted to tell them, they looked alarmed. Bob cleared his throat, as though he was expecting the worst, and Freya thought he was waiting for her to say she knew about being adopted, so she said quickly, 'It's all right. I just wanted to explain about me and Neill and — '

Bob slammed the saucepan he was holding on to the bench. 'All those years,' he said, almost sobbing. 'All those wasted years. Taking you away from us like that. He had no right.'

Freya didn't know what to say. She had never seen him lose his temper. She wanted to put her arms around him; instead she remained glued to the stool as he began to wipe up the water he'd spilled, slowly at first, building to a frantic rubbing, until Shirley finally took the cloth and told him to calm down.

'I can't believe we've hardly seen our grandchildren,' he said. 'It's a bloody crime, that's what. A bloody crime.'

'I just wanted to explain about why we split up,' Freya continued softly.

'Split up?' said Shirley. 'What do you mean?'

'Neill and I are divorced, Mum . . . I'm sorry. I wanted to tell you in person. It's only been a few months.'

Bob looked as though he might collapse. He sat down heavily and stared at the floor. 'But why? Just because a bloke strays away a bit there's no need to go overboard with the dramatics.'

'Who's looking after the children while you're away?' said Shirley.

'Neill,' she said. 'They're fine. I call them

every day for a quick chat. They're fine.'

Bob fell into a deep silence, but as the evening wore on, he seemed better, less wound up. After dinner they sat in the lounge, chatting about changes in the area, in particular the new white footpaths, and the fish co-op where you could sit at the bar eating fresh oysters with your beer.

'I don't want you to think the divorce was my fault,' said Freya suddenly. 'It wasn't. Oh, I know I'm a bit mad and it drove Neill crazy sometimes. But I'm a good mother. And I was a good wife, too. Neill is a born philanderer. He can't seem to help himself. He doesn't just stray; he's rampant. Even now he's found religion I'll hedge my bets he'll still be on the prowl.'

'How awful for you, dear,' said Shirley. 'I'm so sorry.'

'I'll kill the bastard if I ever see him,' said Bob. 'I knew the minute I set eyes on that pommy idiot there'd be trouble. That stupid bloody leather coat he turned up in. On a summer's day! Ninety bloody degrees and a floor-length leather overcoat. Only a pom would be that up himself.'

'He accused me of never bonding with them,' said Freya. 'Which is ridiculous, of course. I mean, how can you not bond with the child you are destined to care for, unless you are callous or there's something wrong with you?'

She paused, and took a deep breath.

'Even if they weren't my own flesh and blood, I would still bond with them.' She hesitated. 'Say if Neill and I had adopted them — for whatever reason.'

Good. She had said it — adoption. If they

378

wanted to talk about it now, they could.

'I would have loved them just as much,' she continued. 'But for a while I believed him, I actually believed Neill was right.'

'I know what you mean, dear,' said Shirley. 'We've felt like complete failures too.'

'Oh, but you're not,' said Freya. 'I mean, I'm a qualified nurse. I went to the top of my profession before quitting to practise herbal medicine. I've got a diploma in herbal medicine now, and I'm a member of the National Institute of Medical Herbalists, and I've just achieved my BSc with the College of Phytotherapy in London. I'm not a drug addict or an alcoholic or a child abuser or a thief — I'm a good person. And that's because of you. Both of you.'

'Good Lord, you've got a few achievements under your belt, haven't you?' Bob beamed. 'That's our girl.'

Shirley rallied, scurrying off to put the kettle on.

'We always had faith in you, dear,' she said, returning a few minutes later with a tray. She sat on the footstool, closer to Freya. 'It wasn't because of us. It's because of you. You were born special. Different. If anyone asks me about my daughter I always say, 'Freya's different to other people. She's a nature-lover. She's a dreamer. She cares about the world.' '

They settled in for the evening. Bob showed her his certificates for services to the funeral industry, and his medals from the war. Shirley showed her some of the booties she'd been knitting for a neighbour's grandchild. They had expected she would stay the night, and asked if her suitcase was in the car. When she said she was going back to the hotel, they looked devastated.

'I can't stay. I've got to get back to the children.' She hated herself for lying, but it was kinder this way.

'You came twelve thousand miles and you're only spending a few hours with us?'

'I'm sorry.'

'Well, I suppose it's better than nothing,' said Shirley. 'Of course you must get home. They'll be missing you. What about bringing them with you next time?'

'If I can afford it, of course I will. I just wanted to see you on my own this time. To tell you in person about the divorce. Last time we were here they were little, and it was impossible to talk about things.'

They looked at each other, then at Freya, and nodded. 'We understand, dear,' said Shirley.

Later, as they stood at the gate saying goodbye, she noticed that much of the tension had gone from their faces.

The sun — unnaturally big, little flames flicking at the edges — was setting in the west.

'I'll write to you,' said Freya.

'Call us any time,' said Bob, 'and reverse the charges.'

'One more thing,' said Shirley. 'I want you to know how sorry we are.'

Freya opened her mouth to say, Don't say it, don't dare say it, please, but Shirley said, 'You mustn't get us wrong. We thought about giving you a brother or a sister. We thought about it a lot. But we had to keep working to pay the bills. We couldn't afford for me to take time off to look after another baby.'

'Don't worry,' said Freya. 'Please don't even think of it. All that jealousy, fighting over possessions and who gets the biggest bedroom. I'd have hated it. I liked being an only child. I was the centre of attention.'

They laughed.

'I couldn't have wished for better parents,' Freya added. She hugged them, and tears welled up in Shirley's eyes. Freya felt ripples of pleasure flowing through her mother's body.

'We're just glad to see you,' said Bob.

Freya walked to the end of the street. Before rounding the corner she turned to wave. To her surprise, they were already busy inspecting their handiwork on the new drive.

44

You're glad she's gone. She made you feel uncomfortable, with her piercing eyes and wild hair. Your heart can't take much more. First Deborah Anne, now Katherine. Next thing they'll bring the whole bloody tribe on to the ward.

You don't want to think about any of it now. You want to forget. You want your body to melt into the mattress and absorb your pain.

A nurse comes in to adjust your catheter. She gives you an injection and asks if you are comfortable.

I am now, you say.

Family? she says, referring to Freya.

No, you say, nothing to do with me. Some friend of a friend. Thought she'd look in on me.

Pity, says the nurse. I was hoping she might be your daughter.

I haven't got any daughters, you snap. I haven't got anyone and that's how I aim to keep it.

When you close your eyes you see Ester standing next to the homestead. The iron roof is red with rust. The struts on the veranda are broken, the deck is buckling. She is hanging washing on the clothesline. Her cheeks are pink and rosy, her eyes bright. She is almost plump she is so healthy.

You are up on the brow of the hill, standing

382

under a gum tree smoking, with your men. They still have another four hundred sheep to shear today, sweating it out in the pens. Their bellies are huge and heaving. Other people are down by the house, measuring windows, taking down notes on a clipboard, sweeping dust off the windowsills, and poking holes in the rotting timber.

There's a sign by the gate saying the house now comes under the jurisdiction of the New South Wales National Parks and Wildlife Services and Kosciusko Huts Association, who are currently restoring Tinderry Homestead as part of a broader project covering the Kosciusko National Park.

Your lawyer Nathan Hamilton is talking amiably to the strangers, and you wonder what sort of deal he has cut. He goes into the house and comes out a few minutes later carrying boxes, which he stacks in the rear of his Land Cruiser.

The hand-made skis you fashioned from fence palings are stacked at the side of the house. You hope Nathan remembers to take them; you told him to donate them, along with some of the older pieces of farm machinery, including a small steam engine that once powered a chaff-cutter. You said he could have all the furniture, too. It was being taken away, to be restored, then brought back when the house and outbuildings were ready to be opened as a museum. It amazed you to think they'd want any of it, but Nathan said the curators were thrilled, in particular with the wagonette, which was still in good working order and only needed a few coats of paint.

Ester pegs out the last pair of hand-knitted socks and walks around the back of the house to the laundry and slips inside, unseen by the young volunteers who are mending a wall of the shearers' quarters. The alpine ash has a silvery-grey sheen in the late-afternoon sunlight. Another man in jeans and a red-and-black check shirt is inside the two-seater dunny, hammering and whistling.

You are embarrassed about the state of the place, especially the bedroom, which you and Ester papered with newspaper to keep out the icy winds. You liked to read the articles when you couldn't sleep at night. Some of the pages are over seventy years old. The rooms are musty and everything smells of cabbage and cooked lamb.

Nathan brings out your best saddle and places it on a railing. He carefully rubs beeswax into its dry surface, massaging life into the tired, sweat-stained leather.

You develop an affinity with the mountains, he says to one of the volunteers. The old boy who lived here, he knew every inch of the place like he knew his own face.

The youngster nods solemnly. Is he dead? he asks.

Not yet, Nathan says, but it won't be long.

What about his wife?

Died years ago.

What happened?

Broken heart, so they reckon. Don't know the

full story. Lost their children, something like that.

He'd be happy to see we're looking after the place, then? says the youth.

Yeah, says Nathan. He'd be very happy. Poor old bugger. He loved this place. I reckon he's still here in spirit, so we better be careful how we go.

The boy nods and begins to prise off a flaking window frame.

You are lucky to have a lawyer like Nathan, who understands, who cares. You know you can trust him. When Ester died he helped you pack up her things to give to charity. Some of it went to a city museum; they were especially taken with her collection of short skirts and knitted stockings, which she wore cross-country skiing. Now you wish you'd kept them for the display they were planning for this museum, for Tinderry. Ester was a good woman. Trekking into the mountains in the snow and ice to fetch newborn lambs at the end of a long winter, chopping firewood, growing vegetables, slaughtering chickens, boiling rags used to clean down the boards in the shearing shed. And always with her straw hat pulled low over her face in summer, and a hooded jacket in winter with a thick green scarf. But you knew her secret.

The city museum got really excited when you showed them her collection of bogong moths. You had built a display case inlaid with glass and Ester pinned the moths to calico, dyed with mountain moss. At first you were reluctant to give them up, and then one of the women, a do-gooder type in a grey twill skirt, said the local

Aborigines who inhabited these parts years ago feasted on bogong moths when they held corroborees and marriage ceremonies.

Take it, you said, disgusted, it's the least I can do.

The woman was ecstatic, and you shook your head in disbelief.

Ester is out the back milking one of the house cows. She will make a pot of porridge for your breakfast, and feed two of the orphaned calves with the leftover milk. She's not the sentimental type, but she likes to make sure all the animals are fed and watered, and any sheep that have been cut are put in her care in the new, clean sheep camps, to avoid gas gangrene and tetanus.

She is wearing a long knitted cardigan, which she pulls tight around her breasts against the cold wind, which is certain to change into a blizzard when night falls.

Tonight, as always, you will urge her breasts into the dip in your chest and give her a good seeing-to. It's the only thing that keeps her up here, the only comfort from the long, cold days when the winds blow off the snow-capped peaks. You are afraid she might run back to the city and leave you. But there's something else that will keep her here. Every time you have an orgasm, you pray she will fall pregnant.

The hill where you are standing is bathed in golden sunlight, after the morning thunderstorm that swept through. You marvel at the resilience of the alpine snow grasses and white eye-brights surrounding the creek that trickles down from a gorge. The mountains are shrugging off their wintry weight and beginning the transition into a fresh new season, very different from the one before, but just as challenging.

It is quiet. The blizzard you expected has changed direction and everything is still. You close your eyes and breathe in the clear air, feeling it fill your lungs, then you breathe out slowly, your feet firm as rocks on the land that you think of as home.

45

'What's he like, this Henry fella?' said Peggy.

She and Connie were sitting on the broad veranda of the homestead, two hundred and fifty kilometres north of Alice Springs. They sipped Peggy's home-made lemonade and looked out at the dry land.

Forbes was out in the south paddock, breaking in horses with some of the boys. They were half a mile from the house, but the two women could see the dust billowing and blending into the river of heat haze.

'He didn't like me,' said Connie. 'I could see in his eyes that he hated me. My colour, more than anything. As though he was ashamed and embarrassed I was there. So I left. Not rudely. I chatted to him for a while. About the weather, mainly. And cricket. He complained about the man in the next bed on a ventilator. The poor guy could hear every word. I knew he wasn't our father, soon as I clapped eyes on him. Too white. Mind, he had a good tan. Farmers are out in it all day. No thought for skin cancer.'

'He must've got a terrible shock when we popped out of our mother's belly, aye,' said Peggy, her eyes wide and round. She shook her head slowly, trying to imagine the scene: Henry standing at the doorway, face drained of blood, the midwife — if there was one in those days, in such a remote place — trying to get the babies out alive, at the same time trying not to let Ester see them until she'd figured out with Henry how to tell her. Wrapping their blood-stained bodies in towels, faces barely visible, placing them in the crib as though they were too hot to handle.

'I didn't like him at all,' Connie went on. 'You know the sort. Stubborn. Thinks all blacks are bad.'

'Our poor mother,' said Peggy. 'She must have gone mad from the shock.'

'Yes,' said Connie. 'And you know what they say about cancer. It can start with a terrible trauma. I've heard of people getting it after a bad car accident, or a death in the family.'

'Well I know I'm ugly,' said Peggy, stifling a giggle, 'but I didn't think the sight of me would kill a person, aye.'

Connie smiled and squeezed her sister's hand. 'You're not ugly.'

'Cancer's a terrible, terrible curse.' Peggy's smile faded into a serious expression. She took a long, loud sip of her drink and rested the glass on her breasts, which were pushed up by her pot belly.

Connie nodded. 'It sure is at that.'

She put her arm around Peggy's shoulder. Peggy's shock of grey and copper-brown hair stuck out like a dense halo. Every morning she tried to flatten it with a hairbrush but it refused to be tamed.

'Henry's an ignorant old man,' said Connie. 'I wouldn't want him for my father. You wouldn't either. I don't care if I never find out who our real father is. We've got each other. That's all that matters now.' She squeezed Peggy hard.

Peggy laughed shyly.

'What about Freya?' she said, suddenly serious. 'I feel sorry for her, with him for a father.'

'She'll probably feel mixed up about it,' said Connie. 'Knowing they gave her up, even though she's white. I don't understand it. Maybe our mother was too sick to look after a child by the time Freya came along. Or maybe Freya was an accident. The Pill wasn't invented then, and I bet they didn't have condoms either. Who knows. But every time I mentioned her to Henry he just got angry, so I gave up.'

'We'll never know the truth now,' said Peggy, her eyes sad. 'How long do you reckon he'll last?'

'The nurses said less than six months. Everything's going. His liver is packing up, and his kidneys. He's got problems with his bowel and his bladder.'

They sat in silence for a long time, watching the sun descend over the pale gold spinifex. When it finally fell behind the distant line of low hills they went inside.

Forbes was in the kitchen with the boys, preparing a meal, which they would eat outside on the screened veranda, safe from the flies. Neither sister had noticed him arriving home on Macey, his grey mare. It amazed Connie the way he moved around the farm from one chore to another, popping up in the chook yard one minute, pushing a vacuum cleaner around the lounge room the next. The boys couldn't get away with anything.

'Git out of it, husband,' said Peggy. 'I'll finish that.'

Forbes joined the boys on the veranda for a smoke. Connie offered to set the long table.

'How long have you and Forbes been taking these boys in?' She scooped up the cutlery and a red gingham tablecloth.

'Long time now,' said Peggy. 'It started when Forbes went into town for supplies and came back with two brothers.' She began to peel a bowl of potatoes, her belly resting on the bench.

'He found 'em sleeping rough on the front step of a real estate agent's in Alice. Filthy, they were. The police told 'em they had to get a job or get out of town. They'd already bin in jail for stealing and had a rough time in there. They were servicing some of the men off the boats up in Darwin, aye.'

'Where are they now?'

'Still here. That's them, out by the shed.' She pointed through the window to two older men, probably in their early thirties, leaning against a fence, smoking.

'When they turned twenty-one Forbes gave them jobs as farmhands and horse-breakers.'

'They seem too old, if you don't mind me saying, to still be here.'

'Forbes never makes the boys feel like he owns 'em just because he helped 'em,' said Peggy. 'They're free to go any time.'

'How do you decide who can come here and who can't?' said Connie.

'We don't,' said Peggy. 'They find us. If a kid turns up here he's welcome to stay. We don't need to advertise. Word gets around. The place is government-subsidised now. The authorities, welfare people, the police, they all send kids here.'

'But how do you look after so many boys?' Peggy laughed.

Connie looked embarrassed. 'What?' she said. 'What did I say that's so funny?'

Peggy took a deep breath and replied, 'Them boys look after 'emselves. Me and Forbes just give 'em a leg up. He teaches 'em horsemanship, so's they can get jobs on stations and make something of their lives.'

'Do you feel happy when you laugh?' Connie bit her lip. She didn't mean to sound rude, but she couldn't help wondering if it was a nervous tic more than a sincere reaction to situations that made Peggy such a giggling gertie. Her sense of humour made Connie feel flat and dull. City life had sapped her childish wonder.

Peggy grew pensive. Her eyes were swimming with big, doleful tears. She was peeling a potato and digging out the eyes with a sharp knife. Finally she looked at Connie and said, 'All Aboriginal people have many fears. If we didn't find things to laugh at, we'd never survive, aye.'

★ ★ ★

'Excuse me, madam, would you like some lunch?'

'No thank you,' said Freya. She gave the stewardess a cursory glance. She resented being interrupted. Wasn't it obvious she wanted to absorb every detail of the changing landscape? Hadn't she made it plain she wanted to be left alone? She had turned into the window, clamped headphones to her ears, put on her sunglasses. Australians were so determined to be nice. She even pretended to be asleep, but still the stewardess insisted on waking her up for afternoon tea.

It was hard not to worry about the children. She gazed at the scenery passing below the plane. Neill had sounded so odd on the phone. She had written them an air-mail letter before leaving Melbourne, and posted it near the hotel. It would be her last letter to them; if Forbes and Peggy have a computer, from now on she would only send emails, so that Neill couldn't trace her.

Connie had promised to meet her at Alice Springs, and said she'd try to bring Peggy.

'You'll like it out here,' she'd said on the phone yesterday, 'it's very easy-going. You don't have to worry about dressing up. I've had the same pair of jeans on for three days.'

Peering through the ice-ruffled window, Freya saw how the land was divided by rivers and mountains, and how the great dark forests surrendered to dusty plains, lacerated with puzzling tracks that appeared to lead nowhere, then suddenly ended at a rocky escarpment or a glittering lake, offering sanctuary to a surprising host of animals and plants, all born with the same desire for life. Staring down at the eerie landscape she thought of Tom and Kirsty and asked herself over and over why she had come here, why she had left them in pursuit of something that she might never understand. Something that might not even make any difference to her life.

She longed to be able to pick up a phone and call the children, just to hear their voices, to know they were fine. She closed her eyes and tried to empty her mind. After a while she opened them again and leaned into the window.

Beneath the plane huge round lakes glinted in the sunlight. Silver rivers snaked across the land, and flocks of birds, thousands of them, swept through the sky. The land spread like a living map, red, brown and golden plains pulsating under a vast ocean of rippling air.

A warm rush of exhilaration rose up inside her. It's going to be fine, she told herself. Just fine.

She mopped her brow with a tissue, and took a long drink of water from the bottle she had brought in her bag from Melbourne. There was no phone, no computer, no fax machine on the plane. She would just have to wait.

★ ★ ★

The plane came into sight at the end of the Alice Springs airport runway and began its descent. The right wing tipped, then the left, until both were level with the airstrip.

Twenty-five Aboriginal women had been waiting at the terminal since dawn, tired but uncomplaining in floral frocks and bare feet. It wasn't every day they got to visit the airport and greet someone from the other side of the world.

394

'Come on,' said Peggy. 'Come on, you lot. Your sister's sister is comin'.'

Yesterday some of the Elders had given Connie her own skin name. Now she could talk to them openly. She was making good progress, chatting to them about her life in America, asking about their lives in the desert, padding back and forth from the café with drinks and ice creams.

'Don't spoil those bloody women,' said Peggy merrily. 'They'll get fat.' Everyone laughed.

Peggy had been given her skin name twenty-six years ago, when Forbes brought her down from Darwin.

'Those were the sad old days,' she had told Connie yesterday. 'Forbes rescued me from a bad life up there.' She looked down at her feet, ashamed. After a while she looked up and smiled. 'But I'm okay now.'

Connie had hugged her. 'That's good.' She adored Peggy, and hugged her a lot, to make up for lost time.

The temperature was nearing thirty degrees. Peggy said it was cool for September. Usually by this time of year it was nearer thirty-five.

Flies gathered around the women's ankles. Connie swatted them from her face. Someone said, 'You'll wear yourself out doing that,' and giggled.

Peggy had collected the women from country around the homestead, and some had come in from the Yuendumu community. She told them they must welcome Freya, because she had no one else. In a way she was one of them, said

Milly, a wrinkled Elder with one eye. The women were glad to oblige. Milly would make Freya her adopted daughter. If Freya agreed, they could make it proper, under law. While they waited, the older women sang softly, their colourful frocks billowing in the morning breeze.

When the plane taxied towards the buildings the noise of the jets drowned out the women's banter. The engine stopped, and they stared anxiously at the ground crew wheeling the stairs towards the plane.

The door near the plane's cockpit opened and a stewardess nodded and smiled at each passenger as they disembarked, blinking at the brilliant light.

Freya ducked through the doorway and climbed down the stairs. She kept her eyes on her feet, too afraid to look up into the waiting fray.

Connie cried out, 'That's her. In the blue skirt.'

Peggy said, 'She's white, aye.'

'I told you,' said Connie.

Peggy was nominated to greet her first, seeing as they'd never met. She walked up to Freya as she came through the gate and said, 'Hello. I'm Peggy.'

She gave Freya a big hug and then held her at arm's length and smiled shyly.

'Welcome to Alice,' she said, and giggled, then looked down at her feet, overcome. Tears welled up in her eyes and fell on the sand.

'Hello, hello,' said Freya, laughing, her tension easing.

Peggy was thrilled. She began to laugh uncontrollably and jump up and down on the spot, clapping like a child.

'Calm down, woman,' said Milly.

Peggy pressed her lips together and was silent. She was shorter than Freya, and dumpy. She wasn't at all what Freya was expecting. She was nothing like Connie. She looked old enough to be Connie's grandmother. Her skin was like parchment. Her stomach and breasts combined to make one vast bulge, like a drum. She had on a pink floral muumuu, spotlessly clean and ironed, a style that both emphasised and disguised her full figure. Her frizzy hair made her head look like an electrified raisin, the fringe clipped to one side with a plastic ladybird clasp. Her feet were bare, her legs scarred and scratched. When Milly wasn't looking she beamed at Freya.

Freya's heart melted. She's lovely, she thought. She had not spoken to anyone during the long flight, and her stomach was in a tight knot. She wasn't sure what to say, so she said, 'Thanks so much for meeting me. I like your dress.'

Peggy went into another fit of the giggles.

Freya looked around at the gathering crowd. She had only expected to be met by Connie and Peggy, not half the population of Alice Springs.

'Welcome to Alice,' said Milly. She stepped forward and put her chubby arms around Freya, chuckling bashfully.

Freya opened her mouth to speak but could not form the right words. Did they know simpl

397

by looking at her? She wasn't sure what to say, and for a moment wondered if Del had somehow been in touch with Connie and let the truth slip out.

They clamoured around, all talking and singing at once, stroking her arms, holding her hands, and ruffling her hair, as though she were a toy.

Connie stood back smiling, pleased the women were giving her a good welcome. Peggy left the others to it and stood by Connie, nuzzling into her arm and holding her hand.

Freya glanced across the sea of brown heads surrounding her — trapping her — looking for reassurance, but Connie simply laughed.

'Now you've gone and done it,' she said to Freya.

Freya noticed that Connie looked different. Her hair was untidy and tied in a loose bunch at the nape of her neck. She was wearing a long yellow dress with ruffled sleeves that was frumpy and dated, and a string of tiny white shells around her neck. She had clumpy leather sandals on her feet, which were callused and cracked. The sandals looked mighty uncomfortable, as well as unflattering. There was no trace of lipstick or rouge or fake fingernails. The effect of this pared-down look was dramatic. Her voice was calmer, not as shrill. She had lost her awkward self-consciousness. Her smile seemed to come from a deeper place. Yet she looked worried too, as though she wasn't quite sure she wanted to be there.

Suddenly a woman broke away from the group

398

and grabbed Connie's hand, drawing her into the scrum. She looked like one of them. She smiled at Freya and hugged her.

'You look so different,' said Freya.

'No need for fancy airs out here,' said Connie, laughing.

The noise of everyone laughing and another plane taking off was overwhelming. Claustrophobia was not one of Freya's quirks, but suddenly she longed to find a quiet spot in which to be alone. On a hill, looking down.

She looked at the sea of brown faces grinning, the scrawny hands pawing, and wondered what they would think of a woman who said she was Aboriginal, but looked white. What would they make of a woman who stepped off a big silver bird from a faraway country they knew little about, claiming to be one of them? Would they think that woman was pretentious? She hoped Connie hadn't said anything about her theory.

She was suddenly acutely conscious of their dark eyes and pink mouths, and their deep matt brown skin. The contrast between her own appearance and theirs made a knot of hot panic rise up inside her. What if Connie was right and Henry was her father? Perhaps the birthmark was nothing but a coincidence?

'Come on, you lot, give Freya some breathing space,' said Milly.

The women stood aside and Connie, Peggy and Milly ushered her outside, where her luggage was waiting on a motorised cart. After retrieving it she was able to breathe freely for a moment, then they surrounded her again.

singing and laughing, and she was borne away to the car park, on a wave of joy.

'Wait here,' said Peggy. 'We're going with Forbes.'

The other women piled into a dusty minibus and settled into their seats, waving at Freya and her sisters through the windows.

'This way,' said Peggy.

She walked along the rows of parked cars, and opened the rear door of a Range Rover. She lifted Freya's luggage into the boot. A man with a sandy complexion was sitting behind the wheel. He made no attempt to get out and greet them, or help with the luggage.

'You hop in the front,' said Peggy, opening the passenger door.

The driver stared straight ahead, elbow resting on the rim of the open window. He was wearing a battered Akubra, brown moleskins and a sleeveless khaki shirt. He sucked hard on the stained stump of a hand-rolled cigarette.

'Go on. Climb in. He won't bite ya.'

Peggy almost pushed Freya into the front seat, then she and Connie climbed into the back.

'This is Forbes,' said Peggy, leaning forward. 'Say g'day.' She slapped the man's shoulder. 'My knight in dusty moleskins.' She threw herself back in the seat and giggled, slapping her bare legs hard.

Forbes barely turned his head. Freya was aware of a tiny gesture of recognition, a barely perceptible nod in her direction, the twitch of a blond eyebrow. He said nothing. A fly shot through the open window on his side, somersaulted along the upper rim of the windscreen, and zoomed off through Freya's window.

'Nice to meet you, Forbes,' said Freya, holding out a hand.

Forbes looked at it but his hands remained on the steering wheel, even though the engine wasn't running.

'How far is it to Paradise?' she said.

Forbes was silent.

'Two hundred and eighty-five k's,' said Peggy from the back seat.

Forbes frowned. He had a large nose and deep lines across his forehead. And a startlingly black colonial moustache, like a live animal. Freya wondered if he'd dyed it. The hair on his head and his eyebrows were blond. Perhaps the moustache was false. It was very impressive.

The front seats had high backs that effectively screened Connie and Peggy off. Freya tried to turn around to chat, but once her seat belt was on it was a strain on her neck.

Forbes struck Freya as a man of few words. She hoped he might switch the radio on. It would be a very long ride to Paradise if he was going to be so cold. He turned on the ignition key and pulled out of the car park with the bearing of a man driving alone.

Before long, they had left Alice far behind. In the side mirror she saw reflected a cloud of orange dust churned up behind them by the wheels. She settled back to try and enjoy the scenery, but it was just a dreary expanse of dry spinifex plains. She hoped they would soon cross rivers and drive alongside lakes, to relieve the monotony. But there was no sign of any water.

What am I doing here? she kept asking herself. I have left my children with two religious nutters so I can find myself — here? She stared at the flat expanse of red and yellow dust and scattered rocks, and a dull tiredness overwhelmed her. Peggy and Connie chatted in the back seat, then silence fell over the car.

Freya nodded off. A loud bump woke her and, embarrassed, she realised she had been dribbling. She quickly wiped her mouth and caught Forbes grinning stupidly at her.

'We're about ten k's south of the Tropic of Capricorn,' said Peggy, leaning forward.

Freya made a few more attempts at conversation with Forbes, but his replies were restricted to grunts and truncated sentences of three or four words. She was uncomfortably aware of his sun-ravaged arms, and the way he held the steering wheel with a thumb and forefinger over his crotch. He left his right arm resting on the window ledge.

Another hour or so passed and he turned on to a dirt highway.

'This is the real Tanami Track,' Peggy shouted.

Freya gazed through the dust-stained window and a terrible pang of boredom and panic crept through her. She had never seen such flat, dull country. She counted four dead kangaroos by the roadside, bloated and fly-blown, and in the distance a flock of grey and pink galahs were the only relief on an otherwise lonely landscape.

Night fell.

402

It happened quickly, like a light going off, preceded by a copper and ruby sunset. Now only the oncoming traffic broke the monotony. Huge trucks hurled past them, silver bull-bars glinting in the blackness. Road trains twinkling with lights lurched along like horizontal skyscrapers. As they thundered past, the Range Rover swayed dangerously from the force of the wind current. Now and then Freya saw the black silhouettes of trees and low hills in the distance. Occasionally they caught up with the minibus, and Forbes slowed to avoid the dust it threw up.

Freya could feel the dust in her mouth, gritty and dry. It was in her hair, too. Her scalp felt itchy with sweat, even though she had washed it that morning. She felt uncomfortable with Forbes; she sensed he didn't like her. She'd known people like him before, arrogant types who made no effort to put a person at ease. He made her nervous and self-conscious, as if every little gesture she made was that of a fool.

Fed up with the silence, she craned her head through the gap between the seats.

'It's very deceptive out here in the desert,' she said to her sisters. 'The distances.'

She knew immediately it was an inane and clumsy thing to say. Especially as the huge space was probably nothing to Forbes and Peggy.

Peggy nodded and laughed. 'You city fellas think youse can hop on down to the corner shop out here, but you're in fer a shock.'

They had been driving for nearly two hours. Suddenly the minibus pulled over in a cloud of dust. Forbes passed it and tipped his hat at the driver. Peggy hung out of the window and shouted goodbye to the women, who had piled on to the roadside. Freya waved too, but somehow felt sidelined. Glancing around, she searched for the lights of a settlement, but there was nothing but blackness beneath a moonless sky.

The bus turned around and started back towards Alice. Freya watched its lights in the side mirror. She saw the shapes of the women walking across the paddocks into a void.

'Where are they going? I didn't see any lights.'

She looked at Forbes. A faint smile formed at the corners of his mouth. He leaned forward and tucked his shirt in at the back. The angle of his head gave him a proud, haughty look.

'Women's business,' he grunted. 'The ones from Yuendumu will get a lift back there tomorra.'

'Oh,' she said.

At least he had actually spoken at last. She felt annoyed by his lack of manners. Perhaps that was how it was out here. The rugged land stripped away any airs and graces a person might have had. He was behaving as though she'd just arrived from the next town, not a glamorous city twelve thousand miles away. He'd probably never been outside Australia, and couldn't compre-hend long-distance air travel — let alone the trauma of leaving your children behind.

'Women's business,' he said again. He nodded towards a rocky escarpment, rising dramatically along the western horizon. 'Blacks only,' he added, looking down the long bridge of his nose at the dark road stretching ahead.

★ ★ ★

They continued into the night on the dirt road. Freya nodded off again, and was awakened with a start when the vehicle slowed down and Forbes crunched the gears as he pulled into a road-house for fuel. The three women got out and used the toilets.

'Hurry,' said Peggy. 'Forbes wants to get goin'.'

They drove for another hour before Forbes made a sharp turn off the highway on to a rough track leading across a huge swathe of flat land. Here the dust was less severe. Freya wound her window down and put her face to the wind. The sky was shimmering with millions of stars.

'God,' she breathed, to no one in particular, 'look at that.'

They came to a white gate with *Paradise* painted across the top beam. Forbes stopped the vehicle. Peggy leapt out and opened the gate. When he had driven through, she closed it again and hopped back in.

The track was suddenly lined with gum trees, marking the entrance to the homestead. Freya could see the woolly silhouettes of sheep huddled beneath trees. The house came into view, lights shining yellow at the windows, throwing beams on to the meshed veranda. Many trees surrounded the buildings, including several palms. It was like a desert oasis.

Forbes pulled up by the front gate and turned

off the engine. Immediately Freya was over-whelmed with the roar of insects singing in the grasses. Several motion lights came on, throwing into relief the ring of trees surrounding the house. They were in full bloom, but Freya couldn't make out the colour or shape of the flowers. She stepped out of the car and stretched her legs. Peggy and Connie got out and stood beside her, yawning.

'Welcome to Paradise,' said Peggy. 'Forbes'll bring your bags in. Come on, I'll show you your room.'

Connie and Freya followed her inside.

'Connie's got a head start on you,' said Peggy, giggling. 'Bin here two weeks and she's part of the family.'

'You mean I'm the chief bottle-washer already,' said Connie, winking at Freya.

There was a flash of the Connie Freya remembered in London, but the blustery bravado had disappeared. She seemed so plain now, all the pretentiousness gone.

'See you tomorrow,' said Connie, hugging Freya. 'I'm off to bed.'

Freya glanced at her watch. It was only eight o'clock, but it felt much later.

Connie noticed her expression and laughed. 'We get up early out here,' she said. 'You'll get used to it.'

'I was hoping we could talk for a while.'

'Not tonight,' said Connie. 'There'll be plenty of time. Don't worry. That's one thing there's plenty of out here. You'll be ready for bed by seven most nights, once you get into the routine of getting up early.'

She gave Freya a quick, awkward hug. There was none of the clingy pawing that had dominated her attitude to Freya in London. She was ambivalent and a little offhand. Freya felt put out. Now that she'd made the effort and travelled all this way, she was expecting Connie to be even more enthusiastic.

'This way,' said Peggy.

She was halfway along a wide hall. As Freya followed her, Peggy briefly opened the doors leading off it and showed her each room. They were full of heavy furniture, much of it brown and green leather. Freya saw little evidence of a woman's touch. Sombre outback paintings, an elegant mahogany dining table and chairs, carved wooden ashtrays, sideboards and dressers groaning with heavy bone china. Saddles piled up on the floor along the hall; bridles, hats, Driza-Bones hanging on hooks. Everything was masculine and dark in the gloomy light. Even the patina of the wood floors. They moved along the hall and Peggy opened several more doors. Three drawing rooms, altogether.

'They all lead on to the veranda,' said Peggy. 'You just can't tell, with the curtains pulled across. They keep the heat out.'

With the sun streaming in the whole place would have a different atmosphere, Freya thought, feeling better.

She spotted a telephone on a side table in what looked like the main living room. She longed to pounce on it and call the children. Perhaps tomorrow she would, if she promised to reimburse Forbes. Since arriving in Australia she had written to them every day. And when she found an internet café, she sent them long and detailed emails. In contrast, their answers were short and lacking information. She wondered if it was Neill writing these terse replies.

'Have you got a computer?' she said, looking at Peggy.

Peggy shook her head and laughed.

'No computers at Paradise. Forbes doesn't like 'em. He hates new technology. He even shears the sheep with old-fashioned clippers, aye. The only machinery he likes is vehicles.'

Freya's heart sank. What would the children think when her emails suddenly stopped? She couldn't write from here: Neill would see the postmark and think she was on some expensive outback tour, then he'd be demanding even more child support money.

'How often do you drive into Alice Springs?'

'Once a month. Sometimes twice. To pick up new boys. And supplies.'

Peggy pointed through a window at a dam that they used as a swimming hole. Freya could see it shimmering under the stars like silver.

'You're lucky. Most times it's dry, but we had a lot of rain this year, so it's full. But you still have to be careful. Two minutes in the shower, no more. You can swim in the dam if you want. Saves on bath water.'

'Is it safe?'

'Course it is. We don't get crocs this far south. You might see a few snakes, some of 'em cool off in there, the ones that can swim, but you'll see them before they see you. We've got a bore, too. But we're still careful about the amount of water we use. Here's your room.'

She opened a door and switched on a light.

Freya gasped. 'How lovely,' she said, admiring the pale floral furnishings and white-painted furniture. It was so different to the rest of the house. Light and feminine. French doors led on to the veranda. Sheer white curtains quivered in the breeze.

'There's a table and chairs right outside your room, overlooking the garden,' said Peggy. 'Not that there's a lot to look at. Too busy to look after it. There's a few roses, and the poincianas are looking good at the moment, aye.'

'It's beautiful,' said Freya.

'You sound surprised,' said Peggy. 'Did you think we lived in a humpy?'

'No. Of course not. It's just . . . ' Freya felt ashamed. 'I just didn't expect you to be so — '

'Well off? Oh, we're not well off. Forbes inherited some money, that's all, and he invested in stocks and got lucky. But we're not rich. It's taken him years to get this place how he wanted it. And he wouldn't have it at all if it wasn't for the local Elders. They let him build on their land.'

'I'm sorry. I didn't mean to be rude.'

Peggy laughed. 'It's okay. Most people are surprised when they come here. Forbes looks like the sort who'd live in a tin shack. You'll see all that if we go for a drive. There's a lot of poverty out here. People don't expect it, especially city types.'

Freya put her handbag on the bed and looked around at the room. There were several paintings on the walls, unframed but striking and raw.

'Who did those?' said Freya.

'I did,' said Peggy shyly.

'How clever,' said Freya, and meant it.

'Not really. Just a fat old black woman.'

'Are they about Aboriginal culture?'

Peggy nodded. 'But they're not original. I copied 'em. From an old calendar. I'm not clever enough to understand what any of it means, aye. I don't dream.'

'I'd like to learn about your culture, if you'll teach me.'

'One of these days I'm gunna persuade Forbes to let me loose on the rest of the house,' said Peggy, ignoring Freya's request. 'He's a bit attached to things, you know. Some of the furniture's as old as he is.'

Freya looked more closely at one of the dot paintings and tried again. 'Are you going to teach me about the Dreamtime?'

'White people think it's something you can just learn,' said Peggy. She looked amused, rather than annoyed.

Freya blushed. She would have to stop making clangers.

'You have to know the land first,' said Peggy. 'Can't know the jukurrpa, can't know me, or your sister, or any of those other women, till you know the land. Jukurrpa's a spoken history of our people; it's our sacred relationship to the land and its creation. It's our knowledge of creation from the past, from now, and for the future. It's ongoing. It's now. White people think it's about the creation of the world and that it all happened a long time ago. But we live it now. We learn it now. It's not about the Big Bang, when everything began. It's more than that. Everything is connected. Even if you and I were not connected by blood, we would still be connected because we are part of the land and all living things.'

'Do you ever wish you knew where your people are? Especially your father.'

Peggy shrugged. 'I know it's not the same, living here in this country, because it's not my country or Connie's. Our ancestors might be from Tasmania for all I know.'

She walked across the room and took a book from the night table.

'This was a gift from Forbes about all the language groups and the areas they're from. Look at this map showing all of 'em. Hundreds, aye. It makes Europe look like Toy Town. Forbes took me on a trip right round Australia and up the middle too, after we first met. I wanted to see if I could recognise my country just by feeling. But I didn't find it.' She shrugged. 'Who knows. It could be anywhere. I'll never find it now. Too old to bother.'

'Do you really think it's possible, to recognise where you're from just by a feeling?' said Freya.

'Yeah. I reckon. The Elders know. Some of 'em have come out here from miles away. They were taken away when they were little, by the authorities. Taken from their families. They came back eventually, but it took 'em years to find

411

their way, to find out exactly where they belonged.'

She was pensive for a moment. She stared at one of her paintings, a childish rendition of a kangaroo surrounded by snaking dots and handprints.

'This is my home now,' she said. 'I've got to know it round here, aye. The people you saw at the airport, they adopted me. I'll never leave. Not now.'

She stepped forward and gave Freya a big bear hug. 'Be careful what you say to Forbes about all this.' Then she held Freya's shoulders and looked straight into her eyes. 'I try to learn off the Elders, but it's an uphill battle. It's a hard culture to learn. It takes a lifetime and you still wouldn't know everything. I haven't got the knack. I'm a coconut blackfella. Not proud of it, but there you go. I can't help the way I am. Bloody white men, interfering with our women.' She shook her head and clicked her tongue.

'Is Connie learning too?' said Freya.

'It's harder for Con.' Peggy let go of Freya's shoulders and sat on the bed. 'Being from America, she's finding it tough. But she's got plenty of pluck, I'll give her that. She's not afraid to get stuck in and have a go, aye.'

'Will Forbes think I'm being affected if I try and learn?'

'You do what you think's right. Just don't go round makin' out you've got black ancestors when you haven't. Henry's white as they come, Connie reckons. He's not my bloody father, or Connie's. You'll never understand our culture,

412

not properly, and nor will I because I didn't grow up with it. I grew up in homes. Horrible bloody places. I was beaten and tortured and locked in a cell. But the Elders are teachin' me stuff all the time. I can learn about it, same as a schoolkid can learn how to add up. I might not have a black heart, but I can still learn the basics. They won't want to teach you because you're white. Anyway, what's the point? Whitefellas, they think it's about painting your body with ochre and dancing around a fire. They don't know nothin' about the spiritual side.'

Freya wasn't sure how to respond. The only thing she felt certain of was her inner voice telling her the truth.

'I thought it might help me get to know you, if I learned.'

She had to be careful. She didn't want to make Peggy suspicious. She would have to be extra vigilant if she went swimming too, and make sure no one was watching. She would wear a T-shirt over her swimsuit, to cover the birthmark.

'The Elders are very proud people. They don't take kindly to people comin' in expectin' them to open up. They're very guarded. Milly said she'd adopt you, but that don't mean she's gunna teach you much. Some whites they wanna come out here and write books and take pictures, but they don't understand the protocol.'

'I'm sorry,' said Freya. 'I don't want to upset anyone.'

'Don't worry. We'll soon get to know one another. You don't have to do anything formal.

Besides, you're not allowed to hear some things or see some things. A lot of it's sacred.'

'I see.' Freya frowned. 'I don't mean to be ignorant. Aboriginal culture wasn't on the curriculum when I was at school.'

'We call it indigenous culture these days, for a start.'

'Oh.'

'It's still not taught in some schools. A few of the universities run courses, but . . . '

'And I've never read any books or met any Aboriginals — '

'Indigenous people.'

'Right. Until Connie turned up I didn't take much interest, to be honest.'

'You're all right. We'll have a good time.'

'I can't stay too long.'

'Gotta get back to your kids, aye?'

Freya nodded. 'Yes, I do.'

'Connie told me about them. You reckon you'll get them back when you go to court?'

'I don't know. Maybe.'

'Well, I hope you do. Kids need their mother. Look at my boys. Their mothers are all alcoholics. Look how it's affected 'em. Glue-sniffers, thieves, we got the bloody lot here at Paradise. Me and Forbes, we sort 'em out a bit.'

She turned at the door.

'Hope you're comfortable. It's a good hard mattress. The sheets are new. Bought 'em at Woolies, aye. If you get cold, there's more blankets in the cupboard. The bathroom's next door. Connie's across the hall. Help yourself in

414

the kitchen if you get hungry in the night. Breakfast's six till seven. All the boys'll be there. We eat all our meals on the back veranda, where it's cooler. Full house at the moment. Thirty of the little buggers.' She giggled.

Freya wished Peggy would sit awhile and talk. She opened her mouth to suggest it, but stopped short when Peggy yawned.

'If you're late for breakfast the boys'll eat all the tucker,' she said. 'Better set your alarm if you don't want to miss out, aye.'

⋆ ⋆ ⋆

A shooting star disappeared behind a black ridge. Cold air wrapped itself around Freya's legs. She pulled her cardigan tight, pushed her feet into her slippers and sipped the camomile tea she had sneaked into the kitchen to make. She had moved the cane chair in her room nearer the French door, so she could look out at the sky.

Her feet were itching to walk and find a hill. She stared through the darkness surrounding the homestead, trying to make out the various shapes of the outbuildings and trees. Strange noises came from the spinifex. A dog howled. She saw something moving in the branches of a poinciana. It would be madness to leave the safety of the house at night, yet she was longing to explore.

She sat in the chair until her eyes began to droop, but by the time she had undressed, washed her face and climbed into bed, she was wide awake again, her body stiff with excitement. She turned on her side and stared through the door. The hypnotic night beckoned. The gilded plains were like an offering. Presently she closed her eyes and fell into a deep sleep.

By the time she had showered and dressed next morning, there was no sign of anyone at the house. She stood at the kitchen door looking towards the corrals. She could hear the men shouting and hoofs banging on the hard earth. Clouds of dust whisked into the sky, and she caught a glimpse of a boot in a stirrup, an arm waving, a hat bouncing, a horse's rump.

She made herself a cup of herbal tea from her own supply, and found a packet of stale muesli at the back of a cupboard. As she chomped her way through it, hoping it wasn't full of weevils, she noticed an envelope addressed to her, propped up on the shelf over the Rayburn. It was a note from Peggy, explaining that the Elders had come for her and Connie at sunup, and that they had gone bush for 'women's business', to teach Connie.

She felt a stab of disappointment.

After breakfast she found a pair of boots in the hall, pulled them on and walked to the corrals in search of Forbes. On the way she passed a group of boys at a white-painted table under a pergola draped with shade cloth. A large Aboriginal man with a bushy white beard was sitting with them, teaching arithmetic.

'Morning,' he said, as Freya passed. 'You Freya?'

Freya nodded.

416

'Name's Terry,' he said. 'I'm the teacher round here.'

'Pleased to meet you,' said Freya. She walked towards him and offered her hand. He took it in his and shook it hard. 'Sorry to interrupt,' said Freya.

'No worries. It's just coming up to morning break anyway.'

She wanted to find Forbes and ring home while the house was quiet, but the boys were looking at her as if to say, aren't you going to say hello to us? They were so vulnerable, their timid eyes peeking out beneath long, unruly fringes. Freya smiled and said hello. They took turns shaking hands with her, and several were overcome with bashfulness, so much so that they were shaking. She smiled at each boy, making sure she gave them all an equal measure of her attention.

'Good on ya,' said Terry, smiling at Freya.

Forbes was helping a young boy break in a horse. About ten other boys were hanging over the railings, watching. They all turned and stared at Freya as she approached.

'Morning,' she said, and smiled.

They tipped the brims of their hats. One or two returned the greeting, but most said nothing.

Forbes looked up and noticed Freya by the fence. She nodded at him and smiled, but he looked away, intent on catching the stallion. When he looked her way a few minutes later, she lifted her hand and gestured that she wished to speak with him. He sighed and shook his head.

'Take over, Billy,' he said, handing the boy the bridle and striding across to where Freya was standing. Her heart beat hard as he got closer. He was tall and gangly. His dark eyes glinted.

'I was just wondering if I could use your phone,' she said. 'To call my children. I'll pay for the call, of course.'

'Is that it? You interrupted me for that?' Forbes pushed his hat back and wiped his forehead with the back of his arm. 'Help yourself.'

'Thank you.'

Freya turned back towards the house. She glanced at her watch. It was seven thirty. It would be around ten p.m. in England. The children would still be up, but it was a little late to be calling.

Neill answered the phone.

'It's late,' he said. 'They were just about to put their lights out.'

'I won't take long,' she said. 'Please, Neill.'

'All right,' he said.

The children were both quiet when they took their turn at speaking to her. She sensed a nervous trembling in their voices. She knew Neill, or Clarissa, would be standing next to them, monitoring, directing.

'Are you all right?'

'Yes,' said Kirsty.

'Do you miss me?'

'Yes.'

'I miss you,' said Freya. 'A lot. I wish you were here with me.'

Silence.

'Are you happy at Dad's?'

418

'Yes.'

'Have you been to church?'

'Yes.'

'Are you getting on with everyone? With Clarissa's kids?'

'Yes.'

'What about Clarissa and Dad? Are they being nice to you?'

'Yes.'

Her voice was flat and programmed. Freya found it heart-wrenching. She longed to get away from this place and go home. But what was the point in rushing back, when they did not even live with her?

Tom's responses were even flatter than Kirsty's. Freya pictured Neill standing over him, perhaps even listening in on an extension. She strained hard to hear any sign of him.

When the children had said goodbye he came back on the line.

'Try and call at a more convenient hour next time, if you don't mind,' he said.

'It's difficult,' she said. 'The time difference makes it tricky.'

'Where are you?' he said, his voice suspicious.

'Melbourne,' she replied quickly. 'I've been to see Mum and Dad. I told them about our divorce. They're very disappointed.'

'Don't lie. I know they don't like me.'

Freya sighed. 'I'm sorry you feel like that.'

'I suppose they hate my guts for getting the children.'

'I didn't tell them. They'd be too upset.'

Neill mumbled an excuse about a heavy

workload, and rang off. Freya put the phone down and sat there feeling numb.

She couldn't seem to shake off her jetlag, and by mid-morning she felt her eyelids drooping uncontrollably. She went to her room and lay down, and woke two hours later when she heard the boys out on the veranda.

She rallied and went to the kitchen to help make sandwiches. Forbes was already there, slicing loaves of bread and spreading them with butter.

'There's some cheese and lettuce in the fridge,' he said.

Freya helped him assemble and stack the sandwiches in neat rows on a tray. Then he put thirty-five glasses on several trays.

'Fill these with lemonade,' he said, 'from the drinks fridge.' He pointed at a large, dilapidated fridge in the walk-in pantry.

Freya did as she was told. It reminded her of her old pantry at Ruislip Manor, shelves stacked to the ceiling with bottled fruit and home-made jam and chutney. She thought of Neill and Clarissa having it off amongst her pickles, and a surge of anger came over her.

Whenever she tried to start a conversation about anything other than the job at hand, Forbes grunted. Freya responded with respect and patience, conscious of the loyalty of the boys he was fathering. They were waiting at the table out on the veranda. Several came into the kitchen for cutlery and serviettes. They were reticent towards Freya, waiting for Forbes to give them permission to speak. But Forbes didn't say a word, and the meal was eaten in silence, with Freya and the boys too afraid to say anything.

Peggy and Connie arrived home after dark. Freya was in the bath. She heard them talking on the veranda, then the screen door into the kitchen banged.

When she had finished her bath she got dressed again and went into the kitchen. Connie and Peggy were sitting at the table in the middle of a serious discussion, voices low and hoarse. They turned around and looked at her, eyes dark and secretive.

'Sorry,' she said softly, sensing their serious mood. 'I didn't mean to interrupt.'

'We're sorry we had to leave you today,' said Peggy. 'But when the Elders want you for women's business, you have to drop everything.'

'That's quite all right,' said Freya.

She stood for a moment, waiting for an invitation to join them, but she could see by their body language, the way they were sitting sideways from the table with their knees touching, that this was a private moment.

She padded back to her room, feeling uncomfortable.

Standing at the French door in her bedroom, she watched the dark shadows stretching beyond the boundary fence, and the low black hills lying across the horizon like sleeping dogs.

★ ★ ★

After the first week she got used to the daily routine and gave herself regular chores, such as helping Forbes make the lunch, or lending a hand in the laundry.

Forbes must have given the boys permission to make friends with her; now they smiled or said hello. Sometimes she listened to them read. Their reading level was rudimentary, and the books were primary-school level, the Mr Men series, Janet and John.

She felt happiest with the boys; there was an easiness between them that she didn't enjoy with her sisters. When they were out of earshot one morning, Terry called her over to the open-air classroom. She sat down in one of the picnic chairs.

'I've spent six months working here,' he said. 'Peggy and Forbes are wonderful people. But I don't know how much longer they can keep this place going.'

'What a shame. Don't they get much assistance?'

'The government helps, and the local community. And all the staff, like myself, work for nothing. Forbes feeds us and gives us a bed in the tin shacks along the dry creek. It's rewarding work, but staff turnover's high. The boys aren't easy. They've had rotten lives. Not a chance in hell of getting proper careers for themselves.'

'It must make your job frustrating.'

'Yeah, it does. But my role is still the same. To give these young people the confidence to start something and the self-discipline to see it through. I can't do more than that.'

'The boys obviously look up to you.'

'A kid can't give you a greater compliment

than his respect and love. I've worked in remote communities like this for years, but this is by far the best. I've got flexibility here. I can work one-to-one with a boy if he won't work with other kids around him. Some of them are very insecure.'

The conversation made Freya's mood downcast. She suddenly saw the hopelessness of the boys' lives, the despair they'd already been through, and the depressing certainty that after Paradise there might be nothing but long, empty days of drinking, petrol-sniffing and depression.

Peggy and Connie spent a lot of time under a large red gum by the dam talking to the Elders, who turned up sometimes as if from nowhere, with their dogs in tow and dilly bags full of ochres. They waved at Freya if she came around that side of the house to pick herbs for soups, a daily job she had given herself, but no one called her over, not even Milly. Aware of the sensitivity of what was being discussed, she kept her distance.

Slowly, in bursts of daring that stopped abruptly or tailed off in embarrassment, the boys began to talk to her at mealtimes out on the veranda. They were curious about London, even more so about life on the canal in a houseboat. They couldn't imagine living on a boat, much less finding enough water on which to put one.

Forbes was clearly uneasy about these conversations, as if Freya might be trying to influence them to leave Paradise and explore the world, but he said nothing. Freya knew they would never leave Australia, most of them, and she felt guilty for talking about a privileged country that was the original source of their plight. Now and then Forbes glanced in Freya's direction and rolled his eyes, as if to say Who do you think you are?

At first Peggy was pleased the boys were letting their guard drop, 'You beaudy,' she said many times, slapping Freya hard on the back. But after a while she developed a fierce jealousy, butting in on conversations and bossing the boys to get back to work. They skulked off, glancing at Peggy as though she'd whipped them.

Freya soon tired of Peggy's childish displays and began to avoid her. She scolded herself for assuming that coming here would be easy. And she ached to be back with her children.

In avoiding Peggy she had to avoid Connie too. Connie took sides with Peggy, though her manners were better. But Freya could sense her resentment. She felt that avoiding them was the cleverest tactic. Pretending to be unaffected usually drove people nuts, and eventually they would climb over the silent wall, humbled.

One day they were in the kitchen preparing dinner. Peggy was busying herself shelling peas and peeling spuds over a basin of water. Freya was preparing a large pot of soup, throwing in handfuls of fresh herbs and pot barley. She was careful not to start a conversation, leaving it to Peggy or Connie. They chatted to each other, ignoring Freya. Inane banter it was too, about the job at hand. Every now and then Peggy would throw in a comment about something Freya would not understand — gossip — then the small talk would start up all over again.

Freya kept asking herself how she could break the impasse without losing face. Her chance came when Peggy cut her thumb while peeling potatoes. It was a bad cut, quite deep, and blood poured from the wound and dribbled down her arm.

'Where's your first-aid kit?' said Freya.

'In the hall cupboard,' said Connie. 'I'll fetch it. We have to keep it locked because of the syringes and medicines in there.'

Peggy had the key on a chain around her neck. Connie eased it over her head and hurried along the hall.

The cut needed stitching. Luckily the first-aid kit was well stocked and Freya set to work. First she cleaned the cut, then sprayed the area with local anaesthetic. Stitching it was tricky; it kept bleeding profusely. Peggy did not flinch once. Freya dressed the wound in a clean, loose bandage. All the time she was working she could feel Peggy watching her. When she had finished Peggy leaned forward and put her arms around her.

'Sorry I've been growlin' at ya,' she said. 'I love my boys like the air I breathe. I'm not too good at sharing 'em.'

'Don't worry,' said Freya. 'I understand. I'd like to help, that's all. I don't like being idle.'

After that things were easier between them, although Freya could still sense a lingering resentment coming from Peggy.

One day Freya suggested the boys get together to paint the wall where the long dining table was set up on the veranda. It was already green, the perfect background for a mural. Freya called a meeting to try and decide on a theme.

Someone recommended a dot painting, but Geoff, an older boy whose alcoholic parents had both committed suicide while in police custody, said they were all too ignorant about the Dreamings to do it justice. He spoke in a morose, bitter voice, then kicked the dust with his boot and stomped off to sulk under a tree.

'What about painting this place?' said Kip, a boy Freya had been trying to get close to during reading sessions.

It was agreed. Kip's face lit up, knowing that everyone had decided to use his idea.

Freya showed them how to map out the picture on newspaper. She felt oddly at ease in the strange gathering of damaged souls. There was a lot of noise and a general air of excitement as they all crowded round. The smell of their bodies was powerful as they got more and more worked up.

At one point Freya glanced up and noticed Peggy glaring at her through the screen door, where she was busy at work in the kitchen. Connie was sitting at the kitchen table, keeping her company.

Freya drew up a list of subjects for each boy to draw and paint. Some were allocated animals: horses, pigs, birds, sheep, and the wallabies and goats that came right up to where they were eating, to bludge titbits. Others chose trees, and three boys offered to do the homestead. Shane asked if he could paint the corral, and the rest of the boys each chose a member of staff. There was a lot of loud arguing over who should paint Forbes, the centre of their world at Paradise. In the end Freya said it should be Geoff, as he was the eldest and had been at Paradise the longest. Someone went across to where Geoff was still moping. Freya watched his face change as he heard the decision, and he scrambled to his feet and trotted across to the table.

'What about us?' Kip was leaning on a post chewing a piece of grass. It rolled across his lips. 'We have to be in it.'

'Of course you do,' said Freya. 'I was saving that for last because it's the most important.'

This part of the meeting took over an hour. Everyone got very heated. Freya had to use a great deal of diplomacy to keep them satisfied.

It was getting late. The long, dry grass surrounding the homestead was singing with cicadas and crickets. The smell of tomorrow's stew wafted through the kitchen window. A large spider was busy spinning a web under the rafters. Forbes would destroy it again tomorrow, as he did every morning, but the spider was crafty and kept coming back.

Forbes came out from the sitting room, where he'd been doing paperwork, with a pen behind one ear. He stood on the dirt off the veranda, in the light of a yellow moon.

'What's all the bloody noise about?'

'We're gunna paint the wall with a muriel,' said Shane importantly.

Forbes smiled, amused at Shane's mistake, but didn't correct him.

'If it's all right with you,' said Freya.

He looked at the wall, and after a moment he nodded. 'So long as youse clean up after yerselves, I don't mind. It's a good idea. That wall's bloody ugly as sin the way it is. But only after your chores are finished for the day. You'll be workin' in the dark, but there's another light I can rig up, a powerful one we use for roo huntin'.'

And so the following day, straight after clearing and washing the supper dishes, they set to work.

Forbes was impressed, but Peggy only gave the wall a cursory glance. She had resorted to banging pots and pans again in the kitchen, and avoiding Freya's eyes. The boys were thrilled with their new, colourful wall.

One morning, fed up with the suffocating air in the kitchen, Freya sprayed herself from top to toe with Aeroguard, and ventured outside with a book. She found an old sun-bleached bench under one of the poinciana trees that ringed the homestead like a flaming hoop and sat there enjoying the shade. The red flame-shaped flower petals were brilliant against the azure sky.

She was just getting into the book — it was the one about indigenous nations and all the different language groups — when Forbes pulled up abruptly in his ute and parked nearby amongst a stand of gum trees. A distressed sheep, bleating loudly, was hanging upside down on the back of the truck, its feet tied to a pole.

Freya jumped up and pretended to be weeding the garden. She found an old kitchen fork stuck in the ground, and began to turn over the earth around the roses. It seemed decadent, lounging around on a working farm, but sometimes she wasn't sure what needed doing. Between mealtimes the boys were over at the corral learning to ride. She didn't want to infringe on set patterns and habits, and Peggy always said there was nothing to do, although Freya sensed she didn't want to encourage her to become more deeply involved in life around the homestead.

Forbes certainly seemed to hate her being there. Perhaps if she offered to help him with the sheep, it might break down some barriers. She slipped on her sandals and went across to see what was up, thinking the sheep must be sick or injured and had been brought in for treatment.

Forbes gave her a brief glance, but she might as well have been invisible. He climbed on to the back of the truck, lifted off the sheep, climbed down again, and set the pole between two forked stakes. The animal struggled alarmingly, its eyes bulging, and Freya worried it might break its back.

Forbes looked across at her, his face expressionless. Then he flashed her a sudden fake smile. An oppressive fear came over her. She moved to the shelter of a tree, peering around it tentatively.

Forbes took a long knife from a leather sheath attached to his belt, and slit the animal's throat. The sheep went into a series of violent spasms, then was still. Forbes worked quickly, slicing its belly clean down the middle from throat to tail.

He reached inside and yanked out the entrails and organs, throwing parts unfit for humans to the waiting dogs, then tossed a few bloody innards towards Freya, laughing as she recoiled. He dumped the kidneys, liver and heart in a white bucket and covered it with a tight-fitting lid, to deter flies. Then he untied the animal's feet and lifted it on to a large wooden block caked in dried blood, and deftly defleeced and dismembered it ready for the freezer.

'I'll take those inside if you like.' Freya was by his side. Without waiting for a reply, she lifted the bucket. She was sickened by his lack of grace, but this was outweighed by her determination not to seem wimpy, when clearly the slaughter of a sheep was a regular chore.

'Thanks.' Forbes gave her a scornful look. 'Put 'em in freezer bags and bring 'em out to the shed. In the big freezer over by the rock-picker.'

Freya had quickly realised over the past two weeks that the more she chipped in, the more Forbes seemed to tolerate her. His cold manner simply made her want to try harder. She thought that if he hated her Peggy would never come round to accepting her.

Later, at supper, she said, 'Do you think I could ride one of the horses tomorrow? I'd like to explore those hills north of the property.'

Everyone stopped eating for a moment. Peggy laughed out loud.

'You can't go there.'

Freya waited.

'Why not?' she said finally.

As Forbes chewed, his ears jerked up and

down like pistons. Freya wanted to pinch them. He continued eating his slab of roast lamb.

The boys did not look up from their plates. She couldn't believe such a humble request could create such a dramatic reaction.

'What's the matter with you all? I just want to go for a ride.'

'It's not that,' said Connie. 'No one cares if you go riding. It's just that you can't go into those hills. They're sacred. See the fence over there?'

Freya nodded.

'No one's allowed to go beyond that without permission from the Central Land Commission.'

'Oh. I see. Well why didn't you say so? In that case I'll go the other way. Do you mind if I borrow one of your horses, Forbes?' She laid down her knife and fork and waited for Forbes to give her an answer.

His face was loosely animated, but the words were slow in forming, as if he couldn't be bothered. He did not look at Freya, nor wait to empty his mouth when he finally spoke.

'You can't go there either,' he said, pushing the food around his mouth and chewing hard. 'But who knows. Milly might let you go for a look-see. Depends how nicely you ask.' He winked at the boys. They giggled over their plates.

'I wouldn't want to intrude,' said Freya.

What was the point in coming all this way, Connie spending all that money on air fares, when they were not even making an effort to get close to her or make her feel welcome? She

431

thought that if she went off riding they might have time to think about their behaviour, and perhaps have a change of heart.

Already this week she had read two books, swum in the dam countless times, drunk endless cups of tea, cleaned all the kitchen cupboards and dusted every surface in every room, touched up the mural, which was still unfinished in a few areas, and polished a dozen saddles.

'We're goin' that way tomorrow,' said Peggy. 'You can come with us if the old man agrees, and if Milly gives her say-so. You could wait by the waterhole while we go up into the gorge. If you get bored you can find your own way back home. Just retrace your tracks.'

'Sounds like a good plan.'

Freya had not been game to venture on foot beyond the boundary fence surrounding the homestead. The buffalo grass was long and dense, an ideal shelter for snakes. Now she was glad she hadn't been tempted. She didn't want to break any rules.

A good ten minutes passed, but still Forbes had not given his decision. Pushing his tongue into the gaps between his back teeth, he glanced at Peggy and said, 'Beaut dinner, Peg.'

'Good enough for the likes of an old ruffian, aye.'

He scraped his chair back from the table and moved further along the veranda for a smoke.

After helping the boys clear away the dishes, Freya went outside. She leaned on a post and looked up at the starry sky.

432

Forbes was leaning on the next post along. He lifted a leg and polished the toe of his boot on the back of his other leg.

'Ever ridden a horse?'

For the first time since her arrival he looked her straight in the eyes. She sensed her answer would go some way to softening his view of her, which so far was not up to much.

'Yes,' she said quickly. 'I have. Not stock horses. Riding-school hacks. Old and fed up, poor things.'

Forbes laughed. 'A bit like me, you reckon?'

'Why don't you like me?' she said, lifting her head haughtily. 'Peggy invited me, but you all act as if you don't want me here.'

Earlier today she had overheard him telling some of the boys she was a stuck-up pommy as well as being white. 'What a combination,' he had roared. Then, more seriously, 'You can't trust whites or poms. So be on your guard.'

She had stepped out of the shadows and said, 'May I remind you I was born on the very same farm as Connie and Peggy, in Victoria. I'm Australian, if you don't mind. I just happen to live in England.'

Forbes couldn't relate to anywhere but the outback, Darwin, Alice Springs, and the one-horse settlements in between. When she mentioned London he looked blank, as though she were talking about outer Mongolia.

'And I wish you'd stop passing me off as a pom,' she said now.

'You're a pommy all right. Only a pommy keeps cheese out of the fridge.'

433

'It tastes better if you take it out an hour or so before eating it.'

'Yeah, well, out here it goes off in five minutes out of the fridge. I had to throw another big piece away yesterday because you left it on the table.'

'I'm sorry. I didn't realise. But that doesn't mean I'm a pom.'

He reached into his shirt pocket for a smoke and lit it with a match. Freya went inside. The man was impossible.

Connie and Peggy were in the main lounge watching television. Forbes came in and sat in his special red leather armchair. Using the remote control he switched from world news to the rural station. An ad came on about tractors. He leaned forward and stared hard at the screen.

'Could do with a new one of those,' he said.

'Yeah,' said Peggy.

It wasn't Freya's idea of a scintillating evening. She tried to make conversation, but all she got were grunts or nods. Even Connie was quiet. Forbes poured himself a generous whiskey on the rocks in a crystal glass. He slurped it back loudly. Freya could see his red lips reaching into the cubes of ice, like a camel. He put his feet up on the cream wool footstool and scratched his instep with a ruler stuffed inside his sock.

'Why don't I saddle up Queenie for you tomorrow?' he said.

Another hour had passed since her original question at suppertime. It was like extracting history from a fossil. She looked at him warily. Was he really prepared to do this for her? What

434

was the catch? He'd probably put the saddle on too tight to make the horse buck. Or strap it up when the horse was breathing out, so it would fall off, taking her with it, once it breathed in.

'You'll find riding boots in the cupboard on the veranda, by the back door,' he said.

Picking his teeth with a fingernail, he got up and kicked the door open with a boot. He disappeared into the hall, and came back holding a riding hat.

'I know you pale pommy bastards like wearing a hard hat. I bought this at the saddlery in town when Peggy said you was comin'. Hope it fits.'

'Thank you,' said Freya, but her words were hushed by the banging door.

She could hear him in the kitchen, telling the boys how the pommy woman wanted to go off into the desert looking for fun, and they all fell about laughing.

★ ★ ★

Queenie reared up as Freya slipped her foot into the stirrup.

'Get hold of her mane and she'll settle,' said Forbes. 'A rampaging bull slashed her stomach with its horn a few months back, disgorged a loop of intestine, but the old girl's come good. She just needs a sure hand.'

'Heavens,' said Freya. 'Are you sure she's all right? Has she been ridden since it happened?'

'Nope. You're doin' the honours.'

She did as she was told and hoisted herself up, whispering words of reassurance in Queenie's

435

ear and gently holding her mane. It had been years since she had been on a horse. She loved the smell of the leather saddle, and the rise and fall of the horse's belly as it breathed. Peggy had come in after breakfast and said Milly had given her permission for Freya to venture beyond the fence, but she was not to go into the hills, in case she stumbled across any sacred areas. Freya had given her word and thanked Peggy for asking Milly, who lived at a camp about half a mile away. Then Peggy and Connie had headed out to the hills with some of the other women, who were already waiting. It amazed Freya the way the women were suddenly there one minute, gone the next. Especially as the land around the farm was flat, with few hiding places.

All the boys gathered around to see Freya off, leaning over the corral fence, waving their hats in the air and whooping.

Fully expecting Forbes to direct her into a fenced paddock, so that she could warm up for a few minutes, she was taken aback when he opened a gate that led into open country.

'Away you go, city girl,' he said. 'See that line of trees over there?'

She peered into the distance. 'Yes,' she said, 'I see them.'

'Head straight for them and keep going along the dry river bed till you get to some rocks at the foot of a hill. That's where Peggy and Connie are. They'll see you coming.'

'How far?' she said.

'Not far. About forty-five minutes.'

'What if I get lost?'

'We'll come looking for you.'

'What about water for the horse?'

'There's a creek further out. You can't miss it. Peggy and Connie won't be far from there. Don't go any closer to the hills than that.'

'Do they know I'm coming?'

'Yeah. But they won't stop what they're doing just to entertain you.'

'That's okay. I'll wait in the shade.'

Billy came running towards the corral just then, waving a plastic box.

' 'Ere, missus, take this.'

When he reached the fence he climbed through and put the container of sandwiches in one of the saddle bags. Freya had already packed an apple and a bottle of water.

'Thanks, Billy.'

'Can you ride, missus?'

'Course I can.'

Forbes grunted. 'Are you going or not? These boys have got work to do.'

'Yes,' she said. 'I'm going.'

She dug her heels into Queenie's ribs and the horse lurched through the gate and trotted across the field.

'Thanks,' she called over her shoulder.

But Forbes had already shut the gate and was climbing into his truck. The boys had disappeared.

Riding across the red earth, the mood of alienation that had persisted since her arrival began to dissolve, and a sense of release and urgency ran through her veins, as though she had just drunk a glass of fiery tonic. The breeze in her hair, the steady clip-clop of Queenie's hoofs on the hard ground, the creak of leather against her jeans, and the blue sky and golden plains stretching endlessly — she felt she could quite easily ride for days without stopping. She wanted to put as much distance as possible between herself and the cynical eye of her brother-in-law.

★   ★   ★

Deep in the blood-red gully, Milly alerted the others.

'Look,' she said, pointing at the sky. 'Brown falcon. Dark one. Don't see themfella too much out this way. Not seen him long, long time, comin' from the sea. Themfella paler out here.'

The women watched as the falcon soared over the cliffs and disappeared.

They continued to paint Connie's bare chest, singing and chanting softly as the designs were lovingly applied. The smell of ochres and female sweat, gum leaves sizzling on a fire, the sound of twigs snapping, and the weird sensation of a strange woman's hands on her skin — Connie was completely mesmerised, though the desired deeper experience was eluding her, like a nun taking her vows for all the wrong reasons, and not feeling the connection she had expected with God.

The Elders kept asking if she'd had any dreams about the Ancestral Beings, but Connie said she rarely had any dreams, or not that she could remember — she was a very heavy sleeper. Milly said they would keep trying to sing up dreams on her behalf, but after two long weeks of trying it wasn't looking hopeful. Not even out here at Blue Rock.

Peggy sympathised with her sister. 'The same thing happened to me when I first arrived at Paradise. I still haven't had the dreams I'm expected to have. But I don't worry too much about it any more. I'm learnin' about it all in a more academic way.'

The Elders had concluded that she was indeed a coconut blackfella, she said. This saddened her for a while, but she had come to accept it, more or less.

'I'm more interested in helping our boys make a life for themselves,' she had confided to Connie.

'It makes more sense,' Connie had said, 'if they want to leave Paradise and get jobs.'

Peggy had laughed. 'That's right. You can't rely on the spirits for a good feed.'

When Connie said she didn't stand a chance of ever getting in touch with her spirituality, Peggy said, 'Pah! What good's the jukurrpa to a city woman from New York? You've got class and money. You don't need any of those silly-bugger dreams.'

Connie knew Peggy was trying to make her feel better, and she loved her for it. But she couldn't help feeling inadequate. The ritual authorities had willingly involved her in the activities of her adopted kin group, and she was grateful, and tried hard out of a sense of obligation more than a deep yearning. She did want to learn, but the realisation that she did not

439

feel connected in the same way that the Elders did, or even some of the younger women, had led her to conclude that it was all futile. Some of the discussions, singing and dancing that took place had relieved much of the stress she felt about her shortcomings, but she still felt foolish and fed up.

The only comfort was in a dream Milly had had, in which Connie was flying through the sky and finally entered an unnamed place, thousands of kilometres east of Paradise, near the sea. This was the closest Milly could get to finding Connie's country, but she was hopeful that in time more details would emerge. She was especially pleased with the dream, because it matched the one she had had about Peggy some years back. It proved beyond a doubt that Peggy and Connie were sisters, and that their real country was near the coast.

46

Riding through the intense heat, Freya pulled her hat low over her face. It was like being on the receiving end of a gigantic welding torch. She screwed up her eyes at the blinding whiteness of a distant saltpan. Because she had not ridden for years, her thighs began to chafe. In the distance a hawk soared over a long chain of blue cliffs, and disappeared behind a ridge.

She dismounted. As soon as her feet hit the hard earth she was overcome with a feeling of having landed from a great height. The sense of belonging that had been missing in Windsor Meadows, and in London too, was not going to suddenly spring up at her out here in the desert, but there was a feeling of ease that intensified when her feet hit the ground. She had expected to be nervous, away from the comforting perimeter of Paradise; instead she was simply happy.

She strolled beside Queenie, enjoying the sensation of the spinifex grazing against her trousers, and the warmth of the morning sun on her back. Until now she had not appreciated the abundance of animal life that lived in the grasses. From the plane the landscape had looked dramatic, the colours and sudden rock forma-tions jutting out of the flat earth like fists. But it had also looked inhospitable and barren. Now she noticed dozens of tiny birds flitting amongst the razor-sharp leaves. A ghostly white praying mantis reared up at her like a boxer. A muscle-bound lizard strutted through the grass and scaled a tree. Weaving her way through the mulga, she was captivated by the deep colours. The earth was so deeply red in places it looked almost black, and the sky so piercingly blue it hurt her head.

Forbes said she would find water, and he was right. There were two claypan lakes beside a small stand of desert oaks. The smaller of the two lagoons was stagnant. As she came closer to the shore of the healthier waterhole Queenie snorted loudly and reared up.

'Easy, easy,' she said, stroking the horse's neck.

The lake was vibrant with reflections and birds preening themselves. Ripples ringed out from each bird. Pelicans and black swans landed and took off noisily. Ducks and plovers weaved their way amongst the water lilies and reeds, playing tag. The air smelled of eucalyptus and sandstone heating in the sun.

A turquoise cloud — wild budgerigars — flew low, screeching like banshees, as though warning of danger, and disappeared into a stand of paperbarks. She gasped as they passed over her head. They were so close the backdraught lifted her hair, making her duck. Camouflaged amongst the trees they fell silent, hidden in a personal place where the stranger couldn't find them.

She sensed this lake was special and deserved respect. Queenie did not know the difference; Freya urged her to drink from the dirty one. She pushed her hat off so that it hung down her back, and knelt by the shore washing the grit from her eyes and neck. She longed to strip off and dive in, but the water looked murky and uninviting.

She was sleepy after another restless night thinking about the children, and Sam Jenner.

He had been kind to her when she left, offering to keep an eye on *Harlequin* and empty the bilges if they drew water. He had kissed her, standing in the car park, and a feeling of panic had filled her heart.

'I'll miss you,' he had whispered in her ear, and the feeling of dread faded.

By the time she and Del arrived at Heathrow, she had begun to hope Sam would meet someone else while she was gone, because it was unfair of her to expect him to wait.

She tethered Queenie to a tree and, glancing around, undressed. She scrambled over the smooth golden rocks and slipped into the water. It felt cold on her hot skin, its texture like thin custard. As her body temperature adjusted, it was soothing and silky. She floated on her back for a long time, eyes clamped against the glare, and a sense of deep peace settled over her. She was sure she was getting closer to dissolving the confusion and finding her real identity, and that it would come to her in a wondrous flash, unambiguous and true.

She opened her eyes.

There was something wrong with the sky. The dazzling light made her squint. Adjusting her focus, she glanced at a stand of tea trees on the far side of the lake.

Someone was watching her.

She couldn't see anyone, but she knew they were there. She didn't feel afraid, but she didn't like being stalked either. She swam ashore, and with as much dignity as possible struggled up the slippery bank. She stood in the sun drying, one eye on the trees, where she was certain someone was still watching.

When she was almost dry she dressed and set off on foot, leading Queenie. She glanced over her shoulder at the tea trees, but there was no sign of life.

★ ★ ★

The women came down from the cliffs to greet her.

'We're just havin' a break,' said Peggy. 'Otherwise you'd be here on your own.'

A few of the older women seemed agitated. They stood back, pretending not to stare, but Freya saw that they were watching her all right.

'Did you see Rosie?' said Connie.

'Someone was in the trees by the lake,' said Freya.

'Which lake?' said an old woman wearing a bright pink T-shirt and a baggy red-spotted skirt.

'The one with the birds.'

'Did you swim there?' said the woman. She stared at Freya's damp hair.

'No,' said Freya, 'I swam in the dirty lake.' She looked at the woman, who glanced down, unable to hold Freya's gaze.

'Come and sit with us in the shade,' said Peggy.

Freya noticed how grubby her sisters were.

'We were just thinkin' about going for a dip ourselves,' said Peggy.

'Yeah,' said Connie. 'Why don't you join us?'

'You go ahead,' said Freya quickly. 'I'm a bit tired.'

'Nah,' said Peggy. 'We won't bother.'

'How is it going out here?' Freya looked at Connie.

'These things take time,' said Peggy. 'Connie's got a lot to learn.'

'Look, here comes Rosie,' said Connie.

Freya looked up and saw a white-haired woman tottering towards them, leaning on a stick. She stopped when she reached the other women and spoke to them in their nation language. Then she stared straight at Freya. The other women followed Rosie's gaze. At the airport they had not made eye contact. Not even when they were crowding around her, singing.

Freya began to wish she had stayed at the homestead. She had interrupted something important, and now she felt embarrassed. She wondered if Rosie had seen her swimming. She hoped the old woman's eyesight was bad.

'Maybe I should head back,' she said. 'It'll be dark in a few hours. I don't want to get lost.'

'You won't get lost,' said Rosie, showing a mouth full of blackened teeth.

Freya looked at Rosie and smiled. Who was this woman with the wily eyes and mischievous grin?

'Thisfella knows who you are,' said Rosie, her dark eyes penetrating Freya's. 'And who you're not.'

'Rosie's an Elder with special powers,' said Connie.

'Really?' Freya grew strangely uneasy. 'In what way?'

'She's ninety-one, for a start,' said Peggy. 'A senior Elder with a lot of ritual responsibilities, and years of experience.'

'Doesn't look a day over sixty,' said Connie.

'Aye, Rosie?' Peggy winked at the old lady. 'Is Freya anything to do with the brown falcon we just saw?'

Rosie glared at Freya. Finally she shook her head. 'Nah,' she said, 'thisfella's not 'im.'

Freya dared to let out a long, low sigh, inaudible to everyone else, but powerfully comforting to her own tense body.

Rosie gave her a meaningful smile, then turned away and walked across to sit on a rock, both hands clasping the stick between her knees. The other women joined her and sat by her feet in the dust, whispering amongst themselves. Freya moved to the shade with her sisters.

'I'm sorry you can't join in,' said Peggy.

'Did I say I wanted to?' said Freya.

'I thought you might be upset.'

'You thought wrong,' said Freya. 'I just wanted to spend some time with you. That's why I came here in the first place. So I could get to know you both. I mean, you've changed so much, Connie. You were friendly in London. What's happened to you?'

Feeling weary, she sat down. The sandy earth was comforting on her itchy legs. She pulled off her boots and socks and buried her feet in the cool grains. She wondered what Rosie was saying about her. She sensed she was the main topic of conversation, and she knew in her gut that Rosie had been watching her at the waterhole.

'I suppose I feel guilty,' said Connie.

'About dragging me all this way to the desert for nothing? So you should.'

'No. About my adoptive parents. And everything they've done for me. They'd have a fit if they knew I was out here doing this.'

She gestured at her painted body, just visible under the neck of her T-shirt.

Freya got up and walked away to be by herself. Connie and Peggy had their own agenda. It was a waste of energy trying to whittle away at their self-absorption. She looked back at them and shook her head.

Connie noticed and her eyes flared. 'Well you haven't changed one bit since coming here.'

'What do you mean by that?' Freya back moved towards her.

'I mean you're still putting too much effort into other people's business, when you should be concentrating on your own family.'

'You invited me here.'

'Yes. I did. To spend time with us. Not to meddle with the boys.'

Connie was right. Freya sat down heavily on a fallen tree trunk. She put her head on her folded arms, defeated, exhausted. Peggy sat down next to her.

'The boys can't handle too many people buttin' in and tryin' to help 'em,' she said. 'They get confused enough as it is, not havin' their own parents around and all us bloody adults telling 'em what's what. The old man's who they look up to most. They get attached to people.'

'He spends time with 'em in the morning,' said Peggy. 'Out on the old couch by the dam. Talks to 'em about their approach to work, budgeting any money they earn, and leadership. We know you've been tryin' to help, and what you've done so far's all right. But just be careful not to get too close. When you go, it'll hit 'em too hard.'

As much as she liked the boys, Freya had already decided not to get drawn in the way she had on the moorings, and had backed off a little these last few days if a boy approached her with his problems. It was a way of deflecting hard truths, keeping her mind off things, listening to them talk at the same time as satisfying her desire to be of use.

On her way out here to Blue Rock she had felt the darkness falling away from her soul, the certainty of life's endless cycle rising up from the earth, unrelenting and strong.

'When we're finished here it'll be better,' said Connie. 'We can spend more time together. It's our fault too, disappearing on you like that on your first day. But it's important I try to learn.'

'I'm sorry,' said Freya. 'I've been selfish.'

'In a few days we'll be home all the time,' said Peggy. 'We'll have a party.'

'We have to go now,' said Connie.

The Elders were heading towards a gash in the cliffs.

'Don't try and follow us,' said Peggy. 'It's dangerous.'

The two women hugged Freya and hurried after the others, breaking into a run to catch up.

'Aren't you going?' said Freya, looking at Rosie.

Rosie remained seated on the rock, hand-rolled cigarette dangling off her bottom lip, unlit. She shook her head.

'Legs hurtin'.'

She leaned down and massaged her ankles, her scarred skin like thin parchment over sharp bones.

Freya weighed up the possibility of speaking to Rosie about her predicament and decided it was worth a go. She sat down near her in the shade, leaning her head on the trunk of a tree and gazing through the casuarina branches at the sky.

They were silent for a long time. A wonderful sense of calm fell over Freya. A soft breeze teased the feathery leaves of the trees, lifting them like down on a baby bird. The smell of wet bark and fresh rainwater pooling amongst sedges and ferns filled the air. Neither woman felt any need to speak. Native red pea flowers curled around the roots of the tree. Freya touched the petals with the tip of her finger.

'Red the colour of joy and happiness. Love colour.' Rosie poked the red dust with her stick. 'Lotta redfellas out here.' She grinned.

'You saw me,' Freya said finally, 'at the waterhole.'

Rosie's eyes were milky with glaucoma.

'Your mob over that way.' She lifted her walking cane and pointed east. 'Some place near the sea, long way.' She nodded at Freya's bare arms, which were turning a deep bronze.

Freya began to tremble. She hung her head and began to cry silently. The relief was enormous.

'Thank you for not saying anything,' she whispered, looking up.

'What's the matter?' said Rosie. 'Why don't you tell them women?'

'They think my father is white,' said Freya. 'I don't want to argue with them. It's too hard for people to believe or understand, even my sisters. I've got no proof. My birth certificate says Henry Nolan, a white man, is my father. I just met him, in Melbourne.'

She grew serious, defiant.

'The only proof he's not my father is in here.' She thumped her chest twice with her fist.

Rosie nodded. 'Saw you swimmin'. Saw that brown mark.' She gestured at Freya's back with the tip of her stick.

Freya reached a hand around and touched the birthmark, felt the raise of it through her shirt.

'No one knows,' she said. 'Only you. It's best to leave it that way. Can you do that?'

Rosie nodded. 'Listen,' she said, hunching her shoulders, casting her eyes over the cliffs, where the last woman in the group slipped like a grain of sand into a rock corridor.

Freya wiped her tears with the back of her arm and listened to the wind whistling in and out of the cliffs. She waited for Rosie to speak but the old lady said nothing, simply stared into Freya's eyes.

'Themfellas up himgully bin learn,' said Rosie. She gestured at the cliffs. 'Somefellas need plenty lessons,' she continued. 'Thisfella wanna learn?'

Freya nodded. 'Yes,' she said. 'I do.'

Rosie narrowed her eyes. 'You havin' dreams?'

'Yes. Lots.'

Rosie smiled. A ragged giggle slipped out. Her stained teeth made her look comical and cheeky.

'White here,' she said, touching the skin on Freya's arm, 'black here.' She touched Freya's heart. 'Won't take much longtime teach youfella. Already got plenty knowledge in there.'

Freya related some of the dreams she'd been having, and Rosie acknowledged that they sounded legitimate enough. But they'd have to wait and see, she said.

Behind them the wind was bleeding its way through gaps in the cliffs, forming a red funnel of dust that whirled towards them.

The hairs on Freya's arms stood up.

The twister passed through the branches directly over their heads, rattling the leaves like foil bottletops. It soared over the spinifex, flattening it, then skimmed over the distant waterhole, stirring the water like an egg beater. The water birds froze, their small round eyes aghast.

When the storm reached the opposite bank it suddenly dissolved, just as quickly as it had formed two minutes earlier. The birds resumed their preening rituals. Everything was still.

'Wow,' said Freya softly.

'Youfella brown hawk,' said Rosie flatly, unperturbed by the spectacle.

Freya looked into the old woman's eyes and saw that she was absolutely certain. She knew Rosie would be offended if she asked for details, the name of the town perhaps, or the language group that her father and his family came from. The old woman would take such questions as scepticism.

Freya excused herself and walked down to the water's edge to splash her face.

When she turned around to say thank you, Rosie was gone.

47

The next day Freya rode out at dawn, before the roosters crowed, before anyone had stirred, and found Rosie at the foot of Blue Rock.

Rosie led the way up a gorge beneath sandstone crags, glowing pink in the morning light. At the top of a rocky incline she worked her way round a huge slab, and stopped to peer through a gap at a panorama that made Freya gasp: a rock arena three hundred metres wide, hemmed in by cliffs and red beehive domes. After winding their way down a stony path, they padded across the sandy palette in silence, as if treading too heavily or talking might damage the ancient magic.

The Council of Female Elders were waiting in a dry creek bed on the west side of the arena. Freya heard them singing softly in the shadows before she saw them. Some were already painted up with ochres.

'Special place this one,' said Rosie. 'Don't tell them other buggers, Peggy, Connie.' She waved her stick in the air impatiently. 'Got rid of 'em today. Told 'em Milly was sick.'

There was much to learn. Freya felt ready. She wasn't a bit shy about being stroked, or painted up by Milly. It was necessary for initiation.

Marrka, marrka, the women muttered over and over, praising Milly's work. They listened closely to Milly's songs and some joined in. Now

453

and then Milly stopped to correct them if they got the words wrong.

Soon the singing lulled Freya into a relaxed, hypnotic state, and a deep sense of contentment filled her entire being. When she looked down and admired the designs Milly had painted on her breasts and upper arms, a chorus of approval rippled through the group. No one had told her to do this; Freya had sensed that acknowledging Milly's efforts was the correct etiquette.

A few important male Elders arrived to join in the rituals and celebrations. Freya knew they were no threat to her safety, although some of them looked frightening, with their scarred chests and painted faces.

'This small *yawulyu*,' said Rosie. 'When them dreams come from *yinawuru*, when thisfella hear about 'em, maybe then have proper big performance. Dancing, singing.'

Later, when some of the women tired and found a place to lie down and rest, Freya opened up to Rosie.

'I've lost my own parents and that's why I've lost my children,' she said. 'I want to heal my spirit, so I can nurture them properly. I heal other people, but with my own children there's a distance. And their father has changed. They're upset, and confused. I want to help them.'

Rosie listened quietly and smiled.

'My husband is right,' said Freya. 'I didn't bond with them to start with. I do love them, but it's a love that has grown out of familiarity, rather than some blinding flash when they were born. Do you understand?'

Rosie nodded.

'I'm a good mother,' Freya added. 'A very good mother.'

'Youfella be all right. Stop worry. Finish this business out here. That bond youfella talk about all time just a little bit worn out.'

A little bit worn out.

They moved into the shade thrown down by the mesas. Every tiny sound was absorbed by the walls of red rock. Freya lay down. The sand smelled of rust. A scorpion scuttled past, drawing a feathery pattern with its tail, and high above in the sky the brown hawk circled the cliffs and landed on a ledge to watch the proceedings.

Rosie left Freya alone and found a quiet spot to wait.

Freya dozed for an hour or so, then Rosie nudged her foot with her stick.

'More work to do,' she said.

Milly told Freya they were now going to focus on aspects of the powerful birth and growth symbols. As the initiation intensified and the singing became louder, Freya felt the negative energy being drawn out of her being, and by the time the sun began to set over the ranges, washing the imperial sky green and red, she felt as if she had been internally cleansed by a cool wind.

When the singing and painting had ended, a woman called Lois stood up and angrily denounced Milly and Rosie's activities.

'What's the matter?' said Freya, alarmed.

'She reckons we sung them songs wrong and did them paintings wrong too,' said Milly. 'Take no notice. She's jealous, that one. Shouldn't even be here. She's a drinker, that one. Got no rights. Pretty soon them dreams'll come and we'll all know for sure. Them dreams you havin' are just forgotten.'

Milly looked at Lois with disgust. Lois walked away and sat cross-legged in the sand.

'She'll soon see,' said Milly.

Milly then sang the most potent song in the cycle, and the other women joined in, all except Lois, who at that point fled the camp towards the cliffs, shouting that her kin group had failed to follow the law, and were treating the *jukurrpa* like a game.

Milly shouted back in her own nation language, then she asked the other women to dance, but they refused. She had overstepped the line. She accepted their rebuff and fell silent.

She looked at Freya, who was curious, and said, 'Don't want to make this mob sick.'

★ ★ ★

Before leaving the site, Freya dabbed her face with water from a pool, careful not to damage the designs on her body.

Rosie drew directions in the sand. 'Head for that old mother,' she said.

'What do you mean?'

'Thisfella.' Rosie drew a large tree in the sand. 'Big redfella.'

Freya nodded. 'You mean the red gum near the waterhole?'

Rosie smiled. From there Freya could follow

456

the prints of her horse back to Paradise.

She hauled herself up into the saddle and dug her heels into the horse's belly. The women stood close together and watched her ride off through a gap in the cliffs. She turned to wave, and they raised their arms and waved back. She rode home to Paradise feeling dizzy with happiness and a sense that time was unfolding before her without fuss.

When she reached the homestead one of the boys took her horse to rub it down and stable it for the night, for the air was cold now and the animals needed to be kept warm.

Peggy and Connie were in the lounge room watching television with Forbes. They saw Freya walk past along the hall, but made no effort to greet her.

The next day she woke feeling energised. She realised how lucky she was to have met the women, a rare, dedicated group determined to keep their culture alive.

'Some of the women who come here have rough lives in the camps and missions that they go back to each evening,' Connie had said one morning at breakfast. 'The mob here do their best to persuade others to give up drinking and fighting and return to the old ways. Most of the camps are dry. Yuendumu, too. But some of 'em sneak bottles in.'

Yesterday Freya had learned through Rosie and Milly that women's nurturing role in Aboriginal society was expressed more symbolically than it had been before they lived on settlements, when their control over the family

457

group and bodily care was more immediate and direct. Now nurturing was expressed through a person's country and relationships. She would not be able to find her country, she knew that now, but being here was good enough. She could take away with her a sense of identity; though not perfect, it would do. Her relationship with the children was what she needed to work on next, and already she knew it would be easier when she got back to England.

One week after the start of the rituals, one of her dreams came back. Crystal-clear this time, and not a bit unnerving, for now she knew what it was: images of the Ancestral Beings. At last she could describe them properly to Rosie, who would try to endorse them, and with luck identify the country of Freya's ancestors.

Anxiety and excitement made her ride hard towards the cliffs, in case Rosie wasn't there. She could feel the critical gaze of her sisters watching from the veranda as she rode off.

Rosie was there, waiting in the dappled shade of an ironbark tree. She was pleased Freya was dreaming again, and wanted to know all the details.

There followed three days of rituals, during which Rosie verified the authenticity of the dreams; the same dreams had also visited her and two other Elders. And they were the ones Rosie had had about Peggy and Connie.

Freya began to feel contented and fulfilled. The dreams were part of a never-ending cycle, Rosie explained. Freya had been chosen as their recipient and caretaker, in spite of growing up in white society.

'Youfella's job keep 'em safe. Tell your own children.'

Rosie was suddenly more relaxed in Freya's company than she had been before identifying the dreams. She showed Freya how to dig for *yarla* (bush potato), *yakajirri* (bush raisin) and *yawakiyi* (bush plum).

'I'm interested in plants used for healing,' said Freya.

'Thisfella think youfella have *ngangkayi*.'

'What's that?'

'Make sickfella better powers.'

She led Freya through a field of wild scrub on the outer perimeter of the arena, and showed her some local traditional healing plants. Some Freya already knew about: acacia, eucalyptus and pandanus.

'Thisfella 'ere good for mouth,' said Rosie, pointing to the spinifex that was up to their knees.

Rosie had a weeping sore on her left leg, on the thin-skinned part of her knee. She stopped at a gum tree, picked a handful of leaves, crushed them in her hand, then pressed them on to the wound. Freya felt it needed closer attention.

'Want thisfella have two-way medicine?' said Rosie.

'You mean Western medicine and traditional?'

Rosie nodded. 'Pah. Bin in one a them hostibals long time. No good. No good. This one's better.'

She lifted her arm and gestured at the wide Tanami plains.

Back at Paradise Freya told Connie and Peggy about the plants Rosie had shown her, rather than lie about where she had been. She suggested they try growing some of them in the herb garden as an addition to the homestead's conventional first-aid kit. They said nothing, simply looked at her disparagingly. Freya left them in the kitchen preparing vegetables for minestrone, and went off to her room for a shower.

'It gives me the shits, big time,' said Connie, once Freya was out of earshot.

'And me,' said Forbes. He was reading an old copy of the *Alice Springs News*. 'I told you whites bring nothin' but fuckin' trouble.'

'She's not causing trouble,' said Connie, 'she's just up herself. Thinks she knows all about life out here. I reckon she's got a secret agenda.'

'Yeah?' Forbes leaned back in his chair and lit a cigarette. 'What might that be?'

'Rosie knows about traditional healing plants. I reckon Freya's cutting a deal with her and the Elders to export wild herbs for her medicinal herb business.'

'Nah,' said Forbes. 'The Elders wouldn't come at that sort of proposition. Even if they did, it'd take years to get it passed through all the red tape they carry on with. Permission for this, permission for that. I mean, that's how it should be, but it won't do Madam Freya any good. Especially if she's in a hurry.'

'I reckon you're right, Connie,' said Peggy.

'She's been goin' out to Blue Rock to meet Rosie every day for the past week.' She turned from the sink where she was filling a pot with water. 'Her and Rosie are gettin' too friendly, aye.'

'You two are jealous,' said Forbes.

'You don't want her here either,' said Connie.

'That's right,' said Forbes, narrowing his eyes. 'I don't want any fuckin' whites at Paradise.'

He scraped his chair back and went outside. Connie watched him from the door. He stormed across the yard and a few of the boys hurried after him, confused by his anger.

'Who does she think she is, coming here and acting like she's Aboriginal?' said Connie. 'I keep telling her Henry's her father but she just gives me a blank look. The Elders will soon cast her out, I reckon.'

'Reminds me of an anthropologist I once met, aye,' said Peggy. 'Thought she knew all about our culture, even wrote a book about it. She was clever, I have to admit. It was her attitude I didn't like. Treated us more like specimens than people.'

'Do you know something else?' Connie's voice was low. She glanced through the screen door. Forbes was a good distance away, chatting to a boy by the chook yard.

'What?' Peggy waited.

'I heard her singing to herself in a nation language. How about that? I mean, she's getting way too far ahead of herself, that's for sure.'

'I heard her too. Yesterday, just before I went to bed. Pressed a glass on her door.'

Connie gasped.

'Don't you dare say anything,' said Peggy. 'It's a bit sketchy, mind you. I can tell she's struggling with it. Only knows a few words. I can tell she's gettin' mixed up. Probably made it up after listening to the Elders.'

Freya could see, as they went about their evening chores, that Connie was fervently trying to convince Peggy that their sister was being arrogant. To make matters worse, after supper Rosie arrived, much to Peggy and Connie's disgust.

'Rosie never comes here,' said Peggy, watching Freya talking to her out in the yard. 'What's she up to?'

'She can't stay here,' said Forbes, coming in with a bowl of fresh eggs. 'She's too good at singing people up and causing trouble.'

He put the eggs on the table and began to clean them with a cloth.

'You can't toss her out,' said Peggy. 'She's too high up. The other Elders would get angry. We can't say anything in case we get chucked off Paradise. You know that, old man.'

'More trouble 'n' they're worth, sometimes,' he mumbled, and went off to the lounge room to watch television.

Freya kept glancing at the house and noticed her sisters watching through the window by the sink.

'You can't stay here,' she told Rosie.

'Got to,' said Rosie. 'Hear about them dreams when youfella wake up tomorra.'

Freya nodded. 'All right. You'll have to sneak in through the French door. I'll show you.'

They walked around the side of the house and Freya said, 'Keep walking, in case someone's watching.'

Rosie did as she was told, hobbling along next to Freya and sucking her teeth.

As they passed Freya's bedroom she said, 'There. That door there. Behind the frangipani.'

Rosie looked, and nodded.

'Hide in the barn,' said Freya. 'Around the back.'

Rosie shook her head. 'Nah,' she said. 'See youfella night time.' She limped away towards the dam and disappeared from sight.

At around midnight Freya was woken by a light tapping at the French door. It was open, but no one appeared. She got up and found Rosie sitting on the doorstep.

'Come in,' whispered Freya.

They sat on the edge of the bed for a while. Freya didn't know how to handle the situation. She liked Rosie, and needed her. But she didn't want to sleep with her in the same bed. Rosie smelled. Her bare feet were cracked and dirty. Her fingernails were not much better. Her eyes were full of a sticky white substance. Her ears were encrusted with dried wax.

Suddenly Rosie lay down on the floor. She closed her eyes and within a few minutes she was sound asleep. Freya covered her with a blanket and wedged a pillow under her head, then climbed into bed. She lay awake for a long time, listening to the soft purr of Rosie's breath.

The next morning Peggy opened Freya's door without knocking and saw Rosie asleep on the

463

floor. Freya lifted her head from the pillow and stared at Peggy in surprise.

Peggy was incensed. Forbes was furious too. He didn't want Rosie in the house, but there was nothing he could do about it. Rosie was a highly regarded Elder and no one ever questioned her authority or motives, except perhaps some of the Elders who were her equal.

Through the days that followed Rosie slept on Freya's floor every night. In the morning she took herself off towards the dam and disappeared into the spinifex.

As they went about their chores sometimes Connie looked up and caught Freya's eye — on the way to the chicken shed, coming back from the stables — and Freya saw confusion and uncertainty in her expression.

Eventually Freya approached her and said, 'I've thought it over and I think you're right, Connie.'

'Oh yeah?'

'About Henry being my father. I was being cocky, thinking otherwise. I'm sorry I doubted you.'

'It's taken you long enough.'

Connie had started smoking since arriving at Paradise. She reached for one now, lit it with a match, and leaned back in the kitchen chair, inhaling deeply.

'You can't blame me,' said Freya, 'having met him.'

'At least you know who your real father is,' said Connie coldly, 'which is more than me and Peggy can say.' She pushed back her chair, stood

464

up abruptly and went outside to finish her smoke.

The sky was turning a deep purple, the horizon tinged with pale gold. Crickets sang in the long grass, and the air around the yard smelled of horse sweat and sickly-sour goat's milk. Connie shooed two goats off the dining table and wiped it with a damp cloth. She sat for a while watching the sky change colour.

The timing now seemed right to tell Peggy.

She waited until Freya was occupied in the bathroom, and found Peggy out by the stables rubbing down ponies with a dry brush.

'Why didn't you tell me you'd been to Tinderry before this?' said Peggy. She sat down on a bench, as if stricken by a hand.

'Because I knew you'd be upset,' said Connie.

'I thought he would have sold the place by now, aye.'

'He has,' said Connie. She sat down too. Her heart was no longer in America. It was here, beside Peggy. Nothing else mattered any more.

'Henry gave me the address and directions. No one's living there. It's being done up. They're turning it into a museum. All the gates were padlocked and the windows on the house boarded up. I climbed over a fence and had a good look.'

'You could've been done for trespassing, aye.'

'There was no one around for miles.'

'What was the point if the place was empty?'

'I didn't expect to find anything, mementoes or photographs. I wanted to see where we were born. That's all. Curiosity.'

Peggy bit her lip and looked at the ground.

'Was it weird, seeing it?' she whispered.

'Yes. It was. Like I said, I didn't expect to find anything. But I did find this. In the shearing shed.'

Connie reached into the tote bag she carried with her everywhere, and pulled out a small black notebook. It was very old, the cover faded and worn. She handed it to Peggy.

'It's Henry's shearing log book. I found it in an old drawer, full of bits of wool and rusty tools and chalk. Take a look.'

Peggy opened the book.

Tinderry was written on the inside front cover. The pages were covered in a series of short, straight lines like the number one, the way a prisoner would tally his sentence on a cell wall, in sets of five. Further on in the book births were registered, as were slaughters. And the names of the shearers and skirters. There was the address of a wool broker in Melbourne. And notes about the weather. Tallies of bales sent to the mill. Wool Henry thought would be suitable for sale as one lot. Lists of orders for wool packs, and the names of two guns his broker had told him about from Hay, who could shear more than two hundred a day. There was the odd personal remark about his best ringers and tar boys. And entries about culls, to even the quality. The pages were stained with lanoline, and a yellow substance, and what Connie thought was tar.

There were near-perfect thumbprints on the top right-hand corner of each page. Henry's thumbprints.

'Keep turning,' said Connie impatiently.

Peggy felt sick. The paper smelled of sweat and wet wool. 'Let's burn it,' she said, holding the book away from her nose.

'Keep turning, for Chrissakes.'

Towards the back of the book Peggy stopped at a page dated 2nd October 1955. It was covered in tallies.

'That's our birthday.'

Connie nodded solemnly. 'Turn over.'

Peggy turned the page.

Under the heading *Births*, in small, barely decipherable handwriting, she read:

Two brown bastards born today. Nearly had a heart attack when I saw them. Thought about slaughtering them there and then, but decided to give 'em away instead. Ester looks like she's about to keel over from the shock. I knew this was on the cards. That's why I didn't want her to go through with it. But she wouldn't listen. Said she couldn't help herself. Now what am I supposed to do with the beasts? I told her I was against it right from the start, but she's a stubborn woman. It's the big smoke, making her cocky.

Peggy read it four times, until the pressure inside her skull began to hurt the bones behind her ears. A long, terrible moment passed before she spoke.

'Is he talkin' about his sheep, or us?' she said quietly.

'What do you think?'

'God,' Peggy breathed.

They sat in silence for a long time, holding hands, both conscious of their simultaneous breathing, the warmth passing between them, their heartbeats.

'Still, I can't help feeling sorry for poor old Henry,' said Peggy finally. 'I mean, he probably felt like killin' our mother as well as us, not to mention the blackfella who got her up the duff in the first place, aye.'

'That's right,' said Connie, squeezing Peggy's hand hard. 'I can't say I blame him for giving us up. I mean, what are we?' She turned and looked at Peggy's yellow eyes. 'We're neither one thing or the other, when you think about it.'

48

Freya sensed her sisters' wariness. She thought that pretending to accept that Henry was her real father would shut them up, but they were still unfriendly. She kept her distance, and they kept theirs. They were like dogs circling one another. It was exhausting, and every night she excused herself soon after supper and went to her room.

Sometimes she telephoned the children, but the calls made her uncomfortable. The children were definitely being coached by Neill; she could hear him whispering in the background, and once she heard him say quite clearly, 'Don't say anything about you-know-what.'

She lay awake for hours, staring through the French doors at the stars, trying to picture her real father: a warrior, a hunter, a jackaroo, an Elder . . . a town drunk?

One night Rosie woke Freya around one o'clock and warned her they were in for a thrashing.

'Dust comin' in. When day breaks, it'll clear.'

Freya shut the window and the French doors. The air in the room was stifling. She lay awake listening to the wind howl around the house and under the eaves.

'Don't worry,' said Rosie, 'himfella's nearly finished.'

When Freya woke, everything was covered in an inch of fine red dirt. It had found its way into her nostrils and ears, and settled on her scalp. The back of her throat was parched.

Rosie went off as usual and Freya began to clean up. Her room looked as if it was bleeding. When she turned on the shower the water came out brown. She stood near the open window, behind the lace curtains, drying herself in the breeze, rather than wiping the dust back on with one of the towels.

After dressing she went into the kitchen, which was already dusted and scrubbed. Peggy, Forbes and the boys were busy sweeping the veranda, with the resignation of country people who take dust storms as normal. She knew she should stay around the house and help, but they were hostile when she offered, so she went to the stables and one of the boys helped her saddle up.

She wasn't far from the homestead when she realised someone was following her. When she dismounted, she felt another set of hoofs reverberating through the hard ground. She kept glancing over her shoulder, but it was impossible to make out any solid objects through the heat haze that blurred the air.

That night at supper Forbes said, 'Met a bloke in town the other day, reckons he's got blackfella blood, but he's white as snow. Silly bugger, tryin' to jump on the land claim bandwagon. Thinks he can come in and adopt someone else's country. They've got no bloody idea, these bastards. Think country means ownership. Straight up. It's got nothing to do with bits of paper and estate agents. It's in here, and here.'

He slapped the side of his head with the palm

470

of his hand, then thumped his chest.

'Fuckin' coconut blackfellas are bad enough, without these bastards.'

He did not look up from his plate, but Freya knew the comment was directed at her. She felt sorry for Peggy and Connie, too, who looked at Forbes with hurt expressions. She wanted to say, *I'm not interested in land claims, I'm interested in my spiritual heritage*, but she thought he'd just say she was being pretentious.

Although Forbes's words were angry, his voice was calm. No one ever shouted at Paradise. Freya watched him sometimes, and wondered what he said to the boys during their morning quiet time together. She plucked up the courage to ask Peggy.

'He gets 'em to sit close to one another on the old couch out there,' she said. 'That's the first thing. To help 'em get used to caring about each other. And the idea of being cared about.'

No one was ever told off or criticised, Freya noticed. Once, she saw Forbes put a hand on a boy's head and hold it there for a long time, while he repeated positive messages about the boy's capabilities.

'Spell good,' he said.

'G-O-O-D.'

'That's right, good. What are you? What do you want to be?'

'Good.'

Freya looked forward to mealtimes, to listening to the boys talk. She admired Forbes and Peggy, the way they helped the boys find the courage to shake off harmful habits and negative attitudes. She reached over the boys' shoulders for emptied plates, and when Forbes had left the table and Peggy and Connie were in the kitchen, she chatted amiably to them about the horses and their different personalities. The boys would add their views. It made them proud to talk about the horses, a boost to their battered confidence.

She asked about their lives before Paradise, and was happy to let them pour their hearts out for hours. Soon they were asking her for advice. They found it easy living at Paradise, but when they went back to town the trouble started. How could they stay on the straight and narrow away from Paradise, without Forbes and Peggy to help them?

Freya told them they had to look deep inside themselves. To a place that had been neglected. That to be strong and resist temptation required knowledge of their culture. She encouraged them to learn from the Elders, who came to Paradise regularly to teach. Some of the boys, she knew, had turned their backs on the Elders and their old ways.

'There's two-way medicine for physical illness, and two-way knowledge for the spirit,' she told them.

Not knowing where their real country was, or who their real parents were, some said they couldn't see any future at all for themselves — until they came here and met Peggy and Forbes. Many had friends who had killed themselves in police custody. They were terrified of facing the same fate. Just the thought of being

472

locked up was unbearable.

'Peggy and Forbes have rescued us from more 'n bein' poor and bein' in jail,' Shane told her. 'Can't lock up a free spirit and expect it to live.'

Because of their respect for Forbes, Freya decided to give him another chance. She began to formulate a defence speech, and planned to deliver it one night when her sisters were busy. But the timing was never right; someone was always hanging around Forbes, chatting.

One morning she was in the stables getting her horse ready to ride out to the escarpment. She heard Forbes outside talking to Kip, who was having trouble fitting in. He'd been caught stealing sweets from another boy's swag. Kip expected a thrashing; he had cowered when Forbes approached. It was pitiful and Freya longed to take him in her arms. She was surprised when Forbes said to Kip that they'd have a nice talk and sort it all out, no worries. She left her horse and stood in the shadows, listening. She could see them through a crack in the door.

'Kip,' said Forbes, 'if you could have any three wishes come true, what would they be? What do you want most in the whole world?'

Kip's eyes searched Forbes's face. He looked down at the second-hand boots Peggy had given him from the storeroom. He was so proud of those boots. He kept stopping to spit on the toes and polish them with his shirt cuff.

Forbes waited patiently, arms limp by his sides.

'I'd like a father,' said Kip softly, looking up at

Forbes. 'I only want one wish and that's it.'

A wave of emotion washed over Forbes's face. He nodded but said nothing.

Kip swallowed hard and looked into Forbes's eyes.

'That's an important wish,' said Forbes. 'A very important wish.'

Kip waited. Then he said, 'I'd like a mansion too. For my own family, one day.'

He looked down again, overcome with shyness.

'A lot of you fellas wish for a father,' said Forbes. 'It's important you want a father. No one can take the place of your parents in your heart. But sometimes it's good to find another older person to make up for that gap; someone you can talk to who will give you good advice if you need it. Here at Paradise you'll be able to learn a lot of things that will help you when you live in the big world again. You'll have people to talk to, like me, and I'll teach you how to be a good ringer, so you can make money and buy that mansion.'

He pulled Kip close and hugged him. Then he gently pushed Kip away and ruffled his hair.

'Off you go now. Collect those eggs you promised Peggy.'

★ ★ ★

Freya woke to the sound of a semi-trailer pulling up outside. She heard the boys whooping and laughing, and Peggy shouting to Forbes to come outside quick. Rosie hadn't been for a few days;

474

she had business to attend to. Freya was enjoying the break, and was especially glad Rosie wasn't here this morning, holding her up.

She put on her dressing gown and went into the kitchen. Everyone was outside in the yard, standing next to the truck. There was a red tractor on the trailer. The driver and his companion lowered the ramp, and the driver hopped up on to the seat of the tractor and started the engine. He reversed it into the yard and the boys shouted and jumped up and down.

Freya went to her room for a shower, and when she came back into the kitchen half an hour later Peggy, Forbes and Connie were there making tea for the two men.

'I just don't get it,' said Forbes. He sucked hard on a cigarette and tipped his hat off his forehead. 'Haven't you fellas got any idea who paid for it?'

The two men shook their heads. One said, 'I wouldn't worry about it, mate. You've got yourself a little doozy.'

'Yeah,' said the other man, 'can't go far wrong with the Massey 130. It's only got two thousand nine hundred hours on it. And the engine's just had a complete rebuild. Make the most of it, mate.'

'Maybe it was the government takin' pity on us at last, aye?' said Peggy. She poured the men another cup of tea.

'I just don't understand it,' Forbes said again. 'I mean, the gov'ment's bin talkin' about shuttin' this place down 'cause it's costin' too much to send these kids 'ere. Why would they turn

475

around and do this?'

Freya stood by the door leading into the hall, listening. Peggy handed her a cup of tea. Connie was over by the sink peeling potatoes. She kept her back to the men. As she dropped the peeled spuds in a pot of water on the stove, Freya caught her eye. Connie looked away quickly. She put down the peeler, wiped her hands on a towel, and went outside.

Freya watched her walking quickly to the henhouse, her shoulders hunched.

★ ★ ★

'Youfella want to go back that England place soon? See youfella's children?'

Rosie sounded tired. She had been meeting with the Elders every day for a week. The strain was showing. And the sore on her knee wasn't healing.

'Yes,' said Freya, 'I do.'

'When you workin' at that hospital you learn reasons to put needles in sick people, not just how to put 'em in?'

Freya hung her head. 'Are you saying I don't truly understand what you've taught me?'

'Youfella pretty clever. Now you know when you sleep how to lay so them spirits can leave and come back without making pain. Don't forget this.'

She came to Freya's room again each night, and listened patiently every morning when Freya had a dream to tell.

Peggy and Connie couldn't understand why

Rosie was so giving of her time, and said so.

'We talk,' Freya told them. 'That's all, really. I'm interested in your culture, and she's happy to tell me. I figure if I learn about it I'll get to know you better, and understand.'

'I hope she's not telling you any secret stuff,' said Peggy.

'Rosie's a stickler for doing things properly,' said Freya. She thought this was a good answer; neither the truth, nor a lie.

When Rosie had fallen asleep, Freya often lay awake trying to work out, like an algebraic calculation, the kinship system, ritual reciprocity between clans, descent-based relations to land, the web of circulating relationships between people and land, and how everything was intricately linked.

Rosie's ancient breath filled the room. Freya reached down and touched her cheek. It was the texture of soft suede.

When she thought about how chaotic her life had been in England, how befuddled she was through lack of sleep and the mysterious longing that had constantly gripped her, she saw how easily others had misjudged her, and why.

But there was still work to do.

One afternoon Rosie took her to the camp where she lived, a small settlement not far from the farm. She wanted Freya to spread the news of the dreams she'd had, because they were so clearly linked to *jukurrpa*.

'We have to keep this Dreaming,' she said. 'We cannot forget it again.'

The collective impact of the recurring dreams

Freya had experienced confirmed her control of the material, but did not guarantee performance. Rosie said she needed more training.

The camp consisted of a series of corrugated iron shacks in the shade of a few spindly acacia and gum trees. The women were either sleeping or lolling about outside on blankets, a chaotic mess of bodies surrounded by cooking utensils, sheets of iron, water drums, dogs and goats. Freya was careful not to show her feelings, and smiled courteously at them. Out of respect for this strange white woman who had *ngangkayi* powers, they did not look her in the eye, a gesture she found powerfully humbling.

The flies were appalling. Freya tried to ignore them, and Rosie gave her a piece of netting to drape over her hat. Freya felt like an idiot. No one else was bothered by the flies. She concentrated on making sure no one was offended by her presence, though it was impossible, with her white skin, to blend in.

At the women's quarters Rosie reached up on to the roof, which was made of brush, and took down a bowl of cooked meat. She began to arrange it on a bark platter. A young girl appeared with a huge round of hot damper, and an older woman brought a billy can of sweet tea, fresh off the fire.

Freya sensed the honour bestowed by bringing her here. She wanted to please Rosie, who had been so generous with her teachings. She sat quietly, watching the activities, absorbing the excitement her presence had generated.

Rosie passed the meat platter and Freya

478

reluctantly took some and bit into it, sure she might die of food poisoning. It tasted salty and full-bodied. She knew the salt probably made it safe, so she tucked in heartily. Rosie offered her baked yams, spread out artistically on a palm leaf. It pleased the women enormously to see her eating, and they all chatted excitedly in their nation language. For dessert, a young girl offered her a wooden bowl full of small, knotty bush tomatoes and quandong.

'I wish they'd told me I was adopted,' Freya said suddenly, looking into Rosie's dark eyes.

Rosie said that to properly activate the Ancestral Beings residing inside her spirit, she had to stop dwelling on things she could not change.

'Better be loved by them strangers in Melbourne than parents who hate 'im.'

When the meal was finished, Rosie asked Freya to join her and the other business people in the shade.

'Youfella paint them designs now.'

Rosie, Milly and two other women from another camp removed their T-shirts and bras. The ochres were given to Freya in a dilly bag, and she began to paint the women and sing songs telling the stories of her dreams. She did all of this flawlessly.

Rosie was very pleased. She indicated that they would now move off from the camp into the hills for the big performance Freya had waited for so patiently. After this, she hoped, her initiation would be complete and she would be a fully integrated member of her adopted country.

Then she could go back to her children, Rosie said, 'fully, completely.'

They turned west through manuka trees and clumps of spiky blue-green spinifex, their long stems moving in the breeze, giving the air a shimmering, hallucinogenic quality. After an hour they climbed to a ridge. Acres of smooth, flat rocks covered in a thin layer of sand were carpeted with a dazzling assortment of wild flowers. They stopped for a moment to admire the view, then Rosie urged them on.

Dropping down to the other side into a dusty valley over fallen trees and huge boulders, Rosie led the way along a dry river bed. Squeezing through a narrow gap they entered a huge open gorge with limpid dark pools full of green moss, and red cliffs towering high above. In the cool shade of the canyon pine trees and palms grew side by side.

Now and then Rosie faltered, but no one tried to help. Her knee was playing up, but she made it clear she didn't want any sympathy. Occasionally she stopped to show Freya purple mint and wild parsnips. White herons circled overhead, and a kingfisher with a red-striped head landed on the branch of a tall white gum tree.

At the head of the canyon was a large, dark waterhole. Freya was surprised to see about a hundred people standing near it, waiting. While Rosie and the other women made ready wooden poles linked by hair string, marking the location of the cleansing ceremony, the others watched solemnly. One of the male Elders stood at the mouth of the canyon swinging a bullroarer, to mark the beginning of the ceremony. The whirring sound echoed around the canyon like a primeval wind.

Freya tried to calm her nerves. She stood to one side by herself, watching fish pop their heads up for air. Huge lime and sapphire dragonflies hovered over the water, dipping in and out of the reeds. The air was so clear it felt like pure silk going down her throat and filling her lungs.

Rosie told Freya to begin the session.

Milly stepped forward and danced with her, and together they mimicked with perfect precision the dance of the Ancestral Beings. Out of respect for Freya's status, all the other sisters stood a short distance away, singing. During the earlier small ceremonies Freya had been quiet and reflective. Now she showed the confidence of a *yamparru* who was in control of material she knew would not be challenged. Her voice rang out loud and clear, absorbed into the surrounding rock.

Once the ceremony was over, there was no sensation of a big victory. The sense of having won her rights as a healer would consolidate slowly.

'Youfella goin' long way away, but thisfella share your dreams,' said Rosie.

Freya nodded and looked up at the sky, a broad ribbon of deep blue between the cliffs. The sun was beginning to set in the west and stars were already appearing, like pins held in a woman's mouth.

Two hours had passed since they'd left the camp. Rosie said they should get back to

Paradise; it was a long way and they'd be walking in the dark. Freya said goodbye to the Elders, and they set off.

They hadn't gone far when Rosie fell over on the hard rock. She didn't make a sound, but Freya could see by her expression that she was in pain.

'Rosie,' she cried, 'are you all right?'

Tears welled up in Rosie's eyes. She lay there looking up at Freya helplessly, unable to move. She had landed on her bad knee and now it was bleeding. Pus poured down her shin, and on closer inspection Freya could see that the wound had become gangrenous.

'We've got to get you to the hospital,' she said.

'Pah. Thisfella not goin' in that big bird.'

Freya hoisted her up. She calculated Rosie weighed about five stone. They were too far from Paradise. Rosie would never make it, even with help. She was weak with fever. Freya supported her with one arm, and with Rosie's directions helped her hobble back to the camp.

The women gathered around, alarmed. Someone brought hot water in a billy, and crushed eucalyptus on a bark coolamon.

'Keep her warm,' said Freya. 'And make sure she gets plenty of water. I'm going for help.'

★   ★   ★

Rosie kicked up a terrible stink when the Flying Doctor Service landed near the camp the following morning. She began to cry, and the other women stroked her gently.

482

'She has to go,' Milly said firmly. 'Two-way medicine sometime the only way.'

The dogs went berserk, barking their heads off as the plane taxied slowly towards the camp. Everyone ran to greet the captain and his colleague, a young blonde woman with large white teeth.

'I'm afraid it's not looking good,' said Freya, pulling the captain aside. 'I hope they can stop it in time. I wouldn't want her to lose her leg. I'd never forgive myself.'

'Don't worry,' he said. 'She'll be right.'

The airlift took less than twenty minutes. Rosie's face was a picture of pure fear as they strapped her on to a stretcher and hoisted her aboard. Some of the women had begun to wail uncontrollably. They watched the plane until it was a speck in the distance. One old woman sat under a tree and hit herself on the head over and over with a stone.

Freya went back to Paradise, full of remorse for not treating Rosie's knee. Look what happens when I don't follow my instincts, she reproached herself. Forgetting other people's needs through an obsession with my own is not my way, and never has been. Right at the moment when her special qualities were being certified, she had neglected her responsibility to be vigilant.

The ceremonies suddenly seemed meaningless. She felt like a fraud.

49

Freya paced up and down the veranda, furious with herself for not stepping in. At midnight Peggy came out and handed her a cup of hot chocolate.

'No point torturing yerself, aye. It's not your fault.'

'Of course it is. I'm a nurse with years of experience. I should have done something about it when I first noticed the infection.'

'She'll be all right. She's in good hands now.'

Peggy went back to bed. At sunrise Freya went into the lounge room and telephoned the Alice Springs Hospital. The switchboard put her through to Rosie's ward.

'Staff Sister Rachel Phillips.'

'I'm enquiring about an indigenous woman called Rosie. She was taken in by the Flying Doctor Service last night. I believe she's been asking for me?'

'How do you know? You blacks, I dunno. You're all bloody telepathic. Are you a relative?'

'No. A friend.'

'Do you mind if I ask your name?'

'Freya.'

'That's right. The old gal's been asking for you all night. Any chance you can come in?'

Freya was quiet for a moment. She wanted Rosie to get well, but Alice was a long way.

484

Where would she stay? Yesterday she'd been thinking about making plans to fly back to England. If she got too involved it might be months before she could leave. Gangrene was a tough customer, and if the prognosis was bad and amputation was necessary, she'd feel obliged to stay and help Rosie recover.

'She's very poorly,' said the nurse. 'She seems to think it would help if you were here. She's kept the rest of the ward awake all night, shouting and moaning. Are you a *ngangkari*?'

'Yes,' said Freya. 'I am.' She sighed. Perhaps she could see Rosie and then take a flight on to Sydney, without having to come all the way back to Paradise.

'Can you come? We can't have her disturbing the peace like that again. I'll have to have her transferred to the prison hospital if she keeps it up.'

'No. Don't do that. I'll see what I can do. It might take a day or two to organise. I have to ask my hosts to drive me in.'

'Thank you. I'll tell Rosie right away. It might shut the old bird up.'

'What about her leg?'

'Too early to tell yet. We've got her on a course of antibiotics. But she's very old and she's diabetic. It's hard to get them better at that age. It's difficult to get a good response when they're away from their own people.'

'Tell her I'll see her as soon as I can.'

Freya went into the kitchen and put the kettle on. As soon as Forbes woke up, she would ask him very nicely to drive her into town. She went back to her room with a cup of tea and began to pack.

When she heard her sisters stirring, and Forbes shooing a possum off the roof with a broom, she went outside to find him.

'I wasn't planning on driving into town until next week,' he said, rubbing his chin with his thumb and index finger.

They went into the kitchen. Freya made him a cup of tea.

'But old Rosie's more important than any routine we might have,' he said. 'Where will you stay?'

'Is there a YMCA in town?'

He nodded. 'Not too glamorous, though.'

'I can't afford a hotel. It'll have to do. If there's a cheaper youth hostel, I'll get a room there.'

'No you won't.' Connie was standing at the door. 'I'll pay for a motel. And no buts about it.'

'Thanks, Connie.' Freya gave her a hug. 'Rosie's been asking for me, apparently. Made a fuss all night.'

'You'd better go for the sake of the other patients, aye.' Peggy came into the kitchen in her pyjamas. 'Poor old woman. She'll lose that bloody leg, I reckon. I've bin on to her for months to get a lift with Forbes into hospital. She's stubborn all right.'

They were all being surprisingly gracious. Freya had expected a flat no from Forbes, and was surprised by his willingness.

'I won't be able to wait around, but,' he said.

'When you're ready to go back to England we'll drive in again to see you off at the airfield,' said Peggy. 'Won't we, old man?' She gave Forbes a dark look.

'Course we will,' he said.

'We can't go today,' said Peggy. 'Too late to get started. We'll leave early tomorra. Four o'clock.'

'I'll book a motel,' said Connie. She went off to use the phone.

'Thanks,' said Freya. 'And I'm sorry for all the trouble. Me and Rosie, we've become good friends. If she's going to lose that leg, well, I'd like to be there.'

★ ★ ★

The drive seemed to take longer than it had when she first arrived. She enjoyed the scenery now, but her mind was on Rosie. And she felt oddly guilty for leaving the boys, some of whom had cried when she said goodbye last night.

'They might tease you,' said Peggy, 'but they're fond of you, aye.'

'I didn't realise how close they'd become to me,' said Freya.

'I warned you,' said Peggy.

'We won't come in,' said Forbes, when they pulled in to the motel car park five hours after leaving Paradise.

Connie went inside with Freya and showed the receptionist her credit-card details.

'Why didn't Peggy come in, at least?' Freya asked her.

'One black's enough for them to cope with, she reckons.'

487

Peggy was right. The receptionist kept giving them odd looks.

'It's not every day a black woman comes into an outback motel with a credit card,' Connie whispered, when the woman went into a back room to phone for verification.

As soon as Freya was settled in her room, which overlooked a palm-fringed swimming pool, Connie said goodbye.

'I'll call you,' said Freya.

'I'm sorry we've given you a rough ride, me and Peggy. We've been foolish. You've got every right to be mad at us.'

'I'm not angry. I just wish I had more time.'

Connie leaned her head on Freya's shoulder. 'I love you, Freya.'

'I love you too, Connie.' Freya stroked her sister's hair. 'It's not easy for any of us. But I will come back one day. What about you? Are you staying on?'

'Yes. I am. I'll have to go back to the States to see my parents one day. But for now I need to be with Peg.'

She went across to the door and opened it.

'I'd better get back. It's a long drive.'

★ ★ ★

Rosie was asleep when Freya got to the hospital. She sat by her bed and waited. After a while she reached over and stroked Rosie's hair. The old woman had her back to her. Freya watched the rise and fall of her small body under the sheet.

Two nurses arrived. They woke Rosie, who

began to swear profusely in spite of her raging fever. She was so weak she could hardly move.

'Hello, Rosie.' Freya stood up and leaned over so that Rosie could see her face.

'About time you got 'ere.'

With enormous effort Rosie stretched her arm around and searched for Freya. Freya took her hand and squeezed it. She kissed Rosie on the forehead.

'No more nonsense now,' she said. 'Rest up.'

Rosie smiled.

The nurses applied a topical dressing of raw honey to Rosie's knee. They pulled faces at one another. The putrefaction in the abscess was severe. Rosie saw their expressions and became agitated.

When they'd finished applying the honey, Freya pulled them aside.

'I'm a senior nursing sister,' she said. 'One of the first rules of nursing is to hide your feelings.'

'Sorry. We can't help it,' said the younger girl.

Freya looked at her name tag.

'Listen, Susan, I'm a middle-aged black, but I'll still have the same feelings inside when I'm old.'

'You don't look black,' said Susan.

'Looks can be deceiving,' said Freya.

'Rosie's a pain,' said Susan. 'Keeping everyone awake at night. She should be with her own people.'

'I don't think your superiors would care to hear you saying that.'

'I don't mind if you report me. I've had

enough of nursing. I'd rather go back to working in Woolies.'

'Fair enough. Meanwhile, show some respect.'

Freya settled next to Rosie and held her hand.

'Bloody fuckers,' said Rosie. 'Not usin' the right honey. You get some. Go on with ya.'

She waved her hand up and down, shooing Freya away.

'Acacia honey. From Afghan Traders, behind Springs Plaza off the mall.'

'Are you sure?'

Rosie nodded. 'What do you reckon? This-fella's bin around long time.'

Freya left her and walked to the Todd Mall. Rosie was right: certain honeys had stronger anti-bacterial properties than others. She just hoped they had the one Rosie wanted in stock.

★ ★ ★

'The freight train comes tomorra,' said the shopkeeper. 'Come back on Friday, when we've unpacked.'

'I need it today,' said Freya.

'Try Woolies or Bi-Lo. They might have some.'

'Thanks.'

As Freya walked through the Todd Mall, a quiet stretch of shops, four black women in floral dresses and bare feet approached her. One said, 'You that *ngangkari* from Paradise?'

Freya looked at her, surprised. 'That's right. How did you know?'

They giggled and hurried off.

Inside Bi-Lo she found six jars of acacia honey

and bought the lot.

'Got a sweet tooth, have ya, love?' said the woman at the checkout.

Now she had to persuade the nursing staff that Rosie wanted this honey — not theirs — applied to her wound.

Staff Sister Phillips was open to Freya's suggestion.

'We have to respect their ways,' she said. 'Rosie's got a better chance of getting through this if we do some things her way. It has a psychological effect, you see.'

'Yes,' said Freya, 'I do.'

'And you can stay all night if you want to. So long as she's quiet, we don't mind. I can bring you a Z-bed and you can squeeze it in next to her.'

Freya wasn't too pleased about this. She had been looking forward to going back to her room at the motel to try and sleep.

'I've got some things to do this afternoon,' she said. 'Then I'll be back.'

She walked back to the shopping centre and went into Coles and Woolies. She found another, smaller supermarket, too. Altogether she managed to find sixteen jars of acacia honey. She hurried back to the hospital and gave them to Nurse Phillips. Then she went in to see Rosie, who was dozing peacefully. She moved the chair to the other side of the bed, and held Rosie's hand and stroked her hair. She spoke to her in low tones in her own mysterious language.

A week went by and Freya began to notice an improvement in Rosie's leg. Her appetite returned and the fever went. Freya had gone back to the shops for more honey after the freight train came with supplies on Thursday, and she also bought Rosie a tube of aloe vera gel for her cracked lips.

One night as she slept next to Rosie, she had a nightmare about Kirsty and Tom.

They were shopping in Richmond with Clarissa, who was more intent on looking after her own brood. Richmond High Street, a narrow one-way system with constricted footpaths, was congested with traffic. The crowds were thick and unyielding. Tom was forced to walk with one foot on the road. He tried to keep his balance and stay on the path. The wheels of the traffic spun in the gutter. Kirsty pulled his sleeve and tried to help him on to the pavement, but there was no room and he was forced back into the gutter. Kirsty looked ahead anxiously for Clarissa, who was oblivious to the danger. Tom mounted the footpath once more, and tried to keep his balance as he moved forward with the crowd.

A double-decker bus rounded the corner, opposite Dickens and Jones, and at the same moment a group of people came out of the bank, forcing Tom on to the road, where he disappeared under the front of the bus.

It happened so fast he did not have time to cry out.

Freya heard the crunching of bones and th
splitting of flesh. She smelled blood and diese
and the sweet final breath of her son.

The wheels of the bus kept turning toward
the station. The driver had not even noticed.

She woke up wailing.

'Thisfella better phone 'em,' said Rosie, when
Freya had calmed down enough to describe the
dream. She said there was no time to waste.
Freya should get on the phone, to make sure
they were safe, then she should book her flight
home.

Freya agreed. She had been away long enough.

Before leaving the hospital she spoke to Nurse
Phillips.

'I have to go,' she said. 'Something's come up.
A family crisis.'

'Well, old Rosie's out of danger. It looks like
we won't have to amputate. Thanks to you and
all that honey.' She laughed.

'Look after her,' said Freya.

She went back to Rosie's bed and said
goodbye.

'Youfella come back soon,' said Rosie.

'I'll try,' Freya said truthfully. 'It might take a
while. I have to look after my children. And their
father, he's English. He won't want them to live
over here.'

Rosie closed her eyes, and when Freya was
sure she was asleep she slipped away quietly,
leaving another bag of acacia honey on the floor
by the locker.

★ ★ ★

493

The children had been waiting for her call. Kirsty said she'd been having weird dreams and couldn't sleep.

'It's driving Clarissa and Dad crazy because I wake up crying and can't get back to sleep. It wakes everyone up.'

Kirsty began to cry, and so did Freya.

'I love you, Kirsty, and I want to be with you and Tom, but Dad and Clarissa want you there with them and so does the court, so I can't do much about it, and anyway, you and Tom don't like the houseboat — '

'Yes we do. We do like it. We've told Dad we want to live with you and at first he wouldn't listen, but now he wants us to because he can't afford to keep us and Clarissa's sick of us fighting with her kids . . . '

Freya couldn't believe what she was hearing. She let Kirsty ramble on about the fights and the misunderstandings and the petty injustices. Finally Kirsty was quiet on the end of the line.

'The dreams you're having,' said Freya. 'Are they strange, really strange — are they about funny-looking animals, and birds?'

'How did you know?'

Freya had thought about the possibility of the children getting in touch with their Aboriginal spirituality, but feared it might have been bred out of them somehow.

'I have the same dreams,' she said.

'That doesn't surprise me.'

'How come?'

'You're my mother.'

'I'm coming home soon.'

'When, Mum? You've been gone for ages. I can't stand it any more.'

'Put your father on.'

Neill came on the line and confirmed Kirsty's news. Freya's hands began to tremble.

'But what about the court?'

'We'll cancel the appeal, shall we — as soon as you get back to London.'

'But Neill, I'm not ready to have the children with me full time, there isn't room.'

'I've sorted that out too.'

'What?'

'Remember I told you about that fellow, the boat-builder? Name's Julian.'

'Yes.'

'I took him on to the moorings to show him the space you've got. He took some measurements and said it'd be no problem getting a bigger boat moored there. I told him you've been trying to find a place to rent to run your herb business, and he came up with a brilliant idea.'

'Really?'

Freya was suspicious. It was so unlike Neill to be nice.

'I've been sending you money, Neill. Isn't it helping?'

'You're not listening to me.'

'Yes I am.'

'I'm trying to tell you that Julian has come up with a solution. A financially viable one that will mean you don't have to rent an outrageously expensive shop somewhere on some poxy high street.'

'Oh, you mean set up a stall at the waterways

festivals? I've already thought of that.'

'Not quite.'

'You seem to have it all worked out.'

'Do you want me to help you or not?'

'What's the catch?'

'There's no catch. Okay, I can't have the kids here any more, but obviously I want them to be happy and comfortable. Julian can build you a three-bedroom boat, with enough space for a small consulting room and shop. With an engine, so you can take your business wherever you like. Think of it, Freya. You could putt on up to Little Venice and hold consultations. Or Oxford.'

Freya was quiet for a few moments, taking it all in. She was both pleased and disgusted. His ulterior motive was to get the kids off his hands, because they were emptying his bank account. And she also knew he was terrified she might report him for diddling the Department of Social Security.

'Does this Julian know what he's doing?'

'Yes. He's a British Waterways adviser.'

'Listen, Neill, what if I said I wanted to visit Australia every year, and bring the children with me? During the summer break, for instance?'

There was another long silence.

'I'd probably say okay, fair enough. They should experience your country of birth as well as mine.'

'Thank you.' Freya let out a long sigh of relief. The huge cloak of resentment she'd carried all these years suddenly melted. Just like that.

'You know, Freya, I don't like taking money from the DSS. So Clarrie and I have decided to sell up and downsize to the country. We thought about going out to Cheltenham, but I persuaded her to stay closer to home, so we're looking around Oxford, near the canal. You can sail up the Grand Union and the kids can visit us.'

'That's very noble of you.'

He was quiet for a moment, then, 'To be honest, it's not just the pressure of having six kids under one roof. They miss you.'

'But Neill, you said I've never bonded with them. You made me look like a useless mother.'

'I was out of order on that particular point,' he said. 'I've asked for God's forgiveness. I hope you'll forgive me, too.'

'Are you sure you haven't put them up to this? Just to get them off your hands?'

'No,' he said firmly. 'Definitely not. They've been nagging me for weeks about it.'

'But why, Neill? Why did you do it? It's caused me so much pain. The children too.'

'I don't know really. I'm sorry, truly I am. I can't help myself sometimes. Always did like being in the right.'

This wasn't how she'd wanted things to turn out. She'd mentally rehearsed what she would say in court for weeks now. She had planned to confess her indigenous origins, and explain her reasons for travelling to Australia. Whatever the outcome, she'd decided to accept it and get on with being the best mother she could be, whether they lived with her or not. Her children were coming home.

'Nobody's perfect,' said Neill.

'Put Kirsty on again,' she said.

'Mum?'

'I've got something to tell you,' said Freya. 'But you mustn't tell anyone. Is your father listening?'

'No.'

'What about Clarissa?'

'She's out.'

'You've got to promise. Make sure Tom doesn't say anything either. This is top secret. I'll tell Dad when I get home.'

'What is it, Mum? Have you met someone else? I thought you liked Sam? I hoped you two would get together.'

'Really? Well, we'll have to see. I've been away a few months. He may have met someone else by now.'

'He hasn't,' said Kirsty.

'How do you know?'

'I saw Ryan. In Richmond. He said Sam's been missing you.'

'That's nice.' She took a deep breath. 'Listen carefully, Kirsty. I want you to know that I've had some wonderful news about my family. Our family, actually. You see, we've got Aboriginal ancestors.'

She would fill in the details later. For now, she wanted a gut reaction.

'Cool,' said Kirsty.

That was all. Just *cool*.

'Put Tom on.'

Tom was silent for a few seconds when she told him, then he said, 'Can we go and visit Australia, if Dad says it's all right? I want to see Ayers Rock and meet some Aboriginal people.'

Freya smiled. 'Yes,' she said. 'Yes, we can.'

Neill came back on with the news that he'd bumped into Luke Pirkel. 'Looked like a reformed character,' he said. 'You won't recognise him. Said he's sold his car yard and his boat, bought himself a designer barge. Massive thing, all mod cons.'

'Really?' said Freya. She was only half listening.

'It'll be much better for you to have someone in your life,' said Neill. 'Clarrie and I can only take the children off your hands once a month. You'll need support from someone else. You've still got a few years to go with them yet.'

'I'm not interested in Luke,' she said.

'Oh, so it's Sam you're after, eh?'

'I wouldn't have put it quite so crudely.'

'Well, good luck to you. Everyone needs someone special in their life. I wasn't much good to you. I'm sorry for everything, Freya.'

'So am I.'

Typical, she was thinking, he wanted her to have a partner, she realised, not out of a desire to see her happy and in love, but to take the pressure off his own love life.

50

Senior Staff Nurse Diane Moriarty, a big-boned woman from New Zealand, was watching a video in the day room, a stuffy terrarium with fixed windows and leatherette sofas and formica card tables. Ordinarily she could see the patients through the windows, but tonight she had drawn the blinds so as not to disturb anyone. She was just getting into the movie — a story about a woman whose husband dies in a plane crash and who then discovers he had another wife — when she heard a noise coming from one of the beds.

It was so irritating, being interrupted just when she'd settled, and she resented it greatly. She pressed pause on the video machine and went to investigate.

Moving briskly from one bed to the next, she finally arrived at Henry Nolan's posturpedic. She expected Henry to gesture that he wanted a drink, or for his bag to be emptied, but when she placed a hand on his shoulder there was no response, just a terrible smell of expelled gas and old skin. She prodded him in the chest and knew immediately that he was dead. She checked his pulse. Nothing.

Diane could have killed the man — if he was still alive — for ruining her evening. She'd been looking forward to it all day; she'd bought two blocks of chocolate, microwaveable popcorn, and a Mills and Boon book for the hours after the film when she was expected to stay awake.

She left Henry and went to phone for the duty doctor and someone to help with laying out the body. She notified the hospital morgue; someone would come in an hour's time with a vehicle to take him away.

Sister June Michaels from Kent Ward arrived minutes later, with Dr Simmons. They came up the ramp huffing and puffing after the long trek through the grounds.

'Inconsiderate bastards, aren't they?' said Simmons, winking at Diane and laughing.

'Tell me about it,' said Diane.

'You'd think, wouldn't you, they'd wait for a more convenient time to cark it, instead of always managing to leave it until the middle of the bloody night,' said June.

They followed Diane to the end of the ward. She pulled the curtain around Henry's bed and switched on the nightlight.

'What's wrong with his face?' said June, horrified. 'He looks as though he was in the middle of a really bad nightmare.'

June was right. Henry looked as if he'd seen a ghost at the precise moment of death. 'He must've been in a lot of pain,' said the doctor.

June took Henry's chart from its hook at the end of the bed.

'Probably had a particularly bad heart attack. His first and last, according to this.'

'What was wrong with him, apart from old age?' said Simmons.

'Parkinson's.'

501

'Horrible thing. Like a living death for some sufferers.'

'I know what you mean,' said Diane. 'A long, slow wasting away. It's as if they're rotting before your eyes.'

'Ghastly,' whispered June.

Both nurses had seen their share of corpses and were fairly hardened to death. But Henry was one of the worst they'd seen in a long time. His limbs were thin as sticks, the collapsed veins running under his skin like blue wires.

They waited while the doctor ascertained the time and cause of death.

'Definitely his heart I reckon,' said Simmons after a few minutes. He wrote down the details on the chart. 'He's been dead approximately half an hour. Which makes your job easier, ladies. Rigor mortis hasn't set in, so he should be a cinch to lay out.'

He said good night and went back to the main building. Diane went to the staff room to fetch cotton wool to stuff in Henry's orifices.

June eased the pyjama top off Henry's withered arms, but the rear flap was jammed under his buttocks. She bent his torso forward over his knees and yanked out the shirt-tail. A strong smell of urine rose up, accompanied by a squelching sound.

'Look at this,' she said, when Diane came back.

She lifted the shirt up over Henry's back, and Diane leaned in from her position on the opposite side of the bed. Together they stared hard at the maple-brown birthmark covering sixty per cent of Henry's back.

'Oh, I know,' she said.

'He must've hated it,' said June softly. 'I mean, the rest of him's so white. Look, even his arms. Except for his hands and the back of his neck, he's like a bloody lily.'

'It's not a pretty sight.'

'I've got a birthmark,' said June. 'On my arm.'

'Oops. Sorry, love.'

'That's okay. Mine's pink, not the brown sort with hairs growing out. When I was a kid my mother always told me it was an angel's kiss, to make me feel better about it.'

'That's nice.'

They finished preparing Henry for the morgue, stripped the sheets, washed him down with a damp sponge. Diane dried him off with a fluffy white towel while June cleared his bedside cupboard. The top drawer was full of used tissues, betting slips, boxes of matches. She pulled out his riding boots, cracked and worn from years in the sun and dust. There was a small address book, a wallet, a set of keys, and two photographs. One was of an Aboriginal woman, quite young and attractive, standing in front of an oak tree, under which bloomed a carpet of daffodils and violets. The other photo had the name Ester on the back. 'That's his wife,' said Diane.

June turned over the photo of the black woman. Neat printing identified the location: *Hopeville, VA. April 2000.* She showed it to Diane.

'Who do you suppose this is?' she said.

'Oh *her*. I was on duty when she came to visit a while back. A real glamour puss. Had all the trendy gear. Said she was Mrs Nolan's daughter, but when I mentioned her Henry got real cranky and said she wasn't his wife's daughter at all, but some woman from the church taking it on herself to visit people without families. He was very, very angry about her being here.'

'I don't understand,' said June.

'Henry was in denial, you see. The birthmark made us all curious, then when she turned up, well . . . The old boy had Aboriginal blood, no doubt about it. She's definitely his daughter.'

June put the photo on top of the locker and said, 'I can't say I blame him for being ashamed, even if she is attractive.'

They dressed him in fresh pyjamas and draped a clean sheet over his bony frame. Out of habit, Diane mitred the corners of the sheet. June applied Vaseline to his blue lips and polished his false teeth with paper towelling.

'You don't need to worry about his bloody teeth,' said Diane, noticing June's efforts. 'He's for the chop; he put himself forward for research.'

'I like to see them going off looking their best,' said June, prising his mouth open and slotting the upper dentures into position. 'Looking for a cure for Parkinson's, are they?' she said, pulling the sheet up over his gaunt face.

'Not this time. They want to investigate the whole throwback phenomenon. This sort of thing doesn't happen too often.'

'I'm still not sure I get it.'

'It doesn't take a genius to see what's happened.'

'Well, I must be thick,' said June.

Diane smiled. 'It's an incredible fluke. One of the doctors in the cancer ward knew Henry's wife, Ester. She was white. But someone in her family must've been at it with a blackfella a few generations back, you see. Henry's too. It takes two recessive genes to create a throwback.'

Diane nodded. 'Yep.'

June peered at the photo again, fascinated. 'She doesn't look like an Abo. She's too pretty.'

'I know.'

'Incredible,' breathed June.

'Incredible,' agreed Diane.

June put Henry's belongings in a plastic bag and attached a name tag. The resident undertaker would arrive any minute, discard the sheet and take Henry away in a body bag to the morgue. Tomorrow he would be transferred to the research centre in the hospital, to be dissected on a stainless-steel bench in front of thirty-five eager students.

51

At the Alice Springs airport Freya bought cold drinks for her sisters. They stood outside sipping through straws, avoiding eye contact. Peggy was edgy, she couldn't keep still, but Connie's relief was obvious. She was impatient to get it over with, and kept looking at her watch. She wanted to get back to the homestead and attend initiation.

'I don't want to be a hypocrite,' she'd said to Peggy that morning, 'but I'll be glad to see the back of that woman. She's so . . . not like us. Sister or not, it's like she's from another place, another planet.'

'Some people never seem to realise when they've outstayed their welcome, aye,' said Peggy.

'She took things a bit too far in my opinion, shacking up at the hospital with Rosie. People are gossiping all over the district.'

The early-morning air was unusually crisp. Thick fog hung low over the airport buildings. It reminded Freya of Middlesex on a cold morning, and she felt strangely comforted by this thought, that a country far from her own could be so similar.

She looked at her sisters and wondered if there might come a time when she could talk to them about the truth.

Connie had painted her toenails a defiant shade of blood red. They looked hideous poking out of her ugly brown leather sandals. She'd put matching red lipstick on her mouth, but her clothes were dishevelled and grubby.

'Thanks for having me,' said Freya, at the departure gate. She hugged them.

'Have a good trip, aye,' said Peggy.

'Good luck with your new boat,' said Connie. 'I hope your kids like it better than the other one.'

Freya turned to Forbes, who stood apart in the shade of a tree, and thanked him for the use of the horses, and the phone. He tugged the brim of his hat. After a moment he said, 'Don't mention it. Come back any time. The boys got on well with you.' He smiled briefly and their eyes locked in a moment of mutual respect. Freya knew that Forbes understood the truth of who she was.

She walked across the tarmac through ripples of heat whooshing from the jets.

At the top of the steps she turned and saw Nurse Phillips pushing Rosie towards the fence in a wheelchair. Freya wanted to run back to the enclosure and hug her, but everyone else had boarded and the ground crew were waiting for her to step inside. Instead, she turned and lifted her arm and waved. Rosie waved back.

When she was settled in her seat, Freya leaned into the window. She could see Rosie talking earnestly to Peggy and Connie. She was clearly angry.

Connie and Peggy suddenly looked towards the plane, their eyes searching each window for Freya. She could tell by the way they squinted that it was impossible to make out any of the faces at the windows, because of the sun, which had now leapt out from behind the clouds. All at once they began to wave frantically at a window towards the back of the aircraft, thinking they had seen Freya's face, but it was not Freya at all, and when she craned her neck towards the rear seats she saw they were waving at a middle-aged white woman, a complete stranger, who stared out at the desert with a bitter expression as if she had just visited hell.

The plane pulled away and trundled towards the runway, and Freya settled back and opened Wally Caruana's book on Aboriginal art, which she had found in a bookstore on the way through town when Forbes stopped for cigarettes and a newspaper.

Modj, the Rainbow Serpent, the dynamic curve of its body showing its sheer strength; Narrangem and Naldaluk, the Lightning Spirits who created curtains of lightning during the wet season; Irramaru, the wedge-tailed eagle who introduced fire to the Tiwi world; a batik painted by Edie Kemarre from the Utopia Women's Batik Group. She turned the pages, fascinated, until suddenly her eyes grew wide and her palms began to sweat. She stared at another painting of the Rainbow Serpent, with serrated teeth, tiny human figures tumbling down its throat along the length of its body. It was her dream. She pored over the picture, heart pounding, then read the text adjacent to the black-and-white plate.

The Serpent is depicted swallowing people whom it will regurgitate later, in a transformed state, as features of the landscape. The theme of swallowing and regurgitation is commonly used through much of Aboriginal Australia as a metaphor for the transition from one metaphysical state of being to another. It is a feature of many ancestral stories concerning the genesis of the world, and it is employed in ceremony to effect the transformation of initiates to a higher spiritual level.

The plane careered towards the end of the runway and lifted itself shakily into the sky. The stewardess came round with prepacked trays of sandwiches and a pot of coffee. Freya sipped water from a plastic cup, leaving the synthetic snack on the empty seat beside her. The open book lay on her lap and she stared at the picture, her breath held deep in her chest, her heart still. Then she closed the book and gazed down at the intricate web of Dreaming paths covering the land, her sharp eye drawn to the winding track that stretched east to the coast.

It was another hour before she saw signs of human life on the ground. No wonder they could not find their families. All spread out, dispersed like dandelion spores. She couldn't imagine being taken from her parents and sent to a mission thousands of miles away at the age of eight, say, old enough to know the meaning of loss and separation, but not old enough to object. Being adopted at birth had been a blessing. Being adopted by people who loved her was a double blessing. Peggy, poor wretch, had run like a wildcat from the orphanage, from the cruelty and loneliness, into a far worse situation in Darwin, at a time when Aboriginal people were banned from the towns, so that she had to hide from the authorities and sell her body for food and shelter.

Freya closed her eyes and did not open them again until the stewardess thrust a silver tray brimming with Minties under her nose. As the plane veered south over plains and mountains and lakes, she thought of Sam. His face was clear in her mind. She could hear his voice in her ear. She thought about the possibility of something developing between them.

At one point she leaned down to retrieve her shoes, which she had removed before take-off. The soles were caked in red earth. The stain was under her fingernails, too — blood-red, gritty, persistent. And in her pocket was another memento of her stay: gum leaves, gum nuts and a small, fire-scorched waratah.

She closed her eyes for the rest of the flight, and when she opened them again they were already over Sydney, all shiny with glass and steel and imported marble, clustered on the edge of the water, the Opera House straining like a ship in full sail, as if it might suddenly snap off with the city in tow and travel back to where it had all begun.

Author's Note

Although *The Past is a Secret Country* is a work of fiction, it is possible for apparently white parents to have recessive genes, or alleles, that recombine after several generations, producing a child who is obviously of mixed race. When researching the subject of biological throwbacks, I discovered that though this type of genetic phenomenon is unusual, even in countries such as Australia and Africa where early white settlers employed blacks as servants and took advantage of the isolation to exploit them, it is possible. Recorded cases, such as that of Sandra Laing, the Afrikaner woman born to white parents in 1955, show this to be true.

For meiosis to take place, both parents must have had non-white ancestry on both sides, usually linked to great-great-grandparents who at some point had a black partner. By a biological quirk, the pigment of an unknown black ancestor can lie dormant for generations and manifest itself in unsuspecting future children. Although I have focused on Freya's father, Henry Nolan, being the possessor of a recessive allele and therefore the immediate source of her and her sisters' mixed blood, their birth mother, Ester Nolan, must also have had a recessive allele for this to occur.

With regard to Aboriginal words used in the text, Freya's 'secret language' is taken from the language group of the Warlpiri, who occupy country in the Central Australian Desert. Because the language is not learned but rather 'spiritually inherited' by Freya, some of the words she speaks are out of context, and one or two are composites of several words. Since I am not a linguist, and had no direct contact with any Warlpiri, I had to rely on limited resources from research. Translations are as follows:

country: in Australian Aboriginal terms this refers to not just a physical place, a piece of land, it is also a basis of identity and an analogy for emotional states
Jukurrpa: the complex, plurally employed concept invoked by the Warlpiri when discussing their cosmology. Commonly translated as the 'Dreamtime', 'Dreaming' and 'Ancestral times', *Jukurrpa* provides the Warlpiri with links to their past, their land, their ancestors, and each other, converting abstract ideas into concrete objects or living persons
yawulya: women's ceremonies and ritual designs
pura-mi: follow
kawarirri-mi: wander
marna: spinifex
warnirri japiya: important
kapati-mi: be uneasy

All the names attributed to Aboriginal characters are fictional. I emphasise this because in Australian Aboriginal culture to speak the name of a deceased person is a speech taboo. If any of the names I have chosen cause offence to the Warlpiri, I apologise.

Finally, this book and my previous novel, *Under The Green Moon*, are my small way of saying 'sorry' to the original inhabitants of Australia whose way of life was destroyed by the invasion of white man.

Maree Giles
February, 2005

We do hope that you have enjoyed reading this large print book.

Did you know that all of our titles are available for purchase?

We publish a wide range of high quality large print books including:
Romances, Mysteries, Classics
General Fiction
Non Fiction and Westerns

Special interest titles available in large print are:
The Little Oxford Dictionary
Music Book
Song Book
Hymn Book
Service Book

Also available from us courtesy of Oxford University Press:
Young Readers' Dictionary
(large print edition)
Young Readers' Thesaurus
(large print edition)

For further information or a free brochure, please contact us at:
Ulverscroft Large Print Books Ltd.,
The Green, Bradgate Road, Anstey,
Leicester, LE7 7FU, England.
Tel: (00 44) 0116 236 4325
Fax: (00 44) 0116 234 0205

Other titles published by
The House of Ulverscroft:

THE SUMMER I DARED

Barbara Delinsky

What comes after the moment that changes your life forever? A question that haunts Julia Bechtel, Noah Prine and Kim Colella, the only survivors of a boating accident off the coast of Maine. Julia, a forty-year-old 'loyal' and 'obedient' wife and mother, realizes after her brush with death that there is more to her than she imagined ... Feeling strangely connected to Noah, and to Kim, Julia explores the possibilities offered by the island of Big Sawyer ... Resolving that she must have more from life, Julia fearlessly embraces uncertainties in a way she couldn't have imagined only a few weeks ago.

HOW LONG HAVE YOU GOT?

Katie Pearson

Molly is facing a new future. She hasn't worked for seven years — well, not technically, although looking after a demanding family has been trial enough. And given her recent multi-tasking at home as nurse, chef and peace negotiator, surely she'd be a catch for any employer? . . . Her ex-boss is persuaded to give her work filming a documentary starring a cantankerous eighty-three-year-old actress called Florence Bird. As filming progresses Molly realises how complicated life can be. But despite their differences Molly and Florence forge a remarkable friendship — one that helps them both confront their fears and answer the all-important question, how long have you got?